DEATHWATCH IGNITION

A rocket burst just behind Cassius, throwing two Ultramarines off their feet – Donatus was sure that Adelmo was one of them. The Chaplain was almost at the control tower, bringing the rest of the force in his wake. He looked up at the war machine now advancing from the forge, and at the cannon being levelled right at him.

'*Do you see their blasphemy, brothers?*' cried out Cassius. '*They fear the divine right of mankind, and to face us they have crafted a graven image of–*'

The cannon roared.

A split second later, a huge shell slammed into the base of the control tower. A blackened plume of debris and smoke ripped out of it as the lower floors were pulverised by the explosive impact. The ork gunners and their anti-aircraft artillery were swallowed by the explosion and the tower toppled, its shattered windows like the black eyes of a skull.

Cassius and most of the strike force were swallowed in the wash of smoke. Secondary explosions crackled through the impact zone as ammunition cooked off.

'Chaplain!' Tatianus shouted into the vox. 'Speak, brother! Do you yet live?'

DEATHWATCH
IGNITION

EDITED BY LAURIE GOULDING

BLACK LIBRARY

A BLACK LIBRARY PUBLICATION

First published in 2015.
This edition published in Great Britain in 2017 by
Black Library,
Games Workshop Ltd.,
Willow Road,
Nottingham, NG7 2WS, UK.

10 9 8 7 6 5 4 3 2 1

Produced by Games Workshop in Nottingham.
Cover illustration by Raymond Swanland.

A CIP record for this book is available from the British Library.

ISBN 13: 978 1 78496 498 6

See Black Library on the internet at

blacklibrary.com

Find out more about Games Workshop
and the world of Warhammer 40,000 at

games-workshop.com

Printed and bound by CPI Group (UK) Ltd, Croydon, CR0 4YY

It is the 41st millennium. For more than a hundred
centuries the Emperor has sat immobile on the Golden
Throne of Earth. He is the master of mankind by the
will of the gods, and master of a million worlds by the
might of his inexhaustible armies. He is a rotting carcass
writhing invisibly with power from the Dark Age of
Technology. He is the Carrion Lord of the Imperium for
whom a thousand souls are sacrificed every day,
so that he may never truly die.

Yet even in his deathless state, the Emperor continues his
eternal vigilance. Mighty battlefleets cross the daemon-
infested miasma of the warp, the only route between
distant stars, their way lit by the Astronomican, the
psychic manifestation of the Emperor's will. Vast armies
give battle in His name on uncounted worlds. Greatest
amongst his soldiers are the Adeptus Astartes, the Space
Marines, bioengineered super-warriors. Their comrades
in arms are legion: the Astra Militarum and countless
planetary defence forces, the ever-vigilant Inquisition and
the tech-priests of the Adeptus Mechanicus to name only
a few. But for all their multitudes, they are barely enough
to hold off the ever-present threat from aliens,
heretics, mutants – and worse.

To be a man in such times is to be one amongst untold
billions. It is to live in the cruellest and most bloody
regime imaginable. These are the tales of those times.
Forget the power of technology and science, for so much
has been forgotten, never to be re-learned. Forget the
promise of progress and understanding, for in the grim
dark future there is only war. There is no peace amongst
the stars, only an eternity of carnage and slaughter, and
the laughter of thirsting gods.

CONTENTS

ONE BULLET

BEN COUNTER

Donatus slid into the cover of a ruined devotional cogitator bank, letting its bent and bullet-riddled frame shelter him for the moment it took to switch ammunition.

The rest of the Sternguard were weathering the storm of heavy-calibre fire stuttering around the chapel interior. Brother Adelmo was backed against a pillar and Felidus had dived into a side shrine as explosive fire tore up the floor slabs beneath him.

Donatus rejected the Hellfire round, too rare and precious, its core a reservoir of bio-reactive acid. The Metal Storm shell was also dismissed – against unarmoured flesh it could wreak carnage that a regular bolter shell could not, but in this situation it would be a poor choice. Donatus ejected his bolter's load and replaced it with a single Kraken round from the clip at his belt. These were rare, too, and Donatus had only a single magazine of them in total. They were not to be fired off lightly.

'Keep moving and flank it!' commanded Sergeant Tatianus, the Sternguard squad leader. The sergeant bolted from cover and sprinted across the aisle between the chapel's stone pews. Explosive fire followed him, filling the air with shards of hot stone. Felidus hefted his heavy bolter and rattled a volley of fire at the enemy, while Adelmo ran, head down, for the cover of the altar.

'No effect!' shouted Felidus over the vox. 'The damn thing's armoured like a tank!'

Donatus put his head above the wreck of the cogitator. The enemy was in the centre of the chapel, laughing bestially as it sprayed an endless torrent of fire at the Sternguard, mocking their attempts to bring it down.

Donatus had learned to hate the greenskins simply by virtue of being human, albeit a heavily modified one. The orks were the enemy of the very concept of humanity. They tore down the order mankind built around it to survive. They toppled the empires that men raised to bring sanity to a galaxy of madness. They were anarchy personified.

Donatus compressed his hatred into a thread that wrapped around his limbs and steadied his aim. His peered through the preysense sight of his custom bolter, leaning into the extended stock.

The enemy was a greenskin specialist. Some orks were leaders, others psykers, others pilots or vehicle gunners. The creature fighting the Sternguard was an ork engineer, one of the insane inventors that built their ramshackle war machines and unpredictably explosive weapons. It wore what Donatus guessed was its own creation – a massive suit of armour, driven by a smoke-belching power plant on its back, with dense plating that had turned aside every bolter shell the Sternguard had thrown at it.

The ork was armed with a pair of rapid-firing cannons, one mounted on each arm. Hissing hydraulics powering its limbs gave it the strength to heft the enormous weapons and keep up a withering wall of fire. Even as Donatus took in the sight, sizing up the greenskin's armoured mass for avenues of attack, Brother Adelmo broke cover again and ran into a blind spot created by a heap of fallen masonry.

'I'm making a detonation run!' Adelmo voxed.

'Go for the joints!' replied Sergeant Tatianus. 'They are the most vulnerable!'

Adelmo ran straight at the ork. He had a krak grenade in his hand, an explosive with a small radius but a high-powered charge designed to rip open armoured vehicles. Placed correctly, it would split the ork's armour open and leave the xenos inside ripe for killing.

The creature saw Adelmo before he got close enough to plant the grenade. It swung one of its cannons and slammed the length of it into Adelmo's chest. The Space Marine was hurled across the width of the chapel and crunched into the wall, dislodging chunks of broken stone as he tumbled to the floor.

The ork laughed again, the metallic sound issuing from the steel faceplate. Its metal mask was in the likeness of an ork, with red-lensed eyes and a huge grinning, jagged maw.

Donatus played his preysense sight across the ork. The sight picked out body heat and motion, lining the armoured ork in red and yellow, and the heat billowing from the power plant; the cannons glowed white-hot and the hydraulics were edged in cherry-red. The crosshairs etched onto Donatus' lens hovered over the ork's chest, where beneath the armour plating the alien's heart had to beat.

Not even a Kraken round, with its shaped reactive charge to punch through ceramite and plasteel, would get through the armour there. Donatus needed another way.

The ork wheeled around to face Tatianus, who was still trying to outflank it. The sergeant rolled out of a volley of fire, but the shockwave of the chain of explosions threw the Sternguard sergeant off his feet and sent him sprawling behind the chapel's altar.

The ork's power plant was facing Donatus now. He had, he guessed, two ways through the ork engineer's armour, and the power plant was one. It did not have the same armour plating as the ork's body and there was a good chance a penetrating shot would create secondary detonations or cause the armour to fail.

He weighed up the chances in his head. At times like this, with a target in his sights, Donatus' mind could hurtle through a series of probability equations that a scribe would need days to write down. He made his decision and pulled the trigger.

The Kraken shell speared through the brass-cased cylinder between the smoke-belching exhaust stacks. From the neat hole and larger exit scar shot a whistling plume of steam.

No explosion of fuel blew the armour apart. The ork didn't slow down. It turned to face Donatus, suddenly aware of the fourth Sternguard in the chapel.

But there were *two* ways through the armour.

Donatus slid a second Kraken round into the breech of his bolter, and felt the click as it fitted into the firing chamber. His crosshair found the red lens over the ork's right eye. A reflex action kicked in, and he fired.

The Kraken shell shattered the lens and bored right through the faceplate. It punched through the ork's real eye and the bone of the socket. The armour covering the back of the skull held and the bullet rebounded inside its head, sending a shower of gore spraying from the ruptured lens.

The cannons fired a few more rounds as the ork's hands clenched the firing levers reflexively. Then the guns hung limp at its sides and the whole contraption slumped, the head hanging low, the cannon barrels resting on the floor.

Tatianus picked himself up. Adelmo was on his feet, too, the deep blue of his Chapter livery caked in white dust from the pulverised stone of the chapel. His armour had been repainted upon his return from service with the Deathwatch, and it had made him look like a new recruit. Felidus had mocked him for it at first, but now Adelmo looked as battle-worn as the rest of them.

'A good kill, brother,' Tatianus commended Donatus, approaching the ork to check it really was dead. A trickle of gore from the punctured lens suggested there was little doubt of that.

'Not so good,' said Adelmo. Though he wore his helmet, crowned with gilded laurel leaves, Donatus could tell that he was smiling. 'It took two rounds.'

Chaplain Cassius took to the pulpit as if he were born to it, the ruddy sunlight edging his polished black armour with dull fire. Behind him rose the industrial mass of Skemarchus, the manufactoria city belching smoke and flame in vast columns that reached the steel-coloured sky.

'Brethren,' said Cassius. 'On the eve of battle we turn our thoughts inwards, towards the strength we shall call upon tomorrow. A million orks hold Skemarchus. We are but eighty. And yet, we shall win.'

The battle-brothers of the Third Company stood ranked up in the centre of the Ultramarines' landing zone, surrounded by the command and sensorium buildings that had been dropped from orbit. Nearby were the Storm-raven gunships and Rhinos that would take them into the storm that awaited them in Skemarchus. The eight squads stood hooked by Cassius' words, the young Chaplain fixing each one with a look as he spoke. He did not wear the traditional skull-faced helm of his position, relying instead on his own face, not yet marked by battle, to relay the intensity behind his words. Most Ultramarines gave decades of service before they could be elevated to the ranks of the Reclusiam and wear the black armour of the Chaplain – Cassius was exceptionally young to serve in such a role.

In spite of his youth, and the fact that most of the Ultramarines now listening to him had more battlefield experience than he did, Cassius' words seemed to lock the congregation in place. His very presence demanded that he be heard.

'What is it that makes a single Ultramarine worth ten thousand of the enemy, and more?' began Cassius. 'Is it wargear from the forges of Macragge? The bolter and the chainsword, and the blessed power armour, are more than the equal of anything the greenskins can field. Is it the wisdom of the Codex Astartes that guides us in war, flowing from the hand of the Primarch Guilliman? Is it the augmentations within us all that make us more than men? No. All these things make us strong, but not victorious.'

Donatus watched the sermon from the passenger

compartment of the Stormraven that had brought the veteran squad back to the Ultramarines staging post. Having fought the greenskin mek and so needing to observe their wargear rites, the veterans had been excused from attending the sermon with their other battle-brothers. Donatus opened up the casing of his bolter, cycling the weapon to check the smoothness of its action.

'He has a way with words,' said Brother Adelmo, who was forcing out the dents that the greenskin had left in his armour. 'I'll give the boy that.'

'Just because we count ourselves as First Company veterans,' said Sergeant Tatianus, 'that doesn't mean he has nothing for us to hear.'

'It was not flowery words that bade me fight,' said Brother Felidus. 'The Codex gives any of us reason enough. Is this what the newly blooded among us react to, though? Sermons and exhortations? Just knowing the orks exist should be enough.'

'You were like them once, Felidus,' Tatianus muttered. 'You were not born into the galaxy a fully formed Sternguard. Cassius is young, but he deserves our respect.'

'And he's right about one thing,' said Adelmo. 'There are a *lot* of greenskins in that city.'

'You're not bored with killing orks?' asked Felidus mockingly. 'I would have thought the Deathwatch had fed you your fill.'

Adelmo tapped the silvered skull that hung among the purity seals and battle-honours on his chestplate. 'The first lesson the Deathwatch taught me, brother,' said Adelmo, 'is that there are *never* enough dead xenos.'

Donatus watched Chaplain Cassius spread his arms, brandishing his crozius arcanum, the short club-like power weapon topped with gilded eagle's wings. 'Yes, brothers – it is our fury that makes us victorious!' he exclaimed. 'Our rage! The unrelenting fruits of our hatred! This is what makes us the equal of an army of orks. Drink deep of that ocean of fury within you. Let it drive your arm, your bolter and your blade, into the hateful corpse of your enemy!'

The Chaplain pointed to the Sternguard. A dozen heads turned to regard them.

'Witness the slaying of the greenskin mek by Brother Donatus of the First Company! It was with rage and hate that he brought the alien low. Learn from such examples and turn your own fury into a weapon deadlier than a whole army of xenos!'

'Behold the rage of Donatus,' said Felidus, smirking as he cleaned the chapel dust from the eye-lenses of his helmet. 'Grab a handhold, brothers, lest the storm of his anger blow us all away...'

Donatus shot him a look. He let his bolter's action slide home and shut the casing. It had not been fury that had brought down the ork mek. It had been a cold, level-headed and thorough approach to war. A suppression of his anger, not a release of it.

'If that is what they need to hear,' said Donatus, 'then let him say it.'

'Let the greenskin stand before us!' Cassius continued. 'For we shall mow him down! Let the ork defy us, for we shall scorch him in the flames of our rage! I give thanks for the battle almost upon us, for we shall sweep away the greenskins on the great storm of our fury!'

The Ultramarines clapped their fists to their breastplates in a warrior's salute. In the distance, beyond the Astra Militarum encampments and motor pools, the ork-lit fires and smokestacks of Skemarchus billowed their smoky foulness into the sky.

This planet was already a place of smothering heat, but within hours it would be completely aflame.

Atmospheric silicate dust rained against the lower hull of the gunship, forcing it to pitch and yaw as the pilot wrestled against the fierce updraughts. The shifting expanses of molten rock below welled up from the planet's mantle, belching the raw geothermal heat of the core into the air.

Donatus held onto an overhead handle and watched through the armoured gunport as the Stormraven headed in low beneath the level of Skemarchus' streets. The city was built on a series of enormous platforms, its foundations sunk deep into the lava flow. Vast furnaces stood among heaped-up tenements and machine shops, part solid and fortress-like, part ramshackle death trap, all baked in the merciless heat hammering up from beneath. The sky over Skemarchus was smudgy darkness, fed by the foundry smokestacks and the new fires that consumed whole districts.

Even from a distance, the city was a torn and agonised wreck. Towers were toppled. Whole foundry-fortresses were torn open, laying bare their steel entrails to the sky, riddled with flame. One of the main platforms had sunk into the lava and was slowly being consumed, a brick and girder at a time.

'The greenskins despoil even that which they can turn to their use,' said Felidus, watching through the gunport beside Donatus. 'Like some in-built allergy to civilisation, they have to tear it down.'

'There's enough of Skemarchus left for them to

repurpose,' replied Sergeant Tatianus. 'If we don't dislodge them they'll turn the place into a factory for their war machines. That thing we fought at the chapel was just one of their meks – this place has drawn a thousand of them and their warbands.'

'Orks are vermin,' spat Felidus. 'They won't surrender. They're too stupid to give up.'

'Do not dismiss the greenskin mind,' said Adelmo. 'A single ork is bestial and crude. But in sufficient numbers they show a cunning that too many of the Emperor's armies have underestimated. Underestimating the intelligence of the alien will get you killed. I saw that much in the Deathwatch – we lost many good brothers who failed to learn that lesson.'

'I know well how dangerous the ork can be,' said Felidus. 'I am saying they will not break like an army of men. We're going to have to kill them all.'

'*One minute!*' came the vox from the pilot, Brother Otho. From below the edge of the nearest city-platform, it was possible to see the spaceport, a wide expanse of rockcrete overhanging the edge, the underside festooned with fuel pipes and coolant ducts. Control towers and comms-aerials rose over the landing pad, and as the gunship rose over the edge of the pad the scattering of ork emplacements came into view.

'They're holding it in force,' said Felidus.

'Of course they are,' said Adelmo. 'Like the sergeant said, they're not stupid.'

'They're standing in our way,' said Felidus grimly. 'That's the most stupid decision they'll ever make.'

The gunships had come in low to avoid any anti-aircraft capacity the orks had at the spaceport. Along with the

Sternguard Stormraven, another pair of gunships carried a force from Third Company led by Chaplain Cassius. As they crested the level of the landing pad, fire stuttered towards the strike force, ill-aimed but heavy volleys that traced burning chains between the gunships.

Donatus felt the Stormraven banking, and the view of the landing pad and the foundries behind it tilted as the gunship swept in towards the designated landing point.

The landing pad was covered in ork fortifications and firepoints, and the gunships would be hard-pressed to make a safe landing. With all the orks and their fortifications cleared away, the landing pad would be capable of receiving much larger ships, from bulk cargo craft to troop transports. That was the purpose of the Ultramarines' mission – to seize the spaceport, and open up a way for the Astra Militarum to land their troops directly in the centre of Skemarchus. Already units of soldiers were grinding into the edge of the city, supported by the rest of Third Company, but it would take them months to make headway fighting room to room through the outskirts. With a spaceport under Imperial control, armies could be sent into the heart of the city to begin forcing back the orks on multiple fronts.

If the spaceport was captured. If Chaplain Cassius and the Sternguard could break the greenskin hold, and open up the gates of Skemarchus.

The Stormraven swept over the landing pad. Scurrying orks shot by in a blur as they ran to take up firing positions. A few anti-aircraft rounds thunked into the hull and the Stormraven bucked.

'*Ten seconds,*' Otho's voice came again. '*Deploying ramp.*'

Donatus felt the Stormraven rearing and slewing under

Otho's control – the pilot had trained with the Chapter's Techmarines, and his skills on the controls were as honed as Donatus' behind a bolter. Donatus felt a spark of admiration for him, for though he might not be named in Cassius' sermons he was needed just as keenly if the Ultramarines were to wrench victory from the greenskins. As the Third Company's best pilot he had been assigned to transport the Sternguard, the most resilient and disciplined of the First Company's veterans.

The rear ramp of the passenger compartment swung open. The fuel-heavy air of Skemarchus swirled in with a roar. Brother Felidus hefted his storm bolter and fixed it to the mount on the open rampway, aiming the weapon out of the back of the gunship. The pilot tilted the gunship onto its tail as the front retros fired and Felidus opened fire at the greenkins running for cover, stitching explosive bolts across the stained rockcrete of the landing pad.

'We're down!' voxed Sergeant Tatianus.

'We are moments behind you,' replied Chaplain Cassius over the strike force's vox-net. *'Heed the word of Guilliman! As it is written, so it shall be!'*

The lower edge of the ramp touched down. Brother Adelmo was first out, firing as he jumped down onto the landing pad. Donatus and Tatianus followed, ducking low, Felidus' heavy bolter fire hammering above them.

The nearest cover was a massive steel docking clamp covered in bright ork graffiti, with a clutch of severed heads hanging from a crossbeam. A grimacing ork vaulted over the clamp and Donatus ran right at it.

A normal soldier would run from the enemy and seek safety, but a Space Marine knew that fleeing was the best way to give the enemy a chance to kill him without worrying about a return shot. Donatus raised his bolter, leaning into the stock as he ran, and let a tight cluster of shots fly. Three bolter shells smacked into the ork, ripping through its patchwork armour of blue-painted steel and detonating inside. The ork's chest was burst open and the xenos pitched face-first onto the rockcrete, dead before it hit the ground, lungs blown out through its back like shredded crimson wings.

Donatus slid into cover beside Adelmo. Behind him, Felidus was hauling the heavy bolter towards them.

'There's too much fire,' Otho voxed. 'I'm covering from above, where I can go to evasive.'

'We wish you clear skies, brother!' Sergeant Tatianus replied.

In battle the Sternguard served as an anchor point, a walking fortification that would hold the whole line intact while the rest of the Ultramarines prosecuted the battle plan. Roboute Guilliman had seen the need for such Space Marines to be organised together and deployed as one to maximise their effectiveness, and thus the doctrines of the Sternguard were found in the pages of Codex Astartes. Now they were the first down, the Ultramarines battle line would form.

The other pair of Stormravens touched down and the Third Company Ultramarines jumped out, spreading their fire in all directions, stuttering disciplined volleys at any ork in sight. Cassius landed just as a group of greenskins charged at the Ultramarines, the aliens eager to reap the glory of cutting down the intruders.

Half of the orks died as they leapt the barricade they had been sheltering behind. One was blasted to crimson mist by a burst of heavy bolter fire from one of the

Stormravens. Others were shredded by bolter shells. Cassius ran forwards, crozius in hand, and slammed into the lead ork.

The greenskin was an oversized brute clad in armour scraps and tattered xenos hides. Its left forearm had been replaced by a huge claw with blades like a set of industrial shears. The claw jabbed forwards and Cassius met it with his crozius. The weapon's power field discharged and the claw shattered, its blades spinning off, broken and scorched. The ork bellowed and Cassius rammed a fist into its mouth, splintering its teeth.

Cassius brought the crozius up into the ork's ribs. Another greenskin tried to get behind the Chaplain but the Ultramarines were spreading out around Cassius and one of them put a bolter round through the ork's spine. Cassius tore the crozius out again, bringing entrails and shards of broken rib with it, then slammed the weapon down to hit right between the huge ork's eyes.

Donatus heard the cheer that went up from his battle-brothers as the front of the ork's face caved in. It slumped to its knees, and Cassius smashed the crozius into the side of its head. The recharged power field discharged again and the upper half of the ork's skull was obliterated, spilling brains like wine from a chalice.

More anti-air fire was streaking overhead, dangerously low. It was too high to threaten the Ultramarines on the ground but the Stormravens were in danger of being picked off. The pilots took them up higher where they could weave out of the orks' gunsights and support with strafing runs from the air. The Ultramarines made for cover near the Sternguard, continuing to fire on the few orks that showed themselves.

'He could have stood back and let the bolters take those greenskins down,' said Donatus. 'No need to risk himself.'

'But then, what would we have to cheer?' replied Adelmo.

Cassius ran over to the Sternguard. Donatus saw he was already liberally spattered with orkish gore. 'Sergeant Tatianus! We have our foothold. Now we must exploit it.'

'Your plan?' asked Tatianus.

'We must not lose momentum. Keep pushing forwards. Advance and sweep the greenskins from this spaceport.'

'If we establish a firebase here then we can capture the spaceport point by point,' said Tatianus. 'Use our heads. Break them down a piece at a time, capture the pad then move on methodically. If we charge ahead we could become surrounded.'

'Hold back, and become swamped with reinforcements? The Codex is clear, sergeant. We must not hand the enemy the initiative.'

'Reinforcements are exactly what we should be worried about, Chaplain,' Donatus interjected. 'If we are caught in the open when they arrive, we will be done for, and we are fools if we think the greenskins do not have them close to hand.' He pointed over the steel bulk of the docking clamp, towards the far edge of the landing pad past control towers and refuelling stations. 'See? That factorium is lit up. It's at full capacity – I can feel its fires from here. The orks have had weeks to build their war machines. The Sternguard tactic is sound in this situation, Chaplain: win each patch of ground and ensure we are not exposed to the counter-attack.'

'You speak out of turn, brother,' said Cassius. 'I am the commander of this strike force. I know the Codex as well as any here and it is Guilliman's own fury that will win this battle, not a slow and tortuous advance that invites the greenskins to strike back.'

'It only takes a single bullet to turn a battle,' said Donatus. 'A round well placed can do what all our anger cannot. Find the right target and the greenskins will crumble.'

'Then until you find that target, brother,' replied Cassius, 'this battle will be fought my way.'

The Chaplain turned to the Ultramarines sheltering in the cover of the docking clamp, sniping with their bolters at the greenskins trying to outflank them. 'Brethren! With fury and steel the greenskin shall be swept aside! Give them not one second to gather their strength! With me, brothers, and show these vermin what rage burns in the sons of Macragge! Charge!'

Cassius jumped up onto the leg of the docking clamp, and for a moment he was silhouetted against the fires of the forge across the landing pad. The Ultramarines followed him, vaulting out of cover and breaking into a run as Cassius led the way.

'Damn,' spat Tatianus. 'Sternguard! Advance and support!'

The Sternguard followed the bulk of the force out of cover. The landing pad was an open space of battered rockcrete broken up by makeshift orkish defences. Some were barricades of fuel drums and rubble, others were based around the control towers and the structures that studded the landing pad. The cityward side was bounded by an enormous foundry, a glowering fortress that flared orange in all its windows and cavernous doorways. It was bad ground to take, covered by overlapping fields of fire from the orkish strongpoints. As the Ultramarines charged, the ork gunfire fell, spraying showers of rockcrete shrapnel, pinging off power armour and streaking from all sides.

One of the Stormravens swooped low, anti-aircraft fire pattering off its hull. It strafed one of the ork fortifications, knocking broken xenos bodies from the jagged battlements before a heavy burst of fire threw sparks from its underside and forced the pilot to pitch the nose upwards and out of the firing arc.

Cassius led the charge into the ork stronghold, using the seconds the pilot had bought him to take the fight to the orks inside. He scrambled up the welded metal detritus that formed the front wall, the bolter fire of the Ultramarines behind him raking across the battlements. One of the Ultramarines carried a missile launcher and he dropped to one knee, took aim and loosed a missile that ripped a sizeable bit out of the top of the fortifications. Cassius swung himself up into the gap and Donatus could see the flash of the Chaplain's crozius as he battled the orks inside.

'Watch our backs!' ordered Tatianus as the Ultramarines followed the Chaplain onto the battlements. Donatus glanced behind them to see a cadre of orks running from between cover, hoping to leap on the Ultramarines with cleavers and cutting weapons that looked like oversized welding torches.

Donatus raised his bolter. He didn't have time to swap ammunition – regular bolter shells would do. Eight or nine orks were in the force charging at the Sternguard and if they got among the veterans they could overwhelm them.

Donatus fired into the fuel tank one of the cutter-armed orks carried on its back. The tank exploded and liquid fire blossomed orange, flowing over the orks. Donatus let loose another volley, cutting down an ork that had avoided the worst of the flames, as Felidus' heavy bolter hammered fire into the remainder.

'Keep moving,' voxed Sergeant Tatianus. 'Don't get left behind.'

In a few moments the Ultramarines had seized the position. The orkish fortification was little more than a ring of makeshift barricades surrounding a noisome fire pit and heaps of bedding. It wouldn't hold. Donatus ran up to the front side and joined the Ultramarines that were finding loopholes and firing positions amid the wreckage.

'Brother Otho!' voxed Donatus. 'What do you see?'

'*It's like an ants' nest,*' replied Otho through the crackle of the vox. From his point of view in the Stormraven, the Third Company pilot could see far more than the battle-brothers on the ground. '*Greenskins swarming everywhere. I can't come down low, they've got Throne knows what mounted around the control tower. Talon Beta has already lost an engine.*'

Donatus recognised the call sign of Cassius' second Stormraven. The three gunships overhead were being mauled by the greenskins' anti-aircraft fire, and were struggling to keep up with the Ultramarines as they charged across the landing pad.

'Watch the forges,' replied Donatus. 'Stay high.'

'We cannot tarry here, brethren,' said Cassius. Donatus guessed a fair portion of the ork corpses littering the fortification had been claimed by the Chaplain's crozius and bolt pistol. 'These walls were put up by greenskins and they will not hold.'

'Take down those guns,' said Donatus. 'We cannot afford to lose our gunships.'

'Such aggression from the Sternguard?' asked Cassius. 'Are we not to burrow in and wait for the orks to come to us?'

'I have no less fury than you, Chaplain,' replied Donatus. 'Now you have brought us this far, we cannot go back. We must press on, for all it costs us.'

'Brother Donatus!' snapped Sergeant Tatianus. 'This is not the time to–'

Tatianus' words were cut off by the screech of a rocket exhaust. A split second later the explosion hit home, the shockwave hammering into Donatus as the side of the stronghold caved in. Flame burst and the blackness of churned rubble ripped over the Ultramarines, blotting out the reddish light of the weak sun.

Donatus came to rest on his back, his auto-senses fighting against the sudden darkness. Edged in the greys of his augmented darkvision, he could see a good chunk of the fortification had been blown in, scattering welded plates everywhere. Ultramarines were picking themselves up and running to take aim at this new threat. Donatus got to his feet, running through the mantra he had been sleep-taught as a novice to check himself for injuries. No bones broken, no organs torn, no penetrative wounds piercing his power armour. He still had his custom bolter, and held its preysense scope up to his eyepiece.

A short way across the landing pad was an orkish ammunition dump, well stocked with crates of rockets and bullets. The scope painted bright reds and yellows around the muzzles of the heavy weapons toted by the orks holding the ammo dump – rocket launchers and a heavy shoulder-mounted cannon, scavenged and repurposed from the defenders of Skemarchus who had fallen when the orks invaded. The Ultramarines' charge had brought them into the range of the greenskins' big guns and now the cannon opened up, raking the breached fortification with massive-calibre fire.

Sergeant Tatianus ran through the eruptions of fire, through the smoke and darkness. 'Leave this place!' ordered the sergeant. 'Eastwards, and find cover!'

Donatus followed Tatianus and the other Ultramarines leaving the shattered fortification. Another rocket streaked by, wayward in its aim, detonating against the far side of the fortification and throwing another shower of dust and wreckage into the air. Debris boomed and clattered down. Donatus paused to help another Ultramarine who was supporting a battle-brother – the wounded warrior's leg was twisted at an unnatural angle and even through the darkness Donatus could see the sheen of blood pouring from his knee.

The three made it to the nearest cover looming through the dust cloud – a series of raised coolant pipelines, already well ruptured by gunfire. Viscous coolant sprayed from the pipes and pooled around Donatus' feet. The wounded Ultramarine was placed against a solid-looking pipe junction.

Donatus had familiarised himself with the other battle-brothers in the strike force. The wounded Space Marine was Brother Scevola, being aided by Brother Vibius. Both were from Squad Senekus of the Third Company.

'It's just my leg,' growled Scevola. 'Two good trigger fingers and a mouth to curse the enemy, that's all I need.'

Half the strike force, including the Sternguard, had made for the cover of the pipe junctions. The other half had headed in the opposite direction to a series of half-collapsed machine sheds. Among racks of decommissioned shuttle parts, Cassius and the rest of the strike force were organising themselves into a firing line to suppress the orks still firing rockets and cannons at them.

'We still need to take that control tower,' said Donatus as he rejoined the Sternguard. He saw Brother Adelmo was not with them. The Deathwatch veteran had been separated from the Sternguard squad, or had fallen.

'And silence those damned big guns,' said Felidus.

'Cassius!' Tatianus shouted into the vox as another volley of rockets howled overhead. 'We cannot push forwards. The enemy has the field and he can bring fire on us from every direction. Consolidate and move by sections, one side covering the other. If we charge on, we'll be torn apart.'

'The greenskins will swamp us if we hold back,' came Cassius' reply. *'It is the fury of Macragge that will win this day!'*

'If the orks try to cut us off then we will mow them down,' replied Tatianus. 'If we charge again, we will leave the fury of Macragge bleeding on this landing pad!'

Donatus glanced up above the coolant pipes. More gangs of orks were sprinting across the open space, hauling heavy weapons and ammo boxes towards the command tower and ammo dump. The Ultramarines could use the split in their force to their advantage, one side moving to the next patch of cover while the other suppressed the worst of the ork fire with bolter volleys. It would be tough and bloody work for every step, but it was better than charging across the expanse of rockcrete again.

But Donatus was not in command. He was not the spiritual guardian of the Ultramarines, with a duty to preserve the wellbeing of their souls as well as secure victory. This was not his choice to make.

'If the greenskins want blood,' Cassius cried out, transmitting to the whole strike force, *'then we shall give it to them! We shall leave this whole place swimming in it! But it is not the blood of mankind that flows this day. Drown Skemarchus in xenos blood! Smother its fires with greenskin flesh!'* The Chaplain leapt clear of the cover of the machine-shops, the volleys of ork gunfire leaving him untouched as if he were charmed.

Donatus admitted to himself it was inspiring to see the young warrior leading from the front, brandishing his crozius like a standard raised high for the rest of the Ultramarines to follow. He could feel those fires in himself stoked by Cassius' example, too, in spite of all the passages in the Codex exhorting him to stay calm on the battlefield.

He felt the pull, as if there were a chain attached to his body that was being hauled on by Cassius. Donatus wanted very much in that moment to sprint into the open, to get face to face with the greenskin and deliver to it the justice of Macragge.

Among the Ultramarines massing behind Cassius was Brother Adelmo, who had been split off from the Sternguard and was now ready to join Cassius' charge. Donatus felt a twinge of envy, for Adelmo could let himself be dragged forwards by the pull of Cassius' words, he could abandon the prohibitions that came with serving in the Sternguard and fully indulge his hatred for the greenskins.

'Back him up!' ordered Tatianus. 'Keep the greenskins' heads down, but do not expose yourselves to fire!'

'Who will spurn the fight this day?' cried Cassius as he ran, an ork rocket spiralling past him. *'Who will wish his armour clean of xenos blood?'* The strike force followed him, firing

as they ran, the storm of ork fire hammering in return almost hiding them from Donatus' sight.

'Eyes north, brothers!' came Brother Otho's voice, distorted by the gunfire and the whine of his gunship's engines over the vox-net. *'The forge opens!'*

Donatus spotted the gunship overhead, weaving between columns of fire. The orks had fortified the landing pad with far more firepower than the Ultramarines had anticipated, and it had robbed them of their support from the air, but at least Otho had been able to use his eyes, even if his guns were quiet.

Donatus ran to the end of the cluster of pipes, leaning around to look towards the northern edge of the landing pad, the cityward side where the forge walls rose like the bulwarks of a fortress. A massive set of doors was swinging open, and the ruddy glow of its fires bled out.

A vast shape was silhouetted in the opening doorway. It was a barrel-shaped machine, easily twenty metres tall, that crunched forwards on a set of enormous tracks. Even at this distance, above the storm of gunfire, Donatus could hear the throb of its engines and the awful grinding of its tracks. Diminutive greenskins scrambled all over its surfaces or scurried out of its way.

The machine was a bizarre representation of an ork, like an idol of some savage greenskin god. On top of the body was a leering face of sheet metal with open portholes for eyes, and banners and totems stood in a steel forest across its shoulders. Its body was covered in blackened armour plates filthy with the smoke of the forge, and greenskin riggers still hammered the rivets that held it all together. One of the machine's arms was a gigantic claw with each of the three fingers covered in spinning cutting blades. The other arm was a cannon so big it was a miracle that the whole machine did not topple over. More skinny greenskin slave-creatures worked the ammunition hoppers on its shoulder to load a man-sized artillery shell into the breech.

'It's a gargant,' voxed Donatus. 'The greenskins have a gargant. Cassius! Brothers! Fall back, they have a war machine headed your way!'

The Ultramarines had fought the orks since the glorious days of the Great Crusade, for the greenskins were one of mankind's oldest and most persistent enemies. The orks possessed, in spite of their apparent savagery, some natural talent for engineering, as evidenced by the heavily armoured specimen Donatus had killed in the chapel. Their finest engineers flocked to major war zones like Skemarchus, and would pool their skills to forge enormous war machines such as the one now grinding its way across the spaceport's landing pad.

That was why the orks had taken Skemarchus – to create machines such as this one. The Imperial war effort was to take the city back before the orks could repurpose its forges, but in this one at least, they were too late.

A rocket burst just behind Cassius, throwing two Ultramarines off their feet – Donatus was sure that Adelmo was one of them. The Chaplain was almost at the control tower, bringing the rest of the force in his wake. He looked up at the war machine now advancing from the forge, and at the cannon being levelled right at him.

'*Do you see their blasphemy, brothers?*' cried out Cassius. '*They fear the divine right of mankind, and to face us they have crafted a graven image of–*'

The cannon roared.

A split second later, a huge shell slammed into the base of the control tower. A blackened plume of debris and smoke ripped out of it as the lower floors were pulverised by the explosive impact. The ork gunners and their anti-aircraft artillery were swallowed by the explosion and the tower toppled, its shattered windows like the black eyes of a skull.

Cassius and most of the strike force were swallowed in the wash of smoke. Secondary explosions crackled through the impact zone as ammunition cooked off.

'Chaplain!' Tatianus shouted into the vox. 'Speak, brother! Do you yet live?'

'Adelmo!' called Donatus. 'Brother Adelmo, speak!'

There was no reply from his fallen squadmate.

Donatus saw gunports opening up all over the ork gargant's body. Heavy mounted guns stuttered fire upwards, replacing the anti-aircraft guns lost moments ago.

Donatus leaned around the corner of the pipe junction and lifted his preysense scope to his eye. The multi-spectrum sight picked out fires burning in the smoky darkness, and hot shards of shrapnel studding every surface. Sundered corpses lay scattered around, their body temperatures registering as a fading glow – the remains of orks caught directly in the explosion. A few forms in the familiar shape of power armour lay on the ground while others moved through the darkness, retreating in good order back towards the machine sheds.

Ultramarines were disciplined. It was that which defined them. When even the bravest men and women of the Astra Militarum would be ruled by confusion and panic, the Ultramarines were still soldiers. That was what kept them alive as the orks tried to capitalise, the greenskins firing their heavy weapons at random through the smoke.

'There,' said Donatus, focusing on a figure that wore no helmet, propped up on one arm as it tried to get to its feet. 'The Chaplain's alive.'

'He does not answer,' said Tatianus.

'I see him,' said Donatus. 'His comm-link must be down. He's injured.'

The surviving orks were emerging from the ruin of the control tower. Dozens of them had survived, and more were running to the centre of the battlefield. Orks loved violence and destruction so the flame and smoke were magnets to them, promising them dying and wounded humans to kill.

Sergeant Senekus was taking the lead, forming the Ultramarines up into firing parties. Within seconds, bursts of bolter fire were scything into the orks, blowing limbs from bodies and ripping torsos open.

'Firebase, brothers!' ordered Tatianus. Felidus and the sergeant were up on the pipework, lending their own volleys to the crossfire that cut down the orks trying to charge through the blast zone.

'Who will bring in the young Chaplain?' asked Felidus between bursts from his heavy bolter.

'I will,' said Donatus. 'I can see him in my scope. The greenskins, too.'

The gargant's savage junk-metal face loomed above the billows of smoke. The greenskin riggers were fighting to reload the cannon, forcing out the massive spent shell. One of the gargant's eyes was thrown open like a hatch to reveal the ork driver, its gurning face surmounted by a pair of crude bionic eyes like mismatched goggles. It leaned out, clearly trying to get a better view of the battlefield. Then it pointed down at the Ultramarines sheltering behind the coolant pipes and yelled an order to its unseen subordinates.

'Displace!' ordered Tatianus. The Sternguard and the other Ultramarines around them ran from behind the pipework as the cannon swivelled to face them. Brother Vibius supported Scevola again, Scevola blasting fire at the orks as he leaned on Vibius' shoulder.

A few scattered chunks of wreckage lay nearby, offering little more shelter than a soldier's foxhole. It was the remains of a crashed lander, brought down in the early days of the invasion. A band of fleeing citizens must have died inside as ork fire brought the shuttle down, leaving scorched sections of its cockpit and passenger compartment smouldering on the landing pad.

Donatus slid into the cover of the shuttle cockpit as the gargant's cannon erupted. The pipework disappeared in another burst of flame and smoke, and a fountain of coolant spurted up high into the sky. The shockwave shuddered the rockcrete floor and gobs of coolant spattered down like greasy rain.

The smoke was clearing from around the tower. The tower had fallen completely, the length of it a sprawl of shattered rubble spilled across the landing pad. A scattering of Ultramarines lay unmoving, the blue of their armour masked by the dust of pulverised rockcrete, and Donatus recognised the battle-honours clustered on Brother Adelmo's chestplate. Chaplain Cassius was similarly caked in dust, but he was propped up on one arm. His bare head glistened crimson with blood.

A chunk of masonry had landed on his leg, pinning him in place. Cassius was trying to tear himself free but the weight wasn't budging. A dazed ork wandered out of the smoke and Cassius put two rounds into its chest without aiming.

Donatus broke cover. He ran towards Cassius and jumped into a shallow crater. The rockcrete was hot and smoking beneath him as he ducked beneath a volley of ork fire. Everywhere was bedlam and smoke, and only the discipline of the Ultramarines forged any order from the madness. Felidus' heavy bolter chattered behind him, forcing the orks to take cover, keeping a few more guns off Donatus as he advanced.

He made it to the length of the fallen tower, the crumbled masonry offering him solid cover against the orks. Cassius was a short sprint away, but the shadow of the gargant's cannon passed over him and he realised it might as well be a thousand miles. Adelmo lay further beyond, still unmoving.

More orks advanced on Cassius. Donatus shot one down with a round to the throat and Cassius shot another through the knee. The greenskin fell and was finished off by a second round from Cassius' bolter.

The gargant levelled its cannon at Cassius. The riggers had almost finished reloading another shell into the red-hot breech. Cassius tried again to force the weight off his immobile leg, but it would not budge.

'You told me that one bullet would turn the battle,' called Cassius, glancing over at Donatus. 'I will show you how one can turn a war. The veterans of the Sternguard think they have seen all of battle, but you still have much to learn. See how one shot stokes a fire in the hearts of our brethren that will never go out!'

Cassius pushed himself up to a sitting position and aimed his bolter at the steel cliff-face of the gargant's hull.

'Defiance, brothers!' he yelled. 'Thus, do I spit upon the works of the alien!'

Cassius fired a single shot. It pinged off the gargant's armour. An act of pure defiance, a final insult to the foe. Even at the moment of death, Chaplain Cassius was inflaming the rage of his battle-brothers. Every Ultramarine there would remember that shot, that defiance. They would speak of it, write of it, have the artisans of Macragge work it into chapel windows and the illuminators ink it into the Chapter's volumes of battle-lore.

Cassius was right. Donatus had much to learn. He had never before heard a cheer like the one that went up over the vox as the Ultramarines watched the Chaplain curse the orks with his single, futile bolter shell.

Donatus vaulted over the section of the broken tower. Orkish gunfire spattered and cracked around him. He led with his shoulder as he ran, taking two rounds on the shoulder guard and another on the armour of his thigh.

He grabbed one of the magazines mag-locked to his waist as he ran. He rejected the Kraken penetrator shell, even though it might have punched through the weaker armoured eye-hatch of the gargant. It might have found the driver, or some critical system – a fuel cell, a reactor shield – to set off a chain reaction. It was possible, but unlikely.

The Metal Storm shells were perfect for ripping through exposed ork flesh, but the riggers on the cannon had finished loading and, even if they were reduced to a gory mist, the gargant would still fire.

Instead, Donatus took out a single Dragonfire shell and loaded it into his bolter. He backed against the slab of masonry that was pinning Cassius to the ground. The barrel of the gargant's gun was aimed right at him, forming a staring black eye with a pupil of fire.

'Sometimes, Brother-Chaplain,' he said, 'defiance is not enough.'

Donatus took aim, the preysense scope cutting through the haze of smoke and dust.

An army of orks possessed a cunning that had slain far too many of the men who had underestimated it. The greenskins had, after all, taken Skemarchus and turned its forges to their own use, churning out war machines to continue their conquest of this planet and the sector beyond.

But that was an army. An individual ork was stupid.

Such an ork had built the ammunition dump where the xenos' heavy weapons were stationed. It had done so ignorant or uncaring of the fact that it was right beside one of the Imperial port's main fuel pumps, where the reservoir of promethium beneath could be tapped to feed the engines of a landed spacecraft.

Such an ork had then laid the heavy fuel hoses leading from the pump to the forge, to fill the gargant's fuel tanks. The same greenskin had jammed open all of the safety valves to send a constant torrent of fuel into the war machine, and the pump's joints and seals still leaked a greasy film across the rockcrete. Hoses had been torn free by the war machine's advance, and greenskin riggers were hammering at the valves with wrenches and lengths of iron pipe to close them again.

What had been a fuelling system sturdy enough to withstand a shuttle crash was now little more than an unexploded bomb thanks to the impatience and crudeness of the greenskins.

The Dragonfire shell was an incendiary, its core loaded with fast-burning explosives to turn the eruptive power of a bolter shell into an expanding ball of flame. The Kraken would have been certain to penetrate, but there was no guarantee the promethium would detonate as the bullet shrieked right through the machinery of the fuel pump and out the other side. The Dragonfire had to be aimed more carefully, at a weak point where one component joined another, but it was sure to have the desired effect.

Donatus pulled the trigger. The weapon bucked in his hand but he held it fast, the stock clamped against his shoulder.

In that moment, his world seemed to fall silent as the shot streaked through the air towards its target.

The shell punched into the side of the fuel pump. The promethium inside ignited instantly and ripped the pump apart in a burst of dirty orange fire. The flames washed through the ammo dump, silencing the orks that had been cheering Cassius' imminent death.

The dump exploded, a thousand detonations going off at once as the unstable munitions went up. Every safety precaution the builders of the spaceport had made was rendered irrelevant as hundreds of explosive rounds ripped through the unsecured fuel lines into the rock-crete beneath the ammo dump. Multiple steel skins were ruptured and incandescent shrapnel tore into the main body of the fuel reservoir beneath the landing pad.

It took less than a second, but Donatus could follow every link of the chain. The fuel reservoir ruptured and near-tectonic ripples ran across the landing pad as the rockcrete rose up in fracturing waves. Gouts of flame lashed up high into the air. The underside of the landing pad gave way and the upper surface caved in, plunging what remained down towards the lava river below.

The hole grew as more and more shattered rockcrete fell. The burning stump of the control tower fell in and brought the chunks of fallen rubble with it. The slab of masonry pinning Cassius to the ground slid into the growing maw and Donatus grabbed the Chaplain by the shoulder guard, dragging him away from the chasm.

The edge of the collapse reached the track of the ork gargant. The riggers were leaping off the war machine's shoulders, their bodies breaking against the rockcrete as they chose to jump rather than face what was coming. The ork in the eye-hatch panicked as it tried to clamber out, but before it could haul its bulk towards safety the whole gargant tilted as its track tipped over the edge of the chasm.

The collapse halted as it reached the massive supporting beams that shored up the landing pad. The gargant was caught on the edge, one track hanging over the abyss, its metal hulk lit by the blood-red glow of the lava rushing past beneath. Vast masses of fallen rubble and machinery were disintegrating in the superheated flow, to be submerged and swept away. Donatus could not help but stare down into the churning lava as he helped Cassius back away towards the machine sheds.

The gargant was immobile for a moment, the ork clinging to the front of its junk-metal head grinning with relief as it sensed safety. Then its face fell as the edge of the collapse crumbled a little more and it slowly, painfully, tipped towards the hole. Artillery shells fell from the open hopper and loose tools and components rained from the open hatches. Riggers too cowardly to jump moments earlier dangled from handholds on the gargant's jagged armour, one screaming as it lost its grip and tumbled into the scalding air billowing up from the lava.

The gargant's fall sped up as the ground continued to give way beneath it. With a roar of twisting metal and fracturing rockcrete, it tumbled into the hole and its vast, ponderous bulk plunged into the lava. It hit hard, the top half buckling in the impact against the surface of the lava, the orks and countless tonnes of steel vanishing in plumes of oily flame. The rest of it was drawn slowly downstream, the metal warping and stretching in the heat, pulling the war machine apart like a body on a rack.

Cassius forced himself to his feet, leaning against the bullet-scarred wall of the machine shed.

'One bullet,' the Chaplain said over the vox. 'One bullet is all it takes... and we have a thousand bullets to spare! The greenskins cower and grovel in despair. They beg for the silence of death. Let us indulge them, my brethren! The fires have consumed their god, and now let the fires of our vengeance consume the alien!' Cassius limped a couple of steps on his wounded leg, bolt pistol and crozius in hand, before Sergeant Senekus ran forwards to support him.

Donatus knew that the Sternguard should lend fire from the back line, but he felt the fire that Cassius spoke of within himself too, now. The Chaplain was right – the loss of their idol had broken the will of the orks and they would never be more vulnerable. The Ultramarines had to hit them hard, relentlessly, breaking them and sweeping them from the spaceport before they could regroup and pin the strike force down again.

They had lost battle-brothers on this landing pad.

Brother Adelmo had vanished in the bedlam of the collapse. He had not been the only one. The grief was like fuel on the fire.

Donatus saw in his mind the bodies of the Ultramarines cut down by the gargant's cannon and the wounds dealt to his battle-brothers, and the burning towers of Skemarchus where thousands of the city's inhabitants had died fighting for their home. He imagined Adelmo's dusty body, perhaps still alive, sprawled on the rockcrete. He pictured the soldiers of the Astra Militarum who had died already on this world, and those who would die in the days to come.

And he saw the greenskin savages who existed solely to tear down the works that generations of mankind had sweated and bled to create.

It felt good to let the rage consume him. Donatus slammed home a whole magazine of Metal Storm shells. A few moments ago he would have preserved every one of the precious rounds, and cursed himself for each that he failed to return to the Chapter's armoury on Macragge at the campaign's end. But now he would seek punishment for every one not buried in a greenskin's body.

Donatus let the young Chaplain's words take him over. He joined the charge, following Cassius' lead as the Ultramarines ran past the enormous burning hole in the landing pad towards the bands of orks who had been strafing them with gunfire. He heard those orks crying out, bellowing panicked orders or simply jibbering nonsensically.

The strike force crashed into them, despatching greenskins with bolters and combat blades. Cassius was aided by Sergeant Senekus as he put a bolt through one ork with his pistol and drove his crozius into the back of another's skull. The Ultramarines moved on from each knot of orks, leaving the barricades and makeshift firepoints draped with ork corpses. Donatus hammered a volley of shredding shots into a trio of orks trying to flee, and they vanished in a mist of gore.

He let the rage drive him on, as the Ultramarines cut their way through a wall of greenskin flesh to open the doors of Skemarchus wide.

He would make the xenos pay.

A heavily modified Chimera drove a mass of smouldering wreckage towards the edge of the platform with its dozer blade and pushed it off, sending it raining towards the liquid fire several storeys below. It was gradually clearing an area large enough to land one of the Astra Militarum dropships, which would ferry hundreds-strong units of infantry into the centre of Skemarchus. It would be a long time before the spaceport could receive bulk landers with its primary landing pad in ruins, but it would soon serve as a makeshift airfield for the Astra Militarum.

Another Chimera, the roof removed from its passenger cabin, was serving as a corpse wagon. It was heaped high with ork bodies, likewise destined to be thrown over the edge. Field engineers were fixing makeshift fuel tanks and laying power cabling under the supervision of Adeptus Mechanicus enginseers.

The Ultramarines meanwhile held the picket, covering all ways in with overlapping fields of bolter fire. A few orks had ventured out of the shadows of the enormous foundry only to be trapped between the dead ends of burning forges and the guns of the Ultramarines. Those few greenskins that had shown their faces since had been shot down with precision fire from the Space Marines.

Donatus finished his post-battle wargear rites, strip-cleaning his bolter and taking a tally of his ammunition. He had fired off all of his Metal Storm shells and half his regular bolter rounds. His Dragonfire magazine was down a single shell. He looked up from the flak-weave barricade of the Ultramarines command post as Brother Otho's Stormraven swooped overhead, banked to slow, and came down to rest on the surface of the platform. Chaplain Cassius, his leg shored up with a temporary bracing splint, limped over to the gunship as the cockpit door swung open. He was still as fresh-faced and unmarked as a novice, though the weight of perhaps a few more years seemed to darken his eyes.

'Any sign of the fallen?' he asked gravely.

Otho swung himself out of the cockpit. 'None, Chaplain.' He stepped through the heat haze rising off the lower hull of the gunship. 'I took the squadron on three passes but there is precious little that hasn't sunk into the lava. We surveyed what we could before the heat and silicates became too much for the engines. They are not there. We have lost them.'

'I see,' said Cassius. 'My thanks, brother.'

'They are gone?' asked Donatus as Cassius turned away from the gunship.

'They are.'

The Codex Astartes required the battle-brothers killed in the battle for the spaceport to be recovered so their wargear and the geneseed that controlled their augmentations could be returned to the Chapter. But the bodies of many had fallen into the hole in the landing pad that swallowed the ork gargant, and had been incinerated in the lava.

Donatus had not known all of those Space Marines well, but an injury to one was an injury to all. Each Space Marine was the culmination of years of training and the distillation of millennia of battle-lore, a rare individual hand-picked by the Chaplains to carry out the will of the Emperor. Each one that fell could never truly be replaced.

And Adelmo had been more than a mere battle-brother to Donatus.

The veteran of the Deathwatch had been his friend – an inspiration, reliable and relentless in battle yet somehow still light-hearted enough to remind Donatus of the reasons why the Ultramarines fought. It would be fitting, thought Donatus, if he could one day do his fallen brother the honour of following in his footsteps by entering the Deathwatch. Adelmo's geneseed might be lost, but his legacy was not.

'We will mourn them,' said Donatus. The words were not nearly enough to sum up what was inside him, but he had never been the most garrulous soul and he could think of no more to say.

'They will serve us still, in memory,' replied Cassius. 'They helped stoke the rage in you, did they not? In all of us. Those fallen brethren killed their share of greenskins this day. And they will tomorrow, too.'

'I felt the anger you spoke of,' said Donatus, 'and I followed it. In all my decades I have not ridden the wave of my rage as I did today.'

'And in all mine,' replied Cassius, 'I have not seen one bullet fell so many.' He paused. 'The same Codex leads us both. The primarch was a master of all forms of war, and so must we strive to be. I have my way and you have yours – so long as neither dies out, the Chapter will have a use for us both.'

An Astra Militarum staff shuttle descended onto an area just cleared by the engineers. It bore the laurels of a regimental commander, and carried the officers who would orchestrate the next stage of the campaign to retake Skemarchus. The opening moves of the battle had been made. Now the next stage was about to commence, and the Ultramarines would be at the leading edge of the advance. Soldiers rushed to secure the shuttle as it touched down and the ramps lowered, allowing a gaggle of ornamented and uniformed officers to emerge, heavy with medals and brocade, in the uniforms of several regiments.

'I must direct them,' said Cassius. 'They will ask much of us. I must ensure they play their part, too. We will have much to speak of when this city is won, Brother Donatus. For now, pray with your brethren.'

'I shall, my Chaplain.'

'And thank your bolter for me.' Cassius gave a smile, the first Donatus had ever seen on his face, and walked away to join the officers.

BAD BLOOD

STEVE LYONS

They dropped out of the warp.

Antor heard the pitch of the ship's engines changing, felt a shudder passing through its hull. His eyes snapped open.

The shutter over his single viewport retracted, and he could see realspace again. It had been too long. At the same time, it was too soon.

The strike cruiser *Incontrovertible Truth* would shortly reach its destination: two hours, maybe longer, depending on how accurate its jump had been. He wasn't ready. His blood was running hot today and his mind was unsettled. He needed more time to cleanse himself.

He closed his eyes again and breathed deeply, sitting cross-legged on his utilitarian bunk. He tuned out all other sounds but for those of the machinery, clicking and ticking in time with his dual heartbeats. He tried not to think about the suit of power armour looming over him, its blank-eyed helm accusing.

The armour was black and silver, but for the right shoulder plate. This was a deep red and bore the image of a drop of blood with angel wings: a stark reminder of where Antor Delassio had come from, and what he still carried with him.

A reminder that he wasn't worthy.

The Cursed Young Prince. That was what his brothers called him – at least, the handful who shared his secret, who knew of his shame. Antor had sworn to them that he could beat his curse, and indeed, he had kept it under control for months now, but it never entirely went away.

What would they say if they could see me now? he wondered.

There were needles in his veins. He could feel his blood being drawn through them into the machine: a half-rusted arcane box with switches and dials and blinking runes, and bubbling glass vials inside it. The machine was supposed to purify his blood, consecrate it and pump it back into him. He knew from experience, however, that it wouldn't be sufficient. He also needed to meditate and pray.

He tried to clear his mind again, to meditate on the glory of the Emperor. But Antor couldn't keep his thoughts from wandering. He couldn't help but remember another day, four years ago. He had been aboard the *Incontrovertible Truth* then too, quartered in this very cabin.

The day the ship had been attacked.

The day the curse had blighted him for the very first time, and overwhelmed him.

Antor had been so proud, then.

Of course, he didn't let it show. Such had never been

his way. Many who had met him had remarked upon the contrast between this junior sergeant's noble bearing and the quiet humility with which he unfailingly comported himself.

Still, when first he had clad himself in the black and silver, with no one but his attendant serfs to see it, he had allowed his chest to swell a little.

Chapter Master Dante himself had awarded him this great honour. Antor had been seconded to the Deathwatch for an indefinite tour of duty. He was one of the very few Blood Angels – at the time – to be welcomed into that august assemblage.

Quietly, he had thanked the Emperor for this opportunity to serve Him and had never really questioned why he, of all his battle-brothers, had been chosen. He had polished his new suit of artisan armour until it gleamed, and had always been the first of every kill team he had joined to report for muster.

He had distinguished himself in a dozen missions already, bringing down the wrath of the Emperor's Inquisition upon the hated xenos across the galaxy.

But that day, he was roused from his sleep by the call to battle stations.

He had already begun to struggle into his armour when his cabin door flew open and a serf – a single serf – arrived to help him. He recited each invocation and performed each necessary ritual patiently. Lights flared outside his viewport. The ship shuddered with the impacts of missiles against its shields, but Antor didn't allow that to distract him. He would have no use for his jump pack here in the ship's narrow chambers and corridors. He inserted his vox-earpiece and sifted through the channels.

The time was an hour before morning prayers.

They had dropped out of the warp early, as Antor had slept. That meant they had probably arrived in the Erioch System of the Jericho Reach. Some of Antor's brothers were to begin a tour of duty at the watch fortress there. Antor himself was bound for the planet Mariach, along with a new kill team, to push back the eldar raider incursions.

A vessel had been lying in wait for them. A grand cruiser.

It had likely been a proud member of the Imperial Navy, many centuries ago. The touch of Chaos had defiled it, warping its very shape. It was a bigger ship than theirs, and smaller escorts buzzed around it like flies.

Watch Captain Gharvil had launched the Thunderhawks. There had been four in the bays, a three-brother response team for each of them kept on standby at all times.

The *Incontrovertible Truth* carried forty-four Deathwatch Space Marines. There was little the remaining thirty-two could do, however, except prepare themselves and report for muster. Their immediate fate was in the hands of their pilots and gunners.

As Antor left his cabin, an explosion rocked the ship violently. He clung to a sconce, riveted to the wall, to keep his balance. More battle-brothers began to emerge from the doors around him.

'That sounded close,' said Brother Casella. He had come to the Deathwatch from the Crimson Fists; his shoulder plate bore their colours of blue and red. 'I wouldn't be surprised if that–'

Another explosion cut him off. This time, the deck plates dropped out from underneath their feet. In the moment before the artificial gravity compensated, Antor judged that they had been thrown into a lateral spin. He drew his hand flamer *Ignatus*, presented to him in gratitude by the Ordo Xenos, though he had no target for it.

He started to run.

He came up short as he rounded the bend of an arterial passageway, to find a bulkhead grinding down in front of him. Casella came to a halt beside him.

'The hull has been breached,' Brother Lokar – a wiry young Space Wolf with red hair and teeth sharpened to points – growled, loping up behind them. 'The starboard mid-sections of decks epsilon through theta have been sealed off.'

Antor was receiving the same information through his earpiece.

'Throne forbid that we should die today without ever setting eyes upon our enemy,' said Brother Sanctimus, seconded from the Ultramarines.

'We won't. We need to find a way around.' Antor was already running several potential solutions through his mind, and he knew the others were too.

Eight of them had gathered in front of the bulkhead, in all. Eight Space Marines – none of whom had ever fought together before – from various Chapters. Lokar took charge, leading them back the way they had come. He was a veteran, a Wolf Guard, in his own Chapter.

Antor saw a flaming Thunderhawk reel past a viewport, and a larger shape – a dark shape, a profane shape – loom behind it. He only caught the briefest glimpse of the enemy cruiser.

He couldn't have described it in any useful detail, nor begun to articulate why it disturbed him so much. He only knew that, in that moment, he felt an indefinable ache in his primary heart.

A chill ran up and down his spine, and he thought he must have bitten his tongue, although he hadn't.

He was sure he could taste blood.

Antor had heard it called the Red Thirst, but in truth he had rarely heard it discussed at all. He had seen its effects, however.

He had seen brave and noble brothers overcome on the battlefield by an uncontrollable fury. He had seen their faces contorted with madness, seen their eyes ablaze with hatred, heard their screams of primal rage.

He had seen some consumed by it, mowed down as they charged the enemy's guns and tanks, heedless of any risk. He had heard of others turning upon their allies, lashing out blindly. Some had been subdued and gradually brought back to their senses enough to fight another day, though this was becoming more rare. Each time it happened, an Apothecary or a Chaplain would blame it on something in the afflicted warrior's blood – if anything was said at all.

Antor had looked at his fellow Blood Angels sometimes, wondering how many more of them might be containing the rage inside them. He had even wondered – but put the thought out of his mind, for that way led paranoia – if he could fully trust them.

Each time, they had buried their fallen brothers with full honours in the red dust of their primarch's home world, Baal Secundus. They had mourned their dead, but rarely spoken of any of them again. Back then, whenever he prayed, Antor was thankful that he did not share their affliction. He had always kept a cool, clear head and an even temperament, no matter how he might have been provoked.

Perhaps his blood was pure.

Alarms were screaming, both inside his armour and outside of it.

Antor could barely hear them. The explosion had deadened his ears.

It had also blown a jagged hole in the *Incontrovertible Truth*'s hull, and one luckless brother had been caught in the blast, his armour shredded. Before he could react, before Antor or anyone else could reach him, he had been whipped out into space.

Antor magnetised his boots. He hauled himself forward, one laborious step at a time. A hurricane was blowing in his face, making his eyes tear up, but he couldn't catch a breath of it. He jammed his helmet down over his head and sealed it, gasping in its recycled air reserves.

Brother Grennon was holding up a bulkhead hatch for him, motioning to him to hurry. Some of the others had already made it through. Antor dived for the narrowing gap, sliding through it on his stomach. Hands caught him by the wrists and hauled him the rest of the way. As he turned to help the brothers behind him, Grennon rolled out from underneath the hatch and let it slam down.

'I could hear the machine-spirits in the shutter, screaming,' he explained, his voice crackling over a short-range vox-channel. 'Another second and this section would have been–'

A voice from behind the bulkhead interrupted. *'Leave*

us. We'll find another way around and join you later. May the Emperor be with you.'

'And with you,' Lokar voxed back. He addressed the others through his speaker grille, brusquely. 'He's right. We must keep going.'

Antor was running again; only now he was one of five Space Marines, rather than eight. They had left three behind, trapped by adamantium-plated shields: one of them certainly dead, the others facing an arduous space walk to the launch bays with limited air reserves, in the deadliest possible circumstances.

Lokar held up a hand to halt them. His head was cocked. 'Do you hear that?' he asked. His senses were keener than those of his brothers, a quirk of his gene-seed.

'I hear more explosions,' said Grennon. He was heavy-set, stolid. Antor hadn't seen his Chapter's symbol before: the silhouette of a grasping claw, picked out by orange flames.

'We are wasting time,' growled Sanctimus.

'Something has changed. The vibration of the deck plates,' said Lokar. 'I think... yes, we have lost the starboard engines.'

A moment later, vox-chatter confirmed it, along with another chilling development.

'All battle-brothers to the port aft cargo hold,' Watch Captain Gharvil instructed from his command post on the bridge. *'The enemy ship is coming alongside. Repeat, all battle-brothers to the port aft cargo hold. Prepare to repel boarders.'*

Antor remembered how he had felt, back then.

He remembered the knot that had begun to form in his stomach, tightening with every blind corner he had turned, every obstacle he had found in his path. It was not fear, far from it.

It was a sense of his duty, imperilled.

But that was only natural, wasn't it?

His ship had been under attack. His battle-brothers were fighting to protect it, to protect him and everyone else on board, and he yearned to fight alongside them – but no matter how hard he tried, how fast he ran, he couldn't reach them.

He knew that the others, his four disparate allies, felt it too.

Lokar had been taking out his frustrations on them.

'Russ, but the greenest Blood Claw back home is faster than the four of you!' he snarled, as another compromised section of the ship was sealed off just as they reached it.

'You brought us this way,' Sanctimus snapped back at him, 'insisting that your "instincts" were superior to our Emperor-given gifts.'

Lokar bridled. 'My instincts are as much the All-Father's gift as–'

'Please, brothers,' Antor intervened, well-used to mediating between those of shorter temper than he. 'Listen.'

He was following the progress of the battle through his earpiece. Three of the Thunderhawks had been destroyed; the last had limped its way back into its launch bay. The Deathwatch had taken out most of the smaller enemy ships, at least. The *Incontrovertible Truth* was crippled, however, and unable to throw off the Chaos vessel as it extended a docking claw and clamped onto the strike cruiser's hull.

'They're blasting their way through the airlock,' Antor reported quietly. His words had the desired effect, refocusing minds upon their immediate predicament.

'I say we stand the best chance if we descend to one

of the lower decks before making our way forward,' suggested Casella.

'Let's do it,' said Sanctimus, seizing the opportunity to take the lead. Lokar scowled at the Ultramarine, a growl rattling in the back of his throat, but he followed along with the others.

According to the vox-net, fifteen Space Marines – around half of those left aboard – had made it to the cargo hold. The watch captain himself had joined them. They were waiting behind barriers hastily assembled from sturdy cargo crates when the inner airlock door was wrenched from its runners. Frag grenades rolled through the aperture and exploded, loosing shrapnel, smoke and confusion. Then their attackers appeared, marching brazenly out of the thick fog, hammering bolt-rounds out ahead of them.

For a long moment, all Antor could hear through his earpiece was gunfire, then Watch Captain Gharvil's voice, clearly under enormous strain, came through.

'*All battle-brothers to the port aft cargo hold, immediately. We're under attack…*' There was a pause then, and more gunfire. '*…attack by Traitor Space Marines – Black Legion!*'

The knot in Antor's stomach twisted. The watch captain could have breathed no viler a curse than that name. And suddenly, he felt that pain in his heart again, sharper this time, as if he had been stabbed through the chest with an icicle. It felt like pain, sadness, loss and the infinite cold of the void.

The ticking of his lashed-together machinery brought Antor back to the present, to his cabin. His heartbeats had sped up.

Even now, four years on, the memory of that day had

that effect on him. He felt as helpless, as frustrated, as he had back then.

He could taste blood again. He was sweating and his robes clung to his muscular torso.

He had never made it to his destination – though his ad hoc team had come close, so tantalisingly close. Casella's plan had been a good one. They had threaded their way through the *Incontrovertible Truth*'s undercroft bilges, through the engine rooms where servitors laboured over spitting rune panels and steaming pistons, though most had already been burnt or crippled in the effort.

They had agreed that the conveyors couldn't be trusted, and had been looking for another way up to the mid-decks when Watch Captain Gharvil had perished.

The battle-brothers in the cargo hold had fought well – by their own accounts – but they had been badly outnumbered. Ten, eleven, twelve Black Legionnaires had fallen, but more had poured through the airlock behind them, until the defenders' barriers had been swept aside and they had been overrun.

It was reported that Gharvil had stood toe to toe with three opponents, slaying one with his power sword and badly wounding a second, giving the remainder of the invading force pause and buying time for his few surviving brothers to withdraw.

'Four of us made it out,' a breathless voice crackled over the vox-channels. *'We have sealed off the hold, but that won't delay them long. We must deny them the ship! They–'* The rest was swallowed by a furious blizzard of static.

'They're jamming our communications,' said Sanctimus. 'We need to reach that hold.'

'No. You heard what happened up there,' insisted Lokar. 'Now is not the time for a frontal assault. We need to employ stealth and cunning. In my Chapter–'

'That sounds like the justification of a coward!' snapped the Ultramarine.

The Space Wolf bristled and squared up to him.

'There must be other groups like ours,' said Antor quickly, 'each cut off from the others. If we could find them–'

'What hope of that, without the vox-net?' asked Casella. 'Our attackers are employing the classic tactic – divide and conquer.'

'We should follow our commander's final orders,' considered Grennon.

'And go marching to the slaughter?' Lokar scoffed. 'The situation has changed. Our watch captain is dead. Most of our brothers are dead, and we can't contact the rest.'

Antor leapt into the ensuing silence. 'They want our ship. Or any ship, perhaps. They can't have known exactly where we'd emerge from the warp, yet they were waiting for us. I wonder how long they were waiting?'

'They could have destroyed us,' agreed Grennon.

'Instead, they sent a boarding party knowing some of them would die,' said Antor.

'What does any of this matter?' growled Lokar, impatiently.

'If we know what they want,' said Antor, 'we can predict their next move.'

'What if there is something aboard this ship?' suggested Grennon. 'Something being conveyed to Watch Fortress Erioch? Is that possible?'

'I don't know,' confessed Antor. 'The watch captain would have known. If there is, they will likely come looking for it. Or for us.'

'We wouldn't have to go to them,' Casella realised. 'We can find a good defensible position and lay an ambush for them.'

Lokar's eyes flashed. 'Stealth and cunning. We can strike at our enemies from the shadows, tear out their throats before they even know we're there.'

Antor Delassio waited.

They had planned their ambush carefully, and not without further disagreement. They remained on one of the lower decks, assuming that anything of value – and so secret that they hadn't been briefed about it – would be hidden down there.

They had chosen a rarely used passageway, but one that – with so many rendered impassable – their enemies were almost certain to pass through. Casella had shot out two lumen-globes, cloaking the Deathwatch in darkness. So much damage had been done throughout the ship that his sabotage would likely go unrecognised as such.

The servitors had failed. The last engine had sputtered out some twenty minutes ago. The *Incontrovertible Truth* was now a dead husk, drifting helplessly. All was silent, but for the occasional creaks of tortured adamantium settling into place.

Antor crouched out of sight. He had made sure that his armour was sealed, giving off no emissions or heat signatures that an auspex could detect. He had cleaned and reloaded his hand flamer.

Brother Sanctimus had agreed to wait one hour. If there were no signs of Black Legionnaires by then, the remaining Deathwatch would seek them out.

'They are probably storming the bridge already,' he had grumbled.

In the event, they appeared long before the hour was up: four of them, to begin with, advancing raggedly by sections. Antor hadn't expected them to be so disciplined. Their black power armour had burnished golden highlights. On their shoulders, each bore an eye symbol staring out of an eight-pointed star, and their bearing betrayed a monstrous pride.

After all they have done, thought Antor, barely noticing that his right hand had curled into a fist, too aware of his own heartbeats in his ears.

He couldn't see his battle-brothers from his position. They had no way of signalling each other to coordinate their attack.

Lokar acted first, as everyone had known he would. Once the traitors had passed his hiding place, he fired a burst of expertly placed bolt-rounds into their backs. Barely had they begun to react when Brothers Sanctimus and Grennon tackled them from left and right. Antor relished the screams their chainswords made as their teeth chewed on the traitors' armour.

Blood rushed to his head as he uncoiled himself and burst through the storeroom door. Red blotches filled his vision and, as he blinked them away, he almost stumbled. Consequently, he was a fraction of a second behind Casella, emerging from the doorway opposite to block the traitors' path, his boltgun already roaring.

The nearest traitor saw Antor's misstep and barrelled towards him, hoping to overrun him as he brought *Ignatus* to bear. He wasn't fast enough, and was met by a gout of flaming promethium to the face which sent him reeling.

Too bad he was wearing his helmet, Antor thought. He fancied he could detect the pungent smell of burnt flesh all the same.

He struck downward with his chainsword, spattering his artisan armour in gore. He had already raised his arm again when he realised that his enemy was dead. Abashed, he thumbed his chainsword's activation rune, letting it sputter to a halt. He turned to face his battle-brothers, but saw no reproach in their eyes.

Antor paused. The battle was over. When... When had he...

He shook his head in confusion. The events of the past few minutes were already a blur to him. He remembered Sanctimus standing tall in the thick of the melee bellowing orders, which Grennon and none of the others had followed. He remembered the smell of electrical discharge, fire and blood.

The Black Legionnaires had fought hard, but the Deathwatch's numbers and the element of surprise had ultimately won the day.

With their deaths, the knot in Antor's stomach unwound a little.

'Four down,' Casella gloated.

Sanctimus nodded curtly. 'We did well. Better than I expected, thank the Emperor.' Casella was nursing a lame arm, while a plasma pistol burst had warped one side of Grennon's chest armour and must have melted the flesh beneath it too. Otherwise, the Ultramarine was right – they were blessedly unscathed.

'The traitors will have voxed for reinforcements,' Antor reminded them.

'We have to move,' agreed Grennon.

They had pre-planned their escape route. Lokar led the way by virtue of being the fastest of them. He had removed his helmet, and he curled back his lips to expose his fangs. 'We'll lay another ambush on another deck. Two, three more times, and these traitors will wish they had never set foot aboard our ship.'

This time, nobody disagreed with him.

Four down, thought Antor. It's a start, at least.

Further along, they climbed a maintenance ladder, squeezing their armoured bulks through a hatchway designed for serfs and mobile servitors.

Emerging onto the next deck up, they were greeted by a sight that dampened their newfound optimism. There had been a battle here too, but with a very different outcome. Three Deathwatch Space Marines lay sprawled across the deck plates, their bodies burnt, slashed and battered. Antor knew their names; he had been due to fight alongside two of them on Mariach.

A Black Legionnaire, too, had been left where he fell. But only one.

'Do these savages not even come back for their own dead?' rumbled Sanctimus.

Lokar sniffed the air. 'They are still close by. We should move on.'

Before they did, Grennon knelt beside the bodies. He salvaged a handful of bolter clips and tossed them to the others. 'In case of need.' He eyed a powerful plasma gun, clutched tightly in the Black Legionnaire's dead hands, before quickly dismissing the idea of wielding a weapon so irredeemably tainted.

Antor was glad when they moved away from that place.

The loss of a brother, any brother, was a tragedy. It was a fact of his existence, however, to which he had grown accustomed long ago. And yet, there was something indefinable about this loss that made it weigh heavily upon him. Perhaps it is the premonition of my own fate, he considered.

Little more than a minute later, they heard footsteps: more than a dozen pairs, by his reckoning, half of them heavily armoured, coming their way.

Lokar, as always six steps ahead of the others, flattened himself beside an open hatchway and waited. For the rest of the Space Marines, there was scant cover to be had. Instead, they drew their weapons, ready to defend themselves.

However, the footsteps turned away from them.

'Sounds like they're descending a stairway,' Grennon whispered.

Lokar motioned to the others to stay put, and crept after the footsteps. Antor was amazed at how silent he could be in power armour.

He returned after a couple of minutes to report. 'Eight traitors, plus degenerate human slaves, headed downward. I don't think they were a search party – if they were, they weren't searching very hard. They seemed to know where they were going.'

'They're headed for the engine rooms,' Antor realised.

Sanctimus glared at him accusingly. 'Then you were wrong. It is our ship they want – and they want it in working order. We should have defended the engines. Or gone to the bridge, as I wished.'

'Should we go after them?' asked Grennon.

'They outnumber us,' said Lokar, 'but if we sneak up behind them, Russ willing, we may be able to–'

'I say we stick to our plan,' said Casella.

Antor nodded. 'I agree. The engines are dead. Let the traitors try to repair them if they wish – if that is indeed what they are doing. In the meantime, we shall be hunting down their allies, trapping and exterminating them like rats. If the Emperor is with us, we may find more survivors too and build our numbers.'

His voice, rarely raised in passion, was rich and sonorous. The others listened to it and – somewhat to his surprise – were swayed by it. 'And if we cannot prevail, and the ship is truly lost... then, brothers, we can take more *drastic* measures.'

They continued on their way. Antor only wished he felt as confident as he had sounded.

Just hours ago, he had known his mission. He had been assigned to a kill team, with a clear chain of command. He had been briefed on his goals, and on the nature of the enemies that would try to keep him from achieving them. He had known exactly what was expected of him. He had been ready to serve – as he always did – diligently.

In spite of his rank in the Blood Angels, Antor had always been content to serve in the Deathwatch, and never to lead.

He hadn't been prepared for this. None of them had.

Antor Delassio had never lost a battle before. Not before that fateful day.

He had almost begun to believe he never would, that even when he was himself struck down – as one day, inevitably, he would be – his sacrifice would only speed his brothers to victory. He had faced that prospect with his usual equanimity.

The first of his brothers to die that day was Grennon.

They had attacked four more Black Legionnaires. This time, one of the traitors had detected them somehow: an inadvertent sound, something out of place, perhaps a lingering heat trace in the air. He had shouted a warning.

This time, their prey was ready for them.

The leader of the traitors wore a lightning claw – three blades wreathed in a dazzling energy field. When the traitor slashed at Grennon, his armour seemed to warp away from its touch and the blades tore into his chest.

He fought on for a minute – maybe even longer – after that, kept going by the stimulants his armour was pumping into him, by his natural adrenaline and his own sheer bloody-mindedness. Sadly, none of these commodities were inexhaustible.

Eventually, his body had to accept that it was dead.

Lokar went down next, a chainsword cutting deep into his stomach.

And just like that, the odds had shifted.

Sanctimus engaged the leader, the clash of lightning claw and chainsword blade lighting up the passageway. Antor and Casella were left with three Black Legionnaires to deal with, although fortunately two of them were already wounded.

Lokar had rent the armour of one between the ribs, and Antor found the same niche with his blade, cutting into flesh and muscle.

As one traitor fell away, another lunged at him, a huge metallic mass crushing him against the wall, pinning the wrist of his flamer hand. A hateful voice blared out of a speaker grille at him.

'You should have found a dark corner to crawl into,

and waited to perish with the rest of them. You would have suffered less.'

Antor's right arm and chainsword were trapped between them. He gunned the blade anyway, cutting into his own armour as well as the traitor's. But he had no hand left free to deflect his foe's pistol, and its muzzle was pressed against his eye lens. A bolt-round at this range would pulp his brain.

The killing shot never came. Instead, the traitor stiffened as blood crested his helm and rolled down his face in rivulets. Lokar had found the strength to stand, somehow, and had buried his blade in the back of the Black Legionnaire's head.

It had taken all the strength he could muster. The Space Wolf swayed for a moment, then crashed to the deck plates again.

'*No!*'

Antor didn't recognise the shouting voice – not until he realised that his throat was raw, and that he was still roaring.

No longer were there three enemy warriors in front of him. There were twice, three times, maybe ten times that number – ghosts picked out in crimson, indistinct. He launched himself into the midst of them with his chainsword grinding and Ignatus flaring, determined to deal out as much pain as he could to them before... before they could...

Pain. Sadness. Loss. The infinite void...

The next thing he knew, he was running. Casella was beside him, supporting him, urging him to hurry. 'Don't look back!'

'L-Lokar?' Antor stammered. He was trembling, ineffably cold inside his armour.

Casella shook his head. 'He was still clinging to life by a thread. He said... no, he *ordered* us to leave him.'

Antor's auto-senses warned him of more armoured figures ahead of them. They turned back, but footsteps were approaching behind them too. Casella kicked open a hatchway and pushed them both through it.

They were in a tiny maintenance bay. Casella wrenched a grille from the wall. He sucked in air between his teeth, and Antor realised for the first time how injured the other Space Marine was. He was limping, and his left arm, already hurt, appeared to have been dislocated from his shoulder and was mangled besides. He had lost his bolter.

He wanted to ask about Sanctimus. He vaguely remembered the Ultramarine falling...

They had won the battle, but at too high a price.

'The service ducts. Go.' Casella helped Antor clamber into the hole in the wall. Then he replaced the grille between them.

'What about you?' Antor protested, through the steel mesh.

'They know we're here. We can only hope they don't know how many of us there are. We must scupper the ship. If I stay behind and engage them—'

'No!' He surprised himself with the vehemence of his outburst.

Casella turned away with a wry smile and headed out into the passageway. Then he was gone, a war cry ringing from his throat. 'There is only the Emperor! He is our shield and protector!'

He was greeted by the sounds of chainblades and bolter fire.

Under the cover of that noise, Antor crawled away through square metallic ducts, scraping his knees and shoulders against the sides.

Casella was right, he told himself. One of us had to stay, and he was injured. The thought gave him cold comfort. It didn't slow his pounding heartbeats.

Did he already know, back then? Did he understand – on some level, at least – what had begun to happen to him? Looking back, from a distance of years, it was impossible to say.

Perhaps he had simply pushed the thought out of his mind, afraid to face it.

Did I not have the right to be angry?

He had emerged from the ducting into a small, empty crew cabin.

The door was locked, but torn from its mountings: evidence that the traitors had already searched in there. He removed his helmet and doused his head in the sink. He gargled to cleanse the iron taste of blood from his tongue.

He lowered himself uneasily onto the bunk, too small for his armoured frame. He tried to blink away the red shapes that still writhed behind his eyes. They filled him with a sense of dread. He didn't dare look at the shapes directly. He was afraid he might see too much.

He had to try to clear his mind. He remembered...

'You should have found a dark corner to crawl into,' the Black Legionnaire had snarled, his helmet pressed up to Antor's face. His eyes had blazed dark red behind his retinal lenses.

'They want our ship. Or any ship, perhaps,' Antor had mused.

'You should have found a dark corner to crawl into...'

'It is our ship they want – and they want it in working order.'

His eyes snapped open in surprise as the deck plates lurched and then thrummed beneath his feet.

'The engines…' he breathed, and in that moment it was as if a prism had suddenly shifted in his mind and made everything crystal-clear to him.

'Do these savages not even come back for their own dead?'

Perhaps not, thought Antor, if they intend to cremate them…

'You should have found a dark corner to crawl into… and waited to perish with the rest of them…'

He knew why the Black Legion wanted the *Incontrovertible Truth* now. They wanted it for the one thing it could do that their own grand cruiser could not: approach the Deathwatch facilities unchallenged. They had been bound for the Erioch System. Some of Antor's brothers were to begin a tour of duty there.

Watch Fortress Erioch!

It was one of the Deathwatch's most important outposts. It served them as a command centre, a garrison, an armoury, a place of study and training, and a repository for holy texts and relics. It was home to the Jericho Reach's Watch Commander – the Master of the Vigil – and the sector's first line of defence against any xenos threat.

Erioch was well defended. Any single hostile ship approaching it would be atomised before it could get close. One of their own strike cruisers, however – clearly wounded in battle, limping home, its communication systems crippled – might give the gunners pause for a moment.

Too long.

If the *Incontrovertible Truth* made it into a docking bay, or even just dive-bombed the parapets with every warhead in its missile tubes armed…

Antor's temples throbbed. He massaged them with ceramite-clad fingers. He had to think clearly, to reason. He was the only survivor of his impromptu kill team, perhaps of the entire ship's complement. There was no one else to tell him what he should do.

Sanctimus was right, he thought, we ought to have defended the engine rooms. Better yet, damaged them beyond repair. Too late for that now, though.

He had come too far. It would take him too long to get back to the engines now, with the ship already underway again. He was closer, far closer, to the bridge. So, that was where he had to go. He wondered how many of the traitors he would have to face there. How many came aboard? How many had died?

It occurred to him, suddenly, that this was a suicide mission for the Black Legion. So, there would be no more left aboard than they might need. The rest would likely have abandoned ship, having ensured – so they thought – that the last of its rightful owners were dead. How many might they have left behind?

Too many...

But only he could prevent what was about to happen. The responsibility was his. He levered himself to his feet, but felt a familiar knot tightening in the pit of his stomach again. 'There is no cowardice in conviction,' he recited, seeking solace in the Emperor's wisdom, 'and there is nothing... there is nothing to fear but... failure...'

He was almost there when it hit him.

Antor couldn't breathe. His vision had tunnelled, dark red, until he could hardly see. He clung to a bulkhead for support.

For a moment that felt like a year, he was elsewhere, another time, in a place of never-ending pain and terror. It felt almost like a premonition... and when it ended, when he finally managed to get a hold of himself, it left him with a dark, sick feeling that he couldn't swallow down, no matter how hard he tried.

'There is no cowardice... in conviction...' he repeated through clenched teeth, willing himself onward.

He had encountered no enemies in the passageways thus far, which suggested that his suppositions had been accurate and few traitors remained. He had been lucky, too, that nothing – no decompressed areas – had blocked his route. He had found more bodies, though – more Deathwatch battle-brothers slain.

The hatch that led to the bridge had been blown open. The gaping hole was unguarded, a sign of the traitors' conceit. Antor flattened himself against the wall beside it, waiting to be certain that they hadn't detected his approach.

Lokar should be here instead of me, he thought. He was the stealthiest of us.

He gathered information through his auto-senses, without showing himself. He pinpointed three traitors on the bridge: more than he had hoped, fewer than he had feared. One stood at the captain's command post, while the others had taken the strike cruiser's controls. They had lain down their weapons and stripped off parts of their battleplate, and howled accursed hymnals as they prepared to meet their dark gods in death. They don't trust their slaves to do this for them, he realised. There were too many traitors for Antor to fight alone.

Grennon should be here instead of me, he thought. He was the strongest of us.

He felt the engines stepping up a note. Assuming that the traitors would be momentarily occupied, he stole a glance through the open hatchway. The first thing he saw was a vast, cathedral-like structure, bristling with spires and towers. It filled the forward viewport, rotating languidly against a velvet backdrop.

Erioch! It was close enough that he could make out the devotional statuary upon its ramparts. He had to act now.

His mind was racing, but he had a plan. He would tackle the traitor helmsman from behind. He would only have a second before the others reacted, but it might just be long enough.

Casella should be here instead of me, he thought. *He was the boldest of us.*

He didn't have to beat the traitors. He only had to wrench the helmsman's hands away from the controls for an instant. He couldn't vox the watch fortress – he could see that the console had been wrecked – but he could send them a message nonetheless. He could throw the *Incontrovertible Truth* off-course – he only had to make it dive, bank, spin or just falter in its approach, and they'd know something was wrong.

There would have been no response to the fortress' hails, no advance warning of their arrival.

He knew that he could trust his battle-brothers to do the rest.

A suicide mission for me too, then, Antor thought, and for a moment, the magnitude of what he was facing overwhelmed him…

He was in that place of pain and terror again. Its blood-red shadows were more distinct than ever; he even thought he recognised some of them, although he couldn't be sure of it…

He clawed his way back to the here and now. He focussed on another thing he had seen on the bridge: the bodies of the crew, heaped unceremoniously in a corner. They may only have been Chapter serfs and servitors, but still they had died for the Emperor.

Antor felt his gorge rising and, this time, he welcomed the anger as an antidote to his fear. He let it blaze inside him, let its heat suffuse him, energise him. Someone has to make the traitors pay, he told himself. No amount of suffering could ever be enough to punish them for their manifold sins.

So, Antor let the anger take him. He rode onto the bridge on its crest, his chainsword screaming, the battle cry of his parent Chapter bursting from his lips.

'For the Emperor and Sanguinius! Death! *Death!*'

Antor remembered.

Blood rushing in his ears, his temples pounding. He remembered battlements framed in the forward viewport, a flash-frozen image steeped in red.

He remembered hurling himself forwards, yanking, wrenching, smashing at whatever came to hand. He remembered black-gauntleted fingers grasping for him, tearing him away, still kicking and screaming.

He remembered a power sword battering at his chest, slicing into his hip, and yet he hadn't felt the blows. He remembered battering at thick, heavy armour plate, making only the slightest of dents. And then...

Then, he was elsewhere. It felt like something else was working his muscles, bearing his pain, screaming in his voice, but he was only distantly aware of it.

He was fighting red shadows, wave after wave of them. He had thought they would never stop coming.

The darkest, most terrible shadows.
Fire.
Spinning metal teeth.
His fists and feet thundering over and over into a bloody,
quivering mass.
And then...
He had removed his helmet and wiped his lips with
the back of his hand.
Something sticky. Something red. Something that tasted
like... his deepest fear made manifest. He had tried to deny
it for four years since then, told himself it couldn't be true,
but... like iron and...
It wasn't real, he tried to tell himself every time the
thought came to his mind.
It wasn't real.

For a long time, Antor Delassio had dreamed, and his
dreams had been drenched in shades of red.
His eyes had opened upon a vaulted ceiling, and dust
motes dancing around bas-relief sculptures. Reverberat-
ing footsteps and the ticking of machinery had filled his
ears. An Apothecary's white mask loomed over his bunk.
'Don't try to sit up,' he had cautioned.
Memories rushed back into Antor's head and, with
them, a stab of dismay. His throat was unaccountably dry.
'You are in the medicae ward,' the Apothecary told
him. 'You were critically injured, but we reached you.
Your hibernator implant did its job. You have spent two
months, one week and three days in suspended anima-
tion under our supervision.'
'The watch fortress,' Antor croaked.

The Apothecary nodded. 'This is Watch Fortress Erioch,' he said.

As he became stronger, over the next few days, he asked more questions.

The *Incontrovertible Truth* had indeed been on a collision course with the watch fortress. Then, even as Erioch's gunners realised what was happening – too late to do anything about it – it had suddenly veered away from them. They had held their fire.

They had despatched Thunderhawks instead. The strike cruiser had been found drifting at the edge of the system, and had been boarded. The hull had already been holed in several locations by improvised breaching charges, the great engines stalled.

There were questions for Antor too. During his recovery, he was visited by several watch captains, an inquisitor and, once, even the Master of the Vigil himself. They had pieced together much of the story, but needed to hear the rest from him. No one else could tell them what had happened aboard that ship, on that fateful day.

No one but Antor Delassio. He was the sole survivor.

They had found him, barely breathing, on the bridge. He had been surrounded by black-armoured corpses, each of them badly mutilated.

The inquisitor, in particular, wanted to hear the details many times over. Antor couldn't answer him. Squirming under a beady-eyed, suspicious glare, he had mumbled excuses: 'I took them by surprise. They were trying to regain control of the ship, they'd been in a fight already, they were wounded, and I... I don't remember...'

The Apothecary came to his patient's aid. 'After such

action, some loss of memory is only to be expected. Even Space Marines have their limits.'

He had wanted to tell them the whole truth – as far as he knew it – but he couldn't. He felt ashamed. He remembered the faces of other Blood Angels contorting with madness. He remembered their eyes ablaze with hatred and their screams of primal rage. He remembered thinking it could never happen to him.

The Red Thirst. The Black Rage.

He could still feel it stirring inside him, two months later. He could still taste the faintest tang of blood on his tongue. He knew that it was a part of him now.

They were calling him a hero. There was even some talk of awarding him the Iron Halo, for what the Master of the Vigil described as 'exceptional initiative'.

He had prevented an attack that would have left the Deathwatch crippled in the local region. He had avenged his slaughtered brethren, and enabled the gene-seed of some to be salvaged. That ought to have calmed his righteous anger.

But it wasn't enough. It wasn't nearly enough.

There were traitors out there still, in their massed legions, revelling in their depravity, scars across the face of the galaxy. They had to suffer for their sins against the Emperor, every one of them.

Until they did – until the very last traitor was destroyed – the rage that boiled in Antor Delassio's veins would never be satisfied.

His hatred of the heretic weighed as heavy as his hatred of the xenos.

* * *

Perhaps it was being on board the *Incontrovertible Truth* again. That might have been why he couldn't clear his mind, couldn't help but remember.

Antor detached himself from his machinery. He washed out the vials that his tainted blood had touched. He had just finished secreting the machine's components in his armoured backpack when there came a knock at his door. He summoned his team of serfs into the cabin, and they helped him into his armour.

His kill team was due to assemble. It would be led by an inquisitor of the Ordo Xenos, so Antor would be under constant scrutiny. He knew what was expected of him. He only prayed he would be strong enough to serve. He could feel the Red Thirst stirring inside him again, despite his precautions.

The Cursed Young Prince...

Three times now, since that day, he had succumbed to the curse. He was fortunate that, each time, his battle-brothers had been able to coax him back from the brink. He had told them there was something in his blood, but he had declined to talk about it. He knew that he should have been honest with them, warned them of the danger he posed to them.

They hadn't yet seen him at his worst. Nobody had.

He ought to have confessed his sins to a chaplain, but he couldn't.

He knew now why he had been chosen for this assignment to the Deathwatch, what had brought him to Lord Commander Dante's attention. He had been sent to represent his Chapter here – rubbing shoulders with witch hunters and the elite of other Chapters – only because of his humble nature. He must have seemed the most reasonable, the most even-tempered of them all, one that surely the curse could never touch.

If Antor's secret were discovered, he would face disgrace and worse. At the very least, the Deathwatch would expel him. Worse still, the purity of his gene-seed itself would be questioned. He would bring suspicion down upon every Blood Angel serving in the kill teams.

He had no choice.

He lowered his gleaming black helmet over his head, to hide the sweat on his face. He checked his reflection and tried to reclaim something of his pride. He had his duty, and he would perform it diligently. He would conquer his curse, as he had conquered it every day – almost every day – for the past four years.

The monster that dwelled inside him could never be slain, but Antor was determined to temper it.

Only, he couldn't help but shift his gaze to the emblem on his shoulder: the blood drop with angel wings. He stepped out of his cabin and couldn't help but remember stepping through that door once before to find his ship under attack.

The rage had saved his life that day. It had kept him on his feet, kept him fighting with a ferocity that had staggered his opponents, even after he ought to have died, as his brethren had. As every battle-brother, every watch captain, every inquisitor in Watch Fortress Erioch would have.

And that was one thing, the one thing above all, that he couldn't forget.

It was the only thing he had left.

Antor Delassio may have been cursed – but once, that curse had saved them all.

THE FLESH OF
THE ANGEL

BEN COUNTER

The stench of the alien was everywhere. It was a heavy, meaty stink, like heaps of butchered animal carcasses left for too long somewhere dank and underground. There was an artificial, chemical note to it too, the smell of the laboratory and the operating room. And underlying it all was an alien sourness that could never come from anything human.

Zameon Gydrael crouched beside the gnarled wall of hardened mucus that bounded the tunnel leading into the Nidus Tertiam. The xenos-wrought structure wound deep into the foundations of Phoenicus Peak, where once a monastic human sect had inhabited the cells and shrines. He could feel the warmth coming off the walls – nutrient fluid pumped through them, channelled to the lower-most reaches of the nidus. He could hear the scrabbling of claws far below, the low groaning of the structure settling, and the hiss of its unspeakable veins and arteries.

But the noise was nothing to the stench.

His olfactory receptors had been enhanced by the surgeons of the Ordo Xenos to pick out the spore-trails of certain creatures, and to recognise a whole catalogue of alien scents. The drawback was that Gydrael could not turn them off.

'Gydrael here,' he said into the kill team's vox-channel. 'I'm in position at the head of Nidus Tertiam.'

'*In position*,' echoed Thorne of the Iron Hands.

'*I'm at Nidus Secundus*,' added Hasdrubal of the Storm Lords. '*Ready to do this, brethren. I'd burn this whole mountain range just to get rid of the stink*.'

'There's movement on the lower slopes,' said the kill team's leader, Sergeant Decurius of the Praetors of Ulixis. He was positioned on a mountaintop watching the main nidi of the breeding ground, where he could warn the rest of the team about reinforcements or despatch himself and the fifth member, Molgurr of the Mortifactors Chapter, to lend assistance if things went wrong. '*Quiet further up. Clear to proceed*.'

'*Acknowledged, brother*,' said Thorne.

'*About damned time*,' said Hasdrubal. '*I have gone seven moons without taking a head. My knife is angry*.'

'*Remember your mission*,' said Decurius. '*Do not give battle unless you must. You will have alien blood to spare on your hands before the night is out, Hasdrubal. Trust me on that*.'

'I am advancing,' voxed Gydrael. 'Fury and blood, my brothers. Soon this world will be clean.'

The interior of the nidus was pitch dark, but Gydrael could see perfectly with his enhanced vision. The architecture of the monastery broke through the crusted mass of resinous matter that the xenos had used to build their nest. The mournful face of a female saint was almost buried in tendrils of alien secretion. Fragments of fallen chitin covered the floor.

Gydrael kneeled down and picked up a smooth, pale shard from the debris. It was a fragment of an eggshell, the curve suggesting it had been the size of a man's torso before it had broken.

'They're hatching already,' said Gydrael.

'*Then we must be swift*,' replied Decurius.

In the close confines, Gydrael holstered his plasma pistol and drew his broadsword.

At these ranges, the powered blade was a surer kill than a bolt of superheated plasma.

As he proceeded, the stench got worse, if that was possible. Below the upper level of monks' cells, the side of a chapel had been torn down to form the opening of a tunnel winding into the depths. A revolting slurping, sucking sound came from further down.

While most of his mind was concerned with the mission-specific details around him – avenues of approach, ranges, hiding places for a lurking enemy – the rest of Gydrael's perception was filing away the other information that came to him. It was a skill he had possessed even before he had become a Dark Angel, the ability to perceive and compartmentalise, and to recall afterwards everything he had seen. The Chapter had honed that skill well. It was one of the reasons that Gydrael had been selected for service with the Deathwatch.

The monks had lived lives of cruel denial. They served for decades before they earned the right to amputate their body parts in the name of the Emperor, denying themselves the very limbs with which they had been born, to understand better the sacrifice the Emperor had made of his physical body. The tale of the monks was told in the sculptures of limbless devotees and the harnesses and supports built into the stone pews that broke through the layers of hardened alien mucus. The small monastic community had existed on Kolagar for centuries before the sslyth had moved in, and in a few hellish nights the xenos had exterminated them and taken over their monastery.

Gydrael moved down through the tunnel and crouched by an opening into a huge chamber beyond. The bulbous shape of the cavity was like the interior of an enormous stomach. It had been carved into the rock of Phoenicus Peak, like a cyst that had rotted away the mountain stone, and the lower half of it was full of a foul grey-green biological soup.

The fluid was writhing. Gydrael's vision focussed on sinuous loops of muscle slithering in and out of one another, forming churning knots of scaly bodies. Clawed, muscular limbs reached from the mass, and here and there a head surfaced – noseless and snakelike, with a yawing, fanged mouth, eyes like flecks of red gemstone, and ridges of horned scales along the scalp and down the spine.

A yowling and roaring reached Gydrael's ears. It was the noise of primal abandon.

The stench was heavy and musky here, an awful mix of decay and fecundity that overwhelmed the air filters built into his power armour and forced his body's augmentations to leach out the toxins from the air.

On the shore of the pool, one of the muscular creatures disengaged from the mass and flopped onto the shore of congealed filth. It had a powerful, four-armed torso, and its lower half was a single long, thick tail. Its scaly body was covered in the sticky fluid and it gasped and contorted as it pulled itself free. Others followed. Some in the mire looked dead, their bodies having given out. The surviving xenos slithered into side tunnels, leaving trails of noxious slime.

'Confirm visual on the sslyth,' voxed Gydrael. 'This nidus has a breeding pool.'

'Have you been seen?' replied Decurius.

'No,' said Gydrael. 'They see nothing in their state.'

'Skirt around it if you can. The hatcheries are likely below you.'

'With pleasure.'

Hasdrubal chuckled. *'Contain your lust, Dark Angel.'*

Gydrael did not give Hasdrubal the satisfaction of an answer. The Storm Lords were of White Scars stock, earthy and brutal, very different to the Dark Angels. The White Scars' primarch, Jaghatai Khan, had apparently lent his Legion's geneseed a certain crudeness of thought which successor Chapters like the Storm Lords had evidently retained.

Gydrael put a hand to the canister mag-clamped to the waist of his armour. It contained enough infectious material to kill everything in the breeding pool a hundred times over. The virus bomb was gene-crafted to the phylum of sslyth that had surfaced on Kolagar, and it would have wiped them all out within three minutes.

If there had been enough of it to spare, Gydrael would have done just that. The sight of the sslyth locked in their fleshly mire turned his stomachs. But the Ordo Xenos had produced barely enough material to arm the three virus bombs the kill team carried into the nidi around

Phoenicus Peak. They had to be used at the right place, in unison, to create the cascading reaction that would wipe out the entire phylum.

'I am advancing,' voxed Gydrael.

As revolting as the breeding pool was, Gydrael filed away its obscenity in his mind. Every contact with the sslyth, no matter how unwholesome, armed him with more knowledge of how to kill them. Of all the lessons Gydrael had learned in the Dark Angels' training halls on the Rock, the first had been the most important.

Miss nothing.

The creature lurking in the makeshift shrine, its four brawny arms holding a pair of swords and a rusted auto-gun, was the first alert sslyth that Gydrael had seen since entering the nidus. It wore a harness of leather straps that clamped crude armour plates around its shoulders, chest and abdomen, and a necklace of fingers and dried-out eye-balls on a strip of leather was tied around its neck. With its muscular tail coiled underneath it, it reared up taller than Gydrael. He could see strips of purple-dyed cloth tied around its four biceps, embroidered with golden thread that seemed at odds with the creature's savagery.

The ssylth stood before the altar of the shrine, which was little more than a heap of battle spoils – severed heads, captured lasguns, a silvery nest of ident-tags, a bowl of human hands – set in front of a carved wooden idol. The sensor-pits along the ssylth's jaw line opened up as they registered the changes in air pressure and tempera-ture that heralded Gydrael's approach. It was impossible for anyone to sneak up on an alert sslyth – many men of the Astra Militarum on Kolagar had tried.

The sslyth whirled around and hissed, opening its mouth wide. Twin crescent-shaped fangs glinted with venom in its upper jaw.

By the time it raised its autogun, Gydrael had lunged across the shrine and was within sword range. The Dark Angel brought his broadsword around in a cut to the abdomen – the creature instinctively blocked with its gun and the blade's power field lit the space up like a bolt of lightning. The sslyth spat and hissed as its weapon was reduced to a shower of metal shards.

The xenos howled, its tail propelling it towards Gydrael. It slammed into him with speed and strength, trying to close its jaws around his neck.

Gydrael didn't fend off the closing jaws. The fangs were blunted against the ceramite of his helmet and shoulder guard. The sslyth was too close for him to swing his sword – he reversed his grip instead, and rammed the hilt up into the sslyth's upper chest.

Gydrael had selected the broadsword from the vaults of the Rock when he had been chosen for the Deathwatch. He was his Chapter's contribution to the ancient pacts which bound the Space Marines to this solemn duty, and he had needed a weapon to reflect that. He had always favoured the broadsword pattern, with its wide, brutal sweeps, its absence of ornamentation and flourish, and the massive, decisive damage that could be dealt with a clean blow. The weapon had a blade of infinitite alloy and a gilded hilt, with a cut red gemstone the size of a man's fist set into the pommel. It was that gemstone that now cracked into the sslyth's chest like the tip of a spear, shattering sternum and rib.

The sslyth was thrown against the pile of spoils in front

of the altar. It let out a high, grating screech that seemed to shake the hardened secretions of the shrine walls. With his blade now free, Gydrael lashed out with a descending crescent blow that caught the creature in the armoured shoulder.

The broadsword sliced through, the power field giving it a keener edge that any mundane blade. It split armour, bone, muscle and organ, slicing all the way through to the sslyth's abdomen. The alien was bisected clean in half, the two sections of its body flopping to the floor in a flood of sundered organs.

Gydrael heard the slithering of more aliens approaching. He shifted his grip on his sword, holding it one-handed while he drew his plasma pistol.

'Brothers, I have encountered resistance,' he voxed.

Three more sslyth rushed in through the side tunnels leading off from the shrine. Gydrael shot the first one through the face with his plasma pistol, the shot blasting the contents of its skull across the wall behind it. The second sslyth had a sword in each hand and a lithe, rope-muscled look to it, faster and leaner than the xenos Gydrael had butchered by the altar. It darted around the defensive arc of Gydrael's sword, slicing out high with two blades and low with the others.

Gydrael had fought just about every form of enemy. Those he had not faced on the battlefield, he had engaged in simulated bouts with combat servitors, configuring their limbs to mimic any one of a hundred different species. Even so, the sslyth's four swords threw him off for a moment as he weighed up each of his guards and parries and found them wanting.

Gydrael abandoned the subtlety of the swordsman. He

trusted in his armour instead, letting three blows ring off the plating over his thigh, shoulder and chest. The fourth strike was at his head – Gydrael ducked under it, pivoted on his forward foot, and brought the broadsword around in a vertical rising strike.

Two of the sslyth's hands thudded, severed, to the floor. The creature hissed, more in anger than in pain, as Gydrael focussed on the third alien, which was lining up a shot at him with a boltgun.

The bolter it carried was larger than those sometimes issued to the officers of the Astra Militarum. It was sized for transhuman hands, but was of an older mark than anything in the Dark Angels' armoury. The alien was strong enough to wield it, but it had none of the marksmanship of a Space Marine. The first shot flew wide and Gydrael lunged at the sslyth, ramming the point of the broadsword home.

These sslyth wore segments of armour salvaged from the Guardsmen of the Astra Militarum, sawn and hammered into shape and held in place by leather harnesses. They were no good against a powered blade. The armour split and the sword transfixed the creature through the stomach. Gydrael felt it sag as he withdrew the blade, knowing the alien's spine was cut through and it would be paralysed before it hit the floor.

The surviving sslyth still had a sword in each of its remaining hands. It leapt up against one wall, bunching its tail in a powerful coil beneath it, to propel itself into Gydrael. He felt the hum of the plasma pistol in his hand – it could punch through the side of a tank, but it needed a second or two to recharge between each shot. It was ready to fire again.

Gydrael shot the sslyth through the throat. Its head flopped forwards, suddenly attached only by a string of charred scales.

The sslyth with the severed backbone was flopping around on the floor, trying to reach the boltgun beside it with jerking, spasming motions of its hands. Gydrael stabbed the broadsword down and pierced it through the back of the skull, slicing through its brain stem.

'Cleared the resistance,' he voxed. 'The sslyth are aware of my presence.'

'Don't tell me Zameon has the first blood,' said Hasdrubal. 'You can have that one, Dark Angel. I'll bring out a heap of xenos heads you can only dream of.'

'Focus, brethren,' said Decurius. 'If one nidus is alerted, the others will be soon. Hasdrubal, Thorne, stay alert.'

'Always,' replied Thorne.

Gydrael studied the altar for a moment before moving on. The carving above the heap of spoils was of an obscene figure composed of mismatched body parts and orifices. It had a heavy, fleshy realism in spite of the crudeness of the wooden sculpture. In the centre of the sculpture's face was a sigil – a circle and two crescents. Gydrael had seen it before, carved into the flesh of maddened cultists or scrawled on the walls of defiled places of worship.

Gydrael picked the sslyth's bolter off the floor. Though it was a Space Marine's weapon it had a patina of filth and corrosion that no battle-brother would ever tolerate. It was a pattern that no forge world or Chapter armoury had produced for thousands of years, and its casing had once been decorated with golden scrollwork that was now peeling off.

'I see evidence of worship,' said Gydrael. 'Devotion to a warp power. To the Lord of Unspeakable Pleasures.'

Hasdrubal snorted. '*It is no surprise. The sslyth are predisposed to perversion.*'

'And they have had contact with the Emperor's Children,' said Gydrael.

'*Then their resurgence is no coincidence,*' said Decurius. '*The Emperor's Children hope to seed this world with them and undo all that the Astra Militarum achieved. That is why this phylum must be exterminated, brethren. That is why we are here.*'

Throughout the Vensine Sector, a massive upwelling of separatism, inspired and coordinated by the traitors of the Emperor's Children Legion, had gained a hold upon a dozen major Imperial worlds and almost a hundred lesser planets. The Inquisition suspected the Emperor's Children had laid the groundwork for the uprising for generations, planting deviant weaknesses in the bloodlines of the Imperial aristocracy and seeding populations with folklore and prophecy that spoke of a bloody revolution.

Heretic militias had seized planetary capitals. Saboteurs had scuttled Imperial battleships and assassins had murdered priests and lawmakers in their beds. The Emperor's Children themselves had been seen leading sermons that devolved into rites of excess and pain. Inquisitorial agents had been turned, obfuscating the full scale of the Traitor Legion's infiltration of the sector.

The Imperium's response was inevitable: a crusade that brought millions of Astra Militarum Guardsmen, dozens of ships of the Imperial Navy and a handful of Space Marine strike forces to the Vensine sector. Kolagar had been one of the first planets seized in a cruel and brutal campaign fought through its subequatorial jungles and across the steppes of its northern continent. The Astra Militarum had committed whole regiments to fighting the combination of corrupted native troops and cultist militias that infested the planet, and after a full year of fighting, Kolagar was subjugated. Its hastily constructed airfields were converted into a staging post for campaigns launched against the nearby rebel worlds, and the planet became a link in the chain feeding men and starships into the front lines of what would become the Vensine Crusade.

Kolagar was supposed to be safe. It was supposed to be an example of the crusade's costly but inevitable victory. But then the sslyth, alien mercenaries who had plagued the sector for centuries as pirates and swords for hire, had struck from the jungle to ambush, mutilate and kill. The patterns and frequency of the attacks suggested more than a simple band of alien predators. The Ordo Xenos of the Inquisition took an interest, and its agents identified the three nidi around Phoenicus Peak as the source of the sslyth attacks.

Gydrael had wondered if the sslyth were there not just as opportunists and scavengers, but as participants in the Emperor's Children rebellion. The Ordo Xenos suspected the same, but investigating the xenos' motives was always secondary to their extermination.

It was no great surprise to learn the Emperor's Children were working directly with the sslyth, fostering in them strange new forms of worship and supplying them with weaponry. A threat on Kolagar, a world already supposed to be conquered, would distract the Imperial forces from expanding the Vensine Crusade and pushing back the heretics from the edges of their domain. It would tie up whole regiments in a campaign of extermination to flush out the resilient sslyth warclades one brood at a time, and turn the campaign's first victory into an unending cycle of massacre and reprisal.

But there was another way to fight the xenos.

Each nidus was too deep to be struck from the air, and too labyrinthine to be assaulted by a regular ground force. But one Space Marine, more than the equal of any sslyth and with the support of the Ordo, could reach the heart of the nest alone. And if he was equipped not just with gun or blade but with an infectious agent gene-keyed to the sslyth nervous system, he could wipe out an entire nidus.

And three such Space Marines, unleashing their virus bombs at the same time, could trigger a cascade that would infect the whole sslyth population of Phoenicus Peak and shatter the xenos presence on Kolagar.

It would be cause enough to exterminate so many xenos, of course, for every Space Marine harboured a particular scorn and hatred for the alien. But to know he was striking at the plans of the Emperor's Children as well would make the operation a particularly satisfying fulfilment of duty.

Zameon Gydrael did not fight for the satisfaction of it. He fought because it was the duty of every Space Marine, of every human being, to strike back at the enemies seeking to bring about the end of the Imperium and the extinction of the human race. But even so, as he left the shrine in the knowledge that the Emperor's Children would rage at the loss of their xenos allies, he allowed himself a glimmer of anticipation of the victory to come.

* * *

'*Five heads!*' crowed Hasdrubal over the vox. '*Five skulls I have taken to be cast into the flame! Ninety-five more and I will carry the jawbone of the last with me. I would wager the count with you, brothers, but you deny yourselves the joy of such things.*'

'*I've breached sea level,*' came Thorne's voice, ignoring the Storm Lord's boasting. '*The sslyth are buried deep. Minimal contact so far.*'

'*You're closing in on the nutrient nexus,*' said Decurius. '*Hold when you reach it. Gydrael, what is your position?*'

'At the hatcheries,' replied Gydrael.

'*Then the nexus will be a short distance below you,*' said Decurius. '*Deploy the virus at the same time, brothers, or the cascade will fail.*'

Gydrael was looking down at a chamber full of sslyth eggs. Each one was translucent, with the embryonic creature inside visible as it writhed and twitched in its nutrient fluid. That fluid was fed by the tendrils coiled along the floor and around each egg, drawing sustenance from the walls of the nidus and feeding it in.

There were well over a hundred eggs in the chamber. Several more chambers branched off, and others off them in turn – Nidus Tertiam contained tens of thousands of eggs, perhaps hundreds of thousands, each one a new enemy of the Imperium. The virus bomb would kill a good proportion of them instantly, but the infection cascade would wipe out every single one.

Gydrael had to pass through to reach a shaft three chambers away, leading downwards. He stepped carefully past the eggs, finding the floor spongy under his feet. He held his plasma pistol in front of him, taking care to avoid disturbing the eggs and rousing the sslyth, but remaining alert for the other dangers he might be walking into.

The xenos guarded their eggs. With so many of them insensible in the breeding pool they had been slow to respond to Gydrael's presence, but the awakened sslyth would consider defending the hatcheries a priority. Gydrael was not surprised when he heard movement ahead, no doubt an egg tender who had to be eliminated or avoided before he could reach the nexus at the lowermost level of the nidus.

Gydrael backed against the wall and glanced into the next chamber.

The noise was coming not from a sslyth, but from a Space Marine.

Gydrael sighted down his plasma pistol. Power armour could turn most mundane blows, but a well-placed plasma blast would bore through ceramite. Gydrael sized up the shot even as his mind told him that something was not right.

Gydrael had been ready to face a traitor of the Emperor's Children. They had been rarely sighted and even more seldom fought by Imperial forces, but it made sense for them to be here to watch over their xenos allies – the sslyth were, after all, rarely beholden to any master for long without the constant threat of punishment. But he was not looking now at the polished purple and gilt colours of the Emperor's Children.

Instead, the Space Marine ahead of him wore black armour with a bare steel trim. He wore a tattered cloak of scaled sslyth hide over his armour, and Gydrael glimpsed the remnants of the Imperial Aquila on one shoulder guard. The symbol had been gouged and defaced.

'*I have reached the target,*' voxed Thorne. '*I'm holding position, but the sslyth are closing in. Move quickly, brothers.*'

'*Almost there,*' replied Hasdrubal. '*I have taken only four more damned heads. I'll claim a third of the final tally, brothers!*'

'*And you would be welcome to them, Storm Lord,*' said Decurius. '*Gydrael, report in.*'

Gydrael didn't reply.

He was watching the Space Marine slowly turn to face him. He wore no helm, and his face was long and drawn, with greyish skin and sunken eyes. He had the appearance of both extreme age and strength, with the sallowness of a greatly extended lifespan.

On his face was a charred handprint, running from the cheek to one temple and the edge of his half-shaven scalp. A smile spread across his face as he looked Gydrael up and down.

Gydrael could have opened fire, but he knew the Space Marine would evade the shot and close in for the kill. Though he had never seen his opponent in the flesh, Gydrael recognised the heraldry of the enemy's armour, and especially the mark on his face. The memory of them rose from the regimented archive of his mind, throwing his carefully ordered consciousness into disarray.

'Well met, younger brother,' said the Space Marine with a smile.

Gydrael holstered his plasma pistol and drew his broadsword.

'Then you're not one for conversation,' said the Space Marine. 'A shame. I wait so long to see a familiar face, and they never want to speak of old times.'

'*Brother Gydrael,*' came Decurius' voice over the vox. '*Report. What is your–*'

Gydrael silenced the sergeant by cutting the channel link. Every part of him was focussed on the figure before him.

'Well?' said the Space Marine. He drew his own weapon, a one-handed power sword with a long, slender blade. It was an archaic pattern that had fallen out of favour with the Chapter's officers long ago. The air crackled and spat around it as the power field activated. 'Are we going to do this?'

Gydrael's feet crunched through sslyth eggs as he charged. He didn't care about alerting the xenos now. A greater duty bore down on him, and its weight forced his sword-arm forward to strike.

His memories were churning. Normally ordered and obedient, now they swirled, fragments of them surfacing to break against his consciousness. One image that surfaced repeatedly, flashing in his mind even as he crossed the ground between himself his enemy, was a place of cold and dark, which had been burned into his mind...

It had been years ago, but it felt like decades. Centuries. Gydrael had revisited that place many times to rebuild those walls within himself, the fortress that concealed the truth even while the rules and philosophies of the Death-watch were built over the surface.

That place was a chapel within the Rock, the fortress-monastery of the Dark Angels that floated through the void, an enormous fortified asteroid riddled with chambers and tunnel networks. The chapel was a silent place far from the surface, a shrine to the Chapter's primarch Lion El'Jonson, large enough to contain a whole company of battle-brothers. There were only two in there now – Zameon Gydrael, and Interrogator-Chaplain Asmodai.

Asmodai rose from his knees, where he had been lighting the incense on the altar. The black stone image of the Lion stared down, approving of their secrecy. Asmodai wore the skull-like faceplate and ivory robes of the Interrogator-Chaplains – Gydrael had never seen him without them.

'Brother Gydrael,' said Asmodai. 'The coincidence of our meeting here is a fortunate one. There are words I would have pass between us, away from the ears of those you will soon fight alongside.'

There had been no coincidence. Asmodai had requested Gydrael's presence there, although his invitation, expressed in sideways and subtle language, would never have been openly acknowledged by either.

'Fortunate indeed,' he said.

'When you leave for the Deathwatch,' said Asmodai, 'it will be many years before you return to us. Our obligations to the Inquisition require us to give you over to Ordo Xenos command completely, and there is no telling where you will be sent or for how long. This will be the last chance we have to speak directly, and without observation.'

'I will stay a Dark Angel no matter what colours I wear,' replied Gydrael.

'I have no doubt of that,' said Asmodai. 'But I would be derelict in my duty if I did not satisfy myself that you understand what that means.'

'I know the matters of which you speak,' said Gydrael, 'and I know my duty. The Chapter demands it of us all.'

'And yet,' said Asmodai, looking up towards the stone

face of the Primarch, 'I must hear it in as many words from you.'

'I will continue the search,' said Gydrael.

'The Fallen think they can hide,' said Asmodai. 'Every one of them is convinced he has found the perfect nest from which to plan his treacheries. But we have found our own ways to hunt them down. The Deathwatch is one of them. You will go to places the Dark Angels will be unable to search, to places where we are not welcome. You will be thrown against the foulest of xenos and the xenophiles who consort with them, but even while you fight with all the zeal for which we are renowned, you must never forget what your duty truly is.'

'I will be on the hunt until I die,' said Gydrael. 'And beyond, if fate wills it.'

'Good,' said Asmodai. 'There is a reason you were chosen above all your battle-brothers when the Inquisition called on us to contribute to the Deathwatch. Your eyes are sharp and your mind is keen. That is our greatest weapon in the hunt for the Fallen. Go forth, Brother Gydrael, and bring us glory.'

'I shall, my lord,' said Gydrael, kneeling for a moment of prayer before the altar.

'And brother,' said Asmodai, as he turned to leave the chapel, 'be sure to miss nothing.'

The Fallen.

No one could really understand what the Fallen were, save for a Dark Angel. They were not traitors, because traitors could be redeemed through sacrifice and made pure again in death. The Fallen could not be redeemed. Their crime was against the human race, not just against the Imperium – against the very concepts of loyalty and duty, not just against the Dark Angels.

His Chpater would never try to explain the Fallen to anyone else. Not the other Chapters of the Adeptus Astartes, not the Inquisition, not even the other members of the Deathwatch. It was a matter for the Dark Angels and their successors alone.

Gydrael charged after the Fallen, parrying a thrust of the power sword and driving his shoulder into the enemy's chest. The warrior pivoted and Gydrael stumbled forwards, momentarily out of control.

The sword lashed up at him. Gydrael barely turned it aside. The impact threw him against the wall behind him and he crunched into it, fragments of resin raining down around him.

The Fallen lunged, leading with the point of his sword. Gydrael caught the blade against the guard of his own, the swords shuddering as their power fields intersected. Gydrael led the warrior past him into the wall, and the impact took his enemy straight through the partition of sslyth secretions.

The two Space Marines were drawn through and into the space adjoining the hatchery. It was a part of the original monastery, relatively untouched by the intrusion of the sslyth. False columns broke up the dark stone walls, and the arched ceiling was hung with cobwebs. Dust and detritus collected in the corners and the cracked paving slabs were discoloured with mould.

Manacles hung on the walls. A rusting framework stood in the centre of the room, of a size and shape for a human to be held spread-eagled against it by the restraints hanging from its crossbars. A trio of cages, each large enough to contain a man, stood against the far wall.

It was a chamber of punishments – or of meditation, where the monks of Phoenicus Peak had once brought themselves closer to their Emperor through pain. The Fallen steadied himself against the wall, jangling the length of rusting chain. Gydrael halted his fall by dropping to one knee, bringing the broadsword up into a solid guard.

He felt the weight of the virus canister at his hip.

Two duties pulled at Gydrael. His role in the mission was clear, and if he did not fulfil that role, the mission would fail. It was an easy decision for any Space Marine.

Any except a Dark Angel. He had a greater duty, one that superseded all others. One driven by the survival of the Chapter, of the Imperium, of the human race.

No one else would ever understand. Gydrael told himself that as he parried a speculative slash from the Fallen, circling around to put the restraining frame between himself and his foe.

'I know what you are,' said Gydrael.

'Do you?' said the Fallen. 'Your mortal ancestors were not yet born when I learned the truth. What I have seen, you would have to dig through ten thousand years of lies to uncover. I think you know very little, younger brother.'

'I am not your brother, Averamus,' said Gydrael.

The Fallen smiled, distorting the scar on his face. 'So, I'm famous?'

'You have the Mark of Scorn upon you,' said Gydrael. 'Where the Primarch laid his hand as you swore your first oaths of loyalty, there the mark of your treachery remains. How many times have you sought to use synthetic flesh or bionics to mask it? But it always comes back. I have learned of Averamus, and how he fled from justice. The shame of your survival besmirches us all. I will clean it away.'

'I had not credited my former brethren with so rich an imagination,' said Averamus. 'What fascinating tales they spin.'

'Do not speak of them, traitor,' growled Gydrael, sizing up Averamus. The Fallen was an expert in his sword form, and Gydrael had never trained against it – fast, slender blades like Averamus' were long gone from the Chapter's armoury. He had faced foes with similar weapons and fighting styles, but never a Space Marine.

The warrior grinned. 'You do not know what treachery is.'

A cut to the head would be met with a slice to the gut. Gydrael might connect, but by the time his own blade hit home he would be disembowelled, even through his armour. A thrust could be turned aside too easily and answered with a close strike inside Gydrael's guard. The broadsword could cut right through Averamus, but the Fallen was too quick to be caught in its arc.

'You serve the Emperor's Children,' said Gydrael. He was buying seconds, goading the Fallen into defending his existence while he searched for a way to land the killing blow. 'Are you just the nursemaid to the sslyth? Or did you broker their subservience to the Traitor Legion? You kneel to the enemies of mankind. I need no other definition of treachery.'

'You have no idea what is happening in this system,' said Averamus. The two of them were still circling, Averamus looking for his own way in past Gydrael's broadsword. 'You think I am a blind follower of those deviants? I will bring down empires of the warp that your kind never even knew existed. I will send the enemies of every human screaming into the abyss. I do it from the shadows, from the very throne room of those I will destroy. You can try to stop me, little brother, but I have been on this path for thousands of years and my will is stronger than yours.'

'You lie,' said Gydrael.

'Maybe I do,' said Averamus, 'maybe not. But you are going to die here, so you will never know.'

Averamus struck first. He went straight through the framework in the centre of the room, scattering its rusted beams. Gydrael met him with a counter-stroke, aiming a sideways swipe at the Fallen's torso. Averamus dropped and rolled under the blow but Gydrael had read the move, and aimed a kick that snapped Averamus' head back.

The Fallen rolled with the blow, hooking an arm around Gydrael's leg and throwing him across the floor. Gydrael sprawled and the Fallen was upon him, the two wrestling now, too close to bring their swords to bear.

'You cannot kill me,' snarled Gydrael as the two grappled face to face. 'Not while my duty is yet undone.'

'I don't have to kill you,' said Averamus. He smiled again. The Mark of Scorn was livid red against his pallid face. '*He* will.'

Something huge slammed against the other side of the chamber wall. Stones dislodged and a clatter of rubble fell. Gydrael let go of Averamus and rolled away, bringing his sword up to ward off the opportunistic slash that Averamus aimed at his neck. Gydrael jumped to his feet and put two long strides between himself and his enemy, ready to face the second threat.

The wall of the chamber collapsed, spilling a drift of broken stone into the chamber. A massive, blocky shape

stepped through, and Gydrael registered the purple colours of the armour plating, the gilded eagle's wing worn
in mockery of Imperial heraldry.

It was a Dreadnought of the Emperor's Children.

It was easily twice Gydrael's height. Both its arms ended
in massive fists and the armoured sarcophagus was as
impenetrable as a tank. The Dreadnought's heraldry was
of a quartered human body, depicted with loving skill on
the frontal armour. The quartered corpse was rendered
in sculpted gold on one leg plate, and again on the left
shoulder unit. Through a vision slit in the middle of the
sarcophagus came a sickly green glow, and those parts of
the Dreadnought not covered in gold plate were painted
in an obscenely sumptuous purple.

It looked as much a monument to excess as a war
machine. The images of a profane feast were worked
into the golden sculptures – plates heaped with human
heads, chalices filled from the slit bellies of spitted bodies, bunches of severed hands and torsos hung like sides
of cattle.

Gydrael's mind dissected and filed away every detail as
he sized up this new and enormous threat. Most men
would only see the Dreadnought's huge size and brutal
crushing fists, but Gydrael saw it all.

The detail you miss will kill you.

Therefore, miss nothing.

'Ancient Xezukoth,' exclaimed Averamus. 'I promised
you a new plaything! And this one will take some real
punishment before it breaks!'

'Are you Ferrus Manus?' said the Dreadnought, its voice
a bass rumble blaring from the vox-casters mounted on its
hull. Its power fists clenched and unclenched as its visual

sensors focussed on Gydrael. 'No, I saw him beheaded by the Perfected One. Are you Guilliman? No, I saw his throat slit. But you are close enough.'

The Dreadnought advanced on Gydrael. It swung a power fist and Gydrael ducked it. The air was seared by the power field crackling above him. The second fist surged down and Gydrael rolled out of the way.

A dark chuckling came from the vox-casters. 'Run!' said Xezukoth. 'Dance for me!'

'Good luck, little brother!' called out Averamus as he retreated from the chamber, leaving Gydrael facing the Dreadnought alone.

Gydrael could have pursued him, but he would not have made it halfway across the room with the Dreadnought at his back. He crushed down his fury, denying it full run of his mind. He would find Averamus and kill him. That duty had not disappeared – it still burned as bright and weighed as heavy.

But to fulfil it, he had to get past Ancient Xezukoth.

The Dreadnought wheeled and crunched through the rubble, seeking to run Gydrael down and crush him underfoot. Gydrael ducked back through the hole through which he and the Fallen had entered, back into the hatchery. Eggs crunched messily under his feet. The nidus was full of sslyth wailing.

'I taste the fires of Isstvan!' cried Ancient Xezukoth. 'I know the colours you wear. You are the Emperor's vermin! You are he who would deny the galaxy its perfection! Do you see my Lord Fulgrim watching? I shall make of you a work of art worthy of his notice.'

The sarcophagus was armoured too thickly for the plasma pistol to penetrate. The eye slit looked like a weak spot but Gydrael knew something of how the Dark Angels' own Dreadnoughts were constructed, and the slit was no more than a decoration to hint at the human being interred inside the machine. Ancient Xezukoth, the crippled and evidently insane III Legion traitor inside the Dreadnought, was well protected and without an obvious weak spot to reach him.

Miss nothing.

The Dreadnought slammed a fist down, shuddering the floor. Gydrael barely kept his footing, and had he fallen the other fist would have pounded down and flattened him. He could not fight like this forever, circling the crazed machine, giving and taking ground. It was piloted by a Space Marine, but it was still a machine. He would falter before it did. And he might cut at it a thousand times before it felt any ill effects – Xezukoth, on the other hand, only needed to land one blow to end the fight.

It charged at Gydrael, who was a split second too slow to get out of its way. It hit him at full speed and he held on to its sarcophagus as it barrelled forwards. Gydrael slammed into the wall of the hatchery and kept going as the encrustations shattered against him. The stone wall gave way in turn as the Dreadnought crashed through.

Gydrael rocked from a blow to the back of his head. He lost his grip and fell, tumbling beneath the Dreadnought, barely avoiding the machine's enormous feet. He forced himself upright, aware that his plasma pistol was gone – he still had his sword, but the pistol was somewhere in the wreckage of the fallen wall.

The sky was open above him. The Dreadnought had smashed through the hatchery and out onto the slopes of Phoenicus Peak. The tips of the mountain range rose all around like the spires of vast stone crown, spinning wispy clouds between them under an ice-blue sky.

Gydrael had emerged on a scarp above the tree line. Below, the lower slopes were covered with dense jungle. A host of birds had taken flight at the sudden noise and disturbance, and were wheeling in dark clouds overhead. Each valley between the mountains was a dark green abyss of choked and tangled vegetation through which the sslyth could slither and writhe, but which was near-impassable for a human soldier. The xenos had chosen their nesting place well.

The Dreadnought turned around, the stamping of its feet against the rock echoing around the mountain peaks. Gydrael could feel the injuries he had sustained – the salves dispensed by his armour had dulled them, but now they were catching up with him. A fractured skull. A wrenched shoulder. Cracked ribcage where the breastplate of his armour had buckled. He could still fight, but not for much longer. He would slow down and become less coordinated, but the Dreadnought would not.

He would not defeat the Dreadnought, not like this. The cut and thrust of combat would favour the war machine over time.

There had to be another way.

The Dreadnought's decoration was covered in the imagery of debauchery. It was suggestive of a foul ritual of consumption. Before he had been interred in the Dreadnought, Xezukoth must have partaken of such feasting. The Emperor's Children were seekers of new and obscene experiences, as demanded of them by the worship of Slaanesh. It was through the profane feast that this one had found such experience.

And he still did.

Gydrael glanced at the front of the sarcophagus even as he ducked another blow and leapt back from another. Would this traitor forgo the ritual of the feast, just because he was locked inside a ceramite-plated war machine? Of course not. Nothing would stop him from slaking his foul desires. And outside the Dreadnought his nervous system would not function – he would be blind and deaf, and stripped of all sense of touch and taste. There was a way in. Xezukoth had to be fed.

He saw it then – a hairline seam in the gilding around the front of the sarcophagus. It described a square below the false vision slit, almost invisible among the sculpted visions of dismemberment.

'You are not Ferrus Manus,' growled the Dreadnought. 'You are not Guilliman. I know the winged dagger on your shoulder. You are the Lion! You are the shadowed one! Oh what joy, for I shall feast upon the flesh of the Angel!'

Gydrael would have one shot before the Dreadnought realised what was happening. As insane as he was, Xezukoth was still a Space Marine and he would still know when an enemy sensed a weakness. Gydrael put his head down and ran at Xezukoth, leaping up onto the front of the sarcophagus.

He wielded his sword one-handed, finding a handhold among the carvings with his other hand. He drew his sword back. It would be easier with a short blade, one designed to stab and punch, but his broadsword would have to do.

All the lumbering Xezukoth had to do was reach up and grab Gydrael with his great power fist, ripping him off and crushing him. Gydrael had only seconds at most.

Gydrael rammed the blade into the top of the section of armour. The blade slid into the seam, forcing it open with a burst of its power field. The hatch sprang open, creating a square black mouth in the centre of the Dreadnought's front armour.

The opening was lined with metallic grinding blades, still stained and clotted with gore. A whole body could be forced into there, reduced to sludge by the grinders. It was through this that Xezukoth could be fed his ritual feasts, churned up and siphoned directly down his gullet. Gydrael drew back his arm again, and drove the whole blade into the opening.

He felt resistance as his sword stripped the teeth from the grinders. He rammed it home again and this time the blade slid all the way.

Gydrael knew well the feeling of muscle and bone giving way beneath his sword's blade. He felt it then as the sword punctured the flesh concealed by the sarcophagus. He felt organic matter parting, before the tip of the broadsword lodged in the power plant at the back of the war machine.

A strangled, gurgling cry came from the vox-casters. Gydrael felt a wave of savage satisfaction as he twisted the blade.

The Dreadnought sank down, hydraulics hissing. One arm fell impotently to its side, cracking against the rock of the mountainside. The other waved aimlessly before Xezukoth lost control of it and it fell limp and useless too.

Gydrael pulled the blade out. He dropped to the ground and the Dreadnought slumped to one side. Blood trickled from the hatchway.

Warily, Gydrael glanced around and reopened the vox channel.

'*Once more – I am deploying the virus!*' came Thorne's voice. '*Then I am falling back! We cannot wait any longer!*'

'*Deploying,*' Hasdrubal growled. '*Taste this, xenos filth!*'

Gydrael looked down at the virus canister hanging from his belt. A terrible howling was coming from the nidus, echoed from the other two nests around Phoenicus Peak. Every sslyth in the nest was awake, dragging itself out of the breeding pool or slithering from its burrow. Gydrael would not be able to re-enter and reach the nutrient nexus, and even if he did, there was little point. The virus had already been deployed elsewhere.

The cascade reaction could not be restarted.

'I know you can hear me,' said Gydrael, knowing that the dying Dreadnought's own vox-feeds would be picking up his voice. 'I will find you, Averamus. I have your trail now. I *will* find you.'

There was no answer.

A figure emerged from the tree line, in the black armour of the Deathwatch.

'I saw you,' said Brother Molgurr. He wore the skull emblem of the Mortifactors Chapter on his shoulder guard. 'You brought the war machine down single-handed. A fine kill, brother.'

Gydrael remembered that Molgurr and Decurius had been watching the area as the rest of the kill team executed their mission. They had seen the fight with Ancient Xezukoth, but Gydrael wished they hadn't.

'*I have a visual on you, Brother Gydrael,*' voxed Decurius. '*Report. You have been silent for too long.*'

'The traitor Dreadnought waylaid me. I could not deploy the virus.'

'*Torment yourself later. Fall back to my position. Cover Thorne and Hasdrubal.*'

Molgurr led the way. Overhead the birds were still

wheeling, the ruby-feathered flocks that had given Phoenicus Peak its name. The jungle they inhabited served as the perfect cover for the sslyth broods that stalked the Imperial forces on Kolagar, and for now, it would continue to do so.

'I will find you,' Gydrael murmured to himself.

And somehow, he was sure that Averamus heard him.

Many thousands of sslyth died in the assault on Phoenicus Peak. The two virus bombs wiped out most of the hatcheries and devastated the warclade that was using the mountains as its breeding ground and base of operations.

The virus did not achieve the pandemic levels required to wipe out the sslyth population entirely. The sslyth in Nidus Tertiam escaped the worst of the infection and so a segment of the population remained uninfected before the fast-killing virus burned itself out. They fled into the jungle, and Imperial intelligence lost track of them among the river ways and swamps of the Blackwine Delta.

The Deathwatch kill team was withdrawn from Kolagar. The task of exterminating the sslyth was given to the hard-pressed squads of jungle fighters drawn from the Astra Militarum's death world veterans. The intelligence that the sslyth were allies of the Emperor's Children was passed up the Imperial chain of command.

Men continued to die.

Gydrael watched the servitors on board the Inquisitorial cutter buckling down the sarcophagus of Ancient Xezukoth. The Dreadnought had been salvaged from the mountainside as the cutter descended to pick up the kill team, after helping to cover Thorne and Hasdrubal's exfiltration from the other two sslyth nests. The Ordos could have much to learn from the Dreadnought, and if nothing else, it denied the ancient war machine to the Emperor's Children.

'The crew say we're heading for the next deployment already,' said Brother Hasdrubal. The lightning bolt symbol of the Storm Lords was emblazoned across one shoulder pad, and Hadrubal's flat, brutal face was topped by a single braid of oiled black hair. He indicated the Dreadnought. 'Of all of us to claim such a kill, it had to be the Dark Angel. Your kind wouldn't crack a smile if you had Abaddon's own head on a plate. Me, I'd have this thing mounted over the gates of our fortress, after the Inquisition had finished their tinkering.'

'They are welcome to it,' said Gydrael. 'My Chapter will know of what I have done. It is among them my deeds will be weighed.'

'We left plenty of sslyth dead on Kolagar. If that doesn't get you crowing, we'll be after the greenskins on the Eastern Fringe next. Reap a tally of them, see how that loosens you up.'

'I do not fight for glory,' said Gydrael. 'I do my duty. I seek nothing more.'

'Everyone seeks something more than that,' said Hasdrubal. 'I can tell, Dark Angel. You're not as mysterious as you like to think. Keep it to yourself if you must, but there's something that drives you on. We all have it. Duty alone is never enough.'

'The traitor's corpse is stowed,' said Gydrael. 'I shall retire to my cell. I must meditate on the mission.'

Gydrael left the Storm Lord in the cutter's hold. The ship was small by voidfaring standards, but it still had enough space to give each member of the kill team a cell insulated from the din of the engines and the hubbub of the crew. It was here that each Space Marine saw to his wargear rites, reviewed his mission archives, and prayed. Gydrael's cell was simple and plain, as befitted a Dark Angel's humility. A shelf of battle histories and war-prayers shared a wall with an icon of the Dark Angels Primarch, Lion El'Jonson, crushing the Void Meridian uprising during the Great Crusade. The opposite wall held dozens of weapons racked up, with combat knives of every size and type and three marks of bolter with maintenance and cleaning tools. A stand for Gydrael's armour took up one corner.

Gydrael knelt on the floor and took down one of the books, a volume of prayers to banish doubt, alongside reflections on actions in combat. He opened the book, and from the hidden hollow cut into its pages he took out a slender dataslate. He thumbed the activation rune and the screen lit up. He felt his injuries now – the ship's Apothecary had patched him up but his body would do the healing, knitting back together the torn muscles and bone during the voyage to the Eastern Fringe.

'Brother Zameon Gydrael,' he said into the device. 'Recipient, Master Interrogator-Chaplain Asmodai. My search has borne fruit. I encountered Averamus on the planet Kolagar. He was as the histories described. The Mark of Scorn was upon him. He was in league with the Emperor's Children, but they intervened before I could bring Averamus to justice.'

The dataslate would convert Gydrael's words into a secure data packet. It would then be sent to a relay station and further translated into a symbol string to be transmitted astropathically to the Rock. The Dark Angels' astropathic codes had never been breached. No one would know the message's contents save Gydrael himself, and Lord Asmodai.

'I broke my oaths to the Deathwatch,' continued Gydrael. 'The mission at Kolagar failed because of me. I pursued the Fallen instead of completing my objective. These are the duties I have to my Chapter and to my Imperium, and I was never in any doubt as to what path I would take if they came into conflict. But... I faltered. For a moment, when I saw I was facing one of the Fallen, I felt that shadow within me. I had to choose.

'Many men will die because the sslyth were not wiped out on Kolagar. Men of the Astra Militarum, and others. I feel the guilt for those deaths within me, for it was within my power to stop them. But I shall crush that guilt down deep within me, and banish it. And instead, I choose to see their blood on Averamus' hands.'

Gydrael turned his helmet over in his grip. It was still grimy from the fighting in the nidus. Sslyth blood and scales clung to the black-painted plating. He slid off a gauntlet and vambrace – they were similarly filthy from battle. The smell of the sslyth clung to him.

'I ask an indulgence from my Chapter, Lord Asmodai,' continued Gydrael. 'When Averamus is brought to justice, if I still live, I shall be the one to execute him. For all that have died and will die by his hand, I would have vengeance on Averamus the Fallen. By my oaths to my Chapter and to the Deathwatch, and all the relics of the Rock, I would take his head. Sealed by the vox-print of Brother Zameon Gydrael, in the name of the Primarch and the Emperor Most High.'

Gydrael deactivated the dataslate and continued to remove his armour, lining up the segments on the floor of the cell. He took a polishing cloth and compound from the tools racked on the wall and began to clean the blood of the sslyth off his armour.

He murmured prayers to the armour's machine-spirit, asking it to remain unbroken, as he settled in to a lengthy session of wargear rites.

It would be a long time before the true dirt was wiped away.

REDBLADE

ROBBIE MACNIVEN

The chosen arena was Arco-Refinery Alpha 1-1's primary firing range. Originally, the low, sloping tunnel had been designed to test Adeptus Mechanicus combat servitors, but with the arrival of the Space Marines on Theron it had been given over to them. If the servants of the Machine God had known what it was being used for now they would doubtless have objected, but a guard had been posted on the door to ensure they didn't interfere.

The chamber's lumen strips flickered to life, a low hum filling the echoing space. Four warriors occupied the fire-scarred range just beyond the empty weapons stalls – two in the black plate of the Deathwatch, two bearing the blue-grey livery of the Space Wolves. One of the former, his quartered red and yellow pauldron marking him out as a Howling Griffon, took the boltgun handed to him by his brother.

'You know the rules, Space Wolf,' the bolter's owner, Caius Vorens, said. 'Combat knives only. First blood.'

Drenn nodded. The young Wolf was almost shaking with battle-hunger, hand clenching and unclenching compulsively around the hilt of his blade, Fang. He could feel the anger of his pack leader, Svenbald, burning into him even as he squared up to Vorens. The Deathwatch kill team leader was terse and stoic, his face unreadable behind his black faceplate. Drenn had left his own helmet off.

They drew their blades and paced out to the centre of the range, boots ringing off the pockmarked rockcrete. Halfway down, Vorens stopped and faced Drenn. Svenbald and the Howling Griffon, Siegfric, took post at the edge of the chamber.

'Before the eyes of the Emperor,' Siegfric intoned. 'Victory to the just.'

Drenn kicked hard, slamming the ork back into the refinery's edge. The alien managed to snatch one of the Space Wolf's gauntlets just as the railings buckled and split. Snarling an oath to Russ and the Allfather, Drenn hacked into its straining limb with his knife, sawing its sharpened edge through slabs of green muscle, tendon and bone.

The ork lost its grip, roaring furiously as it toppled over the platform's side and down, down into the crushing embrace of Theron's swirling gravity well. Drenn watched it go, bouncing off the flank of one of the refinery's engine spheres. Its claws scrabbled for purchase, smearing the grav-machine's flank bloody before the beast vanished into the roiling clouds. The wind's fury snatched its howl away.

'*Report*,' the voice of Svenbald, Drenn's pack leader, crackled over the vox. He grimaced, turning away from the edge.

'Southern plate secure. Six contacts, all purged.'

'*Regroup with the pack at the central hub,*' Svenbald said. '*The fleet is reporting another wave approaching from the east.*'

Drenn bent to wipe the sticky xenos blood from his combat knife, and realised abruptly that the remainder of the alien's meaty forearm was still clamped around his left gauntlet. Frustrated, he prised apart the ork's claws and tossed the limb over the refinery's side. For all their size and resilience, greenskins were hardly a worthy foe. There would be no sagas sung about today.

Drenn sheathed the knife and keyed the activation rune on his jump pack.

The clouds around Platform Epsilon 9-17 looked like diseased lungs, swollen a sickly yellow and shot through with ugly veins of red lightning. The airborne refinery lumbered through the sulphurous banks, the six huge gravitic engine spheres keeping the platform rig aloft.

Thunder split the infected heavens as Drenn landed on the central plate of the refinery. The lightning snapped upwards, a crimson lash from the gas giant's crushing depths. Normally, the Adeptus Mechanicus personnel crewing the platform would have welcomed such a sight, for Epsilon 9-17 was a mobile conductor, channelling a portion of the lightning it harvested to stay airborne. Its central hub bristled with plasteel arrays and blackened earthing spikes, while the bowels of its grav-engines crackled with the energy of the storm. But today the sound of thunder didn't come from the lightning alone. It came from the orks.

Drenn's packmates were watching the second wave coming in. From such a distance the mass of xenos aircraft looked like a black thunderhead, spreading from the hangars of a hulking ork battle asteroid. The looted hunk of debris perched low in orbit, a burly mass of space-scarred rock, rusting battlements and leering skull glyphs.

'Svenbald wants to see you,' one of Drenn's packmates, Karlson, said.

'Where is he?'

'He went into the hub with the xenos hunter. He wants you to wait outside.'

Drenn cast a glance at the three black-armoured warriors of the Deathwatch who stood observing the approaching war planes alongside the Space Wolves, then turned towards the refinery's central hub.

Epsilon's generatorum house was like an Ecclesiarchy church, all crenelated spires and flying buttresses – except instead of the aquila above its arched doors it bore the Machina Opus symbol of the Adeptus Mechanicus, and instead of pews and a high altar, it was crammed with throbbing arco-banks. The vaulted ceiling vibrated with their power, and red light crackled around the coils, throwing the interior into jagged illumination.

The station's crew of six tech-adepts were standing before the hub's primary generator, the air resounding with their binary cant. Magos Zarn was leading them, but turned as Drenn entered. His chief enginseer picked up where he left off.

'My lords,' the magos said. He was addressing the two figures who had walked in just before Drenn – Svenbald and the Deathwatch kill team leader, Caius Vorens. Drenn hung back as they approached the magos. The Martian's face was still mostly flesh, but utterly immobile, as though he wore a corpse mask. The tech-priest's pale lips remained shut, his automated voice issuing from a brass vox-grille sutured into his throat. A canvas pump-lung, a requirement in the inimical upper atmosphere of Theron, pulsed grotesquely from its harness across his chest.

'Magos Zarn,' Vorens said, glancing briefly up at the cog-toothed symbol of the Omnissiah, suspended by great chains above the generatorum.

'My data-streams report the xenos attack has been repelled,' Zarn intoned. The mechadendrites coiling upwards from his robed back were swaying gently in time with the chanting of his adepts.

'Repelled thanks in part to the firepower of your combat servitors,' Vorens said, 'and the oversight of the Imperial Navy. Has there been any word from the other refineries?'

'Epsilon Five-One and Omega Fifteen-Zero have reported similar assaults. Beta Thirteen-Eleven hasn't encountered any contacts, and we have received no communications, for good or ill, from Kappa Six-Eight. Of the refineries beyond my quadrant I know nothing, but my own estimates show that over eighty per cent of the platforms on Theron's northern hemisphere are under attack.'

'Naval fighter command is sparing what it can,' Svenbald interjected, his stony voice a counterpoint to Zarn's monotone speech. 'We've been relying on their orbital presence to detect each incoming wave. There's another one inbound as we speak.'

'I trust your warriors will prove sufficient for the task at hand,' Zarn said. Drenn felt the machine-man's bionic eyes focusing on him over Svenbald's shoulder.

The Wolf Guard sensed the change of attention and turned. His craggy, red-painted face, underlit by the energy surging through the arco-banks, became even grimmer.

'I told you to wait outside, not follow me around like a stray pup.'

'They're coming again,' Drenn said, ignoring the reprimand.

'We know. Get out.'

The greenskin invasion of Theron exuded savage, alien desperation. The strategos of the Departmento Munitorum had calculated that the xenos were attempting to capture the gas giant's arco-refineries in a bid to refuel and rearm before pressing corewards. Kjarl Grimblood, perhaps reading good fortune in the flames of war, had dispatched eight packs from his Great Company to assist the Adeptus Mechanicus forces with Theron's defence. Where the Deathwatch had come from, nobody knew.

Drenn stared at the new swarm of ork aircraft in the distance as they rumbled towards Epsilon 9-17. Svenbald rounded on him, gripping his arm and speaking in hushed but aggressive tones.

'Look at me. Grimblood ordered your transfer to my pack because you're a wild young fool, even for a Blood Claw. My Flame Hunters thrive in the hottest fires, but we don't seem to burn bright enough for your underdeveloped passions, do we?'

'If you stopped gnawing at me, maybe I would respect you more,' Drenn spat, finally looking his pack leader in the eye. Like many of the long-tooths in Kjarl Grimblood's company, he daubed his burn-scarred features with his own blood before battle, the red streaks mimicking the fire that was the symbol of the Grimbloods. Svenbald was a Wolf Guard sky leader, but since Drenn's recent promotion from Blood Claw to the war-hungry ranks of the Flame Hunters he had yet to see Svenbald do anything noteworthy.

The old wolf was all boast and no teeth.

'If you want to remain a part of this Great Company you can start by respecting the decisions of its Wolf Lord,' Svenbald said. 'A place in my pack is an honour, and it burns my pride having to count a whelp like you among my warriors.'

'You want a tame pup who follows all your orders. You'd rather I gave up on personal combat, for a start. I won't. No pistol or flamer can match my blades.'

Immediately after arriving on Theron, Drenn had refused to carry his bolt pistol as a sidearm. The weapon had jammed when he'd needed it most, cut off in the middle of a mob of rampaging orks. Since then he'd relied only on his chainsword, Graam, and his hook-tipped combat knife, Fang.

He'd also discarded his helmet, letting loose his shock of fiery red hair during combat. He had only worn his helm on the day that his bolter had failed, and only then because his power armour had been burning from crest to boot, set alight by the greenskin's crude flamer weaponry. He'd carved his way clear of the mob, like the Fire Wolf of Fenrisian legend, a Flame Hunter worthy of his Wolf Lord. Svenbald had just watched.

'You prefer the blood on your blades to the fire in your heart,' Svenbald accused, accompanying each word with a jab at the Fire Wolf head embossed on Drenn's breastplate. 'You're no Grimblood.'

'You only say that because you know your kill statistics won't match mine at the end of this campaign, long-tooth.'

Svenbald snarled and turned away. 'I don't have time for your toothless biting, Drenn.'

'My name is Redblade,' said Drenn.

'No it isn't. Get back to the pack.'

* * *

Erik, formerly the youngest of the Flame Hunters before Drenn's hasty induction, stepped aside to make room for him at the edge of the refinery. The Wolves were taking up combat positions, flanked by the Deathwatch.

'What did you say to him?' Erik muttered. 'It looks like you pissed in his *mjod*.'

'He still won't acknowledge me as Redblade,' Drenn replied, deliberately catching Svenbald's eye. The Wolf Guard held his gaze, but said nothing.

'The greenskins are using a different trajectory,' Vorens cut in over the vox. 'Stand by for further orders.'

He was right. The first wave had torn into the refinery head-on. Its defenders – hardwired combat servitors, the Deathwatch kill team and Svenbald's Flame Hunters – had picked them off as they approached, smearing the vile-looking clouds with dirty black contrails and spinning wreckage. Only six greenskins had made it to the platform, and Drenn had dealt with them.

This time the orks' crude machines were banking high, climbing above the platform.

'Those look bigger,' said Svenbald. 'Bombers?'

'I doubt it,' Vorens replied. 'They want to take the station, not destroy it.'

'If we kill enough of them, they'll turn the asteroid's guns on us,' Svenbald said, pointing at the vast ork rock-ship still disgorging its airborne flotsam.

'They need the power stored within the arco-refineries. Without the generatorums their most powerful weaponry is useless.' Vorens' voice remained slow and precise, but Drenn got the impression he thought Svenbald was an idiot. His opinion of the Deathwatch leader rose fractionally.

Limping, fat flyers with stubby wings and dozens of

juddering rotors had clambered over the refinery, out of bolter range. Drenn watched, fascinated, as their ramps and hatches were hauled back. Shapes began to barrel from the aircraft, leaping into the abyss with apparent fearlessness. For a moment he wondered whether the xenos were truly so blood-crazed and stupid that they thought they could avoid being dragged down into Theron's gravity well. Then he spotted flares of light winking from the bulky packs strapped to their backs, and he realised he was in fact witnessing a haphazard aerial assault deployment.

'Now we're in for a fight,' he growled. For once, Svenbald didn't reprimand him.

There was a thud of disengaging mag-locks as the Skyclaws drew their chainswords.

'Kill team,' Vorens snapped. 'Protect the central refinery. Hit them as they land.'

'Flame Hunters,' Svenbald roared, 'for Russ and the Allfather, into them!'

Drenn needed no further urging. He was already launching himself into the air, even as the first hard rounds from the orks' crude firearms spanked off the platform around him. The gut-wrenching sense of dislocation matched the adrenaline pounding through his charged body, and he howled with glee as he speared upwards, his jump pack vents throbbing.

He picked his first target. The greenskin's mouth was open, but its bellowed challenge was whipped away by the wind. All Drenn could hear was the keening of his pack as he forced the turbo stud to its limit, pushing his leap as high as possible. He held his chainsword out two-handed, the kraken teeth roaring to life.

Above the surface plates of Epsilon 9-17, Wolf and ork met. The impact almost tore Graam from Drenn's grip, but it cleaved the beast from groin to skull. The rocket lashed to its back detonated, immolating the bisected halves. Drenn left the blast in his wake, drenched in alien gore.

His jump pack hit its peak barely a second after the bloody collision, chiming a warning as the dual-vector thrust shorted out. That was when the second ork hit him.

This one came boots-first. One steel toecap smashed into Drenn's skull, and for a second even the Wolf's super-human senses failed. He felt a crack. Darkness reared up to smother him. The smell of blood – his blood – reached his nose and he snapped back with a snarl.

He was falling. His pack was ringing out a warning, but he couldn't reach the turbo stud because the greenskin that had struck him was now clamping both arms around his waist, locking its hands beneath his jump pack. Drenn got an impression of porcine red eyes glaring from behind grimy goggle lenses, great yellow tusks and breath like a butcher's yard.

Then the alien headbutted him.

There was another crunch. Drenn's vision swam. The world was turning over and under, yet still the ork clung on with savage, stinking intensity. It tried to hit him a second time, but he managed to twist his head back and away and the greenskin's slavering jaw cracked off his gorget.

One of Drenn's hands scrabbled for a hold on the nose of the ork's rocket pack. With a fanged grimace he managed to force the battered nose of the rocket backwards, straining the straps binding it to the ork's broad torso. He thrust Graam into the gap, and revved the weapon furiously.

There was an audible snap of leather and the rocket fell away, launching off on a crazed, looping trajectory.

The ork sensed its sudden weightlessness and tried to gouge Drenn's face with its tusks, but the Wolf just grinned and hit the turbo stud with his free hand. The jump pack's vector thrust roared into life and the ork answered with a howl of agony as the downwash of the twin jets charred its forearms, still clenched around Drenn's waist.

The Space Wolf kicked away, turning and powering his fall into a sideways roll. With a crunch, the xenos brute impaled itself on one of the central hub's earthing spikes.

Drenn slammed into the hub's deck plates an instant later. The pack hadn't had enough time to build a proper thrust, so the impact was hard and clumsy. He rolled, the servos in his power armour grating as they absorbed the fall. He felt a knee plate crack, but then he was back on his feet, Graam in hand, the weapon growling.

Svenbald's Flame Hunters had intercepted a dozen orks on the way up, and a dozen more on the way down, but just as many had made it to Epsilon's plates. A few had come too fast, or their rocket packs had failed them, and their crumpled remains were smeared across the deck. Plenty more, however, had ploughed into the Deathwatch.

The nearest ork had its back to Drenn, too busy pounding at the mangled, sparking form of a combat servitor to notice the Wolf's arrival. Drenn smashed Graam through the alien's thick skull, his own howl joining that of his chainsword. The battle frenzy was on him – the bloody fury the *skjalds* spoke of, the urge to kill so strong that it could fire up even the greyest long-tooth.

It didn't matter any more that the greenskins weren't worthy foes. It didn't matter that Svenbald was an old fool who probably wanted him dead. It didn't matter that even his packmates, themselves headstrong young Wolves, thought Drenn an impetuous firebrand. It didn't matter that every day since leaving his tribe and his home on Fenris, he'd felt like a wolf without a pack, a lone hunter.

What mattered was that his limbs were swift, his armour strong, and that there was alien blood on his blade. What mattered was the way the next ork overextended its lunge, the way Graam's initial strike cleaved off its arm, and the backstroke opened its throat. What mattered was how the next greenskin tried to gun him down, realised its pistol was jammed, and died with his combat knife through its chest.

By the time Drenn Redblade came to his senses, he was standing on the very edge of the refinery, slick with stinking alien gore and staring out into the heavens.

There was a storm coming. The clouds had turned even uglier and more nebulous. The gravity well below was becoming a yawning, black maw. The wind was picking up, and was clawing at him. He spread his arms wide, twin hearts still hammering out the addictive rhythm of combat, a howl building in his–

A gauntlet smacked into his pauldron, shattering the moment. He turned, snarling, expecting to face Svenbald.

The snarl died when he instead found himself confronting the black battleplate of the Deathwatch leader.

'You fought well, Wolf,' Vorens said. His own armour was almost as bloody as the Flame Hunter's. 'What is your name?'

'Drenn,' he replied. 'They call me the Redblade.'

'Listen to the pup,' scoffed Utred, one of the older Flame Hunters, as he slapped a fresh clip into his bolt pistol. 'Not even a single moon with us and he's already given himself a deed-name. He's no true Skyclaw, just an upstart Blood Claw out of his depth. Tell me, who calls you the Redblade? Bar yourself, of course.'

'If I don't deserve the name, then come take this from me,' Drenn snarled, pointing Fang at Utred. Its blade was slick with dark xenos blood.

Vorens pushed between Drenn and the older Wolf, breaking their eye contact. 'The xenos have been purged, but our long-range communications have been disabled. We need to regroup. Come, Drenn.'

Vorens held out a hand, as though to pull the Space Wolf away from the oblivion that beckoned just beyond the refinery's rim. Drenn stepped back from the edge, but didn't take the proffered gauntlet. Utred had already gone.

Epsilon's plates looked like a scene from a skjald's epic. The eviscerated remains of orks carpeted the plascrete. Zarn's red-robed adepts were scurrying between the combat servitors, attempting to effect repairs, their pump-lungs swollen and straining in the thin atmosphere. Sparks flew and saws hummed as pale, dead flesh was stitched back up and rent metal welded shut.

The refinery's servitors weren't the only casualties. Drenn saw the Deathwatch kill team's Apothecary kneeling over the body of one of his brothers, retrieving his gene-seed with a bloodied narthecium. The Flame Hunters were assembling on the eastern side of the platform, and he noted that two of them were also missing: Ivarr and Karlson.

'Lost over the edge,' Svenbald said. 'Ivarr took a hard round through the visor, Karlson was dragged down by two greenskins. May the Allfather guide their souls to the Great Hall.'

'We will feast with them again one day,' Drenn said. The other Flame Hunters growled their agreement, and even Svenbald allowed himself a curt nod.

The sound of armoured boots interrupted the obituary.

'The greenskins that engage in jump-pack assaults are not like the rest of their kind,' Vorens said, parting the circle of Wolves. 'Discipline and determination are their hallmarks. We cannot assume that was the end of their assault, or that any future attacks will be so direct.'

'You think there'll be another wave?' Drenn asked.

'Atmospherics are hampering our attempts to re-establish communication with the scrying Navy vessels in orbit,' Vorens replied, 'but fresh xenos formations are already on their way.'

'We can hold them.'

'That's if they attack us hand-to-hand again.'

'You said they didn't want to damage the refinery,' Svenbald said.

'They don't want to *destroy* it. Damage is another matter.'

'A bombing run this time, then?'

'Possibly. We should prepare Epsilon's shuttles for evacuation. We'll rig the central hub with melta charges before we leave.'

'A true warrior doesn't retreat,' said Drenn, facing Vorens.

Svenbald cut in before the Deathwatch leader could respond. 'A true warrior doesn't speak out of turn, especially before his superiors. Show some respect.'

Drenn fixed the Wolf Guard with a glare.

'I see no superiors here. Only equals at best. If anyone considers himself my better, let him challenge me, blade to blade.'

Svenbald took a pace forwards, fangs bared, and Drenn's

hand went back to his chainsword's hilt. Distantly, the storm's thunder rumbled, heavy with threat.

Then the Lightning struck.

It came from the north, using the rising storm as cover. Two ork bombers were plummeting into the gas giant's black embrace before the Imperial forces even realised they were under attack, scrap-covered fuselages lanced through by heavy las-bolts. Autocannon rounds riddled a third heavy flyer before the formation began to scatter.

They were too slow. The Lightning was followed by five lithe air superiority fighters bearing the matt-grey colours and red talon crest of the local Imperial Navy battlegroup.

The orks had no fighter topcover. Obeying their primitive instincts, most of their war planes attempted to turn and fight, defence turrets swivelling. The Imperial aircraft, however, had been built for this particular type of slaughter. They danced, rolled and darted, whilst the blind rage of the greenskins resulted in their own aircraft colliding or mowing one another down in a confused tangle of fire arcs.

Epsilon 9-17's defenders watched in silence as the Imperial Navy tore the clouds asunder with the weight of the wreckage they sent tumbling into the yawning, swirling gravitational well at Theron's heart. As the final ramshackle bomber was ripped to pieces by strafing fire, Epsilon's cross-command vox-net lit up.

'This is Flight Lieutenant Dall to task force designate Epsilon Nine-Seventeen. Come in, over'.

It was Vorens who answered, tapping into the command frequency. 'Flight Lieutenant Dall, this is Kill Team Leader Vorens of the Deathwatch. We congratulate you on your timing. You do the Imperial Navy great credit.'

'*You honour us, lord,*' Dall replied, '*but my wing can't remain on-station. Another xenos asteroid is attacking platform Sigma Thirteen-Eight, four miles south-west of here. My warbirds need to rearm before we can go to their aid.*'

'The xenos will send another bombing run,' Vorens said. 'We can't protect the platform from that, and the refinery's shuttles are likely too slow for effective escape. Is there any way you can assist with aerial extraction?'

'*Central Command at Alpha One-One can scramble Valkyries,*' Dall said. '*Their ETA would be around twenty minutes. We should be able to make another pass by that time, to see them safely through.*'

'The lives of everyone aboard this station may depend on it,' Vorens said. 'Our thanks again for your assistance, flight lieutenant.'

'*Good hunting, my lords.*'

And then the Lightnings were gone, slamming south-west through the cloud cover, the roar of their jets drowned by the wind's howl.

Drenn looked at Svenbald, but the Wolf Guard was pointedly ignoring him. He felt his anger spike, driven on by the battle lust he'd yet to slake.

'Look at me!' he barked, stung to fury by the older Wolf's disdain.

And that was when the first explosion tore through the heart of Epsilon 9-17.

Vorens was right. These were no ordinary orks.

Epsilon lurched again, yawing towards its southernmost plate. The movement wasn't vast, but it was enough to force Drenn to thought-activate his auto-stabilisers, clamping himself to the deck.

'Hel's teeth,' snapped another Flame Hunter, Hrolfgar. 'What was that?'

Warning klaxons began to wail from the central hub's spire. Adepts were hurrying to the outlying nodes, their mechadendrites writhing in alarm. The platform groaned, tilting a fraction further.

'One of the grav-sphere engines,' Drenn heard Erik growl down the vox. 'It's gone.'

'They're below us,' Vorens added. He was crouching at the platform's side. 'They're on the engines.'

And suddenly it all made sense. The main assault was a diversion. While one mob dropped from above, a smaller contingent had flown their rickety aircraft in below Epsilon and leapt up using their rocket packs. Now they were clambering over the curving plasteel framework of Epsilon's underbelly, rigging the platform with bundles of piped explosives.

'Don't fire,' Vorens ordered. 'We can't risk damaging the gravitic spheres.'

'We've got to get them off,' Drenn said, stepping to the refinery's edge. 'If they take out any more, we won't be able to stay airborne.'

'They're not trying to bring it down,' Vorens said. 'They want to capture the platform intact, and if they want to do that they'll have t–'

But Drenn wasn't listening. He was jumping.

Vorens shouted after him, but it was too late. The young Flame Hunter fell, combat knife unsheathed, fangs bared, his red hair whipping out behind him.

Now was not the time for thoughts. Now was the time for great deeds.

Now was the time for Redblade to make his mark.

The first ork he hit didn't even know it. Drenn's boots burst its skull open and snapped its neck, smashing it off the engine's flank. He activated his jump pack the moment he struck, and the powerful turbos thrust him viciously upwards and to the left. He collided with another greenskin clinging onto a strut binding one of the crackling grav-spheres, the beast's blunt features contorted by a grimace as it tried to bring its crude firearm to bear. The impact of the Wolf, pauldron-first, tore the ork from its grapnel and sent it roaring out into the ether.

Drenn tried to jump again, but his pack chimed. The turbo hadn't recharged yet, and suddenly he was in freefall. There was nothing below, nothing but an endless sea of swirling, sickly clouds and the grinding pressure of Theron's gravity well many miles below.

He lashed out, trying to get a hold on the flank of the sphere sliding past, but his gauntlet could only scrape against the smooth outer plates. With a yell, he lunged with his other fist, plunging Fang into the engine's frame.

His arm jerked and he slowed, but didn't stop. The lightning bolts feeding the gravitic engine's inner core cracked and lashed at the gash he'd torn in the light metal frame, the blade carving its way through the sphere's outer shell. Drenn spat a curse as he gripped onto the weapon's hilt two-handed, but to no avail.

And then, abruptly, he stopped.

The knife struck one of the plasteel stanchions ribbing the platform's swollen belly, the final one before the drop away into nothingness. The metal bent but held, and Drenn found himself dangling helplessly.

Thunder crashed. Beneath his dangling feet, Theron's

swirling maw gaped, seemingly desperate to turn the young Wolf to pulp.

He managed to grip the stanchion with his other hand. His jump pack chimed again, finally recharged, but he had nothing to kick up off. Gritting his fangs, he began to pull. The servos in his power armour whined as they added to his strength, heaving him up onto the narrow strip of metal. It groaned and bent further. Finally he snatched hold of the rent his knife had torn in the engine sphere's shell, and found his feet.

Lightning crashed again, lashing up past him. The arcs caged within the grav-sphere twisted and crackled in sympathy. Drenn heard a ticking in his ears and realised it was his vox, barely audible over the storm.

'*Above you!*'

Drenn looked up and saw two shapes – Vorens and Svenbald – traversing the side of the engine. Svenbald had discarded his jump pack. Both were strapped into harness coils usually plugged into the servitors responsible for maintaining the engine flanks.

There was a crack, and Drenn felt something strike his leg. He turned to see the nearest orks firing at him, their wild aim sending rounds rattling off the stanchions. He mag-locked Fang and bellowed at them, unable to do anything but hold on.

'*Jump!*' It was Svenbald this time. Both figures had paused halfway down the engine's side, just above where Drenn had first stabbed Fang in.

'*We can't rappel past the damaged section,*' Vorens voxed. '*It's too volatile. You have to jump. Now.*'

The plasteel rib underfoot was buckling. More ork slugs

hit him, smacking off his breastplate and his right vambrace. He grimaced, growled a heathen prayer, and hit the activation rune just as the stanchion beneath him snapped.

The jump pack flared to life and he powered upwards, arms outstretched, searing along the vicious rent he'd torn in the engine. Vorens and Svenbald reached out and snatched hold of him, their gauntlets meeting just as the jump hit its apex.

Drenn planted both feet on the engine's side, fangs gritted as he held onto the two tethered Space Marines.

'Bring us up!' Vorens shouted. The harnesses began to whirr in reverse, the taut cables straining as they dragged the three of them back towards the platform.

They reached it just as more thunder split the heavens. The storm was breaking, the winds screaming and hammering at the refinery from all sides. The ork asteroid was moving closer, now barely visible amidst the livid clouds, its armoured bulkheads and bristling guns occasionally outlined by flashes of red brilliance.

The pack hauled Drenn, Vorens and Svenbald up over the edge. Drenn tried to stand, but a sudden stab of pain told him that an ork round had found the weak point behind his knee plate. He'd been so focussed on reaching Vorens and Svenbald that he hadn't noticed he'd been hit. He scowled and pulled himself upright, blocking out the pain.

Svenbald was facing him, grizzled face contorted with anger. Before Drenn could speak, the Wolf Guard slammed a fist into his jaw. The blow sent him staggering. Svenbald snatched him before he hit the railings at the refinery's edge, and the young Wolf went down on one knee.

'You're a stupid, arrogant little piece of gristle,' Svenbald spat. 'If you disobey orders, *anyone's orders*, ever again, I will kill you myself.'

Drenn didn't reply. He could hear roaring and the hammering of bolters, and realised that the orks were attacking up over the platform's edge. Svenbald gripped his vambrace and dragged him forcefully back onto his feet, reopening the wound behind his knee.

'You owe me a life-debt, pup,' the Wolf Guard snarled. 'So in the name of Russ, *fight!*'

The greenskins died.

The Deathwatch and the Space Wolves cut them down on the open plates, bolters and hand flamers blazing. A crackling stab of lightning struck the station as they fought, slamming like the spear of the Allfather into the great rods and spikes projecting from Epsilon's hub. The impact sent fat sparks scattering across the decking and threw the combat into dark shades of crimson. The generatorum thrummed with power, the arco-banks within alive with energy. The whine of the grav-engines, barely audible over the storm, rose to a pained shriek.

'We're losing altitude,' Vorens voxed. 'Magos Zarn is trying to stabilise the rig. All brethren, report to the central hub.'

Epsilon tilted still further. Drenn activated his jump pack, bounding up the plate towards the hub and its halo of energy-wreathed spikes.

Inside, amidst the vaulted, red-shot darkness, the Adeptus Astartes and Epsilon's crew gathered. Magos Zarn stood before the great coils of the generatorum, flanked on either side by his enginseer and adepts. The tech-priest's face was as pallid and lifeless as ever, but he pitched his

synthetic voice in a manner that conveyed the serious-
ness of their situation.

'The xenos have destroyed one of the gravity engines,'
he said. 'And the damage to the second is irreparable. It
is losing its charge as we speak.'

The cowled heads of the adepts turned to scan Drenn,
but he simply glowered. Zarn pressed on.

'I have calculated that the strain on the remaining four
engines is too great. One has already crossed the stress
tolerance threshold, despite our blessings, and I compute
that another will follow within the next eight minutes.
We are losing altitude. I estimate that we will reach critical descent within the next half-hour. After that we will
cross the horizon line into Theron's gravitational well.
Nothing can escape after that.'

'Naval fighter support will be here soon,' Vorens said.
'We will evacuate the station.'

'And we will have failed in our mission,' Svenbald added,
looking pointedly at Drenn.

'At least the xenos won't capture the generatorum banks,'
Vorens replied.

'We'll just have to hope the other refineries are more
successfully defended,' Svenbald went on.

'Would you consider it a success,' said Drenn, his voice
hard and low, 'if we destroy the ork's battle asteroid?'

Lightning pounded the hub, and for a second the power
failed, the only illumination coming from the red energy
crackling behind the murky panes of the generatorum's
banks. The lumen strips overhead blinked back on, but
dimmer than before.

'And how would we do that?' Svenbald asked, his tone
slick with scorn.

'We won't,' Drenn said. 'But Epsilon Nine-Seventeen might.'

Again, no one spoke. Vorens turned to look directly at the young Space Wolf, the light giving his black armour a fresh, bloody sheen.

'Elaborate,' he said.

'We're a lightning harvester,' Drenn said, and as though to underscore his words the lightning struck again. The whole platform shuddered. 'We can't save Epsilon, but we can still use it. Ram the asteroid.'

'The orks will board us long before we reach them,' Svenbald said. 'That's even assuming that there'll be sufficient lightning charge left to damage the rock.'

'I doubt any physical impact could cause sufficient damage,' Zarn interjected. 'But the generatorum has absorbed vast amounts of power in the past few minutes. It may be possible for my adepts to overload the coils, and compress the magnetic flux using combat servitor munitions. We could create a minor electromagnetic pulse that would likely shut down the majority of the xenos' technological systems and cause them to drop into the gravitational well. As for directing the refinery's course, we shall remain on board. I have served this station since I was an adept, still mired in the ways of the flesh. Regardless of your intentions, I will not leave now.'

'With all due respect, magos, I doubt you can hold off another wave of greenskins,' said Vorens.

'The defence servitors will remain in place,' Zarn replied, 'and we will bar the hub's blast doors. We need only hold until we have rerouted and overloaded the power couplings. And if all else fails, we can fight. Do not underestimate the servants of the Omnissiah, Space Marine. The fury of Mars is ours to command.'

Vorens nodded. 'If you believe it can work, Magos Zarn, then I see no reason not to try.'

'I compute the probability of causing critical levels of damage on the xenos craft at forty-eight-point-eight per cent. The odds are not in our favour, but now that Epsilon's loss is guaranteed, it is the most logical course of action.'

'It's settled then,' Vorens said. 'I will inform your superiors on Alpha One-One of your valour, magos.'

'Pray you make it there to do so,' Zarn responded.

The proximity alarms had begun to shriek. The orks were coming again.

This time they attacked from all sides – blunt-nosed fighters, flyers with thudding rotor blades, lumbering bombers that looked like great conglomerations of jagged scrap.

'*I have altered our course,*' Magos Zarn's voice rang out over the platform's vox-masts, '*and I have done my best to stabilise the plates. Accounting for meteorological conditions, engine damage and possible evasive manoeuvres by the asteroid, I estimate a collision in just over thirteen minutes. We will have an optimal electromagnetic pulse primed within five, but we will hold off until your transports are beyond range.*'

Drenn suspected they'd all be dead long before then. The fourth ork wave was vast. The asteroid had emptied its guts, the xenos apparently enraged by the refinery's defiance.

'Make ready,' Svenbald said, chambering a fresh bolt round. Drenn unlocked Graam, his eyes on the storm-wracked skies.

'I'm getting a signal,' Vorens said. 'Stand by.'

The platform's long-range vox-array was down, scrambled

to incoherence by the storm, but the powerful uplinks of the Adeptus Astartes had locked onto an incoming Imperial signal.

Through the clouds came two black Valkyrie assault carriers and two Vendetta gunships, their noses down and throttles open.

'Flame Hunters, assemble on the southern plate,' Svenbald voxed. 'Prepare for aerial extraction.'

The servitor guns opened up, pounding the skies with bolts of plasma and streaking interceptor missiles. The greenskins to the south were unable to get at the two Valkyries as they touched down on the refinery's edge.

The rear ramps dropped, the engines still turning over. Drenn and half the Flame Hunters fought through the brutal downdraught of the left flyer's twin engines, the remainder joining the Deathwatch in the other. The troop hold was immediately full, the space for its usual compliment of a dozen men barely sufficient for six armoured Space Marines.

'*Hold on,*' came the voice of the pilot over the internal vox. There was a lurch as the Valkyrie lifted, overburdened by its new cargo. The rear ramp was still closing. Before it clamped shut, Drenn caught a final glimpse of Epsilon, its plates streaked with blazing firepower. '*We have incoming contacts. With all due respect, lords, we need those heavy bolters working. Keep them off us.*'

Normally the Valkyrie's twin side-mounted guns would have been manned by Naval crewmen, but they'd been left behind to make more room. As Hrolfgar hauled back the left-hand hatch, Drenn swung the heavy weapon out from its housing, checked the belt feed and chambered the first round.

A swarm of junk flyers was closing in on the fleeing Valkyries. The two Vendetta gunships covering their escape were sending rounds thumping back into their pursuers, but the sheer number of aircraft meant that some were getting past the fusillade. Even as Drenn watched, a corkscrewing rocket clipped the wing of one of the Vendettas, shearing straight through. The gunship began to spin out of control, plummeting towards annihilation in Theron's grim embrace.

Drenn howled into the wind and opened fire, the heavy bolter slamming back on its pintle. He guided the bright stream of shells onto the fuselage of an ork fighter that was barrelling straight at the Valkyrie. The heavy rounds chewed through its rusty plating and sent it tumbling nose over tail, flames licking from its front grille.

More greenskins were coming at them from behind. Another rocket, daubed with black and white jags, twisted wildly past before lurching randomly upwards and detonating. Tracer rounds skipped overhead, laddering back and forth as they tried to get a lock. The Valkyrie's pilot was dumping clouds of chaff and blazing phosphorous flares in a desperate effort to throw the greenskins' crude targeters.

A rotor flyer began to drag itself alongside the Valkyrie, little more than a long platform mounted on an open fuselage and bearing two massive fore and aft blades. Clinging to its rear were more orks.

They roared and scrambled off the transport as the two flyers levelled up, smacking their rocket packs. Drenn turned the heavy bolter on them, but it was too late – four of the greenskins were reduced to a gory mist and whipped away by the wind, but the rest slammed into the Valkyrie.

The aircraft lurched, its bare metal interior bathed with warning lights. An altitude alarm began to wail. Drenn heard metal-shod boots pounding against the fuselage.

'No room for chainswords!' Svenbald barked. 'Knives only.'

The ork flyer, its cargo unleashed, wanted more. Its pilot was swinging inwards, a manic grin on its bucket-jawed face. Drenn sent a burst of bolts into the greasy mechanism of the rearmost set of rotors, seconds before it could ram the Valkyrie. The thudding blades came to an abrupt stop, and the greenskin pilot's expression turned to one of panic as the machine lurched away. It began to spin on a crazed downward spiral as its remaining rotor tried to keep it airborne.

Then the first ork was flinging itself in through the hatch.

It came from the top of the Valkyrie, swinging down on one thick, green arm. Drenn's fist met its face, crunching tusks and sending the beast hurtling back out through the gap. He managed to get his hand on the heavy bolter's trigger just as the ork hit its rocket jets, launching itself back up with a roar. The heavy rounds shredded it a split second before impact, and the detonation of its fuel tank slammed Drenn into the armoured shoulder of Erik behind him.

Grunting and the thump of blades told him that more greenskins were trying to clamber in through the other hatch. The voice of the Valkyrie's pilot came in over the vox as an almost incoherent shriek. *'They're on the cockpit! They're on the cockpit!'*

The carrier began to drag to the left.

'Hrolfgar, take the bolter,' Drenn snapped. Without waiting for a response, he unlocked Fang and swung out through the hatch, hitting his pack's boosters as he did so. The wind nearly whipped him away, but his jump pack fought against it, thrusting him up onto the Valkyrie's sloping wing. He activated his stabilisers as he scrambled for purchase.

There were two orks clinging to the flyer's scarred hull. The nearest was trying to prime a primitive stick grenade and thrust it onto a whirling turbo-jet intake, whilst the other was repeatedly slamming a chainaxe at the pilot's cockpit, each furious strike fracturing the reinforced glass.

The closest spotted Drenn as he landed. In a rage, it threw its grenade at him unprimed, the shaft bouncing off Drenn's breastplate and spinning away. Drenn lunged, the ork unable to dodge without losing its grip. Fang found the beast's neck and Drenn backhanded it with his other gauntlet. The greenskin let go, and was gone.

The one perched on the cockpit turned. Beyond it Drenn could see the second Vendetta gunship going down, mauled by a trio of greenskin craft. Rounds from the fighters tore past, punching through the Valkyrie's wing plating. Neither Drenn nor the ork on the cockpit could move without losing purchase, but the greenskin didn't seem to care. Chainaxe revving, it jumped and slammed its rocket jets.

Drenn ducked. The ork scythed overhead, the downward swing of its chainaxe scoring jagged grooves across the back of his armoured jump pack. Then it was gone, carried off into the storm. Drenn turned to see it furiously trying to angle itself back for another run, but then the shrieking bulk of a blazing ork bomber tore past, swatting the greenskin into oblivion. The doomed aircraft rolled onto its back as it fell, armour plates shearing off, one wing a bullet-riddled wreck.

The bomber's killer blasted overhead, banking left in search of fresh prey. It was a Thunderbolt heavy fighter, and it wasn't alone. Drenn crouched and watched as two more Imperial fighters barrelled past, chasing down a red ork jet that was bleeding dirty black smoke from its engines.

Drenn mag-locked his knife. Flight Lieutenant Dall's Naval reinforcements had arrived.

An enhanced pict-caster from one of the Thunderbolts caught Epsilon 9-17's dying moments. The Space Wolves watched it on the Valkyrie's uplink monitor bank.

Epsilon was limping through the storm. Most of the ork attackers had peeled off in pursuit of the escaping Valkyries, and the remainder weren't enough to silence the weapon servitors. The asteroid was trying to turn away, its plasma drives blazing white where they burned through black clouds, but it was too slow. Its weaponry roared too, hammering the refinery, tearing its armoured hull to pieces. Still it struggled on, one deck structure shearing off and tumbling away, another blazing with blue, oxygen-starved flames where an ork fighter had rammed it.

Just when it looked as though the remains of the refinery would finally come apart, Magos Zarn unleashed his final attack.

The electromagnetic pulse, coupled with the overloading of the refinery's hub, caused the platform finally to split apart with a spectacular flash. The pict feed blazed a fuzzy white as the central hub detonated, mushrooming into a blinding corona of raw energy. As Epsilon 9-17's remains spun away into oblivion, the asteroid started losing altitude.

The orkish machinery powering the looted rock was already dangerously unstable. Whipped by successive lightning strikes, those systems that hadn't fused out following the pulse swiftly overloaded. Something within the asteroid's bowels detonated. A section collapsed inwards, red energy dancing and sparking from its armoured bulkheads.

As more explosions ripped through the asteroid's guts it began to fall faster, its descent now unstoppable. It was trapped in the embrace of Theron's gravitational well, caught in an irresistible vortex that pulped those still onboard and smashed the rock into ever-smaller chunks of blazing wreckage. The bulkheads and weapons batteries crumbled and collapsed, as though struck by the armoured fist of an angry god. The overburdened plasma drives were the last things to go, the fury of their detonation momentarily shorting out the feed.

When it came back online, both the asteroid and Epsilon 9-17 were gone, swallowed by the gas giant's fathomless depths.

The Space Wolves said nothing.

Alpha 1-1 was Theron's foremost refinery, and it dwarfed Epsilon 9-17. It was a mountain cast up into the heavens, its hub riddled with secondary blocks housing administrative centres, data banks, hab cells and weapons defence systems. A complex converter array, a whirring mass of spheres and orbs to rival anything from the Dark Age of Technology, crackled with power from the hub's top. A dozen conjoining plates, each alone larger than Epsilon had been, provided auxiliary earthing spires against which the surrounding clouds constantly lashed bolts of energy.

The remains of the Valkyrie's fighter escort peeled off as they neared Alpha 1-1. Drenn could hear Vorens thanking Dall over the vox. Of the Lightning wing's original six fighters, only Dall and one other remained.

The Valkyries touched down on a landing spur jutting from Alpha 1-1's flank. As soon as he stepped out onto the platform, Svenbald grabbed Drenn.

'Those tech-priests are dead because of you, young pup.'

Drenn swiped the Wolf Guard's hand away. 'Maybe if you showed more leadership, long-tooth, then I wouldn't have to do everything myself.'

Svenbald tried to strike him, but this time Drenn caught the blow. For a moment they both strained, muscles taut, their blood-streaked features inches apart. Abruptly, the younger Wolf jerked back, his eyes filled with fury.

'This has gone on long enough,' he spat. 'I will prove what I know you to be, Svenbald – a weak old worm undeserving of the rank you hold. I challenge you.'

'I accept,' the Wolf Guard snapped. He pulled himself up to his full height, holding Drenn's glare. 'I have tried to be patient with you. That ends now. If you won't learn respect, you'll no longer be a part of this Great Company, let alone my pack. The Allfather will decide your fate.'

Vorens visited Drenn as nightfall turned Theron's endless skies an impenetrable black.

He was seated in a tech-adept's commandeered sleeping cell. He'd stripped off the poleyn and greaves from his left leg and was seated on the cold metal slab the adept would usually have recharged on, probing the wound behind his knee. The limb was numb, flooded with painkiller stimms and counterseptic. He grunted as he dug through his flesh with Fang's hooked point, trying to tease the battered ork slug out.

The cell's hatch hissed open and Vorens ducked inside. Drenn had never seen him without his helmet on. His face was like tanned leather, beaten by a hundred different suns and carved by a dozen alien blades. The three service studs at his brow gleamed in the flickering light of the cell's only lumen strip. He looked even older and more battle-hardened than Svenbald.

'I know what you're about to do,' the Deathwatch leader said as the hatch hissed shut.

'I'm about to get this damned thing out,' Drenn growled. He dug a little deeper into his leg and the slug finally slipped free, a pulse of fresh blood slowing as the wound clotted. 'Why are you here, xenos hunter?'

'You won't fight Svenbald.'

'I will. I'll kill him.'

Vorens shook his head.

'You know they'll exile you forever if you do. Send you out into the Fenrisian wastes to die or lose your mind to the curse of your gene-seed. That's what will happen if you win – if you lose, Svenbald will banish you from the Flame Hunters. You'll have to petition your Wolf Lord to join another pack, and the shame will haunt you forever. No one will ever respect your warrior prowess again, not when the blood on your blade would be that of a fellow Space Wolf. Is that what you want?'

Drenn said nothing.

'You won't fight Svenbald,' Vorens repeated. 'Because you'll fight me instead.'

Drenn looked up, scowling. 'This isn't your quarrel.'

'Maybe not, but I lost a battle-brother today. His name

was Kamron of the Storm Wardens. He was a fine warrior, a slaughterer of xenos, and I'd like to have him replaced before we go back into action. The fighting on this world will go on.'

'I don't understand.'

'Fight your duel with me, Drenn. If I win, you will join me in the Deathwatch. You will match your blades against the most dangerous and terrible creatures the galaxy can spit at you. Fang will remain forever red, and when you eventually return to your packmates the skjalds will sing of your glories for an age to come.'

Drenn laughed. It was a short, humourless bark. 'Svenbald won't allow it,' he said.

'I've already spoken to Svenbald, and he is in agreement. Best me, and he will overlook all of your past transgressions and afford you the respect you deserve. Lose, and he will release you to the Deathwatch. He has sworn me an oath.'

'I always knew he was a coward...'

'He saved your life, and it will be many decades before you have won as much honour in your Chapter's service. You are still young, Drenn, and that fact can cover a multitude of sins. But it will not always be so. Your pack will learn discipline in time, and be promoted. You will continue to strain against all authority, and for that you will remain a Blood Claw until the day you die.'

Drenn frowned. 'If that's true, why do you want me for the Deathwatch?'

Vorens nodded, admitting that the question was a valid one.

'I have spoken to my brethren, and they are united in their belief that you are a hot-headed young fool.

But I've seen you fight, Drenn. Your talent is raw, your vigour unfailing. I won't deny that the loss of Epsilon Nine-Seventeen means our mission on this world has been far from successful, but few would have had the initiative to do what you did. Your determination helped to destroy that asteroid. Sometimes rashness produces results. That is why I'm here.'

'And yet you came here for nothing,' Drenn said, 'because I will defeat you, Caius Vorens. Just as I would have defeated Svenbald.'

'Come then, Space Wolf. Let us see if you're right.'

Drenn hadn't been expecting Vorens to strike first. Everything about the Imperial Fist spoke of stoicism and bastion-like defensiveness, yet no sooner had the initiating rites left Siegfric's lips than the Deathwatch leader was lunging at him, his own knife a silver blur.

Drenn parried, swiping the first strikes aside, and backed up two hasty steps. Pride surged up in him. He bared his fangs and met the next handful of thrusts blade for blade. The instant Vorens left his guard open, the Wolf lunged, scoring a deep groove across his silver Deathwatch pauldron. Vorens leaned in, trying to use his weight to regain the initiative, but still Drenn came at him, hammering his left fist into Vorens' breastplate and stabbing again with Fang.

Vorens took the hits against his armour and countered, jabbing hard towards Drenn's unprotected eyes and face. The young Wolf was forced to scramble back again, and his anger rose even further. He turned one of Vorens' blows, and this time the other warrior was a moment too slow in recovering. Drenn lunged, his face contorted in a rictus of anger, aiming towards the joint where breast-plate met plackart, just below the abdomen.

But Vorens hadn't let his guard down at all. At the last moment he bent forwards a fraction, taking Fang squarely on his breastplate. There was a crack as the blade's hooked tip was deflected towards the Imperial Fist's left. He locked Drenn's overstretched arm, twisted it so that the Space Wolf dropped his weapon and, in the same instant, slammed a boot into his injured left leg.

The Space Wolf howled as his limb buckled, the pain of his wound flaring through him. Vorens kept the pressure up, forcing the Flame Hunter down onto his knees, the arm still locked. He clamped his other hand over Drenn's head, resisting every effort he made to regain his feet.

'The duel is over,' Siegfric said. 'First blood to Vorens.'

Drenn could feel blood from the reopened wound running down his leg. He made one last, furious effort to rise, cursing floridly, but Svenbald and Siegfric took him by his pauldrons and restrained him. Vorens let go.

'That was dishonourable,' Drenn snarled as the Death-watch leader stepped back.

'Have you never used an enemy's wound to your advantage?' Vorens said. 'The galaxy is full of countless alien races, Drenn, and all of them are united by a single characteristic – they have no honour. Go searching for it, and you will die disappointed.'

Drenn stopped struggling, allowing Svenbald and Siegfric to release him. He stayed on his knees and felt the anger flush from his system, his heartbeats slowing.

'You're fast,' he allowed. 'And you trusted in your armour to turn Fang. If I'd been using Graam you would be dead.'

'But I would have fought differently. Only fools refuse

to alter their style of combat. You weren't expecting me to be so arrogant with my opening attack, and that stung you. You reacted in kind. Then I used your weaknesses against you – your lack of helmet, and your wound. You responded with speed, savagery and skill, but there was no thought behind it. You are all raw instinct, Space Wolf.'

'And you are only the leader of a kill team, yet you speak with more authority than anyone I have fought before.'

'Within the Deathwatch I am Kill Team Leader Vorens. When I return to my brethren in the Imperial Fists, I will be Captain Caius Vorens of the Sixth Company once more.'

Drenn looked up, uncharacteristically lost for words. The Imperial Fist was the equivalent in experience and rank to Kjarl Grimblood himself...

'Your blade is a good one,' Vorens said, retrieving Fang and handing it back to the Space Wolf. 'But it should not be the only weapon you trust in. If you join the Deathwatch, you'll leave your old life behind, at least for a while. The duties and habits you have now – none of them will matter. The path to your new life starts here. As a warrior of the Adeptus Astartes you have been blessed with numerous ways to deal death to the Emperor's enemies. You should make use of them all. Take this.'

Vorens gestured to Siegfric, who held forward the Imperial Fist's bolter. It was a beautiful weapon, its oiled barrel gleaming, the black stock etched with prayers of wrath and smiting. A tattered purity seal affixed behind the ejection port proclaimed centuries of service. The Space Wolf stared at it.

'Its name is *Xenobane*,' Vorens said. 'And it will teach you to rely on every tool in your arsenal. Take it.'

Drenn clasped the boltgun, still staring. The grip was

fashioned around the lower half of a polished femur, its smooth, yellowing surface scrimshawed with dozens of interlocking names.

'That bone is all that remains of its first owner, Brother Weiss,' Vorens said. 'And the names belong to all those who have wielded it since. It is a custom in my Chapter to venerate the dead in such a manner.'

'You honour me,' Drenn murmured. The wound behind his knee throbbed, but he ignored it, meeting the eyes of the captain.

'You knew the terms of this duel. What do you say to them now?'

Rather than reply, Drenn limped across to Svenbald. For the first time the young Flame Hunter lowered his gaze respectfully, acknowledging the Wolf Guard's rank.

'I owe you a life debt,' he said. 'I swear upon my honour that I will repay it, whether you release me to the Deathwatch or not.'

'It is already done,' Svenbald said, curtly. 'I hope Vorens can teach you something of respect, for I cannot.'

Drenn felt a rare stab of shame, and looked up. The Wolf Guard sighed.

'You have more than Russ' lineage within you, Drenn. You have his untameable spirit as well. Go with the primarch's blessings, and may we meet again.'

Vorens put a hand on Drenn's shoulder.

'The kill team will assemble to observe your oaths tomorrow,' he said, 'and I will send word to the Watch Fortress regarding your appointment.'

He held out his hand, and the Space Wolf took it, vambrace to vambrace, the warrior's grip.

'Welcome to the Deathwatch, Drenn Redblade.'

DEADHENGE

JUSTIN D HILL

I

Brother Ennox Sorrlock lay wounded in the panelled reading room of Planetary Governor Ajax Finne's personal library. His helmet rang with the dying shouts of his squad, and through the hazed eye lens of his Mark VIII 'Errant' armour he saw the darting shapes of the eldar: all blades and skin, and thin, pale, grasping fingers.

He fired three wild shots. His bolter magazine flashed empty. His secondary heart was failing and his breath came in long gulps. His arms were weakening. He tried to reach a fresh magazine, but as he did so a sickle blade stabbed down at his throat. He caught the hand, almost by instinct, dragged the eldar warrior in close, found his combat knife and drove it deep into its body, before throwing the corpse aside. The exertion left him weaker than before, but he gritted his teeth against the pain, flexed his muscles and tried again for the magazine.

'*Brother Sorrlock!*' a voice rang out in his vox-link.

He tried to answer, but could not make a noise.

'*Sorrlock!*' the voice came again. It was Brother Lenhk.

'Leave me...' Sorrlock tried to say, but all that came from his lips was a froth of blood and spittle. He looked about. The fight had moved on, and all around him were the enemy dead, lying in deep piles. Mixed in with the dead were leather-bound volumes in disorganised heaps, scraps of singed paper in the spreading pools of blood, much of it his own.

Warning runes flashed in his helmet: secondary heart collapse, liver failure, blood loss critical, too severe even for his Larraman cells to staunch. Sorrlock found a krak grenade and tried to set the charge, but his fingers were clumsy, and he couldn't see properly anymore. He was trying to toss it towards his enemies when, from the corridor leading towards the library chamber, there was a flash of bolter fire. The screams and shouts of xenos. The vivid gout of promethium flames.

'*I've found him!*' he heard Lenkh call over the vox.

'Leave me,' Sorrlock tried to say again. Warning runes flashed inside his helmet. His consciousness faltered. He felt himself being dragged backwards.

'Cover me!' Lenhk was shouting to Renz, the other surviving member of the squad.

'Covering.'

'We have him,' Lenkh voxed the Stormraven pilot. 'Get us out of here!'

Flames filled the chamber again. More xenos screams and howls.

'*Coming in,*' the pilot voxed.

Sorrlock could hear the whirring of the console, the

repetitive beep of the homing beacon through the pilot's signals as their Stormraven gunship circled, looking for a good place to land.

'I have Sorrlock,' Lenhk voxed.

The pilot's voice crackled back. *'And the rest of the squad?'*

'Dead,' Lenhk shouted. 'Now, get us out of here!'

Then they were out into the open. Sorrlock saw the twin yellow lights of the Stormraven, descending steeply through the rain. It was the last thing he saw before his vision faded, but he heard a sudden roar as missiles streaked overhead. He felt the explosion, but it came to him only as a dim and distant sound.

There was the whine of the gunship, the grate of his power armour against the ramp as he was dragged into the hold. The Stormraven was already lifting.

Something was clinging to the hull. He could hear it scraping to get inside.

'The others are lost?' a new voice said.

'Affirmative,' Lenkh said.

'All of them?'

'Yes.'

Someone was kneeling at Sorrlock's side. For a moment he was able to see clearly. It was an Apothecary with black hair and a ragged scar across his neck. His blue-lit augmetic eyes looked down at Sorrlock.

'Throne,' the Apothecary hissed. 'What did this to him?'

'Xenos,' Lenkh said.

Sorrlock felt his power armour being stripped away, a hand at his neck. 'His gene-seed is compromised,' the Apothecary reported.

The words cut through his pain. Sorrlock felt intense shame. Not only had he led seven battle-brothers to their deaths, but now he could not even pass on his genetic legacy to the Chapter.

As the Stormraven began to climb through the rain clouds, the vox-link crackled. There was a whisper in his ear.

'*Brothers,*' a voice said. It felt like a dream, but the voice was so real and familiar that it roused Sorrlock for a moment. '*Brothers, don't leave me here...*' the voice came again.

The accent was Grimmack's.

Sorrlock moaned. He tried to tell them to go back, that they had left a brother behind, but he was unable to speak.

'Inserting needle,' the Apothecary's voice came.

'No!' Sorrlock tried to say, but the drugs were spreading cool within his veins. They removed all the pain, but there were things worse than pain.

Things like failure and defeat.

II

Space was silent, and here, in the viewing chamber of the Reclusiam spire of the Deathwatch fortress Sentinel IX, the silence was palpable. It was so quiet that Chaplain Ortan Cassius could hear the footsteps from the bottom of the long black marble staircase, nearly five hundred yards below him. He waited, listening to the sound, then turned to the armourglass window where the darkness of the galaxy seemed to suck all light from his chamber.

More than a decade ago, he had donned the black power armour and taken the silver shoulder pad of the Deathwatch; his purpose was to defend humanity from the xenos.

In that time he had sought out and destroyed more aliens than he could remember. But there were always more.

It was a battle that had started long before he was born.

It would last for generations after him.

The thought did not disturb Cassius. He was a weapon of war. It was his fate to die on the battlefield and he was content with that – he would serve until that day.

He drew in a deep breath and put both hands on the vellum of the book he was reading. *The Beatitudes of Arch-Confessor Paladine*. The illumination showed the victorious Paladine himself with one foot on the greenskin, aquila banner held high.

Cassius looked up as his visitors reached the top of the stairs. The first was a red-hooded Inquisitorial serf. He stepped forward to bow and spoke in a deep, weary voice.

'Chaplain Cassius. As requested, I have brought Battle-brother Sorrlock of the Iron Hands.'

Cassius looked past the serf into the shadows at the top of the long staircase. Three red eyes glowed in the darkness.

A metallic voice spoke in clipped tones.

'Chaplain Cassius. I am Ennox Sorrlock – formerly of the Iron Hands, now Deathwatch. Greetings.'

'Why "formerly"?' Cassius asked. 'You came from the Iron Hands and will return to the Iron Hands, when your service with the Deathwatch is done.'

'If they will have me,' Sorrlock replied.

'Why would they not?'

'My flesh was weak.'

'Weaker than steel?'

'Of course. But that is not what I meant. I failed my Chapter. I failed my brothers.'

As he spoke, the Iron Hand strode forwards from the shadowed archway. With each step there was a muted hiss of extensive cyber-enhancement. Sorrlock was tall, even for a Space Marine. His face was half steel – a mess of wires and tubes, with three marble-red optical augmetics where the eye had been.

Cassius put out a gauntlet. The fist that gripped him back was not human. He could hear the gentle whine of motors and metal tendons, felt the cold grip of iron fingers.

Sorrlock did not let go. 'You think my enhancements crude?'

The voice was as monotone as a servitor's, but it did not lack intelligence. Sorrlock had an odd manner; it was methodical, clinical. Too much enhanced inhuman intellect, Cassius thought. Typical of the Iron Hands. They did not trust flesh. They did not trust their greater-than-human bodies, nor even entirely the gene-seed legacy of their own primarch.

They did not trust themselves.

'Crude? Yes,' Cassius said. 'In my Chapter we at least attempt to make a face that is human in aspect.'

'That is foolish,' Sorrlock replied flatly.

'Why?'

'It wastes time and resources.'

Cassius did not try to argue. He turned to the window ports and looked out into the haunted space known as Deadhenge.

'Do you know why you are here?'

'No.'

'Can't you guess?'

'I do not guess. I input data, and assess the best course of action.'

Cassius smiled. He had heard that Brother Sorrlock could be a little difficult at times.

He turned from the window. 'What do you see when you look at the vast emptiness of Deadhenge?'

'Enemies,' Sorrlock said. 'Lurking. Hiding. Pretending not to be there.'

Cassius smiled. When he looked into the darkness of space, he too felt it watching him in return. 'Good. We have that at least in common.'

'We have much more in common,' Sorrlock's monotone voice said.

Cassius turned to look at the metal face and wondered what he meant, but Sorrlock was staring out through the vast reinforced pane, one hand upon the grip of his combi-melta.

III

Pain flooded Ennox Sorrlock as he lay in the Apothecaries' chamber. The drugs were wearing off. His body stiffened, his mouth a snarling rictus, consciousness and memory flooding into him like a fresh shot of agony...

His orders had been to locate the eldar flesh-smith known as the Black Spider. He had done so, but rather than waiting for support, he had led his squad straight in. Surprise, he believed, was worth more than numbers, and all seemed well as they had trapped the Black Spider in the governor's personal librarium.

'We have him!' Sorrlock had declared in righteous triumph as the Black Spider had dashed up a grand wooden staircase. Sorrlock laughed as he aimed his bolt pistol. 'Death to the xenos!'

But at that moment, flesh-constructs had burst from within the vast axelwood bookshelves. All about the Iron Hands were hulking monsters with blades implanted into their flesh, simian heads snarling and hunched, ichor dripping from venom-guns. Sorrlock's squad was surrounded by darting shapes – whips, coils, and searing blasts of poisonous liquid flashed at the Iron Hands, and the Black Spider's narrow alien face changed from an expression of fear to inhuman delight.

'Back!' Sorrlock commanded, and his squad had fought as they retreated.

But the corridor was blocked with more of the foe. They had fought until the enemy dead lay three deep. And as they fell, the Black Spider raised his own weapon. Sorrlock had never seen this type of gun before. He had backhanded the barrel as he charged at the flesh-smith, but moments too late. A spray of sticky green liquid covered his side. The eldar stumbled back but did not fall. Hunched low, it edged forwards, firing over and over again.

Sorrlock had felt the slime splat against his armour. He was confident in his battleplate but the creeping gobs found the weak points – damaged areas, and the joints – and started to dissolve his flesh.

His fury had turned to alarm as the liquid filled up his armour and started eating him alive.

As Sorrlock lay in the medicae bed, the nightmare of the assault returned to him again and again. And it always ended the same way, with the hissed voice from Grimmack.

'Brothers... Don't leave me here...'

Sorrlock knew only too well the pain that the wretched eldar could inflict, and he twisted and writhed at the thought of it. 'Go back!' he shouted out in his nightmares, but he was lying wounded, and could not help Grimmack.

The thin metal arms of the medicae servitor moved quickly to hold the sutures closed. The Apothecary bent over him, the glowing blue eyes staring into his own. 'Be still, brother. We have done all that we can. There is no way back,' he said. It was a simple truth. 'No way back for any of us.'

Sorrlock didn't understand, but felt more life-supporting fluids being pumped into his body.

'Be still, brother. It is time to let go.'

Sorrlock snarled in answer, but the drugs were stronger than he.

IV

Amongst the abandoned orbital platforms over the planet of Shenden Port, deep in the region of space known as Deadhenge, a vessel waited. At the hour foretold by the reading of the Emperor's Tarot, a single Storm Eagle began its descent. Its colour was black, its only insignia the mark of the Inquisition. As it started its dive towards the planet, Kill Team Torrent prepared themselves for their mission.

Chaplain Cassius stood strapped against the steel walls. His briefing had not explained why Deadhenge had been abandoned, but there were humans living on this planet regardless. And, despite the odds, the population was swelling.

In the decades that had passed, they had bred. There were now thousands here, tens of thousands, perhaps. Weak, vulnerable and beyond the shield of the Imperium: to the sentient enemies in the galaxy, these defenceless humans were prey.

To the Ordo Xenos of the Inquisition of Mankind, they were bait that had finally drawn their target in.

Cassius looked towards the members of his team.

Stentor Pranus, Novamarine. An expert in fighting the eldar.

Skarr-Hedin, Space Wolf. A new recruit. One of the fiercest fighters he knew.

The third, Ennox Sorrlock, Iron Hand. A fearsome logic engine.

He had handpicked each warrior. They were the best at what they did. He was going to need them – Vael Donatus, his Chapter brother and favoured kill team leader, was on a posting to the Hurn Wastes. Cassius closed his eyes, and focussed on his fury.

As they entered the outer atmosphere, the air within the gunship began to heat up. Cassius breathed deeply. He could feel Sorrlock's augmetic eyes watching him.

'Sorrlock?' he called across the hold.

Sorrlock made no response. The Storm Eagle rattled as it hit the lower atmosphere.

'You're thinking,' Cassius said.

Sorrlock's metallic voice came back. 'I am always thinking.'

'So, tell me what is going through your mind now.'

'I am reviewing our mission, Brother-Chaplain. Deathwatch kill team specified target: the eldar listed in Ordo Xenos archive Sentinel-Four-Four-Three as Archon 2296-46a. Commonly known as Archon Tehmaq, killer of twelve worlds, first noted in Imperial records in the Opal Sector. Responsible for the Scouring of Lijan, shrine world. Estimated losses of two billion. Ninety-eight per cent losses in the Cadian 1076th, including General Plume and all support staff, Lord Commissar Tranz von Gunten, and Inquisitor...'

Cassius let Sorrlock go through his data files. Sorrlock found facts comforting in a way that became almost painful. He knew the Iron Hand would list each atrocity that the archon had committed.

He let the details sink in, let them stoke his own righteous ire.

No one possessed a fury like he did. He could control and hone it, using it as a weapon of war in itself. It was a black fire within him, a geyser of rage at the traitor, the heretic, the xenos.

He breathed the fury out. His eyes blinked open suddenly as he sucked his anger back through flared nostrils. It filled him.

'The Black Spider will be there,' Cassius interrupted.

There was a moment's silence. It was unusual in Sorrlock.

'The Black Spider,' he said. 'Common Imperial designation for haemonculus of the Dark Coven. Haemonculus listed in Ordo Xenos Archive Sentinel-Four-Four-Nine as Haemonculus 862-CW-5. Responsible for–'

'Responsible for the loss of seven members of Iron Hands Squad Morag, Clan Kaargul.'

There was another pause.

Cassius watched him. 'Your own squad, Ennox Sorrlock.'

Sorrlock said nothing as the Storm Eagle's rapid descent levelled out. They were flying low to the ground now, to avoid detection.

'How do you know this?' Sorrlock said at last.

'You fought well. You brought death to the xenos. They were stacked three deep about you.'

'I brought death to my brothers.'

'We all die,' Cassius said.

'Machines do not,' Sorrlock said.

Cassius sighed. 'Today is your chance for vengeance, brother.'

'Negative. Today our mission is to kill Archon Tehmaq.'

Cassius stared at him, but it was Pranus, the Novamarine, who spoke. 'The Black Spider. He did... *all this* to you?'

Sorrlock's metal head turned to the fair-haired warrior next to him. 'Affirmative.'

'If he did this to me then I would tear his arms from his body!' Skarr-Hedin said. 'The galaxy seldom gives you a chance for revenge like this, Sorrlock. Do you not savour it?' The Space Wolf's fangs appeared as he snarled. 'I can almost taste it. I would rip out his heart.'

Sorrlock slowly faced each of them in turn. The movement had the odd air of a practised behaviour, as if he had no interest in the gesture, but had learnt it was expected. At the end he appeared unmoved.

'Negative. We should all remember. Our mission is to kill Archon Tehmaq. The Black Spider is not our target.'

There was a long pause.

'Query – what does vengeance taste like?' Sorrlock asked.

The Space Wolf grinned, his yellow eyes as inhuman as Sorrlock's. 'Hot blood. It tastes like battle joy. It tastes like laughter. It is like a Great Company charging in fury. It is the roar of battle in the emptiness of the void, when the boarding torpedoes launch.'

Sorrlock watched without reaction, or even interest. 'We are approaching the target,' he said.

At the same time a red light began to flash. *'Approaching target,'* the servitor vox-system announced. *'Contact in ten, nine...'*

'Brothers,' Cassius rumbled. 'Join with me.'

Together they uttered the Litany of Hatred. They were

just speaking the last lines as the servitor reported again. *'Contact.'*

The Storm Eagle landed, bracing harnesses released.

Chaplain Cassius was first out, Kill Team Torrent right behind him.

V

Sorrlock remembered.

He remembered human pain. Human frailties. The enemies of the flesh.

He remembered having a human body again. Running, flexing, twisting, laughing. He remembered the fury of being weak and trapped. He remembered the last moments of his charge, cutting down one, two, four of the foe. He got so close to the Black Spider he could see the back of its throat as it opened its mouth in a roar of hate. There were words there, though Sorrlock did not care for them.

He bludgeoned one of its guards with his bolter's stock, punched the other, took aim... but had fired too slowly.

'Brothers,' Grimmack's voice haunted his dreams. It summoned the ghosts of his Iron Hands back to him. They stood in a circle about him, his dead brothers, in full battle dress, their red lenses staring accusingly at him from beyond the grave.

'You failed us, Sorrlock,' their faces said. *'Your flesh was weak.'*

VI

The low clouds of Shenden Port hid the tops of the buildings in the warehouse district. Between the vast structures were dark canyons, thick with derricks and gantries and ancient, rusting chains. Water dripped in a continuous stream. Sorrlock had plans of the planet and the city stored within his memory coils. He led them towards their destination, taking care to avoid detection from the hunting xenos.

'Canyon fifty-six,' he said. 'This is it.'

Cassius nodded.

'Target structure lies north of here,' Sorrlock voxed. 'Five minutes at current speed.'

Something darted into the canyon a hundred yards from where they stood. Cassius saw a half-starved human, barefoot, in ragged clothes, with what looked like a hatchet in its belt. It kept low, moving furtively, looking over its shoulder, clearly frightened.

Sorrlock's brain worked in data. 'Male,' he said. 'Approximate age, thirty-four. Life expectancy, plus six years. Threat, negligible.'

A flock of sharp shadows plunged down on the man like striking eagles. There was a hum of air, a scream, and then they were gone, wild shapes veering maniacally down the street.

'Eldar reavers. Threat: extreme.'

The human lay in a widening pool of his own blood, moaning in agony.

Skarr-Hedin let out a low growl but Cassius touched his shoulder. 'I hear your fury, brother.'

Sorrlock ignored them both. 'Precision wounds have left the spine untouched. Human experiencing extreme pain levels,' he noted. 'Revised life expectancy, plus thirty seconds. Reavers bear the kill-markings of Archon Tehmaq's coven. Target is likely to be close. Follow me, brothers.'

* * *

Ten minutes later, Sorrlock held up a hand at the base of a vast rockcrete warehouse.

'This is it,' he intoned.

Cassius led Kill Team Torrent forward. The corrugated metal doors hung open on broken hinges.

Sorrlock noted the details. 'It appears most of the warehouses in this area dealt with the shipment and processing of foodstuffs – animal carcasses and organic residues such as dried sorghum stalks, compressed fava oil, gantha root gum...'

He paused in the doorway, taking a moment to scan the room.

'All clear.'

Kill Team Torrent moved slowly up through the empty warehouse floors. The refrigeration units had long since shut down. A vast square container had blown open and slabs of grox flank rotted inside. It was covered in thick blue algae.

The stink was acrid, but the Space Marines could still detect the scent of fresh blood.

Sorrlock halted at the open doors of a conveyor shaft. The bottom was piled deep with rotting bodies. Skinned, headless – human.

'Why would they do this?' Skarr-Hedin growled.

'It is what they are like,' Pranus replied. 'They take pleasure in pain. They feed on fear.'

'Will they be waiting for us?'

'Negative,' said Sorrlock. 'Guards will most likely be flesh-constructs. They will be defending the warp gate. The eldar will most likely be indulging their sadistic temperaments.'

Skarr-Hedin nodded and hefted his heavy bolter. 'Let us continue, brothers.'

Sorrlock led them across an empty refrigeration unit to another conveyor. The iron cabling that supported the cage had rusted through but there was an inner ladder within the shaft that was still firm.

'Sorrlock, take the lead,' Cassius ordered.

The Iron Hand nodded and started to climb. The lift shaft rose through a series of storage floors filled with empty silos and granaries. The shaft ended twenty-five floors up, opening out into a large counting room. Wooden chairs lay overturned along a long central table. The walls were hung with peeling pictures of the colony's founding fathers. They looked out with short beards and solemn faces, hands resting on the various implements of their trade.

Sorrlock raised his combi-weapon.

'Flesh-construct,' he voxed. 'Close-combat unit, serrated blade-arms. Danger: significant. Life expectancy: zero.'

As he spoke the last words, his combi-melta's bolter bucked.

The muffled report of the shot rang out. The construct fell. The entry hole was a neat round puncture through the metal visor, the back of its head a fleshy ruin.

'Left eyeball,' Skarr-Hedin murmured as they stood over the body. 'Good shot.'

'We have entered the sentry zone,' Sorrlock intoned.

'Then we must be coming close to the warp gate,' Pranus said.

'Affirmative.'

Sorrlock led them up a rusty file of wide steps through a doorway into a ramshackle clerk's chamber. Scraps of human flesh hung from walls, with hooks, chains, manacles and fresh dripping skins swinging gently in the breeze from the lower levels. He put another shot through the skull of a second sentry construct, then led the kill team inside.

They were moving faster now. The xenos warp gate had to be close.

Sorrlock dispatched another sentry standing at the end of the next corridor. It slid backwards down the wall, leaving a long dark stain. At the same time an alarm rang out. It was something between a scream and a siren.

'We have been detected,' Cassius cursed. 'Move quickly!'

VII

'There is no other way.'

Ennox Sorrlock drifted in and out of consciousness. He was being devoured by the green slime. His flesh was steaming. His bones were dissolving. He burned from the inside.

He arched his back, and raised his hand to try to fire his boltgun, but he wasn't holding it anymore. He was lying on an apothecarion gurney. A face bent over him. He tried to bat it away before recognition came to him. It was not an enemy.

'Brother. There is not much time. You will need all your strength. There will be pain.'

Sorrlock braced himself.

'Insert probes,' the voice came again.

Ennox Sorrlock's teeth ground together as the barbed neural implants seared into the soft grey matter of his brain. His fingers clenched. His body heaved against the restraints. A low tortured moan escaped through his snarling teeth.

There were hot wires in the meat of his mind. The agony was unbearable.

The voice said, 'Turn it on.'

Sorrlock braced...

...but this time there was no pain. Or rather, the pain was distant as a shouting man, who falls far behind and is soon forgotten.

Pain and emotion existed on the other side of an unbreakable screen in his mind. He could see them. Recognise them. But he no longer *felt* them. There was only a sense of expansion, of elevation, of elation.

His mind spiralled in exacting multi-functional lines of thought and logic. It revelled in the speed of his precision thinking. He calculated the chances of his survival. The rate of healing. The probability of his return to active service within the month. The chances of a bolt shell hitting a Medusan auroch at half a mile.

The voice summoned him back. 'Ennox.'

He opened his one remaining eye. His sight was blurry and indistinct.

His three augmetic eyes did not need to open. They focussed on the face above him.

Iron Father Stovek. Space Marine. Iron Hands Chapter. Age, two hundred and fifty-seven years. Seventy-four per cent augmetic. Life expectancy (organics), in excess of five hundred years, assuming no further enhancement or combat damage.

'Brother Sorrlock,' Stovek spoke. 'You have been blessed.'

'Thank you, Iron Father,' a mechanical voice said in response, and the voice was his own.

Sorrlock sat up with a hiss of pistons. He looked down. His body was metal and wires.

'Over eighty-three per cent augmetic,' Iron Father Stovek said.

'Yes,' Sorrlock said, as he analysed his own body. There was a whine of motorised parts as he looked up. 'Eighty-three-point-seven...'

'You were a great warrior, Ennox Sorrlock,' he said. 'But your flesh was weak.'

'I led my brothers to their deaths.'

The Iron Father nodded. 'I have seen the pict-feeds. You let pride drive you. But you fought well. Better than any I have seen. We have elevated you. Machine and human, melded as one. You are a true Iron Hand now. The finest we can build. Take your shame and hone it to a fine blade. You will fight for the machine. You will fight for the Imperium. You will kill in the name of the Emperor.'

'Yes, Iron Father.'

Sorrlock stood. He took two steps. He moved his left arm, his right arm, flexed his metal fingers.

'I am truly an Iron Hand now.' His metallic monotone had no trace of humour. As his augmetic eyes looked about him, his mechanical cortex scrolled with data and targeting relays.

The flesh was weak, it reasoned.

The machine was perfect.

VIII

From all across the warehouse, xenos flesh-constructs came for them. They were mindless things, but they were not slow or stupid. They followed their master's commands, and their commands were to stop the intruders.

Sorrlock kept the kill team moving, his memory coils continually analysing modes of attack, possible routes to the rooftop, proposed opposition.

As Pranus killed the last constructs in the stairwell behind them, Sorrlock ran to the top and kicked the gantry door open. There was a long, half-lit rockcrete corridor behind it. He did not pause but kept moving, his combi-weapon bucking as each red target lock blinked out. Cassius was right behind him. Pranus was catching up, Skarr-Hedin firing his heavy bolter in support.

As he rounded the end of the corridor, Sorrlock punched his melta barrel into the mouth of the thing that jumped at him, and seared off its head.

Sorrlock's augmetic hand caught the creature's claw. It dripped hissing yellow venom. He snapped the hand free and slammed it into the chest of another flesh-construct. It fell back, heels drumming on the ground as the toxins boiled within it.

Skarr-Hedin filled the corridor with heavy bolter shells, throwing the xenos things back. Behind them stood their flesh-master: an eldar degenerate, human-skin cloak flapping about her.

Skarr-Hedin kept firing. More shells smashed holes in the rockcrete walls where she had been standing.

Sorrlock fired his bolter three times. Two of the rounds hit the eldar in the back and tore her slender shape to shreds.

'On your left!' Cassius hissed as they hit the top of the stairs.

Pranus' bolter was on semi-automatic. The muzzle flare cast a ruddy light on his close-shaven face as he hosed the antechamber. The Space Wolf was right behind him, howling in hatred until the fighting was too close for his heavy bolter and he was forced to draw his combat knife and fight them hand-to-hand instead. He broke a thin eldar warrior backwards over his knee. He struck another in the face, his genhanced senses picking up the distinctive sound of shattering nose bones being driven into brain, then swung around looking for the next kill.

The others were already running towards another flight of wide rockcrete stairs.

'Do not be distracted,' Sorrlock said flatly over the vox. 'Our time is running short.'

More and more siren alarms sounded, calling the eldar from across the city back to the safety of their warp portal.

Now Sorrlock took the stairs four at a time. The stairwell wound up, doubling back over itself at plain rockcrete landings fifty steps apart. As he approached the third landing he tossed a frag grenade up onto the stairwell, timing the explosion to the millisecond, and reached the landing as the last fragments of shrapnel flew by.

His augmetic eyes were running at combat speed. It had the effect of expanding time – the pulling of a trigger seemed almost a minute long. The cyber-optic connections within his brain moved at a speed that not even the eldar could counter. He targeted and fired, the combi-weapon kicking slowly in his hand as each bolter shell exited the barrel. He watched as the rocket accelerant fired in a fierce explosion of yellow flame, his mind calculating the trajectory of each round, the movement vectors of each target, the percentage hit probability, how many more shots it would take to achieve the ninety-nine per cent death/ maimed/inoperative threshold he had learned to trust.

At this speed, his arm seemed lazily ponderous. He had seven bolt shells in the air at one time. Each one was aimed at a different target. He watched each one strike home, confirming the hit.

As they smashed into a four-doored chamber, more flesh-constructs fell on them, wrapping serpent arms about them, serrated knives searching for weak spots.

There were hundreds of them, snapping and clawing. Within moments Cassius was pinned against the wall, and Skarr-Hedin was wounded and slowing rapidly. Pranus filled the room with bolter fire, but even as the attackers fell away more dropped in to replace them.

Sorrlock killed eight in mere seconds, reloaded and started to fire again, but as he reached the end of the corridor a tail caught him about his throat and dragged him back. Its skin shifted in texture as the muscles within it tightened. Sorrlock's metal throat creaked with the strain, which would have snapped any other Space Marine's neck. The tail kept wrapping about him, constricting about his chest and arm as a fanged mouth snapped at his face.

Normal augmetics would have buckled against such pressure, but Sorrlock's were the work of an Iron Father. Even so, the finely calibrated ball sockets creaked and a hydraulic pipe on the bicep bulged and began to leak. Alarms flashed within Sorrlock's retinal display even as he reached across with his bionic hand. From the fingers slid thin knife blades. He grasped the thing's body and his hand snapped shut, shearing straight through muscle, bone and nerves.

The serpent creature whipped round. It was fast, even by Sorrlock's standards. It wrapped around his wrist three times, and a flailing appendage drove a poisoned blade into his plackart, squirting hissing venoms into a gut of wires and pistons and nutri-cabling. It stabbed again, higher this time, seeking flesh, veins – the agony that would paralyse its foe, venoms that would down even a Space Marine within moments.

Sorrlock twisted, braced his feet and slammed his enemy against the wall, but his foe's grip grew tighter. Chances of success began to decline rapidly. Consequential probabilities began to fall as well. Life expectancies of his fellow kill team members. Success of the mission. Probabilities of kill team extraction. All falling.

The machine within him snarled as it processed alternative solutions.

The probability of success was too small.

Too small. Too small.

Options were limited. The consequences were dire, perhaps critical. All probabilities were against them. Sorrlock's logic circuits froze as the variables spiralled beyond his ability to compute.

IX

Sometimes, when Sorrlock slept or powered down, his human mind would remember life when his body was still merely flesh and blood. The tingle of skin. The imperfections of a human body. Sometimes, when he dreamt, the armourglass barrier within his mind dissolved and emotions filled him as they had once done.

Anger. Hurt. Pride.

Pain.

When he woke, the separation from sleep and emotion was always a shock.

The machine gave him so much more. It was precise and logical.

It was not weak.

Not even the Emperor could live without it.

It kept Ennox Sorrlock alive. It gave him power. It made him more than he had been.

Iron was strong. It did not fail.

Now you are strong. You are man and machine. You are more than an Iron Hand. You are iron limbs, iron spirit, iron will. You will not fail.

Do not fail yourself. Your Clan. Your Chapter. The Golden Throne.

You have been given a great honour, Sorrlock. You will not forget. You cannot forget.

The machine does not forget.

The machine is perfect.

I am a machine.

I am perfection.

But sometimes, when the data failed him, all that was left was Sorrlock's fierce, *human* will to survive. That refused to die, even when the data was stacked against it.

He dragged the serpent to his head. Butted it. Trapped it. Bit it. His metal teeth tore through the flesh.

The blood of the creature tasted foul. He spat out chunks and bit again.

Mouthful by mouthful, he gnawed it down to the spine and cracked the bones between his teeth. The creature went slack. He spat again as he threw it to the floor, lifted his combi-weapon and pumped six shots through its body.

The predictive scroll of statistics began to slow, and then moved into a rapid reverse as he fired about the room, putting bolt rounds into the snarling faces that ringed him.

The room was a blur. These xenos moved faster than even he could see at times.

'Sorrlock!' Cassius hissed through gritted teeth. 'Pranus is injured!'

'I will try to aid him,' Sorrlock said, but statistics from Pranus' power armour showed that his systems were collapsing under a wash of toxins. The chances of the team's survival were already low. He ran the cogitations in milliseconds. He had to aid Cassius first.

He put a bolt round through the back of the creature that embraced Cassius in its serpent coils, and two more into the five-armed thing that lunged at Skarr-Hedin. Both rounds hit. Skarr-Hedin threw the clawed hands off, and the creature's sting-tipped tail made a few last efforts to stab through his armour before it fell dead. Sorrlock kept up a storm of fire, keeping Cassius and Skarr-Hedin free to fight.

'I will cover you!' Pranus choked as he reloaded his bolter. 'Move, brothers!'

X

Sorrlock burst out onto the open roof. The warp portal flared in the air above him. It was oval, like an egg, bulging on all sides. As he slowed, three eldar jetbikes powered through the air towards the shimmering alien vista beyond it.

Sorrlock identified them as the same ones who had killed the human in the street. He threw himself back as they swept just over his head, razored blades thrumming in the air as they passed. The portal crackled blue and purple as they approached, strands reaching out to swallow them whole.

He let them go and spun about, looking for the mission target. He spotted an open-topped raider skimmer that was careering up the canyon from the south. It swung under gantries and archways, around rusting chains. His augmetic eyes zoomed in.

There on the deck stood their target: Archon Tehmaq.

Behind him was a face he had seen a thousand times in his nightmares.

The Black Spider.

About them were the archon's retinue, all dressed in black armour, their faces hidden behind horned masks.

He pointed. 'Ident positive. Target acquired.'

'Skarr-Hedin, engage!' Cassius shouted.

The Space Wolf was bleeding from a wound in his side, but he did not slow as he strode to the lip of the building, heavy bolter primed to fire. But Sorrlock did not have time to offer a warning before a hulking figure burst through the floor at Skarr-Hedin's feet and threw him backwards. It was monstrously large – huge slabs of muscle, with a slavering head ending in a knot of tubes that hung about its head like hair. It had six arms. Each one ended with a terrible blade or drill or long, venom-dripping needle.

Skarr-Hedin swung about. It was difficult to hit something coming at him with such speed. He fired as he fell, rounds going wildly astray. Some hit. Others trailed up into the sky. The six arms wrapped him in a dreadful embrace, a fanged mouth gnashing at his throat. Behind the creature the raider's guns opened fire, blazes hurtling up towards them.

Cassius ducked. His crozius was sizzling as he ran to

help the Space Wolf. 'We must slow them,' he hissed. 'Sorrlock!'

The thing tore at Skarr-Hedin in berserk fury. Its snout snapped at his throat. The arms stabbed and tore and crushed. Sorrlock calculated that he had six seconds to engage this threat before the archon came within range.

'Affirmative,' he voxed, aiming at the hulking flesh-construct's head first, but his rounds failed to penetrate the armoured skull. Sorrlock's sensors scanned the creature again, searching for vulnerabilities.

The movement slowed in his enhanced vision.

He took in every twitch of muscle beneath the skin, saw the pump of blood through its veins.

The pattern was clear. This thing possessed two hearts.

He targeted each one. As the metal coils in his brain spiralled away, assessing alternative weak spots in the internal bone mass, his human instincts saw only *twin heart, fused ribcage.*

It took a long moment for Sorrlock to believe what his data showed him. Despite all the changes, the thing felt familiar. It looked like a son of Medusa, the same dark planet that had raised him. The same clan, in fact...

The evidence was clear: this hulking thing had once been a Space Marine. A brother of the Iron Hands Chapter.

The realisation chilled him. Not only was this a Space Marine, he also recognised it. He knew its name. They had been scouts together, had been through gene-implantation and training together. And here they were now, on an abandoned planet, years of warp travel away from their home, each changed in their own way. And now the creature was tearing Skarr-Hedin apart.

The strength of the emotional response startled him.

'Grimmack!' he cried, as if he could call the spirit of his brother back to him. 'Stop!'

But the thing did not stop. It snarled and savaged and punched a blade-fist through the front of Skarr-Hedin's armour, kept driving the blade up towards his vital organs.

'Grimmack!' he shouted again.

Warning symbols flashed in his helm.

Sorrlock had run out of time.

XI

The eldar raider came on at seemingly impossible speed. Its bladed sail swung as the craft flew, strange runes in black on a purple background. Heads hung by their knotted hair from the craft's railings, their slack mouths open in wild terror. The archon's black-armoured retinue drew sickle blades from their belts, lifted their pistols to fire.

The archon himself was piloting. His mouth was open in a fey smile. His white face was flecked with blood, lit by the searing flashes of lance fire.

Skarr-Hedin battered at the thing that had once been Grimmack. The two of them raged at one another, berserk fury on both sides.

'I have this one, brother,' Skarr-Hedin hissed as he drove his combat knife into the second heart. He was gasping for breath. 'Kill the archon!'

'Archon approaching,' Sorrlock voxed. He engaged his combi-melta, focusing his augmetic eyes on the foe. 'I have him.'

As the raider swung up towards the warp portal, Sorrlock aimed and fired. The air shimmered with the sudden heat, and the shot hit the craft in the bows. It should have cut through and hit the archon as well, but the raider veered wildly, caught a hanging gantry, swung about like a ball on a chain and did almost a full rotation before slamming down in a ruin, fifty yards from the gate.

Sorrlock leapt towards it as eldar warriors were thrown onto the ground in crumpled heaps. He focussed on one figure – the archon – who bounded unscathed from the wreckage, pirouetting through the air. Behind him, the Black Spider swung on its many limbs.

Cassius was shouting, but all Sorrlock saw was Archon Tehmaq moments from the safety of the portal. He lifted his bolter and his augmetic targeting systems worked so fast that time seemed to slow. The archon went from a blur to a slowly cartwheeling humanoid in sharp-edged black armour. The three members of his surviving retinue sprinted after him – to shield their master or to escape with him, Sorrlock could not tell.

And there, again, was the Black Spider.

Sorrlock's data stream locked on the thought of what the haemonculus had done to Grimmack. What it had done to *him*. He wished that he could feel hatred for it. Wished he could fire on the Black Spider...

But he was a battle-brother of the Deathwatch, an Iron Hand, perfected through augmentation into a weapon of war. The hatred was there, but it was distant and faint.

He fired.

The two bolts moved with a beautiful slowness. The rocket cores were like flowers of fire with blue centres and shivering petals of yellow and red. The first bolt, a hellfire round, spun as it flew. Light glinted off the microscopic scratches like starlight on the hull of a turning spaceship, almost black against the darkness of wilderness space.

It struck the archon low in the gut, where the lobster panels of his black armour bucked and crumpled as the shock waves rippled. But it exploded without penetrating. It gave off a shower of shrapnel and droplets of bio-acid, shifting and reforming as they flew through the air. It scored spreading lines in the archon's shining arcane armour, like the impact of an asteroid on the dust of a moon.

The second bolt hit the same spot, now acid-weakened by the first. It was a dragonfire round that smashed through the armour, into the archon's gut, where it exploded with a sudden glare of green flame.

Tendrils of fire spread from the wound. They wrapped about the archon in a tortuous embrace. He stumbled and fell. The other xenos, the screeching Black Spider amongst them, were already leaping for the warp gate.

Then they were gone, and the gate shuddered out of existence like an air bladder bursting in reverse. An aching purple afterlight hung in the air, flickering and casting strange un-shadows across the rooftop as it faded.

The archon crawled towards the place where the portal had been. He clawed feebly for purchase on the rockcrete, his scorched belly flat against the floor, his face a rictus of astonishment and pain.

Sorrlock stood over him and put a third bolt shell into his head.

'Mission complete,' he reported.

They dragged the remains of Grimmack from Skarr-Hedin and the Space Wolf propped himself up. There was blood in his beard. The toxins were making his movements laboured and weak. When his voice came, it was rasping and pained. 'I killed it for you, Iron Hand. We fought each other to the death. Your shame is cleansed.'

Cassius knelt, and pulled back the ruined power armour to inspect Skarr-Hedin's wounds.

Even for a Space Marine, they were mortal.

Skarr-Hedin knew this and was not afraid. He laughed messily. 'I shall go and feast with my brothers. I shall tell them that I died bravely!'

'Hold, brother,' Cassius said. 'The gunship is on its way.'

Skarr-Hedin snarled against his pain. As they waited, the purple light in the air above them continued to boil away into nothingness, colours and patterns forming and dissolving.

Sorrlock could see faces in the patterns. They came forward, as if to peer at him, and then faded back. Cassius powered up his crozius, but Sorrlock shook his head. 'They will not fight.'

'Then why do they linger?'

'They have come for their master's body,' Sorrlock said.

'Not to take vengeance?'

'No. The xenos are cowards.' Sorrlock stopped inches from the fading mist. He reached out to touch it, but Cassius stayed his hand.

'Don't,' he said. 'You do not want to know what lies beyond there.'

Sorrlock lowered his hand. 'I know already,' he said. 'Pain. A place of many screams. Many nightmares. A place without hope.'

* * *

XII

The Storm Eagle's engines roared as it returned the survivors of Kill Team Torrent to their waiting ship. Skarr-Hedin's body lay beneath a shroud. Pranus was being tended by two medicae adepts, the Novamarine having mercifully lost consciousness. Sorrlock sat bolt upright, his metal hands braced on his knees, and Cassius watched him. The Iron Hand still appeared to feel nothing. He had the same silence as the darkness of Deadhenge.

Sorrlock knew he was being watched – Cassius could see that from the dull glint of his augmetic eyes.

At last the Chaplain spoke. 'You could have killed the Spider, brother.'

Sorrlock turned his augmetic eye and regarded him. 'Affirmative.'

'Then why didn't you?'

'He was not our designated target.'

'But I would have caught the archon before he escaped.'

'Yes. My calculations say you would.'

'So, why? Look what he did to you. Your squad. Your brother, whom he captured. I brought you not only for your insight and your logic, but also to stoke the fire in your cold heart once more. You could have taken revenge.'

The half-metal face made no response.

'Part of me wanted to,' Sorrlock's monotone voice came at last.

There was a pause, a long pause, and when he spoke again it was almost as footnote.

'But that part is weak.'

FIRST TO HUNT

CHRIS DOWS

Jetek Suberei opened his eyes and looked up to the blazing twin suns of Ballestae, their harsh white glow unfiltered by helmet or visor. Reaching down with his ungloved left hand, he touched the barren rocky surface of the planet and, like any good son of Chogoris, tried to read its secrets.

Sheer walls of granite towered hundreds of yards above him on either side. Their shape and form funnelled a vicious wind that whipped dust and tiny fragments of rock onto his exposed face, flicking the ends of his drooping moustache and long, braided topknot. Suns and breeze were scorching in their own way, but none of this registered on the kneeling Deathwatch warrior, too focussed on learning what the floor of the yawning chasm had to tell him about what lay ahead.

Unfortunately, the tale being told was of little use.

'Difficult to say how much further we must travel,

Vengla. You will have to take flight once again and be the eyes of Suberei. The xenos scum cannot be too far away.'

Rising to his feet, the White Scar strode over to his idling bike and snatched his helmet up from the broad seat. Thrusting it back on, he reached for his gauntlet and clicked it into place, but instead of mounting the battered vehicle, he extended his left arm and took the weight of the magnificent cyber-eagle as she glided from her perch on top of the bike's rear wheel cowling. His impulse-link with the hunting bird might be at the most feral, basic level when they were not in direct communion, but during the long and isolated scouting missions that Suberei favoured, he spoke to her as though she understood every word.

Vengla took flight and climbed swiftly, using the swirling currents and rising heat of Ballestae's unforgiving surface to twirl into the open sky. It filled Suberei's heart with joy to see her soar. It brought back his memories of being a child on Mundus Planus, when he would go hunting with his tribe on the brutal Chogorian steppes. It mattered not that Vengla carried the augmentations of the White Scars Techmarines, that she was not a pure-breed – in fact, with her enhanced vision, power and reactions she had proved a great ally and, on occasion, a formidable weapon.

Canyons. Harsh rocky outcrops. The distant horizon.

Images of her hunting perspective formed in his retinal display as he mounted his bike and gunned the accelerator. He felt the deep treads of the rear wheel bite into the chasm's rough surface and set off. If Vengla was his companion, this bike was his most beloved possession.

Every time he mounted the iron steed he felt at home. There was some truth to the saying that Chogorians were born in the saddle; he felt a feeling of absolute freedom and power every time he went out riding. However, there was something unique about this bike. It had served him so well for so long that he found it unthinkable that he would ever replace it. When he had first met his new Deathwatch brothers, he'd had to fight, and fight hard, to keep it. They couldn't understand his attachment to the dented, scarred machine when better and newer technology was available. When it became clear that Suberei's usual good humour and bluffly eccentric manner didn't extend to losing his bike, a compromise was finally reached and the old bike had been given a fearsome weapons upgrade. Such was the state of its once-white livery that the need to paint it black had been questioned.

With a sudden lean to the left, Suberei deftly avoided a massive sheet of rock thrusting up from the ground and sped onto a wide, flat ledge – one of thousands that ran along the jagged walls of Ballestae's myriad canyons and ravines. This world had been harsh enough before the eldar had invaded, and had continued to provide no comfort or tactical advantage as wave after wave of the xenos battered against the embattled Imperial presence.

But then, when one final assault would have likely engulfed the Imperial forces, the eldar had inexplicably stopped their onslaught and withdrawn deep inside their own territory.

'That is why Suberei is here – to find out why, and to bring the storm.'

Suberei might have been addressing his eagle, but whether or not she heard he didn't care. He liked to talk to himself. On more than one occasion fellow battle-brothers had commented on it. He did not care about that either.

He was the Living Hurricane, the master of the Chogorian steppes, always first to hunt, and–

A flash of red. Then another. Very fast, closing.

'Higher. Go higher.'

Again – there. Two vehicles with xenos riders.

Eldar jetbikes. 'Return. Now.'

Suberei went up a couple of gears, the sudden increase in speed jolting him backwards and bringing the broad front wheel inches off the upwardly angled granite. In front of him was a steep incline leading to an overhang of rock from the mesa running along the top of the sheer canyon wall. Vengla's commanding view showed that the grav vehicles were heading towards him down the same valley, and the last thing he needed was to be discovered out in the open like this.

He had been travelling constantly for nearly two days, moving as fast as he could across the wide-open spaces, then ducking and dodging through twisting passageways to avoid any long-range patrols. Curiously, there had been none. The reconnaissance pieced together from the single functioning Imperial orbital recon unit had been imprecise, but the impression was of a significant concentration of eldar forces fairly close to this position. Attracting their attention and bringing them down upon him before he'd even managed to discover what was going on was not part of his plan, nor his usual stealthy approach.

Pulling back again on the throttle, he made his mount buck with raw power, vapour streaming from the exhausts as it hurtled up the glassy slope. Suberei leaned forwards, anchoring his weight so the bike could not flip over.

Within seconds he was at the top of the incline and slamming on the brakes, juddering to a stop and cutting the engine with a stab of his thumb. Vengla plummeted past him then arced gracefully back, outer wing feathers and razor-sharp talons outstretched. She dropped onto Suberei's forearm before taking her usual perch behind his seat. Reaching into a small container to the rear of the bike, Suberei pulled out a lump of meat and tossed it backwards without looking. Vengla snatched it with a darting nod and devoured it gratefully.

Suberei could feel his surroundings whisper through the sole of his boot. The planet, it seemed, talked to him when it chose to.

Dismounting with an easy grace, he slipped onto his chest and inched towards the outcrop's edge. Luckily, the valley below curved steeply on his left then straightened out for a couple of miles. Far to the right was the huge rock he had dodged to ride this slope. The approaching eldar would likely have to gain altitude when they spotted it, and hopefully they'd be too preoccupied to look up any higher. For a few seconds his blood boiled and his hearts pumped in anticipation of combat, but he suppressed the reaction.

Now was not the time to attack. Now was the time to gather intelligence.

Fine dust began to fall from the huge, sheer rock face dozens of yards opposite, and the cyber-eagle clacked its beak behind him.

'Still, Vengla. They will pass any time now.'

The dust turned to a mist of stones shaking loose from the walls on both sides, raining down onto Suberei's armour. He heard the high-pitched whine of the eldar engines, amplified and distorted by the canyon. And suddenly there they were – two, riding at a frantic pace side by side. The closest, slightly smaller in frame than the other, had the better line and nosed ahead on the turn. Despite the angle, Suberei could see the white emblem of the Saim-Hann craftworld painted on the long, sloping fairing, and the flapping pennants fixed to their backs. The markings were not identical – both had subtle variations, signifying that they were from different kin-bands. That in itself was not unusual.

The fact they were both hacking at each other with swords most certainly was.

They passed by Suberei's position in a flash, the outer rider catching up despite its rear left aileron nearly hitting the rock face. The other took another swipe back at its rival's gleaming white helmet, but in doing so unbalanced itself momentarily and drifted to the right. This was all the space the larger rider needed to accelerate into, leaving the other with the option of pulling up and away over the rapidly approaching sheet of fallen granite, conceding first place, or colliding headlong into it.

Suberei was incredulous. 'Are they trying to kill each other?'

As the leader crouched down and flipped the jetbike on its side, it was clear that no thought was being given to the one behind. The larger rider disappeared through the narrow gap, leaving the outmanoeuvred smaller rider banging his fist on the top of his cowling before pulling up sharply. But despite the eldar's fast reactions, the bottom of one of its stabilising fins snapped off and spun away. Then he, too, disappeared out of sight.

Vengla squawked loudly and flapped her wings as larger rocks and debris fell from the walls above and opposite her master's position. Realising the danger of the situation,

Suberei remounted his bike and headed back down the slope, ducking and dodging the rock falls. Judging the maximum height he could safely jump to the canyon floor, Suberei wheel-spun the bike sharply to the left and launched it into space, ahead of the obstacle the eldar had just passed. The landing was harsh, jolting Suberei from his seat and throwing Vengla violently to one side, but the bike's suspension absorbed the worst of it. Quickly checking that his shield and weapons were still attached, he flicked the bike one hundred and eighty degrees and gunned the engine.

'Yes, Vengla – Suberei will follow the route they have taken here.'

Directly behind him, the eagle screeched and wiped its hooked beak across the seat's ridge.

'You are correct. They may return this way again. The actions of the xenos scum are… unusual.'

Vengla ruffled her feathers and tightened her grip around the small bar upon which she perched. Protected in the slipstream of Suberei's power armour, she almost casually took to preening as her master used the deep shadows created by the high canyon walls to hide his progress. While the morsels he provided had kept starvation at bay, her hunger for fresh meat would be growing. Very soon, she would hope to feast.

Suberei looked down at the auspex built into the controls of his bike and frowned. It still provided less detail than normal vision, and was nowhere near as good as the view Vengla could give him through her superior eyes. He didn't need the scanner anyway, as Ballestae was beginning to talk to him directly. As the miles and hours passed, hints and suggestions of unseen terrain whispered from the wind's directional change and the arrangement of rocky layers. As he took a long, broad slope to avoid yet more fallen rock, his thoughts turned back to what he had witnessed.

Replaying the events through his mind, he focussed on different details – the variations in the eldar symbols, the riding techniques they had adopted and, in particular, their ferocity against each other. He knew that it had been more than a race.

'The xenos were fighting each other, Vengla. But for what?'

In the far distance, Suberei could see evidence of heavy weapons fire on the opposite canyon wall where a rough entrance to the valley had been fashioned. Recognising it from the fractured images the orbital unit had transmitted days ago, Suberei came to a crunching halt and turned off the bike's engine, surveying the base of the sloping cliff before him. It was a dead end, the barrier wall rising up and backwards out of sight into the darkening sky. He knew that on the other side, nestled in a well-protected valley, were the eldar forces. It wasn't impregnable by any stretch of the imagination, but the towering granite created a perfect defensive base. Ballestae clearly favoured the xenos' way of war, but if the Imperium had been lucky enough to land there first, the course of this long and bloody battle might have been quite different.

Suberei saw the shadow a fraction before he heard the howl of a Vyper's engines.

Heaving his bike into the quickening gloom of the chasm's floor, he watched the skimmer slow near the base of the incline, its rear gunner turning slowly from left to right before the blood-red machine gathered speed and roared away.

'Nothing more than a routine patrol,' Suberei murmured. 'Suberei will await darkness, then go hunting.'

Finding some excellent cover underneath a pile of fallen boulders, he cleaned his weapons as Vengla attended to her feathers. Once night began to close in, Suberei looked towards the purple darkness of the slope.

'Blades or bolts, Vengla?'

The cyber-eagle clicked her beak and cocked her head quizzically at the question.

'Suberei agrees. Blades it is.'

Suberei reached to the rear of his bike and retrieved his power sword and shorter duelling *kindjal* from its ceremonial animal-skin sheath. Examining both curved blades in the fading light, he nodded to himself with satisfaction. Vengla opened up her wings and stretched, waiting for Suberei to extend his arm, but he shook his head.

'No, I think not. You must stay here and guard the steed.'

Ignoring her indignant wing flapping, Suberei flicked the kindjal around in a couple of rapid circles, delighting in its perfect balance.

Now he was ready.

By day, Ballestae's twin suns beat down onto its desolate surface, scorching what passed for flora and burning any living creature exposed to their harsh rays. The night offered no better comfort, the thin atmosphere and lack of cloud plunging the temperatures well below freezing. As far as finding cover on this inhospitable world went, crawling up an ebony cliff face in black armour was about as good as it got.

Occasional Vypers soared overhead, and while it was difficult to find foot and hand holds on the near-vertical slope, when he stopped moving he blended in with his surroundings perfectly. The only real problem was maintaining grip. The night brought with it frost and ice, making progress slow and precarious. An occasional slip and loss of a few yards was a trade-off he was willing to make, as long as he didn't start a rockslide that might give away his position. That had been the main reason he'd not brought the eagle with him – if she had to take flight to save herself, she might attract attention.

As the sky brightened with an artificial glow in front of him, he was even more convinced that he'd done the right thing. All he could do was hope the ridge he was crawling towards was nothing more than a silhouette to the enemy.

The view that finally met him was extraordinary. A few hundred yards below, virtually every part of the rough valley was covered with elaborate temporary structures, grav-machine tethers and floodlit open workshops nestled in between. Clusters of ornate scarlet dwellings and lines of jetbikes stretched at least two miles into the distance, penned in by near-vertical cliffs on every side. Any gaps between the enormous walls were heavily guarded, but as Suberei scrutinised the mass of red bodies moving around, he realised that this was not, in fact, a single eldar encampment.

They were all Saim-Hann, of that he was certain, but the differing pennants and banners flapping from half a dozen satellite camps suggested this was an assembly of disparate kin-bands.

He found it curious that there was very little movement *between* the sectors. The xenos seemed to be keeping to their own boundaries, and even the sentries standing at the jagged entrances to the valley were subtly different in appearance and deployment. His eyes fell upon a large, steeply raked rectangular arena directly below his position. Even though it was in near-darkness and deserted save for a few eldar attending its outer structure, the position and enormous size was significant. He considered that it might be there to serve as neutral ground. However, its exact purpose eluded him.

There was no unity here. They had surely all arrived on Ballestae together but, unlike the Deathwatch he proudly served, these aliens did not move as one.

The way the outer camps had clear avenues between them suggested a deliberate attempt to remain separated, and his Chogorian sensibilities picked up a deep unease. As if to confirm this, his attention was drawn to the assembling of several dozen eldar from facing camps in the middle distance. It was difficult to make out details this far away, but he didn't need to – the body language of the opposing factions was becoming increasingly belligerent, and when blades appeared from nowhere, they were brandished with clear intent. Within seconds, the straggled front lines were joined by dozens on either side, the ensuing jostling and pushing narrowing the gap between their camps. Just as it looked as if they might come to blows, several elaborately dressed eldar moved swiftly into the middle of the pack, wielding their ceremonial spears in a flurry of robes and outstretched warning hands.

At first it appeared that the two groups would back down, but the pushing continued until the stand-off erupted.

The brawl would likely have continued long into the

night had the sky not been lit with a brilliant display
of power by the tallest of the eldar warlocks. Suberei
watched as the factions shuffled back hesitantly from one
another, leaving several armoured bodies lying prone on
the ground to be tended by their kin. The leader, resplendent in black robes and red glowing jewels, pointed towards
the dimly lit arena.

An audible roar went up not only from the two conflicting kin-bands but the entire valley, as the other camps had
gathered to watch the outcome. Lights burst into brilliance
around the arena, and Suberei ducked out of sight as
thousands of eldar stampeded towards the amphitheatre.

He took in a very deep breath and exhaled slowly. It
was likely that this was something never before witnessed
by an outsider.

A flash of red registered in his peripheral vision, and
he flattened himself immediately onto the freezing rock,
clutching the edge for anchorage. He didn't move for long
minutes after the patrolling Vyper had turned away, and
by the time he looked back down into the valley the arena's steeply raked platforms had filled to overflowing.

Standing on a central dais facing Suberei's position, the
tallest warlock rose from its seat and pointed slowly to
the warriors arrayed on its left, then those opposing them
on the right, eliciting more cheers and, Suberei fancied,
furious insults from every side of the arena. Banners were
waved to show clan affiliation and blades were readied
under the harsh lights. Every xenos rose as two single eldar
strode into the empty floor from opposite entrances. Both
were armed with long swords, and both wore no helmet.
Having fought several of their number over the last few
months, he also recognised the style of their garb.

'Clan chiefs. Now *that* is interesting.'

There was no announcement needed, no further cere-mony required. The two Saim-Hann ran at each other, swords held high and behind as was their way. With the first clash of blades came a tremendous roar, the audience forgetting their own petty squabbles and focus-ing instead on the melee unfolding before them. The slightly larger of the two chieftains spun on the ball of his foot and rotated his body to the left, avoiding a slicing downward blow from his opponent. In a split second he countered with an upward arcing slash, but the smaller eldar flipped backwards, the blade glancing off his right shoulder.

The speed was frenetic, the intention clear – to draw blood and to win.

The first whirled his body in a spiral and leaped into the air, but instead of using the height advantage to strike down onto the exposed head of his foe, he instead sliced through the pole carrying the opposing kin-band's pen-nant. It fluttered to the floor and, on landing next to it, the triumphant warrior ground it into the dirt with his boot heel.

One side of the arena erupted in fury and, within sec-onds, a much larger battle was taking place. Eldar fell and jumped from the terraces onto the bare ground below, engulfing the two clan chiefs in a sea of red.

This was not the dignified race that Suberei knew. The scene was one of utter chaos, with non-aligned groups who had come to watch throwing themselves into the fight for good measure. Things were little better outside the arena, where bystanders were enjoying their own con-tests. In less than a minute, every xenos in the valley was at another's throat. It was an astonishing sight, breathtaking and exciting in its ferocity.

Suberei wished he could call in a Naval bombardment right now and finish the whole gathering off in one deadly salvo, but he knew that was impossible. They'd lost their support ships when the eldar had last reinforced their own numbers, and while Imperial forces were doubtless making their way towards Ballestae and would certainly drive back the xenos invaders upon arrival, the Astra Militarum were currently without support. It occurred to Suberei that any action he might personally take at this point would not only be suicidal, but likely go unnoticed in the pandemonium.

While he didn't yet know the motives behind this hostility, his scouting experience was taking over and telling him to get away. He now knew the lie of the enemy land, even if he couldn't explain why the eldar had halted their attacks, and with this information, the Imperial forces could bring the fight back to the xenos.

At precisely the same moment as he came to this conclusion, the ledge onto which he was clinging broke apart.

Given the ice-rimed surface and the steep angle of the rock face, Suberei didn't have a chance of preventing his fall. Despite spreading his arms and legs out as wide as possible, his speed increased rapidly and within seconds he was hurtling down the cliff face, his breastplate and the forward rims of his pauldrons taking most of the grinding impacts. He tried to keep vertical but his foot connected with an outcrop, spinning him wildly. Instead he threw his left shoulder forwards, quickly flipping himself onto his back. His armour was, of course, capable of withstanding such a battering but he could not afford to strike a rock headfirst at such speed. Opening his arms, he scrabbled around for a hold, the stars flashing by in a blur. When he finally got one, the shock nearly tore his arm out of its socket but it had the desired effect, arcing him around so he was now sliding down the ledge feet-first and on his back.

If he felt that his situation had improved, spotting the two eldar jetbikes tearing towards him from left and right quickly dispelled the illusion.

The rock erupted with shuriken fire on either side as the red machines hurtled towards him, but their angle of attack and the speed with which Suberei was travelling meant that their lethal hail sliced wide of the mark. Suberei credited the enemy with the sense to turn quickly and come in for another pass, and with no stomach for dying in such a fashion he urgently looked past his feet to the rapidly approaching ground below.

As one jetbike banked sharply to the side, Suberei lifted his knees up towards his chest, sliding on his armour's backpack down the unforgiving rock, his vision immediately blurred by the vibration. Tensing his stomach muscles, he thrust both hands down and threw his body forwards so that he was perpendicular with the cliff face. He knew the contact between his feet and the rock would be brief at the speed he was travelling, and if he did not time his manoeuvre precisely he would topple forwards onto his chest again. As soon as the flat of his boots met the speeding rock below, he kicked away as best he could.

Now he was in freefall, the vast dark mesa stretching out from the base of the mountainside below him, but his sudden leap from the rock face caught the closing eldar riders by surprise. The one on his right tightened its turn and began firing, but stopped as the closer one on the left hurtled into the line of fire. Suberei could sense the ground rushing up to greet him and tensed himself for the impact, but the eldar wasn't going to be cheated of his prey. Pointing his jetbike straight at the falling Space Marine, the pilot opened fire at near point-blank range, but overshot, grazing the armour on his shoulder.

Suberei seized his chance. Activating his power sword, which mercifully had remained mag-locked at his hip during his crazed descent, he connected with the underside of the jetbike's tapered nose, slicing through its slaved weaponry and severing vital control systems. The machine immediately flipped onto its back, hurling its rider out of its seat and towards the canyon behind. Suberei roared with delight, but his victory cry was thumped out of him as he slammed hard into the surface of Ballestae.

The few warning runes that were not already red immediately changed colour in his visor, and Suberei lay on his back for dangerous seconds, waiting for the rush of adrenaline from his hearts to clear his head.

Then an image intruded upon his vision, one of wheeling dots of light and shadows.

Vengla had taken flight, and was on her way to help.

Through her eyes, he saw the second Saim-Hann jetbike speeding towards his prone position, likely believing him too stunned from the impact to realise that his attacker was nearly upon him. Suberei fought the urge to stand, instead remaining still and counting on the nature of his enemy to engage at close quarters rather than shred him from a distance. Sure enough the jetbike levelled out only yards before his position, its rider leaping into the air, blades drawn, before the sleek machine had come to a whining halt.

Suberei sprung to his feet, the weight of his armour providing vital purchase on the icy rock. The eldar might have the advantage of speed but the blades it wielded, while dangerous, were nothing compared to the power sword that now hummed in Suberei's right hand. In his left, he held the kindjal in a dagger fashion, and used it to block the xenos' first thrust. Its second blade moved in fast to Suberei's right, but the blow was parried with his power sword, the sheer brute force of his move knocking the warrior to the freezing floor. Rolling into a kneeling position, the Saim-Hann brought its blades up once again and pushed itself forwards with extraordinary speed. Unfortunately, the surface underfoot did not give the creature the momentum it had expected, and Suberei leaned in to capitalise on the split second of poor coordination. His power sword entered the eldar precisely in the middle of its abdomen and didn't stop until the hilt was blocked by what remained of its armour.

Suberei wrenched his crackling blade back and the xenos collapsed to the ground, a gentle cloud of steam wafting upwards from the gaping wound.

Vengla cried from high above, and Suberei focussed his thoughts on her vision. Shapes were flying into the inky sky, myriad shadowy forms backlit by the glowing lamps of the encampment. The eldar had mobilised in force, alerted to his presence by those just slain.

'To your perch, Vengla! Hurry!'

Suberei powered down his sword blade and sheathed his kindjal, then strode towards the shelter under which his beloved bike was waiting.

He was on it in moments. Jabbing at the ignition, he slammed one foot onto the ground, pulled back on the accelerator and spun the howling machine around just as Vengla shrieked into place behind him. High above, the sound of multiple xenos grav-turbines added to the cacophony as they echoed from the stone. Suberei roared into the gloom, riding as fast as he dare given the limited range of his vision. At times he stopped dead, using the darkest parts of the valley for shelter, and at others he drove with scant seconds' warning of deadly barriers looming in his path. He called on every trick he'd learned in the White Scars vanguard to avoid capture as Vypers and jetbikes flashed overhead and, when he took to the ledges of the cliff walls, below his position.

Given a couple more hours of darkness, the broad slope on which Suberei sped could have led him out of danger. This section of canyon was arrow-straight and the ledge relatively free of obstructions. Unfortunately, the first rising sun of Ballestae was already picking up the rough-hewn sides of the path, the angle of the rays chasing away the shadow cover masking his progress. Suberei edged closer and closer to the canyon wall until his handlebar grip was scraping along the rock, but with the second sun also climbing he knew discovery was only a matter of time.

A blur of movement passed overhead, and a shower of rock exploded all around him in a maelstrom of Vyper fire. Vengla squawked loudly, as much in protest as concern, and Suberei ducked low to avoid a boulder as it bounced overhead. More debris fell, clanging off the forward plate arch and wheel guards.

Glancing to his left, Suberei saw the Vyper had descended for a clearer shot. He laughed at their impertinence.

Grabbing his bolt pistol, he fired off-handed at the xenos gunner, putting a bolt through the head of the creature and cracking the pilot's cockpit screen into the bargain. The machine spun upwards and away, disappearing out of view onto the flat plain above. A second Vyper took its place, gliding in and strafing the wall ahead. Granite shards spun and flipped in all directions, and while Suberei's intention was to accelerate through the lethal spray, a slice of rock flipped through the front wheel fork and jammed itself underneath the bike's fairing.

The entire machine flipped forwards with the instant deceleration. Suberei spun over the ledge, barely managing to remain in the saddle, and smashed into an overhang before dropping the bike onto the canyon floor below.

Head reeling, he fired upwards into the belly of the Vyper machine. But instead of turning in to finish him off, it unleashed a point-blank salvo onto the ledge overhanging his bike, cracking the rock above and bringing down several tonnes of shattered stone on top of it. Suberei scrabbled out of the way of the descending avalanche, chunks clanging off his armour.

By the time the huge cloud of rock dust had cleared, the eldar machine had disappeared from sight.

Suberei didn't stop to question why they had not pressed their advantage. Instead he leapt up to where his bike's rear wheel could just be seen protruding from the rock fall, drawing his power sword in readiness for attack.

When seconds turned to minutes, he shifted his weight slightly and lowered his pistol.

'Suberei will not fall for xenos trickery,' he murmured. Stepping cautiously forwards, he peered up and scanned the brightening sky to his left and right.

The enemy were nowhere to be seen.

More debris cascaded down onto his helmet and shoulders. Throwing himself back, Suberei waited for the growing landslide to pass in front of him. With a sinking heart, he realised that he could no longer see any part of his bike. It would take an age to dig it out, and even then there was no guarantee it would be salvageable. At that single point in time, if a thousand eldar had appeared before him then he would have torn them all apart in revenge for his loss.

But something equally pressing occurred to him.

'Vengla. Do you live?'

The answer came almost immediately in a beating of wings and high-pitched shrieks. The cyber-eagle landed heavily on Suberei's right pauldron, traces of blood on her beak and around the augmetic implant encompassing her eye. The son of Chogoris extended his right arm and she hopped down onto it, seeming to favour her left leg over her right. Dropping his bolt pistol and throwing off his left gauntlet, Suberei ran an expert hand over her, checking for any obvious wound or injury. She in turn pecked at his fingers, stretched her wings and opened her talons.

'It seems we both live to hunt another day.'

He was relieved, and felt no shame in admitting it.

An hour or so after the landslide, the skies still remained silent. The filters in his helmet reduced the glare from both suns, which now peeped over the ledge.

'Something is not right here, Vengla. Why would they call off the attack when Suberei was in such a vulnerable position?'

The eagle shuffled along Suberei's vambrace and tapped

her beak on the deactivated power sword's blade. Suddenly she darted her head up and around, her mouth opened slightly and tongue tasting the air.

'What is it? What do you sense?'

The bird took flight without bidding. Suberei replaced his gauntlet, grabbed his pistol and followed her for a few hundred yards down the chasm's littered floor, making a mental note of where his bike lay buried.

With the rock so weak and unstable, it no longer provided reliable cover.

And he knew – both from the eagle's unease and from the planet itself – that the enemy would be coming.

Spotting a thick ledge high on the vertical striated wall to his left, Suberei took three mighty leaps onto a line of crumbling outcrops and landed heavily, sword now fizzing with energy and bolt pistol ready to unleash a hail of destruction. Closing his eyes, the impulse-link with Vengla crystallised in his auto-senses and razor-sharp images of sky and land filled his mind's eye.

The canyon in which he crouched was little more than a jagged line across the vast black plain over which the bird flew. There were relatively few other valleys in the vicinity, so any search was bound to concentrate on this chasm sooner rather than later. The eagle climbed higher, the twin suns an occasional flash of brilliant light as she scanned the wide, open sky of Ballestae and the forbidding ground below it.

Shadow. Low to ground. Moving slowly.

Closer. Investigate.

Vengla dropped like a stone, arrowing towards the planet's surface, her gaze fixed on a closing Vyper. From its raised platform, the rear-mounted gunner warily rotated the long barrel of his shuriken cannon in a methodical search pattern, oblivious to the approaching eagle. When the cyber-eagle's augmented vision picked out the kin-band symbol on its prow, Suberei grunted in surprise.

Movement. Fast. To the right.

Turn and descend. Careful.

The second Vyper appeared from behind a distant peak, following a criss-cross pattern over a tributary valley. Both machines were conducting quite separate searches from one another, which at first puzzled Suberei.

But then he nodded to himself.

Furthest target. Identify.

Vengla banked sharply to the right and sped towards the Vyper. Suberei focussed his concentration on the front of the twin-pronged cowling. As soon as he saw the white pattern and black chevrons, he recalled his cyber-eagle. Opening his eyes again, he took in a deep breath.

The puzzle fell into place.

The kin-band symbols on the Saim-Hann Vypers were the same as the duelling jetbikes that had nearly crashed into the rock on the valley floor yesterday. They were the clan chiefs who had fought so viciously in the arena last night. Suberei didn't know a great deal about the specific xenos craftworld traditions, but he did know a thing or two about the feuding tribes from his own world of Chogoris.

He knew the importance of being the strongest, the fastest. The first to hunt.

Now it all made sense. The reason that the eldar campaign on Ballestae had faltered was so the rival factions could vie for the honour of delivering the killing blow to the Imperial forces.

The clan chiefs had taken up his pursuit personally.

'Such hubris! Such arrogance!'

The words were spat rather than spoken. Anger rose once again in Suberei's chest with the realisation that these two rival leaders had clearly decided that he, the Living Hurricane, master of the Chogorian steppes, would be the final prize in their competition. *They* had called off the attack that might have finished him on the valley floor, so that he could be their sport.

Well, that was not going to happen.

Spotting the eagle as a dot on the horizon, Suberei extended his sword arm. In the seconds it took for her to swoop down into the gaping canyon and come to perch on his vambrace, his decision had been made.

If the disunity he had seen in the eldar camp was bad now, how would they react to the elimination of their two strongest champions? The other lesser factions would throw themselves into the power vacuum, giving Suberei enough time to return with his intelligence and orchestrate a full-scale pre-emptive attack. He wouldn't even have to reach the Imperial front lines – he could break communications silence as soon as he was in range, and they could meet him halfway. Suberei raised his arm and looked into Vengla's piercing eyes.

'Yes, proud friend. You are right. It is time for Suberei to bring the storm.'

Vengla shrieked once then hopped up onto his pauldron, gripping tightly with her talons. Looking out into the brilliantly lit valley, Suberei scanned the opposing rock face for a vantage point but couldn't quite find what he was looking for. Striding back down to the canyon's floor, he jumped and hopped over the rubble, scanning the cloudless sky for any enemy movement. In the upper face of the cliffs, he spotted a large, ragged hole just beneath the plain's edge. To get to it, he would have to climb up and traverse part of the mesa above, but that did not bother him at all.

In fact, it just might work to his advantage.

Ballestae stretched out into the distance all around him and, around half a dozen miles away, he saw the small red speck moving slowly from right to left. With a smile, Suberei strolled boldly out into the open, keeping watch on the Vyper as he did so. It only took a few seconds for it to spot him and, as it turned and sped closer, Suberei mag-locked his power sword, dropped off the ledge into the chasm below and swung himself into the cave mouth with his now free hand.

From above, Suberei heard the howl of the Vyper's engines echo into the valley. Just above his head, the red pincer prow of the grav-machine crept into view, the pilot clearly deciding that caution was the better part of valour. The further it edged forwards, the more Suberei retreated into the body of the cliff, the planet itself hiding him from the sophisticated eldar scanners. If they could not see him, they could not attack – so that meant they would have to fly over and into the chasm to find him.

Crouching at the side of the cave wall, Suberei watched the Vyper descend.

The starboard rear fin floated past his eye line, then the base of the gunner's platform and, finally, the gunner himself, white helmet gleaming under the rising suns. Eldar reactions were lightning fast, but even they could be surprised, and the sight of a Deathwatch Space Marine leaping through the air from seemingly nowhere was more than enough to give Suberei the advantage.

The eldar tried to bring his weapon to bear, but was too late. Suberei cleaved the cannon in two with a stroke of his sword and grabbed hold of the now useless stump of a barrel, smashing his right boot into the eldar's chest. The warrior struggled to draw his side-arm, but another impaling thrust from Suberei's sword pinned the xenos to the seat. Suberei wedged himself between the platform and the cockpit and was reaching for his bolt pistol when the Vyper suddenly accelerated upwards, throwing the Space Marine violently forwards onto the twitching body of the gunner. As the speed increased, Vengla dived in to help her master but the brutal gravitic slipstream hurled her onto the vehicle's floor, behind the cockpit.

Suberei was completely exposed to the battering wind and realised that if he were thrown from the machine at this height, he would likely not survive the fall.

He sliced into the base of the gunner's chair, the frame and its occupant coming away and tumbling backwards into the valley some thirty feet below. Realising what had happened, the enraged clan chief pilot threw the Vyper into a near-vertical climb, forcing the stunned Vengla to scrabble for extra grip with her talons and hurling Suberei over the mangled rear of the vehicle. Grabbing hold of the gunnery platform's stump, Suberei stabbed down with his power sword and thrust it into the exposed xenos workings, giving himself two handholds instead of one.

The machine tipped and pitched, throwing Suberei from left to right and up and down, but he only grinned. His people were born riders, and he would prove more than a match for this bucking beast. Rolling to the left, the

Space Marine kicked out violently with his foot and connected with the rear of the port fin's tip. A good chunk
came away, exposing sparking circuitry and naked framework. The Vyper lurched violently with a sudden loss of
control, and Suberei hoped this would convince the pilot
to descend.

Sure enough, it did – straight down, in a power dive.

Suberei felt himself become weightless as the arc put
him into freefall. The sky tipped upside down, and he lost
his grip on the platform stump. Luckily his power sword
kept its place buried in the deck, but his wrist popped as it
took the sudden weight of his entire body and he crashed
into the rear of the cockpit, making the Vyper judder even
more as it fell from the sky. Again the pilot flicked the
machine from right to left; Suberei was tossed over the
broken fin and then the other, the movements too violent
for him to grab his pistol and bring it to bear. Instead he
concentrated on keeping his grip on the sword, his view
flashing from sky to ground to the red of the Vyper itself.

A brief glimpse through the rear window revealed
the clan chief struggling with his controls. This pleased
Suberei hugely.

The fact he could no longer see Vengla did not.

A hail of shuriken sliced into the deck below Suberei's
gauntlet. Squirming around for a better view, he spotted
the Vyper of the opposing kin-band closing rapidly, its
own gunner trying to get a shot at Suberei's arm. It was
clear that this eldar wanted its prize alive.

Reacting to the sudden appearance of the competition,
the stricken chief piloting Suberei's reluctant ride tried
climbing again but the machine was not up to the challenge. Seeing their advantage, the other crew flew in even

closer, the gunner pushing away her console and rotating the frame towards Suberei's position. Dragging himself back onto the deck, Suberei punched a hole through the cockpit screen in an attempt to strike at the un-helmed pilot, but the clan chief leaned forwards, infuriatingly out of reach.

As the machine flipped to the right, Suberei fell back once again but this time let go of his sword, using the newer, better handhold of the broken cockpit frame while he made a grab for his pistol. He was just bringing it to bear when the other Vyper's gunner landed right in front of him.

The eldar's blade buried itself into Suberei's vambrace, slicing through the armour and into his arm. Suberei roared a Chogorian curse and smashed his fist into the eldar's helmet. The gunner fell backwards, only her grip on the sword planted in Suberei's arm saving her from plunging to her doom. Searing pain flamed up from the twisting blade, but Suberei ignored it and let go his grip on the cockpit, grabbing onto the haft of his still-buried sword instead. Staggering sideways, the eldar came with him. At first her feet scrabbled and her free arm flailed, but then she found her balance and reached down to her belt for the dagger sheathed there.

Gritting his teeth, Suberei yanked his skewered arm back, pulling the eldar off-balance again. Bellowing with rage, he spun his body forwards, throwing his arm out at great speed and dislodging the xenos' blade. The sudden momentum threw the gunner off the platform into free space. She made a brave attempt to grab hold of her own Vyper, which was flying alongside the rival machine, but instead collided with the underside of the rear section. The eldar's neck snapped backwards at an unnatural angle, her lifeless body sailing out to the rapidly approaching surface.

Steadying himself, Suberei could see the two clan chiefs gesticulating at each other through their canopies, his own pilot nodding something in agreement. Suberei grabbed his bolt pistol and aimed at his pilot's head, but the Vyper lurched down and his shots went wide, hitting the other machine and striking the armoured canopy. Pulling away and out of danger, the opposing chief kept his distance and a wary eye on Suberei as the Space Marine grabbed for the stump of the gunner's platform to avoid falling. The craft ducked and weaved.

He roared in defiance, hoping the xenos could hear his words.

'In the name of the Emperor and the spirit of Jaghatai Khan, Suberei will end your–'

An image flashed into Suberei's mind, dim at first but then clearer. He closed his eyes.

He could see the sky and the ground, but not from his perspective. In the middle distance was the range of mountains surrounding the eldar encampment, then the two Saim-Hann Vypers drifted into view. One was manoeuvring furiously with a bulky figure – Suberei himself – clinging to its rear, the other keeping pace, one side of its canopy smashed, its pilot's hair flying wildly in the wind.

The angle steepened, and the hole in the cockpit grew larger as it came closer. Suddenly there was confusion, a burst of movement and a dark shape in the blinding light, then a furious shrieking and screams in an alien tongue. Blood clouded the vision, but then was blinked away, leaving a scarlet wash over the action.

Vengla struck over and over at the clan chief's eyes. His hands frantically clawed at her, but to no avail. The shrieks became a long scream and the world seemed to tip in on itself.

The image disappeared, and Suberei opened his eyes to see the opposing clan chief's Vyper bank sharply to the right, its occupant thrashing around in agony. Suberei's pilot had to stop his destabilising movements to avoid a mid-air collision, before the other machine dived past and ploughed into the ground far below, breaking and rolling in the dirt. As his craft levelled out, Suberei holstered his bolt pistol, hurled himself forwards over the damaged stern, retrieved his power sword with a mighty pull and thrust it into the back of the pilot's neck.

The grav-machine dropped sharply and spiralled towards a deep ravine between two sloping cliff faces. Suberei pulled his sword from the pilot as he slumped onto his controls. The forward-mounted weapon beneath the prow began firing continuously, spraying the rapidly approaching ground with a hail of shuriken fire. Suberei waited until the whirling machine was only a dozen yards from impact. Then, with a howl of triumph, he leapt clear and crashed awkwardly down the rocky ravine wall.

The Vyper came down harder. Something exploded inside the fuselage before the conflicting energies of its damaged gravitic drives detonated the machine in a shower of fractured crimson pieces.

Suberei did not wait to see if the other xenos from the camp would come to investigate; he needed to get his information back to the Imperial forces. As he limped away as quickly as he could, a shadow flashed overhead then circled around him once.

'Vengla! Come to Suberei!'

Nothing.

As he slowed his pace, Suberei's delight was slowly clouded by concern. Why was the cyber-eagle not calling to signal her return? Had she perhaps seen a massed enemy group pouring out of the ravine between the mountains to find them? No. She would have shared that vision with him. Was she injured? Again, he would have sensed that.

Then, as she suddenly appeared, he laughed heartily at the reason for her silence.

'Suberei extends his thanks to you, proud friend. Now, enjoy your feast.'

In her beak were two glistening orbs dangling from red, dripping stalks.

The eyes of the other Vyper pilot.

The two had travelled over sixty miles before the first eldar patrol went overhead. This did not surprise him. He had no doubt the deaths of the clan chiefs would have thrown the Saim-Hann forces into disarray, and it was likely that they had wasted precious time trying to coordinate themselves. As he hid and observed from cover, he saw a single Vyper attack and cripple two jetbikes from opposing clans in a surprise attack, and it became obvious that the conflict between them had escalated significantly. Suberei and Vengla were able to skulk and slide their way further and further from the eldar encampment, unnoticed.

Why had the xenos become so fractious? Was it something he had missed? Something to do with this world in particular?

Suberei realised that it did not matter.

Finding a suitably high location, he sent a message by coded data-burst back to the forward Imperial lines. Once acknowledged, he made his way down to the great black plains once more, but instead of continuing his journey he took a seat on a large granite outcropping and considered his situation.

'The Militarum forces are mobilising as we speak, Vengla. Our work is done. But Suberei has one last mission to fulfil before we leave this accursed planet.'

The sounds of battle thundered in the distance as Suberei surveyed the scene from the bottom of the canyon. Flurries of rock and stone fell around him, but he took no notice. Perched above and to the left of the buried bike, Vengla shifted her weight from foot to foot then launched herself into the air, swooping low over what remained of the ledge partially buried under glistening black rubble.

Suberei closed his eyes and surveyed the scene through her vision. Spotting an exposed lip large enough to support him, he calculated the best way up to it without bringing yet more rocks down and followed the route as carefully as his power armour would allow. Vengla remained airborne all the while to keep watch, though it seemed that the Imperial forces had the eldar contained.

Suberei studied the way in which the rocks had fallen. Most of them had settled towards the top of the sloping rubble, and a few swift kicks had them crashing down into the valley below. He was rewarded with a small patch of dull grey metal he immediately identified as the exhausts. Good. At least the bike hadn't been flattened beyond recognition.

One large boulder held the rest of the landslide in place,

so Suberei put his right shoulder to its massive rough side and pushed as hard as he could. Straining with the effort, he felt his arm throb, but kept on going until the rock began to move. Slowly, it ground its way towards the ledge until gravity finally took hold and it toppled over. Waiting for the loose shale to clear, Suberei moved through the choking black dust to inspect the damage to his now exposed bike. The front guard was badly dented and the barrel of one bolter fouled with grit, but miraculously, it appeared intact.

There was, of course, only one way to be sure.

Dragging it free from the smaller rocks, Suberei brushed the dust from the saddle and mounted it. He jabbed the starter and the engine spluttered and complained. He grunted, and stepped back to inspect the grimy systems.

He cleaned and adjusted the fuel injectors as best he could, then climbed back on and tried again. His reward was a throaty roar and clouds of dirty smoke spewing from the rear.

With a cry of delight, Suberei rolled the bike slowly forwards, allowing pieces of rock to work their way from under the front and rear wheel housings. Gradually increasing speed, he followed the still fragile ledge upwards. A more cautious rider might have decided to take a longer, safer route to ensure that their machine had no hidden damage that could prove fatal to the rider at high speeds, but not Jetek Suberei. Pulling back fully on the throttle, the bike leaped forwards, eating up the space to the sheer drop. Faster and faster he went, and wider and wider his grin became until he finally launched himself skywards.

The landing on the plains wasn't the most elegantly

executed, but it served to shake the last few bits of stub-born debris from the frame. Slamming on the brakes and skidding sideways to a halt, Suberei revelled in the raw power of the bike as it idled beneath him.

There was now only one thing missing. With a squawk of welcome, his cyber-eagle dropped onto her perch behind her master. Suberei revved the engine as she settled.

'Come, Vengla. Let us away.'

CITY OF RUIN

IAN ST. MARTIN

Not a single breath has left my body but in service to the House.

The words echoed through Sai's head, offered no challenge by the howling of the wind. From the spire's terrace he beheld the metropolis of Pomarii tumbling out across the plains in a breathtaking expanse of gridlines and hab blocks.

Billions of people lived, toiled and died below him, but all he could see was his mother's face, and the glacial reserve engraved in her features.

As the lone male heir of House Trigarta, the course of Sai's existence had been decided and regimented from the day he first drew breath. Of all the opulence and luxury that life within a House of the Navis Nobilite afforded, choice had been a delicacy too rare to taste. While his sisters took to the stars, guiding the fleets of the Imperium, Sai remained cloistered, shut away from anything that might threaten the continuance of the bloodline.

He had sailed through the Sea of Souls to arrive here on Basatani, to be received by the emissaries of House Velon. Sai's future was decided, an arranged marriage with a daughter of Velon to maintain alliances that had existed before man had first set foot on Basatani, and nearly as long as the Imperium itself. Sai would never shepherd a vessel through the Immaterium. Despite the priceless value of a Navigator's curse, he was consigned to be little more than a breeder.

He would never even open his eye.

Every beat of my heart has been for the survival of the House, Lady Trigarta had said as Sai departed for Basatani. *And now, so must yours.* He had excused himself from the pomp of the reception, seeking a rare opportunity to be entirely alone.

But the tension in the city below was palpable even from these heights. War had descended over the entire sector, which was in the grip of a xenos invasion, or so he had been told. Sai had only just arrived when the aliens began their assault. Safe within the system's core worlds defensive line, Basatani had avoided the bloodshed thus far.

Other than lessons in naval and military history taught to him by his tutors, he had no experience of war, or of any of the myriad xenos races that opposed the Imperium of Man. His life had been insulated from such things, the perils of the galaxy rendered inert on the pages of parchment scrolls and dataslates.

Sai looked up. The terrace and spire were draped in shadow, drawing his gaze to Basatani's star. The blazing sphere was masked in an eclipse, and a brief smile crept across the youth's face as he beheld it.

Then his wonder chilled into ice that crept up his spine.

He looked closer as klaxons began to wail in the distance. He remembered his study of this world in the long months of his journey...

Basatani did not have any moons.

The eclipse grew darker, casting the spire and all of Pomarii into deeper shadow. The object continued to swell, growing larger, and Sai's eyes widened as it caught fire.

There was a noise like the sky ripping open. The intense heat of the atmospheric plunge stripped away pieces of debris from the object, which arced downwards on columns of fire. Stone fragments the size of hab towers smashed into the city in shattering explosions. Individual sounds ceased to be. Numberless impacts and the din of destruction swelled and overlapped into a monstrous cacophony like the roaring of a nightmarish ocean. Tremors rocked the spire. Sai grabbed hold of the railing of the terrace and crouched behind it. He shrank against the thunder of explosions as debris rained down, demolishing entire city blocks below.

Sai touched a hand to the elaborate headdress he wore, carved into the image of angels with platinum wings swept protectively over his mutation. His third eye throbbed and pulsed beneath the covering. He peered over the railing upon the city. A swelling cloud of dust from the impacts boiled over the metropolis like churning fog. It rose, billowing and licking at the roots of the central spires but failing to reach their height.

His gaze lifted from the shrouded devastation below, and ice plunged into his veins.

A gargantuan meteor of blazing rock and jagged metal, far larger than anything else that had fallen, broke through

the clouds, descending towards Pomarii like the fist of a
livid god. Flickering streams of fire from the city's defence
batteries carved ineffectual scars into it, and hasty arrows
of fighter craft hurtled out from hangar bays, rising to
intercept the looming colossus.

Sai's breath caught in his throat as the meteor responded.
Clouds of ordnance lashed out in all directions, and the
fighters blinked away in tiny sunbursts.

This was no meteor. Someone, or *something*, was controlling it.

It was a ship, and it was not slowing down.

The hulk began to tumble, rolling slowly like a great
ocean leviathan as it hurtled towards the city. Fire-wreathed
debris continued its hellish rain, obliterating spires and
reducing entire city blocks to rubble.

Sai of House Trigarta realised that he was going to die
at the top of this spire, on a world he did not know, for
a reason he would never understand.

Rodricus Grytt stood in the scarlet light of the Thunderhawk as he was armoured for battle. Robed thralls and
servitors surrounded him, anchoring massive plates of
ceramite over the Space Marine's genhanced musculature.
The war-plate was the deep black of the void, save for the
silver bearing the insignia of the Deathwatch riveted onto
his left arm and shoulder. The only thing to hint at his
Chapter allegiance was the gold livery of the Imperial Fists
on his right pauldron. The jet fist of Dorn was scarred and
singed from recent battle, the deepest gouges still stained
with the blood of brothers and foes alike.

Grytt rolled his shoulders as the thralls stepped away, the
power pack on his back thrumming to life. The servants

fell to their knees, offering trembling devotions to appease the spirit of the armour for the haste of its preparation. Grytt ignored them, scratching at the scars that branched over his face before donning his helm.

For a Space Marine, joining the ranks of the Deathwatch was among the highest of honours, worthy of remembrance in the annals of one's parent Chapter.

For Grytt, it was exile. One that he had imposed upon himself.

Through the visor of his plough-faced helm, Grytt stared at the servo-skull that bobbed before him, the whirring clockwork of its optics pulsing in the gloom. The drone served as his spotter, expanding his view of a battlefield as his Devastator squad rained down the fury of Dorn upon the enemies of mankind.

Grytt blinked, and the skull's pict feed overlaid his right eye-lens. He breathed in the armour's stale air, and watched the recording of the battle he had fought mere days ago. He watched himself lead a squad of Imperial Fists through roughly hewn rock tunnels awash with blood and flame, heavy weapons unleashed at point-blank range upon a roaring horde of greenskins.

He watched as his brothers demonstrated the iron discipline and restraint that defined Dorn's sons as they waged war.

He watched as he himself did not, striking ahead and casting abandon behind. He witnessed his loss of control mar the cohesion of his squad, and he saw his battle-brothers die because of it.

'Never have I witnessed one so strong display such weakness,' Grytt remembered the words of Captain Kyradon, now counted amongst the fallen as the vile xenos burned the system to ashes. The words dug into the core of him, taking root with barbs of cruel truth.

Grytt possessed a furious temperament, more in common with his zealous cousins of the Black Templars than that of the Chapter that had once been Legion. In a brotherhood where control was paramount, his recklessness was a mark of shame.

When the Deathwatch summoned him, requesting he join their ranks, Grytt had accepted without question. War's intoxication had eroded his discipline, and the fight to not drink deep of it was the only battle he had ever lost. In order to atone, he would drown himself in it. He would return to the Imperial Fists tempered and purged of his weakness by the crucible of shadow war, or he would not return at all.

The deck shuddered beneath Grytt's boots as the gunship landed upon the hangar deck of the Deathwatch frigate *Kisertet*. The Imperial Fist stepped down the embarkation ramp into the ordered pandemonium of the hangar bay, towards the figure that awaited him.

Like Grytt, the warrior was a Space Marine of the Deathwatch, his black armour edged in blue and etched with esoteric runes. A crystalline hood rose behind his head, crackling faintly with unnatural energies. The heraldry of the Silver Skulls displayed his origins, while his wargear marked him as a Librarian.

'Brother Grytt,' said the psyker, his tone soft for a Space Marine. 'I am Adomar. You have arrived in haste, but we cannot tarry here. Kill Team Almuta gathers. We must join them.'

Grytt removed his helm again with a gasp of equalising air pressure, and carried it in the crook of his arm as he followed Adomar. The servo-skull whirred as it floated at his shoulder.

'Tell me,' asked Grytt, as the two Space Marines departed the bustle of rushing auxiliaries and hangar crew, walking through the darkened corridors of the *Kisertet*. 'Have you crusaded amongst the Deathwatch long?'

'No,' replied Adomar, his steps silent compared to Grytt's hulking gait. 'I am a replacement for their fallen, as are you.'

'This invasion has spilled much noble blood,' said Grytt. 'My company has been engaged with the greenskins assailing these worlds for weeks. My boarding party had only just returned from one of their wretched vessels when I was seconded here.'

'It is an honour to serve,' said Adomar. 'Your experience with these orks will do us credit in the strife ahead.'

'So long as this filth is burned from our dominions,' Grytt replied. 'If the Deathwatch is to be at the throat of this horde, I intend to be the blade that cuts it.'

Three warriors stood in the gloom of the strategium, fresh from the fires of battle. The Space Marines of Kill Team Almuta bore the scars of intense fighting, the damage clear to see as Grytt and Adomar entered.

A warrior of the Iron Hands crouched behind a Space Marine of the Revilers Chapter, hands and snaking mechadendrites attending to his comrade's power pack. The Reviler leaned heavily against the polished onyx of the strategium table, bearing the full weight of his unpowered armour. With a few ministrations, the Iron Hands warrior sealed the power pack as the gooseflesh hum of power returned, and both straightened while adepts and serfs attended to and prayed over their sacred war-plate.

The third warrior, bearing the twin-blade livery of the Executioners, stood silently, looking down upon the power axe held in his hands. The weapon's craftsmanship was exquisite, inlaid with pearl and ruby teardrops, its double blade fashioned to resemble outstretched wings. It was not an aesthetic style he would credit to the Chapter, but Grytt had seen its like before, forged in the armouries of Baal and carried into battle by the descendants of Sanguinius.

The Executioner looked up at the newcomers, his armour creaking with the stalling clicks of damaged servos. He stepped forwards, mag-locking the axe to his back.

'Brother Adomar,' he said in greeting. The Silver Skull inclined his head in reply, his face cast in the shadow of his psychic hood.

The Executioner looked to Grytt. 'I am Ralon, now leader of Almuta.' Grytt noticed the Reviler and Iron Hand look briefly to the warrior, before their eyes returned to him.

The successor, then, thought Grytt.

'Brother Imre,' said the Iron Hand in a mechanical snarl of introduction, pressing his cybernetic fist to his chest.

The Reviler inclined his head fractionally, no emotion disturbing the urbane calm of his pale features. 'Kitra.'

'We must be brief,' said Ralon. 'Brothers Grytt and Adomar have joined our ranks from amongst the forces conducting operations alongside us in the system. We were marked for withdrawal and recovery, but new orders have diverted us here.'

The hololithic projector at the centre of the table chattered. A blizzard of flickering light winked into the air, rolling and coalescing into the planet Basatani, where the

Kisertet now perched at high orbit. The planet was sedate and verdant, with continents of rolling plains and calm oceans. A blinking dot arced down onto the surface with a flash, and from its impact spiralling clouds and storms bloomed over the world.

Kill Team Almuta studied the hololith of Basatani as it turned gently before them, the planet's former beauty smothered beneath continent-spanning veils of dust like a sphere of curdled cream.

Grytt leaned forwards, planting his fists upon the table. 'This is our target?'

Ralon cleared his throat. 'Basatani. Ten days ago, a xenos hulk made landfall within the outskirts of Pomarii, the planetary capital. The city contains the majority of the planet's population, and casualties are estimated to be catastrophic. The force of the impact has triggered ash storms that shroud nearly the entire globe, significantly inhibiting any scans of the surface from orbit.

'We received scattered vox-transmissions that large numbers of orks emerged from the hulk. The Astra Militarum presence on the surface was little more than a token garrison, their regiments having been diverted to hot zones across the system. They now number among the dead.'

'So what are *we* doing here?' asked Grytt. 'The entire system burns, rife with greenskin incursions of greater scale than this. What down there is so important?'

'Not what,' replied Adomar, 'but *who*.'

The members of Almuta turned to the Silver Skull as the psyker continued. 'We are here by mandate of the Navis Nobilite.'

'We are the scourge of the xenos,' said Imre. 'Not thralls to task with the errands of the Navigator Houses.'

'There were envoys of two great dynasties on Basatani when the xenos hulk made landfall,' said Ralon. 'Our orders are to infiltrate the surface, confirm whether there are any survivors, and extract them.'

'We are committing a full kill team in the middle of a system-wide invasion for a rescue mission?' asked Grytt.

'The two Houses have served the Imperium of Man since the time your gene-sire walked among mortals, son of Dorn,' replied Kitra. 'Navigators are prized, and carry much influence in the Council of Terra. Should they require aid, none but the Emperor's elite shall do.'

Grytt made to reply, but Ralon raised a forestalling hand.

'We all have our role to play, brothers. And if any leadership of this horde is below as well, killing it here and now could shorten the invasion by months.'

'Greenskins are an infestation,' said Grytt, running a gloved hand through his stripe of silver hair. 'Their microscopic spores now carpet that city as surely as the ash. It is only a matter of time before millions of them taint its surface. You all have been fighting these xenos scum as I have. I say burn it from orbit, and be done.'

'Our esteemed watch-commander shares your sentiments,' said the Executioner. 'Accordingly, the *Kisertet*'s shipmaster has set a mission timeframe of ten hours before she begins an orbital bombardment of the hulk, survivors or not.'

'There are many unresolved variables,' said Imre flatly. 'Too much is undefined. How are we certain any we seek remain alive?'

'Brother Adomar?' Ralon looked to the psyker.

'I have seen it,' said the Silver Skull. 'There is one with the sight to guide through the Sea of Souls who yet lives upon the surface. A child without a crown, taken by storms of great rage. Fate showed me five who swam beneath the cowl to seek him out, but the storms are bladed, and much blood will be shed.'

Grytt regarded Adomar. *A Prognosticator?* He had heard tell of entire crusades being abandoned by the Silver Skulls based upon such vague divinations…

'Our losses?' asked Ralon.

'They are… acceptable,' Adomar replied, his gaze never leaving the planet's flickering image.

'Squad leader, I object,' said Kitra. 'If this is to be a covert infiltration and extraction of the asset, the Imperial Fist poses an unacceptable risk. I have reviewed his combat record. He is reckless, and will expose us to an ork warhost of which we know neither size nor capability. We are the razor's edge, not a cudgel. His antics will see us dead.'

'My apologies, cousin,' Grytt's eyes narrowed. 'I like my enemies to fall down when I hit them.'

'Oh, yes, very good. Why not enact Exterminatus upon every world our enemies touch? Destroy everything around us so that we might be the lords and kings of cinders.'

'Enough,' said Ralon. 'I will not suffer this. We are elite, and your bickering like neophytes shames your Chapters. Prepare for drop pod deployment. Operations commence in two hours. Anything else?'

'Yes,' said Grytt. 'I need a weapon.'

'Come, my child,' his mother cooed, extending her hand. 'Follow me.'

Sai recoiled, uncertain. Her voice was fluid, unusual. It was not threaded with the iron calm it had always possessed. He was suddenly afraid.

'*Come with me now,*' she said, her voice deepening. 'DO NOT DISOBEY.'

The light in Lady Trigarta's eyes blackened, shrinking and turning the shade of old blood. Veins of dark ivy bloomed over her skin like ink through water. Her skull groaned and stretched, reforming into a squat plug sheathed in ochre-green flesh. Tusks of yellowed bone burst from her lipless maw, broken and etched with crude iconography.

Sai turned to run, but brutish hands seized him. They grabbed hold, spinning him roughly. The thing was massive, growing larger and larger, crushing him in its grip.

It roared, its language an incomprehensible dirge of alien rage. Sai's hands slapped to his ears as the creature shook him. His headdress tumbled away, and though his mundane eyes were screwed shut, wreathed in tears, his other eye snapped open, blinding everything in a searing corona of light–

Sai awoke with a start, drenched in cold sweat.

He saw only darkness, briefly illuminated by flickering sparks that did nothing to tell him where he was. He heard water dripping, and the disjointed thrum of engines in desperate need of repair.

His third eye throbbed in rhythm with his heart. He lifted his head and felt a heavy weight upon it. A cage of rough iron was bolted around his skull. Panic seized hold of him. His face was crusted with dried blood.

Sai reached out. Searing pain shot through his arms as he tried to move, every shift bringing fresh agony. His arms were locked out to his sides. He turned his head, and saw lengths of iron rebar driven through his wrists, pinning him like an insect for study.

A knot of haphazard machinery erupted in a cascade of sparks, throwing brief light into the chamber. Sai saw a cavern of rock, threaded with piping and junkyard steel. Crude pictographs and graffiti covered the walls. Ramshackle devices rumbled and ticked, operating in defiance of any mechanical logic. It resembled some cruel lunatic's nightmarish laboratory.

It was then that Sai heard breathing. Deep, laboured and pained, like that of a wounded beast. Plodding footsteps closed on the Navigator, and a blinding light stole his sight.

When his eyes adjusted, Sai screamed as he beheld a creature standing inches away from him. It was the thing from his nightmare, massive and green, with beady crimson eyes glaring from a sloping brow. A crown of crackling electrodes, which sparked and linked with crimson lightning, was screwed into its skull. Totems and metal tools clinked from hooks on the apron of crude sackcloth it wore, and it leaned heavily upon a staff of rusted iron topped with a cluster of smouldering human skulls.

Sai's memories returned, riding a wave of throbbing pressure boiling within his skull. *The dust. The crash. Crawling through the wreckage, hearing the bestial howl of the things rampaging through the city. Struggling against green hands, opening his eye–*

His blood froze.

What his eye had done to them. They knew what he was.

Sai looked up, and the ork returned his gaze with an uncouth, bestial grin.

The drop pod hurtled through the tortured skies of Basatani like a drop of oil through smoke. The pod jinked and rolled, buffeted by ash tempests that spanned continents. Within, the kill team made their final preparations for planetfall.

'Brother Grytt,' said Imre, 'your Chapter engaged the xenos in this system.' It was a statement, not a question.

'Yes,' Grytt replied. 'It was my last action before being seconded here. My company is entrenched against the greenskins at the system's core, where we believed the flagship of the orks was located. We boarded their ships to cripple them and destroy their leadership. Without a clear ruler, it was surmised that the horde would fall to infighting and scatter.'

He glanced around the confines of the pod for a moment, then back to the deck.

'We destroyed much of their armada, but they were too many. At great cost we destroyed the flagship, but the rest scattered across the system before we could intercept them all. This hulk was among them, and may carry the one who has taken up the mantle to lead the xenos.'

'You were among the warriors who assaulted the flagship?' asked Imre. 'An achievement.'

'It would have been if any of the brothers you commanded got out alive,' Kitra muttered.

Grytt ignored the Reviler, his gaze meeting that of the servo-skull stowed before him. His scars itched beneath his helm.

'Irrelevant,' said Imre. 'Sacrifice will be necessary to contain this outbreak. These xenos are cunning for their race.'

Grytt remembered the fighting in the tunnels. Extracting the gene-seed of the fallen. Regrouping with the fleet as the flagship burned, hearing the rumours of him being considered to lead the company in the wake of Kyradon's death. He shook his head, and focussed.

'These orks are ferocious fighters,' replied Grytt. 'Only

superior strength will crush them. We will be engaged below, and the wrath of Dorn will be waiting for them.'

'We require speed and stealth here, brothers,' said Ralon. 'We hit, pick up any traces from the Navigator Houses, and avoid detection by the xenos. If there are no survivors to extract for the Navis Nobilite, we leave before the greenskins know we were ever there. Let the ship purify the site from orbit.'

'What of the civilian population?' asked Adomar.

'Not our concern,' replied the Executioner. 'This is a fast operation, Almuta, quiet and by the numbers.' His helm turned to Grytt, nodding to the Devastator's stowed weapon. 'You fire that thing without my sanction, and we will have a problem.'

The Imperial Fist nodded, his gaze returning to the skull. 'As you wish, brother.'

The kill team stepped from the drop pod and into the devastation of the city. Ash covered everything like filthy snow, swirling about in drifts at the whims of the howling storms. The sky was black, lanced through with lightning as thunderheads clashed and cast everything in eerie twilight. The dense ashfall marred the armour of the Space Marines, until they resembled living statues advancing through the streets.

Visibility was limited to just a few yards, the auspex crowded with ghosts and false returns. Hab blocks collapsed into heaps of rubble. Any walls that remained standing were vandalised with crude greenskin graffiti. Statues of Imperial saints, and even the Emperor Himself, were torn down and defaced, their faces daubed green. In the distance, pillars of smoke and heat haze curled up from the base of the hulk with the distant din of fledgling greenskin industry.

Uneven mounds of ash littered the streets. Wind swept over a cluster of them, revealing bodies, and pieces of bodies. The level of mutilation cast objective doubt on whether or not the remains had ever been human.

The Space Marines formed a chevron, Kitra stalking ahead on point, Grytt and Imre anchoring the flanks. Grytt's servo-skull rose above them, the spotter bobbing and swaying in the crosswind. The Imperial Fist unlimbered his new weapon, chambering a round with a deep *clunk*.

The Valedictio pattern frag cannon was a massive automatic grenade launcher larger than a heavy bolter. Twin ammunition belts fed from a hopper on Grytt's backpack into the cannon, along with power cabling feeds to his armour. With modifications performed in the armoury, he mixed the belt feeds with solid rounds for soft targets and fragmentation shells designed to obliterate harder defences.

'Remember what I said,' warned Ralon. 'Fast and quiet.'

'Tell that to the orks,' replied Grytt, his voice a metallic growl through his visor.

The servo-skull chirped, the pict feed translating over the Devastator's right eye-lens.

'I've got something,' he said. The team split, taking cover on both sides of the avenue.

'Show me,' Ralon replied.

Grytt twinned the feed to the commander. 'North of us. Ork infantry, two light vehicles.'

'There's something else...'

'Those are civilians,' answered Grytt, watching the

procession of grey figures stumbling through the ash. 'They are rounding up survivors. Forced labour, or sport killing.'

'We should shadow them,' said Kitra. 'They could lead us right into the hulk.'

'Seconded,' said Imre.

'Agreed,' replied Ralon. 'Keep your distance, follow them in. No one fires unless I give the order.'

Grytt guided the servo-skull closer, magnifying the image. The forced march had stalled, as a man scrambled away after somehow breaking free from the group.

The poor human cried out as a blast took his leg off at the knee. He crashed into the ash, blood pulsing from the stump and rendering the ground into a sticky loam. The ork stomped down on his remaining leg, snapping bone and tearing a scream from the man's throat that Grytt heard through the spotter's pickups.

The ork reached down, its clawed fist closing over the man's head. It wrenched its hand back and threw something into the street. The feed flickered with static. It refocussed, and Grytt watched the ork stomp back to the column, the man's corpse left mangled in the dust.

Another greenskin approached, grunting a challenge to the first. Punches were thrown, and the two brawled in the dust, with the first beating the other severely before casting it back to the column to vent its frustration on the other prisoners. Grytt narrowed his eyes, linking targeting runes to the orks and blinking away the spotter feed as three shots rang out.

The ork threw its pistol aside as it clicked empty, and was raising a rusted cleaver when Grytt opened fire. Standing braced in the centre of the street, he unleashed a blistering salvo from his frag cannon. High-explosive shells slashed out into the two ork vehicles in deafening thunder, rupturing their dilapidated construction and littering the ground with chunks of greenskin flesh.

'Grytt, you fool,' barked Kitra. 'You'll expose us!'

The surviving orks turned to respond before solid shot rounds burst their bodies apart, leaving nothing but twitching lumps of meat. Silence descended as smoke mingled with the ash.

The Imperial Fist approached the trembling column of humans, and snapped the length of chain binding them together. The moaning wretches blundered about, unable to focus upon anything or anyone. They scrambled away in every direction. Grytt reached down to lift one up who was sprawled in the dust. The woman recoiled back, howling and clawing at his arm. Nothing human remained in her wide, unfocussed eyes, just the frenzied instinct of an animal to survive. He released her and she fled into the ruins.

'Brother Rodricus Grytt,' Ralon called out and he strode forwards, rapping an accusing fist against the Devastator's chest. 'You are hereby marked for disciplinary flagellation. Your actions have endangered–'

'You would rather watch these people be butchered?' Grytt demanded. 'We are the protectors of Humanity. I will not sit idle while they are slaughtered by these xenos filth.'

'If you seek more greenskins to combat,' said Imre, looking up into the sky. 'You have guaranteed it.'

Flares corkscrewed into the air between the kill team and the ork hulk, exploding in greasy bursts of red and yellow smoke. Roars sounded in the distance, a bestial overlapping din with no unity or rhythm.

Artillery burst behind the kill team.

'They have our position,' said Adomar, racking the slide of his boltgun.

Hundreds of orks poured in towards the avenue, whooping and firing weapons into the air. Their charge grew louder, shaking loose rubble and drowning out all sound in its terrible tumult.

'Displace!' barked Imre, pointing to an alleyway beside them. 'Through the buildings. I will draw their fire.'

A rocket jinked past their position, exploding in the second floor of a hab block and spraying them with debris.

'Go now!' The Iron Hand stood, snapping off precision shots from his plasma gun. The kill team crossed the open street and began moving through the building.

Imre sighted down his rifle, each shot taking the head from a screaming ork. He staggered as a solid round smashed into his shoulder. He leaned forwards and vaporised the greenskin's torso.

Kitra took up a firing position in a doorway.

'Imre, I have you covered!'

The Iron Hand rose, firing his plasma gun into the swelling lines of orks and moving to a mound of shattered masonry in the middle of the street. He made to advance as another pair of rockets corkscrewed into the mound, exploding in a hail of smoke and shrapnel.

'Brother!' Kitra shouted, unable to see the Iron Hand through the smoke. A barrage of artillery howled through the air, and Ralon pulled the Reviler back as the front of the building collapsed, cutting them off from the street.

Imre staggered against the road, his war-plate sundered and covered in ash-clotted blood. He made to rise, but reeled as the orks bracketed him with weapons fire. A grenade exploded, throwing him back to the ground. He rolled to his knees but toppled, his right leg nothing but a shredded stump of fused flesh and plasteel.

The orks surged forwards. Imre's armour shattered under the fusillade of their guns.

He fired a blast into the mob as it encircled him, bringing cleavers and hatchet blades down and kicking the weapon from his grasp. His multi-lung was filling with blood, and his secondary heart had ceased to beat.

Imre faced the glaring maw of a massive ork chieftain. The brute drew a serrated axe, and drove it down into the Space Marine's side as the mob roared. The Iron Hand reached out with his cybernetic hand, fighting through the storm of blades and punches to reach for his fallen plasma gun. The weapon's barrel glowed from rapid firing, and its plasma coils writhed with the unstable energy building within.

The Iron Hand grabbed hold of the weapon as a cudgel smashed into his head. Blind, he cradled the weapon to his chest, overcharging it. The plasma coils shivered and sparked, groaning with inevitable overload.

'The flesh...' Imre choked, his voice wet with blood and oil, '...is weak.'

Reaching for the plasma coil, Imre crushed it in his fist, and the street vanished in a starburst of azure light.

Grytt watched the explosion from the overloaded plasma weapon in the static-laden pict feed of his servo-skull, as Imre's ident-rune blinked out on his display.

Kitra's fist pistoned into Grytt's jaw, knocking him back. Grytt swung back but the Reviler dodged, ducking to swing around behind him. The Imperial Fist managed to seize hold of Kitra and throw him against the crumbling wall of a hab stack with a thunderous crash.

Grytt heard the click of a bolt pistol as he took a step forwards, and felt the weapon press against the back of his head.

'That. Is. Enough,' growled Ralon.

'Dead,' Kitra coughed, pulling his helmet free and spitting a mouthful of blood onto the ash. 'Imre is dead because of you.'

'I don't see much else but death here,' said Grytt. 'Though it seems I am the only one doing anything to avenge it.'

'Blood and fire is all you want,' the Reviler hissed. 'You're no different from the orks.'

'I am here to kill the xenos!' Grytt roared. 'Blood and fire is all they understand. I will finish what my Chapter started and break the back of this horde, and keep the rest of this system from burning. Our focus should be on ending an invasion that threatens billions now, not blundering about this wasteland chasing ghosts.'

Ralon seized Grytt by the collar and hauled his face only inches from his own, the bolt pistol now resting beneath the Devastator's jaw.

'Go against my orders again, Fist, and by the Throne I will kill you myself.' He released him with a shove. 'We need to displace now, before the hell you have unleashed encircles us.'

'Brothers,' Adomar called from the avenue outside the tenement. Ralon pulled Kitra to his feet, and the kill team converged on the Prognosticator, kneeling in the ash.

'What have you found?' asked Ralon, taking the object that Adomar held out to him.

It was an elaborate helm, small even for a mortal,

resembling a pair of angels with broken wings. It bore the heraldry of House Trigarta.

'This was worn by the one we seek,' said Adomar, rising to his feet. 'He lives, and his soul-echoes will lead us to the hulk. We will find him within.' He turned to Grytt. 'It seems that all shall have what they desire.'

Sai cried out, struggling against his bonds to recoil from the leering ork. He hissed as once again it twisted the jagged metal pinning him in place, and he felt warm blood trickle across his wrists as the wounds reopened.

The ork gave a gurgling, choking laugh at the Navigator's suffering as it leaned closer. The beady red eyes of the creature widened and glazed over, as if filling with cataracts.

Sai screamed. He had felt others step within his mind in his training, but never like this. Where his mentors had slipped beneath his consciousness like warm oil behind his eyes, the ork's intrusion was tantamount to dashing his head open against a rock and prying his skull apart. Images stabbed into Sai's mind, jagged and edged in barbs of black malice and ochre rage.

He saw himself, screaming silently from within an iron casket, his third eye pried open by savage hooks and staring out into the void.

Vertigo and nausea soaked into Sai as the vision became rippled and unfocussed. With a stab of heat to his mind it resolved again. *The casket was bolted onto the prow of the xenos hulk ship like a barbaric figurehead. The hulk ploughed through the void, tearing free of Basatani's gravity. Lightning coursed through Sai within the casket, and blood streamed from his warp-eye even as reality itself began to bleed in response. A rift opened like claws tearing through the curtain of stars, and billions of hands reached out, hauling the hulk into the roiling insanity of the warp...*

They meant to use him to take the ship back into the Sea of Souls. The ork's savage grin grew wider.

A roar thundered up from deeper within the hulk, issuing from a single throat but of unbelievable depth and volume. Bolts of sickly colour shot through the meat of Sai's mind, flashes of bright fear and panic. The ork psyker tore its mind from his like a rusted blade. The Navigator collapsed against his bonds in horror and exhaustion.

The greenskin scrambled back from Sai's hanging form, barking at the gaggle of minions toiling within the chamber. It issued growling, threatening noises to its underlings, who recoiled from it and their captive, fearing him despite the cage of iron fastened about his head.

Sai looked down, watching in horror as the alien brutes continued their crude construction below him, locking rebar and metal framework around his legs and torso.

They were building the iron casket from his visions.

'Stand by,' said Ralon through the static of the vox. 'Now!'

Grytt blink-clicked a rune on his retinal display, relaying the signal to his spotter. A booming detonation engulfed the side of the hulk, sending smoke and debris soaring into the sky.

The kill team crouched some distance away, near a narrow trench carved into the rocky hull of the ork war craft. Kitra had set the breaching charges near one of the main points of entry before rejoining Almuta.

Flares burst over the site of the explosion, and the Space Marines watched as hordes of greenskins converged on the area.

'That won't buy us much time,' said Grytt. He received no response from the rest of the team.

'Kitra, take point,' said Ralon. 'Adomar, behind him. I need you to track any trace of the asset. Let's move.'

The kill team advanced into the tunnel. Grytt blinked rapidly, and his visor cycled to thermal vision. His servo-skull flittered above his shoulder, its sensors pulsing scarlet in the darkness.

The tunnel wound into the hulk, threaded with sporadic steel grating and coils of exhaust piping. The machinery was decrepit and volatile, remaining functional seemingly out of spite alone. The air grew hotter as they went, and Grytt tasted smoke and scorched iron through the filters of his helm.

As the temperature increased, so did the noise. Greenskin industry was a frightful cacophony of tearing metal, smashing hammers and the howls of thousands of orks as they laboured, along with the enslaved population of the hive, to restore the colossal ship.

'Adomar, do you sense anything?' asked Ralon as the team stalked past a massive factory cavern, reaching a junction in the tunnel.

The Silver Skull paused, and frost crept over his armour, carving runnels down the ash-caked plate as it melted again in the heat.

'He is close,' said the psyker distractedly. 'There is something else with him. A presence. The warp channels through it, but it is unrestrained, like a wildfire. It wields great power, but the power is killing it.'

'I have encountered ork psykers before,' said Kitra. 'We must be on our guard. Their power swells from combat. I have seen them tear entire armies apart.'

'This way,' whispered Adomar.

The kill team proceeded down a branch of the tunnel, leading to a cavern filled with bizarre machinery. A pillar of iron scaffolding dominated the centre of the cave, with a crowd of orks gathered around, toiling at its construction. A slumped human form could barely be seen within the pillar, pinned in place in a cruciform position.

The chamber filled with booming boltgun fire as the kill team opened up on the orks within and slaughtered them. Unarmed, the brutes had little chance and were quickly reduced to broken, twitching corpses.

'The ork psyker,' asked Kitra, panning his stalker boltgun from corner to corner. 'Where is it?'

'That device in the centre imprisons the Navigator,' said Adomar, pointing with his power sword. The Librarian stared up at the maniacal contraption. 'What *is* this? By the Throne, what were they building?'

'Do not seek to understand the xenos,' said Grytt. 'They are filth to be eradicated, not studied.'

'We need to cut him loose and withdraw,' said Ralon. 'We are running out of time.'

'No,' said Kitra, as once more they heard the howling of alien throats. 'We are already out of time.'

Kill Team Almuta formed into a firing line as fresh mobs of ork warriors approached.

Kitra braced his boltgun to his shoulder, poised as still as a statue as he sighted through the weapon's scope. Ralon's power axe shone blue in the hellish light as he loaded a full magazine into his bolt pistol. Adomar channelled his energy into the psychic core of his force sword, and mauve energy shivered up its blade.

They watched the flickering light of the tunnel fill with

monstrous silhouettes. Gunfire thundered, and howling, wailing roars split the air. Grytt chambered a round into his frag cannon, and squared up alongside Ralon as the orks emerged.

Bolter rounds zipped through the flickering dark, a stuttering report as each one fired before detonating within greenskin flesh. Orks burst apart in welters of foul blood. Limbs swung orphaned through the air, still clutching rusted blades and decrepit firearms. Fyceline smoke filled the cavern, rolling about the ceiling like drifting spirits as filthy xenos innards covered the walls.

Grytt's retinal display swelled with locked targeting icons. Thumbing the safety from his frag cannon and bracing in a wide stance, he fired a burst of solid shot rounds with a booming *chunk! chunk! chunk!*

The screaming anti-personnel shells tore through ranks of orks, coring torsos in clouds of pink mist. The fusillade killed dozens of the brutish xenos, and twice that number fell mewling and wounded on the ground, left to the mercy of their fellows who trampled them to death in their eagerness to close with the enemy.

Kitra fired the last round in his magazine and stowed his boltgun. Lightning claws slid out from the Reviler's gauntlets, writhing with energy. He wove through the onslaught, striking in and out of range, slashing orks to ribbons with each strike of the energised talons. Ralon's axe flared with each killing strike, the glowing blade fizzing and popping as alien blood boiled from its power field.

Adomar carved into the orks, his power sword wreathed in warpfire. Seeing the xenos' attacks with his mind's eye heartbeats before they occurred, he drove through their ranks, his strikes scorching swathes of the creatures with unnatural energies until the flesh ran from their bones like tallow.

Grytt smashed a greenskin aside with the barrel of his cannon, firing point blank into the horde. He stopped picking shots and fired on full automatic, blasting away the roiling host of screaming xenos as if he were tearing chunks from a mountain.

The orks faltered against the weight of fire, until a roar tore down the length of the tunnel, so loud that many of the aliens stumbled from their feet in alarm. The rest brayed, whooping and barking challenges at the Space Marines.

Their leader revealed itself.

The ork chieftain was massive, stomping head and shoulders above the rest of its kind. Veins the size of a man's arm branched over iron-hard muscle, and dense plates of armour covered the creature's body, riveted directly into its flesh. Steel horns had been drilled into its skull and curled out in all directions, their jagged tips sharpened into killing points. Scarlet eyes burned below its sloping brow, furnace-hot with alien rage. Both of its hands had been crudely removed, replaced by enormous pneumatic claws that gushed oil and crackled with caged lightning.

'Adomar,' said Ralon, his voice an anchor of calm. 'Extract the asset from the xenos device, and take care you don't kill him doing it. Kitra, find me an exit, and kill anything in front of you. Grytt, you and I will attend to this beast.'

Grytt set his stance wide and low, and levelled his frag cannon at the greenskin warlord. 'This time, xenos filth, you won't go crawling away into the dark to hide.'

The warboss stopped and roared as the warhost of ork warriors gathered behind it.

The Space Marines braced. Kitra and Adomar leapt to their tasks, while Grytt and Ralon stood before the warboss.

'Grytt, we strike together,' said Ralon, his eyes locked on the hulking monstrosity. 'I'll circle to the right, draw its–'

'Just kill it!' bellowed Grytt, firing a burst from his frag cannon. 'Die now, filth. Face the judgment of Dorn, and the Emperor!'

The solid rounds clanged and ricocheted from the warboss' armour, smacking into the walls and slaying the orks behind it. Those rounds that found flesh burst through in ragged wounds, enraging the alien chieftain further.

In three massive strides, the warboss covered the distance to the Devastator and smashed him into the air with a single sweep of its claws.

Grytt landed hard against the far wall and crashed to the floor. His retinal display blacked out and reset, clouded with static. He blinked blood from his eyes, searching for his spotter. The servo-skull was lost in the smoke, its feed to his display cut.

The Imperial Fist pushed himself to his knees as Ralon leapt through the air to land on the ork's shoulders. Each slash of the commander's axe cleaved iron horns from the warboss' crown as he blasted down at its face with his bolt pistol.

The warboss bucked, twisting to shake the Executioner off. Ralon reared back and buried his axe in the alien's forehead in a spray of dark blood. The xenos swung with the blow, catching the Space Marine off balance. Then it grabbed Ralon in its claws and, without apparent effort, tore him bodily in half.

A cry of rage tore from Grytt's throat as he stood on shaking legs. The warboss turned, throwing the Executioner's remains aside, and stomped towards him. Grytt fired at the charging ork, targeting the breaches in its armour. With a howl of rage, the xenos reared back as an explosive round detonated, blowing one of its claws apart in a burst of flame and bloody shrapnel.

Swinging the ragged stump like a club, the warboss smashed Grytt to the deck once again and seized him with its remaining claw. Raising the Imperial Fist to its frothing, roaring maw, it squeezed. Pistons and crude hydraulics in the claw's talons crushed Grytt's armour, and he felt the overlapping plates of ceramite grind and snap under the titanic strain.

Unable to free his frag cannon from the ork's monstrous grip, Grytt pulled his combat blade, slashing at the bundles of wires and hydraulic feeds weaving over the claw. The hoses snapped, spraying oil and brackish fluid like crazed serpents, but still the claw closed tighter.

Grytt felt his vision narrow as the force overwhelmed him, when his retinal display blinked, reconnecting him with the feed from his servo-skull. Grytt saw the arch of stone the warboss lumbered beneath, dust and debris falling from it with each thunderous step.

Grytt chambered a burst of high explosive rounds, and strained to aim his frag cannon's barrel at the ork's legs. He fired, snarling as the blast also sent shards of metal and stone through his own armoured greaves, but felt the ork's claw relax a fraction as it howled in pain.

He kicked away, freeing himself and landing with a crash on his back. He raised the cannon to the cracked stone of the archway over them.

'To the abyss with you, filth!' Grytt fired, obliterating the arch and burying both him and the ork warlord beneath an avalanche of ruined masonry.

He wheezed, blinking away the procession of urgent runes spilling over his visor display. He squinted, looking through the intermittent feed of the servo-skull. A heap of broken stone covered him and the ork, wreathed in clinging ghosts of smoke and dust.

Grunting with effort, he pushed forwards through the pile, dragging himself towards the flickering light. Razor-edged fragments gouged his plate and scraped the enamel from his armour. The fibre-bundle musculature of his left leg was shredded, and the armour hung as a dead weight.

Grytt punched through, and dragged himself free from the rubble.

The mound of rock shuddered, rolling away as the head of the warboss also pushed free, howling as it thrashed to right itself. It clamped its sparking claw around Grytt's leg, dragging the Space Marine back towards it.

Grytt rolled in its grip, levelling his frag cannon at the beast, and fired.

But the weapon only clunked with an uneven cough.

He wrenched furiously at the firing mechanism, fighting to clear the jam as the ork pulled him closer. With a bark, Grytt expelled a dented shell from the weapon's breech, and fired again. The shell screamed from the cannon in a blast of fire and smoke, striking the warboss in the gape of its maw. The high explosive round ruptured the ork's skull, detonating in a shower of blood and rancid meat.

The Devastator lowered the smoking barrel of the

cannon, dragging deep breaths through his helm as the rusted claw went slack.

'So must the fate of all xenos be.'

Kitra ducked beneath an ork swinging a club of jagged metal and cleaved upwards, splitting the creature from hip to neck with his lightning claws. He leapt onto a gantry, scanning the chamber for a viable exit.

Adomar stood before the half-constructed tomb for the trapped Navigator. The air froze, and ice formed over the metal as the Silver Skull began to tear it apart with his mind. He stripped away plates of iron, taking care not to harm the youth within. Clearing the framework away from the boy's unconscious form, Adomar slid the lengths of rebar spike from the Navigator's arms, and caught him as he fell.

'Brothers,' said Adomar. 'I have him. He yet lives.'

'And I have located a pathway that should lead out of the hulk,' said Kitra. 'Awaiting team leader's confirmation.'

'Ralon has fallen,' Grytt responded over the vox, firing a high explosive round to collapse the tunnel behind him. *'We need to withdraw now. The* Kisertet *will begin its bombardment in minutes.'*

Kitra growled. 'Have you no respect for the dead, Fist?' He loomed before the Devastator as they met with Adomar at the centre of the chamber. 'Another brother lost for your recklessness. Is there no end to–'

The Reviler's words were drowned by a choking cry as he was enveloped in scarlet lightning. Kitra thrashed as he rose into the air and hurtled into a control panel in a shower of sparks.

The ork psyker emerged from the smoke of the burning chamber, uncouth rage ticking tremors across its face.

Grytt bellowed wordlessly, firing a burst from his frag cannon.

The ork did not move. The shells froze, tumbling slowly around the greenskin, before shooting off in different directions to frame the xenos in bursts of fire and shrapnel.

'See to him!' cried Adomar, passing the Navigator to Grytt and charging the ork, his sword burning with psychic flame.

The two psykers clashed in a thunderclap of warring energies. Adomar parried a blow from the ork's staff, rolling his wrists and slashing across the alien's chest. Blood boiled from the wound, and the creature howled in anger, its scream a sonic blast that threw Adomar from his feet.

The ork leapt towards the prone psyker, deflecting a shell fired from Grytt's cannon with a thought and sending it spiralling back towards him. The round exploded at the Devastator's feet, throwing him through the air to crash hard against the ground.

Landing before Adomar, the xenos plucked a crooked dagger from its belt, the rusted blade writhing with poisonous energy. The greenskin slashed the dagger into Adomar's chest, again and again. He made to drive the blade down into the Space Marine's throat, but stopped as the temperature in the chamber plummeted.

Standing silently beside the xenos psyker was Sai of House Trigarta.

The ork growled as it glared down upon him, enraged by his escape. Adomar rolled free, turning his back to the boy.

Slowly, the lid of Sai's third eye quivered free of its crust of dried blood and drew back, locking the alien's gaze with the forbidden sight of his mutation.

The greenskin's eyes widened, their blazing red hue drowned in blackness so complete that light could not escape their surface. The flesh shivered and bulged. With a moist pop, they melted down its face, revealing undulating rifts into the warp within the sunken pits.

Billions of tiny writhing claws tore into the dumbstruck beast, pulling it into the gashes in reality. Flesh ripped liked oiled sackcloth and bones gave way with a sickening crack as it was pulled into the impossibly small rifts. A howl of incomprehensible agony tore from the greenskin's throat as the warp devoured it, the steaming coils of its entrails streaming up and into oblivion in shrieks of flash-frying blood.

The ork's screams died as its throat tore away, pulled into the abyss. The creature's skull broke in half as it was sucked into the portals, leaving two glowing tears in reality floating in the chamber.

Flickering with lightning, the rifts coalesced into a gateway to the Immaterium. Ribbons of nightmarish colour pressed against the thinning veil between the real and unreal, clawed things made from anguish and fury desperate to breach the material realm. Liquid madness began to stretch the portal wider, eager to feast.

'Grytt,' said Adomar weakly, reaching towards the Navigator. The Imperial Fist stood, ignoring the stabbing pains shooting through his body, and limped to the boy.

Sai stared up at the undulating doorway, looking at things that only he could see shimmering before him. Mandalas of pulsing light collapsed and reformed again, flickering in and out of focus.

'Come, my child…' a million unholy voices sang to him. *'There is so much for you to see…'*

Sai took a step forwards, blood flowing from his mundane eyes, and reached for the rift.

Grytt seized hold of the boy, and clamped his hand over the Navigator's eye. A billion cries lashed out from the rift as it seized and withered. Lightning the colour of shame and ecstasy burst from the rapidly diminishing ball of unreality, before coalescing into a sphere of black glass. The sphere hovered in the air for a moment, before dropping and shattering against the ground. The shards twitched with a clink before boiling away into a muffled thunderclap of sparking mist.

Grytt staggered as Sai collapsed, barely managing to get an arm under him. Adomar pushed himself to his feet and, with Kitra supporting him, the Space Marines took flight.

The kill team sprinted through the tunnels of the ork hulk as the chrono chimed down. Grytt stopped at junctions and intersections, blasting the hordes of pursuing greenskins and collapsing tunnel walls to bury the howling xenos beneath tons of rock. He fired the frag cannon one-handed, cradling Sai's unconscious form in the other.

The Space Marines charged through the hulk and into the crash site beyond, ash streaming from their armour as they ran.

Adomar collapsed. At his side, Kitra hauled him to his knees again, though this time his hands came away slick with blood.

'Brother,' whispered Kitra.

The Silver Skull removed his helm with a hiss of venting air pressure, the tattooed face beneath a scarlet mask of blood.

'You cannot tarry. Go, now. Leave me.'

'Tell me,' said Kitra, breathless, 'are these acceptable losses?'

Adomar laughed, a wet choke of blood between his teeth.

'We are dead from the moment we ascend to the ranks of the Adeptus Astartes, Reviler. Even more so when we take the oaths of the Deathwatch. Death is our only destiny, and no loss is too high to eclipse the scale of duty.'

The chrono in Grytt's helm beeped. Four minutes remained. The ground began to shake with the tread of raging orks.

'Go, damn you!' Adomar hissed, driving his sword into the ground and leaning his weight against it. 'See our mission done, and ensure that the blood drunk by the soil of this world was not shed for nothing.'

'By Dorn, your sacrifice shall never be forgotten, brother.' Grytt hammered a fist to his breastplate.

'Die well, son of Varsavia,' said Kitra as he turned away.

Adomar laughed again.

'I shall, brother. And not alone.'

Grytt and Kitra set off to the extraction point at a run. Adomar set his helm in the dust beside him, and watched the street fill with howling greenskins. A growl built in his throat, and a crackling nimbus of light blinked into existence around him.

His growl became a cry, as stones and rubble lifted from the ground, floating and chaining with lightning around the psyker. His eyes narrowed as the orks drew within a few paces, a sea of berserker fury.

The midnight lacquer on the Space Marine's armour boiled away, exposing the bare silver ceramite of the war-plate. Adomar roared, and a blinding light slashed out from his eyes, curling around him as the nimbus of lightning spasmed and swelled. The horde of fury raced towards the boiling wall of energy.

The first ork brushed against the veil, and the avenue vanished in a searing flash. Lightning exploded in strobes of crackling death, the greenskins vaporising and bursting like sacks of jellied meat.

Adomar of the Silver Skulls felt his body boil away, and plunged into the waiting darkness.

Grytt felt the shockwave as it burst through the air, throwing him and Kitra forwards. The Imperial Fist turned, sheltering Sai's body as he fell. He crashed into the wreckage of a ground carriage, his retinal display awash with static and frenzied warning icons. His helm crumpled, the left eyepiece torn away by the impact. He wrenched the helmet free and locked it to his belt.

Hands gripped his shoulder and lifted him to his knees.

'No time for rest, brother,' said Kitra, extending his hand.

Grytt gripped the Reviler by the wrist and stood, lifting Sai from the ground. He punched the release stud of his harness, shrugging the depleted ammunition hopper from his back and dropping it to the dust. Locking the frag cannon to his back, Grytt caught a bolt pistol tossed to him by Kitra, and the two warriors charged down the avenue to the extraction site as the remaining minutes burned away.

Grytt ducked reflexively as an ebon Thunderhawk screamed low over their heads, its retros shrieking as it cut a tight blistering arc to slow at a city courtyard. The gunship hovered over the rubble as the Space Marines sprinted to it, pintle-mounted heavy bolters blasting away at the hordes of pursuing orks.

The embarkation ramp of the gunship lowered as they approached. Kitra leapt up, turning to take hold of the Navigator as Grytt gripped the edge.

A rocket spiralled towards the Thunderhawk, and the gunship swayed aside as the missile flashed over it. Grytt snarled as he clung to the ramp, hearing the chrono in his collar chime.

'Get airborne now!' shouted Grytt, hauling himself up as the Thunderhawk hurtled into the sky. He swung his legs onto the ramp, and Kitra dragged him up as the craft rocketed, rolling and blasting up into orbit.

'*Grab hold of something,*' the pilot called over the vox. '*They've initiated the bombardment already!*'

Grytt and Kitra locked themselves into restraint thrones in the forward hold and secured the Navigator. The gunship wrenched to the side as the first streaking lines of the orbital strike lit up the sky, pushing its engines beyond their tolerances to put distance from the surface.

Fulgurant streaks of light burned through the ash storms, lancing down like the defied fury of the Emperor Himself. The hulk caught fire as the orbital bombardment struck its surface, burning as lance strikes sliced into it. Mass drivers smashed down, blasting the xenos ship to atoms in thunderous detonations that filled the sky with flame. The orks within were boiled alive as bolts of plasma liquefied the craft, and devastating ordnance shattered the ruins of Pomarii. Explosions burst over the surface as the Imperium of Man avenged the death of its subjects with fire and blood.

* * *

Waves of fire and plasma swept the continent, burning the surface to glass. Anything living on the surface, human or greenskin, was obliterated in the searing conflagration. The ash storms amplified, swelling larger and surging across the planet as they drank in the ruin.

Grytt glanced down at Sai, the young Navigator twitching in the throes of some unknown nightmare. It would not be his last, Grytt thought as he tightened the medical dressing obscuring the boy's mutation.

Then he looked from the viewport down at the devastation as they climbed through the upper reaches of Basatani's atmosphere. The ork hulk was gone, the site of its impact nothing more than an irradiated crater of scorched rock. The city was shattered further as another bombardment began. Soon nothing would remain but glass and slag scattered over a scorched open graveyard. His gaze shifted to the Navigator, then his ever-watchful servo-skull, caked in ash and scorched from battle.

Grytt knew at that moment that his decision to join the Deathwatch had been right. The bloodshed below had not freed him of his rage, but would he have succeeded without its fire? He felt clarity descend as the ship rose into orbit, a tempering of his choler that he had never felt before.

It was not gone, but assuaged. If only briefly.

The clarity crystallised within him, a sense of understanding. He was not one to lead, never the implacable glacier of calm that Captain Kyradon of the Eighth Company had been. He was the hammer of Dorn, a weapon for sowing destruction and purging the enemies of Man into oblivion.

If his first mission with the Deathwatch were any

impression, there would be many foes to be destroyed in the time to come.

THE SILENCE

STEVE LYONS

The xenos died without ever seeing its killer.

It was lying on its stomach in the long grass at the lip of an escarpment, overlooking a natural forest path: an eldar scout with pale skin, dark eyes and sculpted cheek-bones. It wore a hooded cloak of animal hide, and had decorated its arms and face with tattoos and bone jewel-lery. It carried only a simple recurve bow.

Up close, it turned out that the bow was sculpted from wraithbone, while the arrows were tipped with explosives.

The scout hadn't moved, hadn't made a sound, for as long as Setorax had been watching. It had cloaked itself in silence – but it didn't know the silence like he did.

He approached it on his elbows, inch by painstaking inch. With each movement, he settled into position care-fully, so as not to snap any twigs or crunch any leaves beneath him. Not once had his prey so much as glanced in his direction. It probably thought it impossible for anyone to sneak up on it – least of all a fully armoured Space Marine – through foliage so dense.

Its mistake.

Setorax waited for the breeze to waft by him again, carrying with it the sounds of the distant battle. He used those sounds to cover him as he had pounced.

The first the eldar knew of his presence was when he seized it in a chokehold with his left arm, driving a knife through its back and into its heart with his right. It expired without a sound, just as he had intended.

He left the lifeless body where it lay, overlooking the path, its bow wedged against its shoulder, eyes open and staring. From a distance, anyone would think that it was still on sentry duty. No one would know that Edryc Setorax had ever been here.

There were two more sentries in the nearby trees.

Setorax had scouted their positions earlier, before dealing with their fellow on the ground. He had to be sure they wouldn't see him, or hear him, as he did what had to be done. He was deep in enemy territory. He was alone. He knew that the moment his presence here was detected, it would be the end for him.

And the eldar were famed for their keen hearing.

He slipped into the shelter of a sprawling, thorny bush, and dropped into a crouch behind it. He raised his bolt pistol and sighted along its barrel. He had a clear head shot at one of the scouts, lying across a low branch. The other was more difficult to target, higher up and nestled in the crook of a broad, gnarled trunk.

He preferred not to use the gun anyway – not until he

had to. Even suppressed, it would make too loud a noise out here.

He circled his prey, using the trees for cover. He worked his way closer, ever closer, towards their positions. It was a meticulous process, almost painfully slow, but Edryc Setorax had learned how to be patient.

At last, he made the tree in which the first scout – the one closer to the ground – lurked. He eased himself into a hollow between the tree's roots. The scout was immediately above him now. He couldn't see the xenos – it was perfectly hidden from him at this angle, as he was from it – but he knew it was there.

In a flash, he uncoiled himself to his full eight-foot height. He reached up and snatched the eldar scout from its perch. Taken by surprise, it fell backwards into his arms, and he twisted its neck until the bone snapped.

He heard a rustle in the larger tree beside him. He cast the first scout's body aside to round on the second, above him. It was just beginning to react to his sudden appearance: too slow, as he had hoped. It had nocked an explosive-tipped arrow.

Setorax fired his jump pack. He winced at its engine roar, but that could not be helped. A rapid burst was enough to propel him twenty feet up in an instant. He cannoned into the second eldar scout, splintering its arrow. He over-balanced it, and they plummeted into the soft bed of the undergrowth together.

He landed on top of his enemy, his fingers locked around its throat. It was stronger than it looked, but still utterly helpless beneath the crushing weight of Setorax's genetically enhanced bulk and heavy power armour. He crumpled the xenos' windpipe, and held it down firmly while it choked.

Like the other eldar before it, it died in silence.

Setorax listened for approaching footsteps. He heard nothing. He concealed the bodies of the scouts in a nearby bush, piling leaves on top of them for additional camouflage. As long as nobody stumbled across them, it would likely be some time before they were missed. Just like the others.

He could make up a little lost time now.

He weaved his way quickly through the forest, sure that the immediate area was clear of eyes and ears. He trusted to his armour – matt black, its silver trim deliberately dulled – to cloak him if he was wrong. He trusted his auto-senses to detect more sentries, or find their tracks, before they heard him.

Setorax was a silent shadow, flitting through the foliage.

The next marks he encountered, however, were making no attempt to hide. He heard them mustering in the centre of a clearing ahead of him. He could probably have found a way around them, but he was curious to see what they were doing.

There were thirty or more of them: eldar warriors, better equipped than the scouts, with several power blades and shuriken catapults among them. A pair of dragon riders stood out from the crowd in their sturdy but elegant wraithbone armour. They had brought their hulking, reptilian mounts with them. Setorax was careful to remain upwind of the creatures, lest they pick up his scent.

He wondered why these eldar weren't out fighting with their main force.

He could only imagine one reason. They were setting up an ambush.

He lay on his stomach, in cover at the edge of the clearing, and watched for a while. He kept an eye out for farseers among the eldar, but saw none. He knew they had to be close by, though. He had learned a great deal about the eldar's psykers on the craftworld of Yme-Loc. It was they who must have divined his kill team's approach.

Setorax had lost vox-contact with them hours ago. He couldn't warn them about what lay in store for them. He could stay where he was, though. He could wait until the ambush was almost sprung, then erupt from hiding behind his enemies and turn the tables on them.

Not this time, he thought. He had come this far behind enemy lines for a reason. He wasn't ready to reveal his presence here yet. His battle-brothers, he decided, would have to look after themselves. They were more than capable. Inquisitor Gravelyn might not like it, he thought; but then, the inquisitor need never know.

The eldar were digging a linked series of pits, setting monofilament tripwires. As ever, their traps were so subtle, so elaborate, that even a Space Marine might find himself ensnared – or at least distracted a second too long. When Setorax had seen enough, he backed away from his vantage point and circled around them.

He hadn't gone much further when he discovered the first formation.

It stood between the trees, in a spot where narrow shafts of afternoon sunlight pierced the canopy, and it sparkled in their radiance. It was four and a half feet tall, a solid slab of crystal, abstract in shape – one side was bulbous, the other almost razor-edged – but, like the eldar themselves, it was beautiful in a dark, twisted way.

Setorax found his eyes drawn to it, despite himself. He regarded his reflection, distorted by the crystal's facets. There was a suggestion of circuitry embedded within the crystal, and he thought he saw xenos machine-spirits working busily, but that might have been merely a trick of the light.

He had seen formations like this one before, on Yme-Loc and other worlds since. He knew what it was, and he knew that it was entirely organic.

It was because of this structure, and others like it, that this world was at war.

An Imperial colony fleet had arrived here, months ago. Surveys had suggested that the planet was uninhabited, an ideal site for new agricultural facilities.

The settlers had begun the process of clearing the forest, which blanketed the planet's only continent from coast to coast.

They had happened upon some of the crystal formations and, believing them to be ancient xenos ruins, had naturally razed them to make way for new construction.

That act of destruction had summoned the eldar here – or rather, back here. Theirs was an Exodite tribe, split off from their decaying civilisation millennia ago. Like many of their kind, they were nomadic. They travelled between worlds, following the seasons or merely their own whims. They hadn't returned to this world, to this forest, in many years; but nor had they abandoned it for good.

They had left their souls here.

The human settlers didn't understand that. They didn't know the eldar like Edryc Setorax knew them. All they knew was that pale, willowy, deadly figures had emerged from the trees and set upon them. They didn't know where their attackers had come from – there had been no reports of any ships approaching the planet.

They had been massacred.

And, of course, the survivors had sent a distress signal. And, of course, the Astra Militarum had despatched an Imperial Guard regiment to find out what had happened here and deal with the apparent xenos threat.

The battle had been raging for several weeks now.

The Exodites were relatively few in number, but they knew this environment well and they knew how to hide in it. The guardsmen had suffered significant losses. They had turned to the Ordo Xenos for help in understanding their foes and their tactics; and the alien hunters in turn had called in the Deathwatch.

They had brought a kill team to this world, ten members strong. One of their own inquisitors had chosen to lead it – that was how important this mission was to the order – and Edryc Setorax had been assigned to join him. He was a Raven Guard, a specialist in guerrilla warfare – and, of course, he knew the eldar.

They had been dropped into the thick of the forest. While the Astra Militarum kept the bulk of the Exodite force occupied, Setorax's kill team were to strike unexpectedly at their heart; specifically, at the psykers whose precognitive powers were guiding the xenos forces, keeping them always a step ahead. There were two Librarians among the kill team's number, keen to utilise their own warp-gifted abilities.

To Setorax's frustration, they had been too slow, too noisy. They had talked too much instead of acting. And, inevitably, they had been detected.

Once this became apparent, as the first wave of warriors sprang from the trees around them, he had slipped away from the others. He hadn't bothered to ask Inquisitor Gravelyn for leave. He hadn't told his battle-brothers, any of them, where he was going. Those who knew him, however – those who had fought alongside him before – would not have been surprised to find him gone.

He knew what they thought of him. Setorax had heard them talking, when they didn't know he was within earshot. They didn't trust him to support them – one of the worst things that could be said about a soldier, any soldier. They speculated that the Raven Guard Chapter had been glad of a chance to be rid of him.

He knew that wasn't true. The Master of Shadows had not volunteered him for service; in fact, the Deathwatch had requested him by name, after reading his record. He also knew that he had more than proved his worth to them.

He had saved the lives of too many brothers to count, sometimes with their knowledge, often without. He expected no gratitude either way. Setorax expected nothing at all, nothing from anyone. He only spoke to his fellows when he had to, during missions. In between these, he shunned their company entirely.

He was happiest – he had always been happiest – in solitude.

He preferred to hunt alone.

Someone was coming towards him.

The stranger was trying his best to be stealthy. To be fair, he was making a passable job of it. He was no eldar, however, and his presence lit up the display inside Setorax's helmet. The Raven Guard flattened himself against a tree trunk and waited.

The stranger crept past him without seeing him.

He was an Imperial Guardsman in fatigues, flak jacket and battered tin helmet. He clutched his standard-issue lasgun one-handed, his right arm in a grubby sling. Setorax felt a flash of anger towards him. After all the effort he had made to get this far, this idiot could have brought an army down on top of him. He had to silence him.

He knew that, if he showed himself, he would likely startle the guardsman, perhaps make him cry out. He crept up behind him instead. Clamping one hand firmly over his mouth, Setorax snatched the gun away from him with the other.

'Be quiet and still,' he hissed in the guardsman's ear as the man panicked and struggled, 'else I will crush your throat.' He considered doing it anyway.

When his captive finally calmed down enough to comply, Setorax let him go. The guardsman reeled out of his grip and whirled to face him. He was sallow-eyed, filthy and unshaven. He must have been wandering the forest for days.

Setorax made the sign of the aquila, the quickest – and quietest – way of demonstrating his loyalties. The guardsman was still frightened out of his wits. He had probably never seen a Space Marine before, let alone had one spring out at him from nowhere, like some macabre forest spirit.

'How long have you been here?' Setorax snapped. 'Have you seen the eldar encampment?'

The guardsman gaped at him, unable to speak.

'I… They ambushed us,' he finally managed to say.

'Three days ago. They were riding these… these huge creatures and–'

'Did you see any farseers?' Setorax interrupted him. Impatiently, he clarified, 'Shamans. Have you seen the eldar shamans?'

The guardsman shook his head.

'My sergeant gave the order to withdraw,' he insisted. 'I didn't desert, I swear I didn't, but I was injured, separated from my squad, there were eldar everywhere and I couldn't get back to–'

Setorax had no interest in his story. He raised a hand to stem the guardsman's babbling. He didn't need an answer from him, anyway. He would likely only have confirmed what the Space Marine already knew.

'Follow me at a distance of twenty paces,' he instructed. 'Stay quiet – as quiet as you can. And don't speak. Never speak to me, unless I ask you a question.'

The guardsman nodded. He seemed relieved to have orders to follow again.

Setorax had been following a set of dragon tracks, and he continued to do so. He winced as, behind him, his companion's boots crunched into the undergrowth. He was taking a risk, but he judged it a risk worth the taking. If there were eldar in the immediate vicinity, he considered, the guardsman would be dead already.

And it was always useful to have a distraction to hand.

Setorax could hear a voice. An alien voice.

It was raised in a lilting incantation. The words were unintelligible, flowing into each other like the rushing of a river. He told his companion – he hadn't asked his name – to stay back. The guardsman was only too happy to obey him.

As he neared the voice's source, he saw another pair of misshapen crystal structures. Sitting cross-legged between them was a bony eldar figure, its pale face painted with natural forest dyes and wrinkled by age. It was wrapped in homespun robes that were fraying at the wrists and elbows and threaded through with faded sigils. The robe was cinched with a belt of twisted vines and hung with fetishes.

It could hardly have been anything but a farseer.

Setorax eased himself down onto his elbows and knee-pads, then his stomach. He watched and planned. His prey, alas, was not alone – it was protected by three rings of eldar sentries.

Three lesser warlocks surrounded their master, each facing away from it. They were tall and wiry, their faces hidden behind carved wooden masks that lent them a ghoulish aspect. They wore breastplates of sculpted wraithbone over their robes, and carried blades of the same arcane material. Each of them wore a spirit stone as a pendant, hanging from a fine silver chain around their neck.

Eldar warlocks were powerful warriors as well as witches. Setorax didn't relish the thought of fighting three of them at once. He knew he had to act soon, though – the far-seer's mind would detect his presence eventually, if its other senses could not.

He raised his bolt pistol, seeking out the clearest sight-line through the trees. He waited until no eyes were turned his way to see the telltale flash of a muzzle.

He squeezed his trigger.

A silenced shell struck the farseer's unprotected head, detonating inside its skull and blowing brain matter in all directions. Setorax took no pleasure in the grisly sight. He was doing his duty – no more than that, no less.

He held his breath as the warlocks separated, seeking cover, hissing urgently to each other. They didn't know where the assassin was yet – not exactly, thanks to his silenced weapon – but their psychic senses would pinpoint him soon enough. Setorax eased his hand behind his back, to his jump pack.

The warlocks, all three of them, turned his way at once. They began to stride boldly towards him. The closest of them was *too* close. It raised its hands, dark energy dancing and fizzing between its fingers. Had it unleashed that energy upon the prone Space Marine, it would surely have crippled or killed him. Having seen the farseer's fate, however, it chose to defend itself until its fellows could reach it.

The air around the warlock rippled as it weaved the substance of the warp itself into a shield. At the same time, Setorax triggered the launcher on his jump pack, firing a blind grenade. The shell rocketed between the warlock's feet and buried itself in the undergrowth, pumping out thick grey smoke in its wake. He launched himself at his enemy as the choking cloud swelled around them.

The warlock didn't see him coming, couldn't even try to dodge him. Setorax's hurtling, armoured form bore it to the ground. Its psychic shield was little use up close, against brute physical force. Setorax hammered his fists into the warlock's head, until his gauntlets were dripping with blood.

He listened for the others, couldn't hear them, knew they would be close by all the same. He fired several rapid shots from his bolt pistol; he heard the rounds bursting against tree branches and roots, but the fog cloud swallowed up their flashes. He also heard two pairs of light footsteps, scampering for cover.

He turned and raced away from his invisible enemies. The fog confused his auto-senses as well as his natural ones, but this was a necessary price to pay. The eldar might have had scanning devices too, in addition to their witch-sight. Many Exodite tribes possessed equipment that belied their apparently rustic lifestyles.

He maintained as steady a heading as he could, tearing carelessly through vines and branches. He ran until the strands of grey smoke ahead of him parted, giving way to dappled sunlight. His armour's sensors could tell him where he was now: not far from where he had left the Imperial Guardsman, as he had intended.

He looked back towards the fog cloud to see the fiery trail of a flare streaking out of it. The flare exploded as it struck the forest canopy, sending tendrils far and wide. The surviving warlocks had sounded the alarm. Soon, too, the cloud would dissipate, and they would be able to use their senses – all of their senses – to find him.

He had made it easy enough for them. He had let them hear him running, and left a trail that even a neophyte could follow. Setorax didn't have much time.

He made his way back to the guardsman. He was in a highly agitated state, almost firing on the Space Marine when he saw him. Setorax waved aside his garbled apologies.

'You want to get out of here?' he asked him, brusquely. The guardsman nodded.

'What happened back there?' he whispered, breathlessly. 'I thought I heard–'

Setorax talked over him. 'When I give you the word, run as far as you can in that direction.' He pointed eastwards. 'Do not engage the eldar, but do not stop or deviate from your course for any reason. When you can run no further–'

'But I thought you were taking me back to–'

The Space Marine pressed a small, metallic disc into the guardsman's good hand, which was trembling.

'When you can run no further,' he repeated, 'activate this. Then hide it as best you can. After that, you may defend yourself if you wish.'

'What is that? Is that a–'

'You will be doing the Emperor a valuable service,' said Setorax, gravely. Then, before the guardsman could speak again, he barked at him, 'Now, go!'

The guardsman hesitated for a second, as if trying to decide which frightened him more, his enemies or his nominal ally. He decided to take his chances, such as they were, with the former.

As the man scurried off eastwards, Setorax slipped away in the opposite direction, a silent shadow once more.

It wasn't long before he detected the first signs of pursuit.

The eldar weren't close enough for Setorax to hear them, but he felt the ground trembling with the footsteps of their dragon mounts. At least two beasts had joined the hunt, he judged. That was good. The more the better, as long as they were hunting the wrong quarry – which they were. The tremors were lessening in severity as the hunters headed further eastwards, away from him.

'When you can run no further,' he had said. He had meant, 'When the Exodites catch up to you, intent upon bloody revenge.' He wondered if they would torture the guardsman before they killed him – could they resist the temptation? They might suspect that he hadn't been working alone. They would find no evidence to confirm this suspicion, however, and with luck they'd have more pressing concerns by then.

Setorax had gone far enough west. He veered northwards again, then north-east, coming around behind his foes. He found another crystal formation, this one with the look of a stunted tree about it, but it was unattended. His auspex informed him that he was nearing his target coordinates.

An icon flared red inside his helmet. He allowed himself a grunt of satisfaction. The Imperial Guardsman – likely the *late* Imperial Guardsman – had served his purpose. He had activated the locator beacon that Setorax had given him. He must have hidden it well, too, or simply flung it far away as the dragon riders pounced on him, because a full minute passed before its signal cut out.

Long enough.

Setorax's auto-senses had a fix on the beacon's position. That meant his kill team knew where it was, too. And that changed everything.

Another pair of dragon riders thundered across Setorax's path.

They were clearly in a hurry to be somewhere. He waited for their footsteps to die down. In their rush, they had left a clear trail for him to follow, back to their point of origin. The Exodite encampment. He knew he was close to it now.

He almost ran into several more eldar hastening up the same trail in the dragons' wake. He hid from a group of eight of them. Most of them were warriors, but there were two among them that he judged to be warlocks, from their dress.

The encampment was where he had expected it to be, based on Astra Militarum reports and a strike cruiser's orbital scans of the forest. It was small, so the scans had been unable to pinpoint it precisely. It comprised a mere half-dozen tents – though each of these was an elaborate, multi-layered pavilion, woven from the dyed fur of some beast or other, supported by an intricate web of external ropes and timber poles. The tents stood in a rough circle around the ashes of a recent fire.

This was only a temporary base, erected by the Exodites upon their return to this world. The portal that had brought them here was probably close by. It hadn't shown on the orbital scans either, so was likely no more than a sliver, only wide enough to step through. Setorax knew he could search for it for months and never find it.

He could hear no sounds, just the flapping of the tents themselves in the breeze. The camp appeared to be deserted. He knew better than to believe that, of course.

It did seem, however, that his strategy had proven successful. The Exodites, their farseers, had seen his kill team coming. They had been prepared to greet them. Then, a beacon had been activated behind the Exodite lines, and the kill team – after wasting much time with discussion, he didn't doubt – had altered their heading.

Whatever they thought of Setorax, they respected his abilities. They would have identified his beacon's unique signature and known he had employed it for a reason. They were no longer marching into an eldar ambush. And the eldar themselves knew this – their farseers would certainly have divined it – and were scrambling to adjust their tactics accordingly.

It was always useful to have a distraction.

Setorax had already killed one eldar farseer. Experience suggested that there would be at least two more; including one more experienced, more powerful than the others, acting as their leader. This one, at least, was unlikely to leave the encampment, unlikely to expose itself to danger. It had sent its warriors away, however – even some of its warlocks, as Setorax had seen – to meet the approaching threat.

It would never be more vulnerable to a stealth attack than it was right now.

There were tripwires set around the clearing. They were strung through the undergrowth, invisible to anyone who didn't know to look for them. The crystalline filaments stretched up to the branches of nearby trees, in which comparatively low-tech warning chimes were concealed.

Setorax stepped over each wire in turn, mindful not to brush against them. Then he slid across a narrow patch of open ground and took cover behind the closest tent.

He had timed his arrival well. The sun was setting. The forest was being gradually leeched of colour and its shadows were lengthening. Nocturnal creatures were beginning to stir in the brush, squeaking and rustling.

Setorax drew his knife and slowly, carefully, scored a vertical slit in the tent. He teased the flaps aside with his fingers and peered through. His auto-senses took a moment to adjust to the dimness within, to confirm that the tent was empty.

He sliced further, eventually creating a gap that he could slip his armoured form through. Setorax crept through the tent and hunkered down behind its entrance. Each time the breeze stirred it, he was able to look out across the campsite. From this vantage point, he could see into three more tents. They appeared to be empty too.

Then the flap of another tent bulged, and a figure emerged from it and stood still, straight-backed. It was another warlock; and it must have sensed something amiss. It cocked its head, alert for the slightest disturbance in the air. In its right hand it clutched a tall spear, silver and studded with gems. The spear hummed quietly, suffused with arcane power.

The warlock's dark eyes roved around the encampment, gleaming through the round holes in its mask. Even cloaked in shadows as Setorax was, he knew its witch-sight would detect his aura. He was going to have to fight it.

An eruption of sound, from somewhere to his left, saved him.

One of the squeaking creatures he had heard burst out of the undergrowth – a small one, it sounded like, perhaps fleeing from a predator – and blundered into the tripwires. It hissed and screeched as it tied itself up, alarm bells clanging in the trees.

The warlock took three strides, turning its back to Setorax, and hurled its spear. He heard a thunk, a whimper, and both beast and bells were abruptly silenced.

By then, Setorax had darted back through the tent and was climbing out through the slit he had cut. He heard a harsh voice, raised in question. He judged its source to be the tent from which the warlock had appeared.

For all his dealings with the eldar, he had never deciphered their tortuous language, nor did he care to. The Exodites had likely evolved their own impenetrable dialect, anyway. He could judge the tone of the warlock's answer, however, which was calm and reassuring. It was claiming to have everything under control.

Belying that sentiment, it was approaching Setorax's tent – the one from which he had just escaped – suspiciously. Its humming spear had returned to its hand, by some sorcery that disgusted Setorax but didn't surprise him. The sound gave away its position as surely as any locator beacon would. Setorax crept around the side of the tent, between its guy ropes, in time to see the warlock disappearing inside.

He slipped through behind it, his knife at the ready.

In the moment that the warlock saw the tear in the back of the tent, as it opened its mouth to cry out and began to turn, Setorax pulled the creature's head back and cut its windpipe with his blade. He kept a firm grip on the body until the last of its life had bled out of it. Then he lowered it carefully to the ground.

For several minutes, he waited inside the tent, letting the silence settle. Only now did he let himself think about the peril he had been in, the risk he had taken.

The warlock he had killed had carried a rare and precious weapon. It must have been a potent psyker, perhaps on the path to becoming a farseer. In a fair fight, face-to-face, he knew it would likely have slaughtered him.

Three or more such warlocks could have given his kill team a fight, had he brought them with him. At least, they'd have held them at a standstill long enough for eldar warriors to make it back here and lend their arms to the effort. The ensuing battle would have been long and hard, with casualties on both sides.

Setorax had been caught up in many such melees himself. Too many.

He had felt the crush of armoured bodies around him, breathed in the stink of burning chainsword oil, felt the hairs on the back of his neck pricking up as psychic energy charged the air. Most of all, he loathed the noise that filled his ears – the resounding clashes of metal on metal, the percussion cracks of gunfire and bursting grenades, the roars of the victors and the howls of the defeated.

He knew that his battle-brothers, many of them, lived for those moments. Setorax had learned better. On Yme-Loc, he had spent three weeks behind enemy lines, moving always in the shadows of the craftworld. He had studied the eldar and had learned their strengths and weaknesses, and frustrated their repeated attempts to scry him out.

The eldar were fast and they were agile. He knew well the frustration of trying to land a blow on one of them, at least when they were aware of him. They weren't especially tough, however; they favoured light armour, trading protection for mobility. The way to beat them was with a blow that they couldn't see coming.

That was what made their psykers – with their warp-enhanced perceptions – especially dangerous. Setorax had learned their weaknesses too, however.

He emerged into the encampment again. He crouched in the leeward shadow of another tent there. His auspex picked up three heat signatures inside the occupied tent. Most likely, he thought, two more warlocks – along with their leader.

Ideally, he'd have waited for the latter to show itself. It couldn't hide forever. He would have despatched it with a shot to the head, as he had the farseer in the forest. What the creature would never see or hear, it couldn't *foresee*; and what it couldn't foresee was likely to make it nervous, afraid, prone to making mistakes.

But the psykers would miss their dead fellow soon, if they hadn't already.

Setorax fired a blind grenade through the flap of the tent.

It was a perfect shot. Smoke billowed out through the narrow opening, between the tent's overlapping layers, through the vents in its roof. A moment later, a masked figure stumbled out. It had thrown up a shield around itself, as Setorax had expected it would. He held his fire. If he could draw this creature away…

It swung towards him, firing a shuriken pistol. Setorax was already running. Tiny star-shaped projectiles shredded the corner of the tent behind him, slicing through its web of ropes. He made the relative safety of the forest, flattened himself behind a mighty spreading tree with needle-shaped leaves and turned to look for his enemy, but it had disappeared. It had taken to the shadows itself.

The warlock knew where Setorax was, but it was hidden from him. He had to reverse that state of affairs if he wanted to live.

He doubled back to the treeline, creeping up behind the farseer's tent.

A thin grey haze still clung to it, but there was no sign of movement either from within our without. Setorax scanned the tent again and found it empty.

He was alone, outmatched. Perhaps he ought to have abandoned the mission, he thought, to melt back into the shadows and find his way back to his kill team. But then, everything he had done so far would count for nothing.

So he waited instead. For several minutes, he didn't so much as twitch a muscle. He was like a dark, metallic statue. He had crouched like this for hours at a time before. When his enemies were sure he had indeed escaped into the forest, when they lowered their guards, he would still be here, a mere breath away from them.

If they didn't find him first. Was that the breeze rustling the leaves above him, he wondered, or an eldar crawling along a branch towards him? Was that the snout of a forest animal poking out of the undergrowth, or was it a gun barrel?

A shadow flitted between the eldar tents, accompanied by a low, familiar hum. Two figures met over the ashes of the fire, and exchanged urgent whispers. Setorax eased himself forwards to get a better look at them. One was the warlock that had fired at him before, now clutching its dead fellow's silver spear. The other carried a glowing blade.

There was something behind him.

He didn't know what had sparked that realisation. He had seen nothing, heard nothing, he just knew. He whirled around, saw nothing still. He raised his bolt pistol all the same; and suddenly, it was as if a gauze had fallen from his eyes, as the warlock – the one that had been there all along – came at him through the trees.

It had clouded Setorax's senses, his very thoughts. It had happened to him before; he should have sensed it. On some instinctual level, he had.

The creature sliced at him with a witchblade, which crackled as it channelled its wielder's own psychic power. Setorax was barely able to twist out of the way of its thrust. The air around the blade rippled, as if it were cleaving reality itself. He didn't doubt that, had the warlock been able to surprise him, it would have stabbed just as easily through his armour, into his back.

The warlock, certainly, had expected him to die – it wasn't prepared for him to fight back. Setorax emptied his bolt pistol into its face. It reeled away from him with a howl. He didn't stop to confirm that it was dead. He could hear its fellows running up behind him, and a familiar hum rapidly growing in volume.

He whirled around as the humming spear streaked towards him, energised as the witchblade had been. It grazed his armour between the ribs, causing startled flashes in his helmet displays. Setorax lowered his head and fired his jump pack.

The remaining two warlocks leapt for cover, but his auto-senses had anticipated their trajectories. He rocketed into one of them, the one that had thrown the spear at him and thus disarmed itself. His momentum carried it clear across the encampment.

A heavy tent arrested their flights, and folded around them. Tangled up in its fabric, they wrestled furiously, the advantage clearly with the stronger of them. The warlock couldn't scramble away from its attacker, couldn't make use of its superior dexterity, couldn't catch its breath long enough to bring its psychic abilities to bear.

Setorax pummelled the warlock relentlessly, shattering its bones.

He heard the spear coming up behind him again and dived out of its way.

This time, however, it hadn't been targeting him. The weapon returned to its wielder's hand, which closed around it reflexively. It was the last move the warlock made. The spear fell silent, clutched between its stiffening fingers.

Setorax rolled to his feet to confront what he hoped was the final warlock. It was marching towards him, eyes blazing, witchblade drawn. He had no choice but to fight it head-on. He drew his knife. He let the warlock come to him.

And it was just as it had always been.

The clamour of battle numbed his ears. There was only himself and his opponent in the world, only this one tiny patch of ground. Setorax swung, thrust, sliced at the warlock, but it danced around his attacks, in the process delivering a few expert strikes of its own. Its own blade scored criss-cross lines across his chestplate, defacing the Imperial aquila and fracturing the armour over his right hip.

Seeing the weak point it had created, the warlock smashed its blade into Setorax's hip again, forcing his leg to buckle underneath him, driving him to one knee. He thought he heard the eldar laughing, taking pleasure in his pain, savouring the taste of vengeance.

Setorax knew it would be a mistake to succumb to rage. He had to tune out all distractions, had to focus. He had to see past his enemy, aiming not for where it was but for where it was about to be. He had to be like the farseers and divine the future.

His knife sliced open the warlock's stomach. It staggered away from him in abject surprise. It dropped its blade, and reality distorted around its raised hands. It must have known it was finished. It was gathering the sum total of its being together for one final, devastating assault upon its executioner.

He lunged after it, ignoring the shooting pain in his hip, his bolt pistol firing. The warlock jerked and howled and toppled backwards. It lost control of its psychic energies, writhing in their excoriating grip. Blood leaked from its eyes and nose.

Setorax left the xenos to die in agony. He was painfully exposed here, and the Exodites' leader must be close by.

He heard footsteps marching towards him. The warlock he had beaten at the edge of the clearing was bearing down on him. He cursed himself for not finishing it off, until he saw that the spirit stone it wore against its chest was glowing white.

He heard a rustle of fabric behind him. Another dead warlock – the first one he had killed – struggled out of the tent he had left it in. Its throat gaped open, it was caked in congealed blood, but it came lurching at him all the same.

This was something he hadn't seen before, and he wondered if – he prayed that – it might be an illusion. Either way, there was no point in fighting already-dead foes. He could be fighting them forever. He fired his final blind grenade at his own feet. As its cloud of darkness enveloped him, Setorax ran, but not too far. He relied on the scans his auto-senses had already taken to guide him across the encampment. He asked himself, if he were the eldar farseer, where would he be hiding?

It would want the best possible view of its surroundings. It must also have had sightlines to the warlocks whose life forces it had rekindled.

He circled another tent. He had to tread especially carefully, because he couldn't see its ropes until they were stretched across his calves, on the verge of being wrenched from their moorings. He could hear the two reanimated warlocks feeling their way around blindly, searching for him. He heard nothing of their master.

It might have slipped away, of course; it would have been stealthy enough. Or it was holding its position, still and silent, waiting for the unnatural fog to lift as it had lifted before. It could be listening for Setorax, just as he was listening for it. He'd have done the same thing in its place.

He crouched and levelled his bolt pistol, although he could see no target.

The fog cloud began to disperse, slowly, on the breeze.

He could make out a few shapes now: some real, some illusions caused by the shifting smoke. He could see the large, elaborate silhouette of the Exodite tent at his shoulder. He could see the knotted tendrils of a scrubby bush at his foot, but the twisted faces that leered out of it were purely imaginary.

He could see a figure ahead of him.

He waited for it to become clearer. It was crouched at the far corner of the tent. It was looking across the encampment, with its back to him. It wore a farseer's robes, finer than its fellows', and a headdress fashioned from some beast's antlers. It was female, he realised, snow-white hair flowing down its back.

It was almost perfectly framed in Setorax's sights.

But he waited an instant too long.

The farseer moved as he fired. His bolt-round grazed its shoulder rather than, as intended, detonating inside its skull. Grunting in pain, it fled behind the tent. Setorax cursed to himself as he sprang after it. It had been a long hunt, too long to let his prey escape him now. As he rounded the tent, however, he saw that he had made a mistake. The farseer wasn't running.

It was standing, waiting for him, flanked by its reanimated warlocks. It was bleeding, clearly in severe pain, but its eyes blazed with hate-fuelled resolve. It was summoning the power of the warp to deal with its tormentor.

Setorax didn't have time to aim his bolt pistol. He simply emptied its magazine in the eldar's direction while he could. Then, a small sun exploded inside his head and his muscles turned to rubber. He was dimly aware of his gun slipping through his numbed fingers as the world turned a fiery shade of red, and then black.

Blessed silence returned to the forest, like a blanket settling over it.

Setorax returned to his senses, lying face down in the dirt. He felt as if someone had sliced open his scalp and pounded his brain with a hammer. He lay perfectly still for some time, letting the silence soothe him. He listened for sounds of movement around him, but could hear nothing.

He had been out, according to his armour chronos, for just a few minutes. He wasn't sure how he had survived at all. Mere strength of will? Perhaps he had gunned down the eldar farseer before it could train its full power upon him?

When at last he lifted his head, he was greeted by a welcome sight.

The farseer lay dead alongside him. The revenant warlocks had fallen too, presumably when their master had perished but, crucially, before either one of them could finish off their helpless enemy.

The Emperor had been with him today. The sounds of the battle, however, must have carried far and wide. Setorax should have slipped away from the encampment while he could, but something stopped him: an instinct, again.

He heard a droning voice, and suddenly he realised that it had been there all along. It came from somewhere among the trees, somewhere to the north.

He approached the voice with caution. Drugs from his armour's reservoir had numbed the pain from his injured hip, but it was still weak and his right leg dragged behind him a little. He would have to do something about that: patch up his fractured armour, so it gave better support. Later, he told himself.

He came upon a cluster of crystal formations. He had mistaken them for tree stumps from a distance in the twilit greyness. He could now see several more of them, stretching ahead of him like trail markers. He picked out fresh tracks between them.

Were there more Exodites ahead of him, Setorax wondered? If there were, they must have heard the battle too, and known he was nearby.

He almost mistook the farseer for another formation, before realising that it was the source of the voice. It was sitting cross-legged in the dirt, unmoving. It had its back to him. A dozen wraithbone runes danced in the air in front of it, glowing white. As Setorax watched them, their lights faded and they clattered to the ground.

The farseer's chant had tailed off. In a scratchy voice, without turning its head, it said quietly, 'You may as well show yourself. I cannot harm you.'

It spoke in High Gothic, with no hint of any accent. Setorax, for reasons that he couldn't define, believed the xenos. He remained in the shadows all the same. He aimed his bolt pistol at the back of the farseer's head.

'I saw you,' said the farseer, 'in my visions. Time and again, I cast the runes, and always they showed me the same: a fleeting shadow at the edge of my perception. I tried to bring you into focus, but time and again you slipped away from me. With each casting, I divined victory over the human invaders, and yet–'

'You,' Setorax breathed. 'You are their leader. The farseer I fought at the encampment–'

'She would have been their leader tomorrow,' the eldar sighed. 'I am old, far older than one of your race could possibly imagine.'

Setorax eyed the hunched figure.

'You are old,' he agreed, 'and unprotected.'

'Yes, I am. And you have your duty to your god on his golden throne. I have already accepted my fate. I see you clearly now. I know you for what you are. Yours is the silence that fell upon Yme-Loc. Yours is the shadow of death, for all of my kin.'

'Yes.' Setorax's finger began to tighten around his trigger.

'I only pray our deaths will satisfy you.'

He hesitated. 'What do you mean?'

'No longer do our warriors fight to repel the invaders,' said the farseer. 'They give their lives only to delay your advance. They hope to buy time for our warlocks to save the World Spirit.'

Setorax had heard the term before. 'The crystals?'

'The spirits of every eldar that has lived and died in this forest. They are the reason we returned here, when your settlers began to wreak their destruction. Break the crystals, and our ancestors lose their tethers to this realm. You condemn them to the hell of the warp, to be devoured by She Who Thirsts.'

'But you can save them?' asked Setorax, uncertainly. He remembered the first farseer he had killed, the ritual it had been performing.

'Take our lives if you must, they are of little consequence to us. But I beg of you, Edryc Setorax, if your emperor has left you any compassion at all in your hearts, spare our immortal souls.'

The old xenos fell silent, then. For a moment that stretched into many minutes, nothing stirred in the darkening forest.

Setorax crept up cautiously behind the eldar. He kept his gun trained on it, as indeed he had done all along. It didn't move, didn't even appear to breathe. As he drew closer, Setorax saw that his first instinct about it had been right. There was no eldar there at all. There was only a twisted, shapeless slab of crystal, to which his eyes had ascribed a curved spine and a bowed head, in the gathering gloom.

A dozen wraithbone runes were scattered in the dirt in front of it.

Setorax crouched beside the crystal. He pressed the barrel of his bolt pistol up against it. He peered into the crystal's depths, as if he might have found the farseer lurking in there somehow, staring out at him with a mute appeal in his eyes.

Then he holstered his weapon, pushed himself to his feet and turned away. He had completed his mission, done his duty. The crystal was no threat to him, no impediment to the Imperium's goals. He had no reason to squeeze the trigger.

And it would have made too much noise.

* * *

Setorax made good time back through the forest.

Night had fallen, so it was easier for him to pass unseen. He also knew the lie of the land now. He avoided the crystal formations in case more warlocks were conducting their rituals among them. Let them do what they have to do, he thought.

Nor was there much chance of encountering Exodite warriors. They were still busy keeping the Imperial Guardsmen at bay. By morning, he thought, most of them would be dead, while the rest would have faded away into the shadows.

In the meantime, the sounds of a smaller, closer battle – even more hard-fought, if that was possible – drifted to his ears from the south-east. His kill team had walked into the eldar ambush, the second one; although, thanks to him, their attackers were unlikely to have been completely prepared for them.

The sounds made it easier for him to pass through the forest unheard.

The flashes of gun muzzles, gouts of flame, the sparks of swords against armour, lit up the night ahead of him. Setorax came up behind an eldar scout, firing arrows from behind a tree at the edge of the melee, and snapped its neck.

He took over its vantage point. He watched and waited.

His battle-brothers were outnumbered six to one, pinned down but fighting furiously. He saw Inquisitor Gravelyn surrounded by eldar warriors, bellowing litanies of battle as he swung his hammer tirelessly.

Brother-Epistolary Malkus had thrown up a psychic shield to deflect incoming arrows and shuriken. Brother Delassio, his own jump pack burning hot, was blazing a swathe through his enemies with a hand flamer. Eldar bodies were mounting up as the jungle burned.

Two brothers had already fallen, however, and as Setorax watched, Brother Torgo almost became the third. He was about to be crushed between a pair of charging dragons. Setorax raised his bolt pistol. He targeted one of the dragon's riders, hoping at least to shake its control of its mount. Torgo, however, saw what was coming and leapt out of the impact zone with a quarter-second to spare. Setorax stayed his hand. He didn't have to reveal himself yet.

It wasn't long before his moment came, however.

The remaining Space Marines rallied behind the two Librarians, who hurled bolts of psychic energy from their hands, and the tides of battle slowly shifted. A knot of eldar withdrew to the edge of the battlefield, and they had their backs to Setorax. He fired his jump pack and was among them in an instant.

The force of his arrival scattered them. His knife cut down three warriors before they knew he was there. He had punched a hole in the eldar's skirmish line, and his brothers on the kill team poured into it. He had probably saved their lives. Again.

He would make that point when, inevitably, Gravelyn challenged him to justify his actions today. He would explain how he had changed the course of the war on this world. He wouldn't mention using his kill team as bait in the process.

Then, no doubt, the inquisitor would write a scathing report for his watch captain, which, no doubt, would be utterly disregarded. The Deathwatch knew what a valuable asset they had in Edryc Setorax. So, as far as his faults – his withdrawn nature, his disregard for authority – were concerned, nothing would be said.

There would be only silence.

THE WALKER
IN FIRE

PETER FEHERVARI

The priests of the Adeptus Mechanicus claimed that teleportation was instantaneous, but nothing was certain in the warp, least of all time. Sometimes an instant swelled in a traveller's perceptions, extending into a fugue state that could last subjective seconds, minutes or even hours. For most travellers the fugue was a maelstrom of bewildering fragments seeded from their souls, each piece gone before its meaning could be divined. For a few it offered flashes of insight that dissolved like gossamer threads at journey's end.

For Garran Branatar, the passage brought only shame.

Once more he walked the temple-lined avenues of Gharuda, scorching white marble to black with the sacred fire of his bonded weapon. He had crafted the heavy flamer with his own hands and refined it over many years, perfecting it with the devotion of a true artisan. His kinship with the weapon ran deeper than blood, for it had been forged in the fires of his soul. It grieved him to belittle their bond with the unworthy foe they faced today.

Tainted by terror, Gharuda's Imperial guardians had surrendered to the xenos raiders who preyed on their world, offering up their own people as slaves or sacrifices so they might escape the same fate. They were contemptible, yet Branatar took no pride in their cleansing. He knew every battle-brother in his squad shared his disdain, so they scoured the shrine city with sombre, subdued efficiency.

'This is no work for the Sons of Vulkan,' Athondar said, striding alongside him, 'least of all for a Firedrake.'

Though his fellow warrior's face was hidden beneath his helm, Branatar sensed the frown there. Despite his ferocity in battle there was a kindness about Athondar that was rare even among the Salamanders, a Chapter that had always enshrined the protection of Mankind at its heart. Some battle-brothers saw Athondar's sensitivity as a weakness, but Branatar believed it elevated his comrade, bringing him closer to the ideal of their lost primarch.

'We are burning out a viper's nest of xenos collaborators, brother,' Branatar said to his comrade. 'In time the human worms who survive may become dragons who honour the Emperor.'

Then the game changed.

As the Salamanders turned onto the promenade leading to Gharuda's basilica, the sky was riven by angry traceries of viridian light. Moments later a shoal of dark vessels slipped from the multiple rifts like predators of the deep sea, their forms sleek and spiny, as though woven from broken black bones bound with thorns. The xenos had returned to claim a final tithe...

The moment distended, then shattered into a thousand mirror images of memory as the teleportation fugue burned itself out.

'*Some souls are beyond redemption,*' Athondar said, a heart-beat before Branatar's world dissolved into white light.

Tamas Athondar had first spoken those words five years ago, shortly before he died.

But death had not silenced him.

Sarastus was a world shrouded in perpetual night. The darkness wasn't caused by some anomaly of cosmic geometry, for there was nothing eccentric about the planet's form, mass or orbit. No, there was curse upon Sarastus, old and devoid of bite save for the blight of absolute darkness, but that had been enough to sour the world's soul.

Carceri, the largest of the planet's hive cities, was a hunched ziggurat of manufactories and tenement vaults, cold and silent, but not quite dead. Things that had once been human haunted its precincts, clinging to a half-life of hunger, hate and the dim memory of something more.

It was this last and cruellest misery that drew the ghouls to the roof of a nameless hab-block when they sensed a tremor in the immaterium, for they scented disorder as flies scented carrion flesh. For a time they scrabbled about the empty expanse, hunting for the nagging *wrongness* that had lured them there. Some raised their cataract-encrusted eyes to the broken sky, as if to invoke the blessing of a god even blinder than they. A thrill of blissful terror ran through the pack as the warp tremor grew stronger...

The radiance burst among them like a compressed supernova. Despite their blindness, the ghouls recoiled and fled from the light, chased by a swirl of tortured air as the portal swept a path clear to make way for something new.

Moments later, five shapes were silhouetted against the

light. They stood rigid as iron statues while traceries of energy played about them, drawing flickering reflections from their helmet lenses. Though they were man-like in form they would have been giants among normal men. Their armour was painted black save for the shoulder pauldrons, whose emblems both united and divided them. While the left pad of every warrior bore a stylised 'I' cast in silver, the right ones differed in colour and design.

Abruptly, the portal winked out and darkness swept over the intruders.

'Kill Team Sabatine, switch optics to full-spectrum night vision,' a voice commanded inside Branatar's helmet. The timbre was clipped and precise, identifying a speaker who was entirely grounded in the present.

For Watch Sergeant Cato Thandios, teleportation is always a silent instant, Branatar reflected. *His soul is untroubled by shadows.*

Sometimes Branatar envied the squad leader's uncomplicated faith. Like all warriors of the White Consuls, Thandios revered the Emperor not only as the master of Mankind, but as the living god whose destiny was absolutely manifest. Few Space Marine Chapters subscribed so completely to the Imperial Creed, but Branatar imagined there was great clarity in such conviction.

Three voices acknowledged Thandios on the squad's vox-channel. Two belonged to proven battle-brothers, but the third was an outsider, a Techmarine newly assigned to Sabatine for this mission. Branatar frowned at the newcomer's inflectionless tone. None who entered the Omnissiah's service were left untouched, but this warrior – Anzahl-M636, his name was – sounded more machine than man. Branatar had met skitarii with more personality. The Techmarine's equipment also set him aside from his squad brothers, for while they were encased in hulking Terminator plate, Anzahl-M636 had opted for lighter power armour. He had modified the suit extensively, reworking the pauldrons and breastplate into angular, geodesic shapes that venerated the Machine God. His helmet was a smooth dome split by a vertical visor that glowed with cold light. It gave him the aspect of one of the Adeptus Mechanicus' soulless automatons.

'Salamander?' Thandios pressed, stirring Branatar from his brooding.

'Acknowledged, watch sergeant,' Branatar said as he activated his optics with a thought sigil. A rockcrete expanse resolved across his lenses, rendered in an abstraction of grey-greens. The flat surface was blemished with boulder-sized debris and deep cracks that could swallow a man. It was a miracle that the rooftop was still intact.

Looking up, Branatar made out the broken shell of the district's dome arcing high overhead. To his trained eye the damage looked like the work of decay rather than munitions, suggesting this city hadn't died in an honest war. It was a disquieting thought, but according to the mission briefing, Sarastus had fallen centuries ago. Its doom was surely irrelevant to his present duty.

We are here for those who came long after, Branatar knew. The briefing had been vague, but that much was certain.

'The teleport homer is unattended,' Anzahl-M636 said. 'Our bridgehead has been compromised.' There wasn't a trace of concern in the Techmarine's voice.

Branatar turned his gaze upon a cylindrical device squatting a few paces from the squad. The indicator on its relay panel pulsed white in his night vision. It was the only source of light on the rooftop.

'Formation Aegis,' Thandios commanded. 'Kill the beacon, One-Thousand.' It was the Watch Sergeant's custom to name each warrior by his Chapter of origin, which occasionally resulted in some odd designations, as had happened with Anzahl-M636, who'd been dubbed 'One-Thousand'.

The Brotherhood of A Thousand, Branatar thought. It was a strange name for a Space Marine Chapter when *all* Chapters aspired to such a number. To his mind it was as drab as the black 'M' that served as the Techmarine's Chapter badge. *Functional...*

'It's said their brotherhood always numbers *precisely* one thousand,' Icharos Malvoisin sent on a secure channel, as if reading Branatar's mind. 'A dismal prospect is it not, brother?'

'An absurd one,' Branatar replied as he turned to cover his pre-assigned watch vector. The squad fanned out around him to scan the rooftop in every direction. 'Next you'll believe we Salamanders can breathe fire.'

'Oh, I never doubted it, brother. What else would account for those angry red eyes of yours?'

'Watching your damned back, simpleton.'

Despite his rebuke, Branatar counted the Angel Resplendent as a friend. Cato Thandios and Sevastin, the Black Wing, were trusted allies, but outside the field of battle they were strangers to him. His camaraderie with Malvoisin had been unexpected, not least because the man's humour had rankled him when they'd first met. In truth, Branatar had wondered how such a frivolous warrior had earned a place in the Deathwatch, but he'd found his answer on their first mission together: there was *nothing* frivolous about Icharos Malvoisin.

'Status report, One-Thousand?' Thandios asked.

'The teleport homer has functioned at ninety-seven-point-three per cent efficiency,' Anzahl-M636 replied. 'Our spatial misalignment was within acceptable parameters.'

The Techmarine had extruded a serpentine mechadendrite from his gauntlet, connecting him to the device that their ship's teleporter had used to triangulate their deployment. Without a homer, the squad might have materialised inside a solid wall or high above the planet's surface. Neither prospect was conducive to survival, so homers were vital, but they had to be placed manually – so where was their contact on the ground?

'Has it been tampered with?' Thandios demanded, obviously sharing Branatar's unease.

'Improbable,' Anzahl-M636 said, deactivating the homer. 'The–'

'Multiple contacts incoming,' Sevastin cut across the Techmarine. If paranoia was a virtue in war then the Black Wing was a saint of battle, for he was always the first to see a threat, if indeed it was *sight* that gave him his edge.

The creatures swarmed from the cracks in the roof like locusts, hauling themselves out with gangling arms and grasping, almost prehensile feet. They were naked and hairless, their pallid flesh stretched taut across skeletons that were no longer quite human, with misaligned joints and backswept skulls that frayed and tapered to thorny points. Their eyes were like shrivelled white mushrooms, sunken behind distended snouts that sniffed at the air as they skittered towards the squad, loping and leaping, sometimes on their feet, but just as often on all fours. Yet despite their bestial aspect, they charged in utter silence, save for the scrabbling of their talons across the ground.

Somehow, that was the most inhuman thing of all.

Mutants, Branatar thought with weary revulsion. He had seen such perversions of humanity before, though never as far gone as these degenerates. *It will be a mercy to cleanse these vermin.*

'Hold fire,' Thandios ordered, 'melee weapons only. Keep it quick and quiet.'

The warp turbulence that had heralded the squad's arrival had lasted scant seconds. If fortune went their way the true enemy hadn't registered it, but sustained gunfire would be pressing their luck.

'Divided we endure,' Sevastin hissed, as he did before every battle, even the least. Branatar assumed it was his Chapter's credo, but if so it was a dark one. He'd fought alongside the Black Wing for years, yet he knew nothing about the reclusive warrior's past.

He is another who entered the Deathwatch seeking absolution, Branatar guessed. *Absolution, or oblivion...*

He tilted his flamer up so it wouldn't be sullied by unclean blood and raised his left hand. It was empty, yet the massive gauntlet was a weapon in its own right. There was a flare of light beside him as Malvoisin's power sword surged into life. Like Branatar, he had customised his personal weapon, encasing the hilt in a chiaroscuro fretwork of silver and obsidian that sang when he swung the blade. The Angels Resplendent were artists without parallel among the Adeptus Astartes and Malvoisin was among their finest.

'Veritas vos viribus!' Thandios intoned in High Gothic as the mutants broke against the Deathwatch like a tide against an immovable rock. Claws and jaws scraped and

snapped against hard ceramite, unable to penetrate or find purchase, while flailing fists battered themselves into bloody oblivion. The squad answered without mercy, culling the vermin in swathes.

Branatar swung about with his fist, crushing skulls or punching through chests with equal ease. The ghouls were so fragile he barely felt them die. It was like extinguishing phantoms...

'This is no work for a Firedrake,' Athondar echoed his sentiment.

Branatar cast the unwelcome memory aside and focussed on the battle at hand, though this slaughter hardly warranted the term. Given time he could put down every one of these degenerates on his own.

Beside him, Malvoisin whirled his blade about in wide, rippling arcs that cleaved through two or three mutants with every pass. Tactically he was in his element here, but Branatar knew that he took no joy in such crude work.

Icharos will sketch this scene over and over when we are done with this world, he predicted grimly. *Whatever foe we face later, this is the one he will remember.*

Watch Sergeant Thandios was intoning a steady stream of canticles as he fought. Like his faith, the White Consul's fighting style was resolute and controlled: he swung his power fist with piston-like regularity, marking every kill with a word of castigation.

In contrast, the Black Wing tore into the mutants with a whirling abandon that strained against his bulky armour. His single lightning claw spiralled through the pack, slicing his foes into ragged fragments that spattered and sometimes stuck to his carapace. Thandios had frowned on Sevastin's choice of a single claw because the Codex

Astartes decreed that *two* was the optimal configuration, but the Black Wing's choice hadn't hindered his lethality.

'This mutant strain appears stable,' Anzahl-M636 observed, 'but it exceeds prescribed Imperial limits for genetic drift. I will recommend a full purgation commission following mission termination.'

Branatar glanced at the Techmarine. The newcomer stood rigid with his arms folded while the multi-jointed servo arm attached to his back whirred about with a life of its own, striking down mutants like a metal cobra. Its clawed head had extruded twin rows of rotary blades that shredded everything they touched.

There was a snarl of disgust from Malvoisin. Branatar turned and saw a ghoul perched on his friend's back, its matchstick legs wrapped around his helmet as it scratched at the lenses. The wretched creature must have vaulted from the shoulders of its kin to gain such a height. His vision impaired, the swordsman swung about trying to shake it off while keeping the others at bay. He was in no danger, but the sheer *indignity* of it appeared to enrage him. With a flourish he spun his sword round and lanced it up through the beast. Its carcass ignited and came apart around the energy-swathed blade, but another mutant leapt forwards and wrapped itself around his right leg. Malvoisin stamped furiously, crushing one of the beast's trailing limbs and sending tremors through the rooftop.

'Caution,' Anzahl-M636 said flatly, 'this structure is unsound.'

The Techmarine was moving now, ploughing through the mob to put distance between him and the raging Angel Resplendent.

'Icharos–' Branatar began as Malvoisin kicked out and

dislodged the ghoul from his leg. Before the Salamander could finish, the swordsman brought his blade down in a vertical swipe that cleaved the mutant in two and bit deep into the ground. With a roar of fury he hacked again and again, pulverising the creature into ragged red shards and sundering the ground beneath.

'Angel!' Thandios bellowed.

A lattice of fissures zigzagged out from the riven rock-crete, widening as they extended. A moment later, the ground under the Angel Resplendent heaved apart and he found himself straddling a chasm. With a grace that belied his armoured bulk, Malvoisin spun to his right and brought both feet down on solid ground.

'That was foolish,' he said to Branatar. A shallower warrior would have said it with a grin, but there was only shame in Malvoisin's voice.

No, not shame, Branatar realised through his relief. *Despair.*

'I–'

Malvoisin's words were snatched away as the ground disintegrated under him and he plummeted from sight, leaving behind a ragged hole. A tremor ran through the rooftop and another great slab tumbled through, widening the pit and sucking in a trio of wildly scrabbling ghouls.

'Structural disintegration imminent,' Anzahl-M636 evaluated.

The slab under Branatar tilted towards the rift as he backed away. He saw that the Techmarine had reached the stairwell at the roof's edge, but the rest of his comrades were caught in the collapse. Thandios was leaning forwards as he tried to navigate a path through the farrago, while Sevastin balanced precariously on a swaying slab.

They won't make it, Branatar gauged. *And neither will I.*

'Kill Team Sabatine,' the Techmarine instructed, 'initiate armour salvation systems. Proceed to ground level, if you endure.'

'He's right!' Branatar voxed. 'It's the only way, brothers!'

As he was pitched towards the rift, he cradled his weapon and triggered his armour's lockdown mode. The muscle fibre bundles lining the suit's interior expanded, sheathing his body tightly as he plunged into the darkness alongside a pair of flailing, but still silent ghouls.

Ten feet... twenty... thirty...

He hit the floor of the level below like a wrecking ball and punched straight through to the next. He'd come down feet first thanks to his suit's gyro stabilisers and the impact sent shockwaves up his legs and spine.

'*...dum spiro spero...*' Branatar heard Thandios praying over the vox, then the thread snapped as he crashed through to another level. Then another.

This would be an inglorious way to die, he reflected.

'*Unworthy of a son of Vulkan*,' Athondar agreed from the deeper pit that had claimed Branatar on Gharuda. The agony in his voice was undiminished.

'Forgive me, brother,' Branatar said. Then the ground surged up like an iron wave to crush him against the anvil of his guilt, and–

Branatar howled as he saw Athondar fall, his friend's legs sheared away from the knees down by an unclean xenos projectile. With a shriek of tortured gravity, the eldar raider that had felled him swept past overhead, lancing more of the Imperium's avengers with black light.

'Go! Finish it!' Athondar yelled, hauling himself against a

wall by the strength of his arms alone. 'I shall hold the road, brother.'

Branatar willed himself to remain beside his wounded friend. This time the xenos wouldn't overrun Athondar and flay him alive. This time he would change it.

But already the irresistible, irrevocable hand of the past was sweeping him on – on towards the basilica where the corrupt Gharudan elders cowered.

They were his primary kill targets. His duty.

And Branatar understood that the nightmare would run its course exactly as it had done the first time and every time after. Except this time Athondar was laughing at him as he turned his back, mocking him with a voice that wasn't his own.

'Garran!'

Snarling like a trapped animal, Branatar fought back, straining his muscles against the vicelike grip of history – tainted history – but it held him rigid as the voice of fate taunted him…

'Disable lockdown, Garran!'

Branatar blinked, recognising the voice and obeying instinctively.

'Icharos?' he asked.

'So they tell me,' Malvoisin answered without a trace of humour.

'It gladdens me to see you, brother.' Branatar breathed deeply and flexed his arms as the tension in his armour eased up. His fall had been broken by the corroded relic of some ancient machine and he was wedged waist deep in its housing. By Vulkan's grace his flamer was intact save for superficial dents.

'How long was I out, Icharos?'

'We've been on this world less than twenty minutes,' Malvoisin said. 'You and I landed in the same chamber.'

The Salamander snorted. This wasn't an entrance they'd regale their battle-brothers with when they returned to their Chapters. 'What of the others?' he asked. His suit's augur was playing up and he couldn't get a lock on the comrade standing a few paces away, let alone the rest of the squad.

'Sevastin is two floors below us.' Malvoisin paused to consult his own sensors. 'The Techmarine is six floors above.'

'He's taken the long way down,' Branatar said sourly as he began to yank at the wreckage encasing his legs. 'What of the Cardinal?'

Malvoisin had coined Thandios' nickname, but now his friend received it with stony silence. Branatar halted his efforts to free himself.

'Where is the watch sergeant, Icharos?'

Malvoisin made no answer.

'Icharos!'

'He was still falling when I lost his signal,' the warrior said quietly.

They descended through the crumbling, shadow-choked corridors of the hab-block in silence. Malvoisin had fallen into a brooding reverie that Branatar made no attempt to dispel. If Cato Thandios was lost then the burden lay squarely with the Angel Resplendent.

Still falling? Branatar wondered. How was that possible? Even if nothing had broken Thandios' passage along the way, the building surely couldn't extend more than a few thousand feet below ground level. He couldn't still be falling...

'*You are wrong, brother,*' Athondar whispered to him. '*A man can fall forever, on a fallen world.*'

They found Sevastin waiting in a cavernous atrium on the ground level. The Black Wing stood by the lip of a jagged wound in the marble floor. He turned as they approached and indicated the rift.

'The Watch Sergeant is gone,' he said without emotion.

Branatar peered into the chasm and frowned. Beyond the first few feet, the rift was an impenetrable void. His instincts told him that Thandios' impact hadn't carved that unnatural pit. No, it had been there since darkness swallowed this world.

Waiting for Thandios?

'You can't be certain,' Branatar said gruffly, unsure whether he was arguing with Sevastin or himself. 'Did you see him fall in?'

'I saw nothing,' Sevastin said, 'yet I know it.' He hesitated. 'My Chapter is familiar with the traps that riddle the darkness between the stars.'

'We will return for the Watch Sergeant after the mission is complete,' Branatar said with a conviction he didn't feel. He turned his back on the pit and surveyed the atrium. It was littered with debris, like every chamber they'd passed through, but here there was a surreal twist: the fragments of a gargantuan statue were scattered about, transforming the place into a tomb for a stone giant.

'They brought down the Emperor here,' Malvoisin said quietly.

Branatar glanced at his friend. The Angel Resplendent was studying the severed head of the colossus. It was tilted towards them, its regal features frozen in the moment of judgement. The statue was crudely rendered – doubtless the product of a servitor-carved manufactory line – but there was no mistaking its subject.

Yes, Branatar decided, *it is Him.*

'Such desecration damns us all,' Sevastin said darkly.

'Perhaps true damnation lies in raising the monuments that invite such desecration,' Malvoisin mused. There was a remote intensity in his voice that Branatar didn't like at all. 'Perhaps we condemn ourselves.'

His words were drowned by a wail of static. Simultaneously, the readouts on Branatar's helmet auspex began to flicker wildly.

Vulkan's blood! Branatar cursed, assuming this was another consequence of his fall until Sevastin looked at him sharply and tapped his own helmet. Disturbed, Branatar focussed on the white noise and his transhuman physiology began to compensate, his Lyman's Ear filtering the cacophony to a low hum.

Some kind of interference, he guessed. *Where's the damn Techmarine when we have need of him?*

He froze. There was something moving on the far side of the atrium, near the building's splintered entrance: twin orbs hanging in the darkness like spectral baubles. Another pair resolved to their right, another to their left. Branatar squinted to calibrate his night vision and the silhouette of a hooded figure resolved behind each pair.

Eyes...

'Beware!' Sevastin yelled as something leapt from the Emperor's granite brow. It was like a skeleton forged from metal, with spindly reverse-jointed legs and overlong arms that brandished a pair of shimmering blades. The thing's head was sheathed in a tight leather mask with bulging goggles set above a breather pipe that looked like an insect's proboscis.

'Divided we endure,' Sevastin whispered as he opened

fire with his storm bolter. The mass-reactive rounds caught his attacker in mid-air, shredding its torso and throwing it back against the stone head. The creature slid to the ground and scrabbled about like a broken puppet searching for its own strings. The Black Wing spun and caught a second attacker's blade in the tines of his claw, creating a flash of opposing energies. Despite its augmetic limbs, his foe couldn't match a Terminator's strength and Sevastin shoved it away, twisting the sword from its grasp in the same movement. The creature crashed to the ground, but flipped back onto its feet and skittered towards him again, spinning its remaining blade like a rotor. He decapitated it with a rapid-fire burst to the skull and it stumbled into the arc of Malvoisin's power sword, which sliced clean through its thorax.

'*Skitarii assassins,*' Anzahl-M636 advised over the vox-channel. '*The Xenarites have registered our incursion.*'

Branatar realised that the absent Techmarine had accessed his optic feed, something that only the squad leader was authorised to do. He didn't like it, but this wasn't the time to argue.

'Into the fires of battle!' the Salamander bellowed as he thumbed the trigger of his heavy flamer and unleashed a torrent of fire upon a pair of charging skitarii. Their masks were scorched away instantly, along with the leprous flesh beneath, revealing skulls that looked almost entirely human. The cyborgs' hyper-alloy bodies withstood the heat, but the fibre bundles at their joints melted and they slumped into each other, becoming a single pyre of twisted metal.

Something ricocheted off his right pauldron. Another projectile shattered against his weapon's casing.

The eyes! He swung round, looking for the hooded figures he'd spotted earlier. They'd kept their distance, but there were five now. Standing rigid from the waist down, they tracked his squad with long rifles, firing precision bursts that slipped between the whirling assassins.

'*Skitarii snipers*,' Anzahl-M636 identified. '*Tactical proposition: advance*.'

'Where are you, One-Thousand?' Branatar asked, irritated by the outsider's presumption.

'*Closing on your position now. My path suffered significant impedance.*'

'Then why didn't you jump like the rest of us?' Branatar snapped as another round struck him. He doubted that the Techmarine's lighter armour would have weathered the fall so well, but that prospect didn't trouble him greatly.

Branatar immolated another assassin and marched towards the skitarii marksmen, eager to bring them into his range, but they registered the threat and circled away, maintaining their formation as they retreated, matching him step for step. The damned things were walking *backwards*, yet neither their pace nor their rate of fire had wavered. It was as if their movements were guided by another mind entirely. Watching that inhuman rigour, it struck Branatar how little he knew about the armies of the Adeptus Mechanicus.

I've never had cause to see them as enemies before, he realised. He would rectify his ignorance after this mission. To the Deathwatch, *everything* was a potential enemy.

Another synchronised barrage hammered into him. This time every shot struck his breastplate and red icons blinked across his lenses, warning that the outer layer of his armour had been breached. Thus far it had proven equal to the snipers' attacks, but if he didn't catch up to them soon this wasn't going to end well.

From somewhere above, a faint ray of red light sliced through the darkness and flitted towards the skitarii marksmen. Delicately, it played across the squad and settled on the warrior at the centre, marking the bulbous lens of its right eye. A heartbeat later, the glass shattered and the cyborg's head snapped back. Its rifle slipped from lifeless fingers and it toppled over. As far as Branatar could tell, the killing shot had been silent.

It seems we have an ally, the Salamander judged. *Our errant contact, perhaps?*

He followed the beam back to its source and spied a figure crouched in the palm of the giant Emperor-statue's hand. The stone fingers loomed above the atrium on the stalk of His right arm, looking like the splayed battlements of a surreal watchtower. By some fluke of physics the broken limb had fallen and balanced at an unlikely vertical angle.

Was it blind fortune or divine providence that made it fall just so? Branatar wondered. *Did He foresee this moment?*

The long barrel of the sniper's rifle recoiled as he fired again and felled another cyborg. He ducked away as the skitarii spotted him and returned fire, blasting away chunks of granite.

The distraction was all Branatar needed. He steamed forwards, teasing his heavy flamer back to life as he bore down on the surviving marksmen. Realising their error, they began to back away again, chittering in curt binaric code as he lashed out with a tongue of flame. It licked the robes of the nearest and set the heavy fabric alight, the flames then leaping to the next. Within seconds all three were engulfed in burning shrouds, yet they kept moving, all the while trying to train their cumbersome rifles on him. Branatar would have respected their tenacity if it had sprung from courage, but he knew the skitarii had no choice in the matter. They were *programmed* to be fearless.

'*And what of the Adeptus Astartes?*' Athondar asked from the open grave in Branatar's soul. '*When did you last taste fear, my brother?*'

Branatar crushed the voice, angered by such profanity. This benighted world was turning his shadows against him, as it had done with Malvoisin, but Branatar was a Salamander and guilt would never rule him. He sent a final burst of fire after the smouldering marksmen and turned his back on them.

'We are nothing like these slaves,' Branatar murmured. 'We choose our wars.'

Abruptly the dormant white noise in his helmet surged up again, straining against the filters he'd erected. He scanned his suit's sensors, but found no clue. Irritated, he dismissed the static and focussed on more urgent matters.

Malvoisin and Sevastin were duelling with the last of the assassins, a three-armed nightmare that danced between them on needle-like legs. This one was a skeletal giant that was almost as tall as its foes, though only a fraction of their bulk. Its multiple swords were a whirlwind blur as it blocked and slashed, then leapt away before its enemies could use their superior strength to trap or unbalance it.

They aren't working together, Branatar realised as he watched his comrades fight. *Each of them wants the kill for himself.*

The mysterious sniper joined the fray, his beam flitting

around the assassin as he tried to secure a shot, but the cyborg's frenzied gyrations were impossible to pin down.

'Techmarine,' Branatar demanded as he marched towards the skirmish, 'what is that thing?'

'*Cross-referencing with data cache,*' Anzahl-M636 answered. He paused briefly. '*Probable identification: Ruststalker, princeps configuration, however it displays significant augmetic and tactical enhancements. It is exemplary work.*' He paused again. '*Caution: the interference on your vox wavelength suggests the proximity of a skitarii infiltrator unit.*'

'What?' Branatar asked, confused.

His question was answered a moment later. Something clanged onto his back and locked spiny metal legs around his shoulders. Simultaneously the hiss in his helmet surged into a shriek and static gnawed at his optics. A memory of the ghoul that had vaulted onto Malvoisin's shoulders flashed up, but he knew this interloper was infinitely more dangerous. He attempted a couple of punches, but his angle was too restricted and the thing twisted out of his reach. Furious, he clawed at one of its spindly legs, but couldn't get a grip with his clumsy gauntlet. He mashed at the metal limb as the cacophony wormed into his skull.

'*–rIan InfiLTtraaTor…*' The Techmarine's voice was garbled almost beyond recognition. '*–neuRaalstATic aUUraAA–*'

The rider struck Branatar's helmet with an unseen weapon and his world exploded into dazzling light as a halo of energy coiled around his head. His nose ruptured and he tasted blood. To his horror, he felt his armour seize up as its systems were overwhelmed.

'*And so we are reunited, brother,*' Athondar's shade mocked as Branatar watched the skirmish ahead, unable to move.

Blearily he saw the Ruststalker Princeps crouch and spring at Malvoisin. It hit his chest with both its needlepoint legs and thrust itself back into the air with heightened speed. The ricochet became an almost vertical dive at Sevastin, the velocity and angle impossible to evade. The Black Wing knew it and didn't even try. With a howl he lunged into the assassin's extended blades with his claw extended, meeting his fate with the frigid fury of his Chapter.

'Tenebrae...' Sevastin hissed with oblique hatred as every one of the Ruststalker's swords pierced his breastplate. The blades keened in transonic harmony as they bit through deep and punched through his back in tripartite ruination. But in dying the Black Wing also brought death, his claw raking up through his killer's torso and disintegrating the fleshy nub of its skull. His arm dropped, but his armour kept him on his feet.

Tenebrae? Branatar wondered hazily as static flooded his optics. The Black Wing's last word had been delivered like a death curse. Was this the darkness that he–

With a screech, his tormentor was ripped away like a leech from its host. The toxic noise receded and Branatar's armour surged back to life. He lurched round and saw that the Techmarine had finally caught up with the squad.

Anzahl-M636 stood motionless as he regarded the writhing skitarius held aloft in his servo claw. The creature's skeletal frame mirrored that of the assassins, but its head was a saucer-like dome inset with a cluster of lenses and antennae that denied any trace of humanity. A torrent of furious static rippled from the cyborg as it tried to reach its captor with the crackling goad clutched in its right hand.

'I advised a stealthy incursion, Salamander,' Anzahl-M636 said, 'but your squad's errors have produced a positive tactical outcome.'

His mechadendrite lashed out and punched through the prisoner's domed head. The skitarius went rigid and its sonic assault warbled into silence as the razor-tipped dataspike burrowed into its skull.

'Accessing neural network,' Anzahl-M636 reported.

Branatar left the Techmarine to his bizarre ritual.

'Sevastin died well,' Malvoisin said as Branatar approached their fallen comrade. The Angel Resplendent had discarded his damaged helmet and his long black hair was plastered to his scalp with sweat. 'It was a hero's death.'

'It was a wasted death,' Branatar corrected bleakly.

'The Salamander is right,' an unfamiliar voice said behind him. 'If you'd fought as brothers, not rivals, the Black Wing would still live.'

Branatar turned to face the sniper who'd come to their aid, certain this was the squad's elusive contact.

'We who watch, atone alone,' the Salamander said formally.

'We who atone, watch as one.' The stranger completed the agreed code-catechism. His voice was the hoarse whisper of a man who rarely spoke out loud.

'If you'd held your post at the beacon both my brothers would be alive,' Branatar challenged.

'More likely I'd be dead along with them,' the sniper said as he coiled his rappelling rope. 'The ghouls smelled the translocation scars you made. You drew at least three different packs. As you can see, I'm not a walking tank, brother.'

It was true – the sniper wore the light armour of a Scout.

Ceramite plates encased his chest, shoulders and knees, but the rest of his body was protected only by hardened leather.

'So you ran,' Malvoisin accused, his eyes glittering in the hollows of his finely chiselled face. His loathing was a tangible, terrible thing, not for what the sniper had done, but for what he *was*.

Monstrous, Branatar agreed. There was no denying that the obsidian skin and burning eyes of his own bloodline lent the Salamanders a fearsome aspect, but this was off-set by an ineffable nobility that elevated them. No such grace redeemed the sniper's countenance. He was ancient, his face a hatchet skull sheathed in skin like grey leather. Scraps of white hair hung from his scalp in long strands, shadowing sunken eyes that were the lustreless black of an oceanic predator.

'You deserted your post,' Malvoisin said coldly.

'I survived,' the sniper said, hooking his rope to his utility belt. He grinned at the other's disgust, revealing the curved yellow spines of his teeth. 'Aye, we're not so pretty, my Chapter. Our veins don't run with angels' blood.'

Branatar sensed no humour in the stranger's mockery, nor indeed much malice. The newcomer was just going through the motions of conversation.

'Evidently you take no pride in your own kin,' Malvoisin said. 'Or perhaps they took none in you, Black Shield?'

In place of a Chapter icon, the stranger's right pauldron was painted black, signifying he had expunged his past and sworn himself entirely to the Deathwatch. Such an act was almost unthinkable to a Space Marine – those who took the 'Black Oath' were driven by the darkest of shadows.

'Pride is a fool's game,' the Black Shield said, widening

his shark's-maw grin. 'My brothers thought I was too soft, so we parted ways.'

'You've worked with Inquisitor Escher before?' Branatar asked, following an obscure intuition. The elusive inquisitor who'd sanctioned their mission hadn't deigned to brief the kill team personally, but Branatar sensed the Black Shield's connection with him – *or her?* – was altogether closer.

'Since the day I was dead to my Chapter, Salamander.' The sniper spat. It was the first honest gesture he'd made. 'I've been tracking these Xenarite heretics since they split from the Stygies forges and went rogue. Been almost a year now – the last couple of months on this corpse world.'

'What do you know of our target?' Branatar pressed.

'Nedezdha Lem?' The Black Shield snorted. 'She's just another magos who got too hungry to stay on the right side of the Ordo. They're all bloody Xenarites on Stygies, but most play the game and keep to the shadows.' He shrugged. 'Maybe a xenos archeotech site gets stripped clean in the Halo Stars or a downed eldar ship vanishes before the clean-up detail arrives. Nobody looks too hard…'

Malvoisin was appalled. 'You claim the Ordo Xenos turns a blind eye to heresy?'

'You can't declare Exterminatus on a cornerstone of the Imperium like Stygies.' The Black Shield laughed without humour. 'Even the Imperial Cult isn't that deluded.'

'Where is the heretic?' Branatar asked coldly, unsettled by the exchange.

'Old Arbites precinct, six blocks east of here,' the sniper replied. 'Lem has it locked down tight, but she's short of cog-soldiers. Salvaging xenos tech is a dangerous business.'

Branatar studied the Black Shield, trying to see past his obvious ugliness.

'You're hiding something,' he said.

The stranger met his gaze in silence, his black eyes as devoid of emotion as they were of irises.

'I am ready,' Anzahl-M636 signalled. 'We must not delay. What the skitarii see, their masters also see. The Xenarites are aware of our presence.'

'They woke up when you brought half this building down,' the sniper suggested sardonically. He turned and stalked towards the portico. 'Let's get this done.'

'Your name?' Branatar asked.

'Hauko.'

The Black Shield didn't ask for theirs in return.

The Xenarite fortress was situated in a perimeter district of the hive's lowest tier. A vast dome covered the entire precinct, yet it was only one of dozens that clustered at the base of the stacked metropolis, and those dozens were merely the outermost extremities of the hive. Judged on such a scale, the fortress was insignificant, yet in its own right it was formidable.

The bastion squatted at the centre of a barren plaza like a monolithic cube. Its walls were reinforced with riveted iron plates and buttressed with watchtowers at every corner. Twin blast doors were set into its facade, each bearing one half of the cog symbol of the Adeptus Mechanicus. Virtually every other building under the dome had been levelled to segregate Nedezdha Lem's stronghold from the rest of the hive.

'The Xenarites have not been idle,' Branatar observed with grudging respect.

'Yet for all their labours they have forged only a soulless monstrosity,' Malvoisin mocked.

The brother warriors were watching the fortress from a crumbling ruin on the outskirts of the plaza. It was one of the few structures that had escaped the Xenarites' purge.

'*I am in position,*' Anzahl-M636 reported on the vox.

'Confirmed,' Branatar replied. 'Black Shield?'

'*Ready to hunt,*' Hauko voxed from his sniper's nest on the roof. '*Multiple targets already marked on the watchtowers.*'

'Confirmed.' Branatar switched back to the Techmarine. 'One-Thousand, you are cleared to go. May the Emperor walk with you.'

'*Acknowledged,*' the soulless voice replied. '*Commencing deployment.*'

Branatar watched as the Techmarine walked into the plaza alongside the Sicarian Infiltrator he had captured. The sentries on the watchtowers spotted the pair immediately and multiple searchlights swept down to mark them as they approached the bastion. Anzahl-M636 was unarmed save for his retracted servo arm and he had removed his helmet to make himself vulnerable to the Infiltrator's taser goad. To all but the sharpest of observers he would appear to be the captive and the skitarius his captor, but his mechadendrite was buried covertly in the back of the Xenarite's head. Reprogramming the skitarius was beyond the Techmarine's ability so he was controlling it like a servitor on a tight leash. It was a dangerous ruse, but the kill team needed any edge it could get.

'The Techmarine wasn't chosen for this mission by chance,' Malvoisin gauged. 'Do you trust him, Garran?'

Branatar snorted. 'I trust nothing about this mission except you, my brother.'

Malvoisin was silent for a moment, considering. 'I am not to be trusted either,' he said finally.

'Your actions on the roof were... rash...' Branatar began, recalling the rage that had overcome his comrade.

'They were the actions of a *madman*,' Malvoisin hissed. 'There's something inside me, brother. A taint, like an iron barb in my soul.'

Before Branatar could reply, a towering bipedal engine clattered across the courtyard to intercept the Techmarine. A servitor hunched in a recess of the machine's lower carriage while a skitarius in ornate black armour rode astride it. The rider tilted its lance towards Anzahl-M636 and questioned his 'captor' in harsh binaric as the machine paced in tight circles before them. The Infiltrator answered in kind.

'This is an unclean world, brother,' Branatar said as he watched the exchange. 'Such corruption kindles rage in every one of us. Your fury was righteous.'

His friend made no answer.

'Icharos...'

There was a buzzing hoot from the plaza and the skitarius dragoon stowed its lance, apparently satisfied. It swung round and strode away, resuming its patrol as the intruders continued their advance. The blast doors retracted as they neared the bastion, revealing more skitarii in the gatehouse, their bulky guns glowing with baleful blue light in the darkness. These warriors wore backswept helmets slit by narrow visors and their armour was swathed in robes that trailed to their feet. Another figure appeared at the threshold, taller than its fellows and sporting a fan-like crest of blades on its helmet. It assessed the newcomers in silence.

The silence stretched.

'That slave hasn't lost its instincts,' Branatar murmured to Malvoisin, watching the tall skitarius intently. It was obviously a leader of some kind. 'Be ready, brother.'

Suddenly the leader lunged towards the Techmarine with a flanged mace, but Anzahl-M636 had anticipated it and his servo claw swung round to intercept the blow. Its buzz-saw jaws snipped off the cyborg's arm just above the elbow, chewing through metal and bone in seconds. Simultaneously the Infiltrator beside him emitted an ululating wail that surged through the skitarii in the gatehouse like a killing current. They howled in almost human torment as their muscles convulsed in the throes of a voltaic seizure. Some fell to their knees and clawed at their vibrating helmets, while others flailed about blindly, crashing into the walls or one another as they sought to escape the sonic scourge.

Only the leader appeared resistant. It staggered back and raised the gun in its surviving hand, but Anzahl-M636 followed and smashed the weapon aside. Before the skitarius could retreat again his servo claw swept down and clamped its jaws around the cyborg's head. The Xenarite screeched like a klaxon as its helmet crumpled.

Branatar was moving before the leader died. He brought down a three-metre stretch of his hideout's wall with a single blow of his power fist and stepped into the plaza. Malvoisin's sword flared into life as he followed. The searchlights found them instantly and gunfire followed a moment later, thudding into their armour in a slow but steady barrage. Fortunately, the sentries lacked heavy weapons, but Branatar's auspex detected rising levels of radioactivity as the bullets ricocheted off his carapace.

The crimson light of Hauko's sniper rifle swooped overhead and silenced one of the sentries, then slid across to another tower. The Terminators were drawing all the fire, leaving the sniper to ply his craft unhindered.

'Keep those doors open, One-Thousand!' Branatar bellowed into his vox as he fixed his gaze on the portal. Anzahl-M636 had pressed on into the gatehouse and he heard muted gunfire, but the enslaved Infiltrator had fallen silent.

Malvoisin grunted as a shot grazed his temple. He was shielding his face with a splayed gauntlet, but it was a crude defence. Branatar had never understood why so many veterans chose to fight with their heads bare – almost as if war were a game to them.

'I told you to put your damned helmet back on, Icharos,' he chided.

'I lost one of my optics in the fall,' Malvoisin said lightly. 'I'll not fight half blind, brother!' He sounded almost cheerful, as if battle had salved his guilt.

There was a raucous hoot of fury from their right and the mounted skitarius thundered towards them, its lance crackling with energy. Clouds of ochre incense billowed from the dragoon's mount as it charged, its reverse-jointed legs hammering across the ground like giant pistons.

Branatar and Malvoisin faced the rider together, standing side by side as it bore down on them. The Salamander's flamer rumbled as he nudged the slumbering inferno within to life.

'We rise on burning wings!' Malvoisin yelled.

And then the strider was upon them, and for a few shining moments the battle-brothers were perfectly at one with the purpose for which they had been forged.

The dragoon arced its iron steed towards Malvoisin and set its lance for Branatar, intending to trample one and impale the other in a single pass. Recognising its intent the Terminators held their ground, as motionless as statues.

Waiting… waiting…

At the last moment, Malvoisin surged forwards and dodged out of the strider's path, swinging his blade backhanded to parry the lance aimed at his comrade. There was a flare of light as he sliced clean through the prong, sending darts of energy swarming up the haft. In the same instant, the Salamander breathed his fire, first immolating the engine's servitor, then tilting the stream up to catch the dragoon. He squeezed down hard on the flamer's trigger, maximising the promethium flow to reach the rider on its high perch. The weapon answered with a belch of fire that hit the cyborg like a guided comet, transfiguring it into a scorched metal shell filled with liquefied flesh and bone. Branatar grinned as the strider clattered past, blindly bearing the funeral pyre of its master. It crashed through the perimeter wall and raced on into the dark city beyond.

'That was well done, brother!' the Salamander said, turning in time to see his comrade's head snap back as something struck his skull.

Still gripping his sword, the Angel Resplendent fell to his knees, held for a moment, then toppled over.

'Icharos!' Branatar bellowed. He stalked over to his friend and turned him over clumsily, for once cursing the bulk of his sacred armour. A scorched rift arced across Malvoisin's forehead where the bullet had torn a path through the flesh, but not quite penetrated the skull. It was a fluke of trajectory so rare that those who survived such traumas were considered blessed, but Branatar doubted whether this wound would be a benediction. The skin around the gash was already necrotising in the wake of the irradiated bullet. It looked like a jagged crown had been carved across his friend's brow.

'Brother?' Branatar hissed.

'It's a lie,' Malvoisin whispered. 'All of it.' His eyes opened, burning with a truth only he could see. 'We condemn ourselves…'

Then his gaze clouded as his consciousness slipped away.

'*Go! Do your duty!*' Athondar urged. His words slurred into a merciless loop of accusation, a noose around Branatar's soul hauling him back to Gharuda, from one betrayal to another. He could almost *see* the shrine world's temples unfurling around him…

'Be silent!' Branatar roared. He closed his eyes, indifferent to the bullets battering his armour.

'*Salamander?*' Hauko's voice crackled over the vox. '*You need to keep moving.*'

The thought that the Black Shield was witnessing his private torment struck Branatar like a knife, silencing Athondar and severing the thread of despair he was weaving.

No, Branatar thought, *it isn't Athondar…*

'It almost had me,' he said.

'*I don't understand.*' For once Hauko sounded puzzled.

'This damned, dead city,' Branatar snarled. 'It's full of… of…'

He looked at the injured Angel Resplendent. There was nothing he could do for his friend until the mission was done.

'I will return, Icharos,' he vowed. Then he turned away and stalked towards the bastion.

'One-Thousand!' Branatar called as he stepped into the gatehouse. There were dead skitarii everywhere, sprawled about in contorted positions like broken mannequins. The enslaved skitarius was among them. Its domed head had erupted into a crown of jagged petals that looked like the result of an internal explosion. Inspecting the corpse, he noted that the plasma pistol Anzahl-M636 had secreted under its robe was gone, as was the Techmarine himself.

'One-Thousand, status report?' Branatar voxed.

There was no reply.

He tried again, but his receiver remained stubbornly silent. It was possible that the Techmarine's vox had been damaged, but Branatar suspected he was *choosing* not to answer. He didn't like the implications of that at all.

He switched frequency. 'Black Shield?'

'On my way, Salamander,' Hauko replied immediately.

Branatar frowned. He was suddenly struck by the thought that Hauko and Anzahl-M636 might be communicating on a private vox-channel. They were both outsiders, but were they outsiders to *each other*?

A cold rage swelled in his chest.

Growling low in his throat, Branatar stormed through the gatehouse and into the courtyard beyond. The open space was like a smaller box within the great box of the bastion. *A puzzle box...* Countless doors led off from the courtyard and a metal staircase zigzagged along the walls, offering access to the upper levels. It would take an intruder days to scour the stronghold if he went in blind.

'But you know exactly where you're going, don't you,

One-Thousand,' Branatar murmured. He spotted a pair of skitarii corpses at the far side of the square. The molten craters in their breastplates were unmistakably the work of a plasma weapon. An iron hatch lay among them, evidently ripped from the doorway beyond.

Branatar had his path.

The Techmarine's trail of violence led Branatar through a maze of corridors to a wide stairwell that descended into the fort's underbelly. There was a lift beside the stairs, but only a fool would trust such a contraption when hunting a rogue magos. Kill Team Sabatine had already lost one of its brothers to an abyss and Branatar was damned if he'd follow.

'Salamander,' Hauko voxed, 'I'm in the courtyard. What's your position?' This time it was Branatar who remained silent.

The trail of dead skitarii ran dry three levels down, but Branatar pressed on without hesitation, sensing in his guts that Lem would be in the depths of her stronghold. Hauko had tried contacting him once more, then gone quiet. Perhaps he'd guessed Branatar's suspicions.

'Secrets and lies, Garran,' Athondar whispered sadly. 'They will eat the Imperium from the inside out.'

'You're not wrong, shadow,' Branatar agreed.

The staircase terminated at a narrow gallery overlooking a circular amphitheatre some twenty feet below. Titanic pistons rose and fell along the perimeter of the cavernous chamber, venting steam as they powered the arcane mechanisms of the bastion. The floor of the chamber was encrusted with a tangle of machinery and insulated pipes woven around a massive central dais. A cluster of glass cylinders rose from the dais like giant specimen bottles. Metal rings reinforced the vessels and electricity spiralled around them at regular intervals, illuminating the chamber with flickering blue light. Scores of robed servitors wandered the mechanical maze, attending to their duties with dull diligence. None of them paid any attention to the intruder.

Branatar stepped onto the moving conveyer ramp that connected the gallery to the dais. As he approached his destination he caught sight of an armoured giant slumped against a cylinder on the far side of the platform. Though the figure was partially obscured by the tanks, it was unmistakably Anzahl-M636.

'One-Thousand?' Branatar voxed. He neither expected nor received an answer.

A few moments later the Techmarine was fully revealed. His right arm had been hewn off at the elbow and his servo claw hung limply across his chest, its rotary blades spinning idly. Deep rifts criss-crossed his armour and a broken blade jutted from his sternum.

Branatar coaxed his flamer into life as he stepped onto the dais and circled around the glass tanks. He grimaced at the dark shapes that hung suspended inside the containers. Though blurred by the murky liquid that held them, those hulking, aberrant forms filled him with a loathing that ran blood-deep. The intensity of the emotion was almost overpowering and Branatar was suddenly certain of the *righteousness* of this mission. Despite his misgivings about the inquisitor who'd sanctioned the purgation, he had none about the kill itself. Nedezdha Lem's hunger for knowledge had lured her into unspeakable heresy.

She had to die.

'*Salamander…*' Anzahl-M636's voice was little more than a sigh on the vox.

Branatar approached the slumped Techmarine cautiously. The upper part of the blue 'M636' code tattooed across his forehead was gone, along with the top of his shaven head. Both had been sliced away with clinical precision to reveal a concentric geometry of flesh, bone and brain. Augmetic implants sparked amidst the cross-section map of his brain like splintered power pylons.

And yet the Techmarine somehow still lived.

His piercing eyes locked onto Branatar and the Salamander noticed their irises were angular rather than round – almost crystalline.

Are those augmetics or a mutation? Branatar wondered. Abruptly the eyes shifted focus to something over the Salamander's shoulder.

'*Secutor…*' Anzahl-M636 rasped.

The Salamander swung round without conscious thought, opening fire as he turned. His blazing whiplash struck the thing behind him as it lunged forwards with myriad blades. A shimmering corona burst around his attacker as the flames were caught in some kind of energy field and spat out as impotent ricochets of light.

Branatar cursed at the techno sorcery as he backed away, slowing his enemy with a steady flow of fire. The thing's shape was silhouetted against the radiance as it pressed through the flames like a man swimming upriver. A flowing robe veiled it from head to foot, but Branatar glimpsed the glittering humanoid spider beneath. It swarmed with razor-tipped mechadendrites and multiple arms that wielded whirling swords. The creature loomed over him, hunched under the weight of its elephantine cranium. Its face was a revolving bronze cog with a nest of serpentine dataspikes at its centre. Every spoke of that abstract visage housed a glowing optic that cycled through the spectrum as its cog-face rotated.

Was this abomination Nedezdha Lem? Branatar knew the priests of the Adeptus Mechanicus could take countless forms so there was no telling how far a heretic magos might go.

'Nedezdha Lem,' he challenged, 'stand down in the name of the Ordo Xenos!'

The eightfold web of eyes regarded him with detached contempt, but the cyborg made no answer as it advanced. It was formidable, but it was moving with a pronounced limp, always lurching to the left, as if its legs were unbalanced. Two of its arms drooped, trailing their swords listlessly along the ground.

'Then you will be judged by fire, heretic!' Branatar bellowed and he increased the flow of promethium to his weapon.

With a final burst of light the abomination's aura collapsed, overloaded by the Salamander's assault. The conflagration engulfed it instantly, incinerating its robes and revealing its adamantium frame. The left side of its torso was a ragged ruin, almost certainly the result of plasma fire. Evidently, the Techmarine had not accepted his fate quietly.

'You fought well, brother,' Branatar said. It was the first time he'd used the epithet for Anzahl-M636.

His back bumped into one of the cylinders. He could retreat no further. With almost loving precision he modulated the flow of promethium to his flamer, sacrificing range and spread to increase the intensity further still.

The weapon shook violently as it struggled to direct the inferno.

'I walk in fire, as fire walks in me,' Branatar intoned as the cyborg bore down on him. It was glowing white-hot now, imbuing it with an almost supernal cast.

'Target acquired,' Hauko voxed.

A ray of light lanced from the gallery above and locked onto one of the cyborg's rotating eyes. There was an explosive crack and both the eye and the spoke that housed it were shattered.

That was no ordinary sniper round, Branatar gauged, *but then Hauko is no ordinary sniper.*

The cyborg emitted an ululating howl of rage and its attention swept to the gallery. Branatar seized the moment and dove forwards, still spewing fire as he barrelled into the giant and rammed the nozzle of his weapon against its thorax. A maelstrom of blades embraced him, along with his own fire, but he held his ground, grinning savagely as his weapon overheated. Sparks flew out from the muzzle as something inside it fractured.

'Unto the anvil of–'

The explosion tore the combatants apart with a violence that threw them into the air as if they weighed nothing. Branatar crashed through the tank behind him, shattering the glass and spilling its contents in a viscous, unclean tide. The cyborg was sundered into a score of white-hot fragments that rained back onto the dais like molten hail.

'A *worthy foe, and a good death, brother,*' Athondar judged as Branatar's world burned away into darkness.

* * *

Death came for him in a black robe, her eyes ancient in an ageless face that was as white as a bleached skull. She appraised him without expression as his senses seeped back from oblivion.

Athondar…

Branatar gritted his teeth and sat up. He was sprawled in the wreckage of the containment tank, covered in a residue of slime and broken glass, but otherwise intact. He whispered his thanks to the ancient Terminator armour that had preserved him, as it had done so many times in the past. As he turned he caught sight of the xenos creature that had spilled from the tank. It was slumped beside him – a four-armed monstrosity encased in an exoskeleton that shone a viscid blue. The thing's elongated skull was lined with gills and its white eyes were set beneath deep ridges that tapered into a tangle of muscular tendrils. Though the creature was obviously dead, Branatar was seized by an almost physical need to burn it. He reached for his weapon… and remembered its sacrifice.

'I shall forge another,' he vowed.

'Your armour's resilience is remarkable,' the black-robed woman observed. 'The Secutor's skeleton was forged from pure adamantium, yet it failed to withstand the blast.' She paused, calculating. 'I estimate his structural integrity has been reduced to zero-point-three-nine-nine percent.'

Branatar's eyes settled on the stylised cog woven into the woman's robes. It was the symbol of Stygies VIII.

'Lem,' he hissed.

Pain wracked him as he rose, but Branatar ignored it. He knew he was broken in countless ways, but none of that mattered now. The sight of the xenos abomination had fuelled his imperative to end this heresy. The magos stood motionless as he raised a clenched fist above her head. She appeared to be unarmed and devoid of augmetics, but Branatar knew Tech Priests were infinitely deceptive. This seemingly frail creature might be deadlier than her giant guardian.

'Nedezdha Lem,' he intoned, 'by decree of the Ordo Xenos–'

'We who watch, atone alone,' she said.

Branatar froze, shocked to hear the code-catechism on her lips.

'I believe the couplet is completed with the refrain "*We who atone, watch as one*",' she continued. 'An unsophisticated verse, but my rendition is correct, is it not?'

'Your spies overheard the code,' Branatar growled.

'Hold, brother,' Hauko said behind Branatar. 'It's no trick. She's the one who led us here.'

'Explain yourself, Black Shield,' Branatar said coldly. He didn't lower his fist.

'Magos Biologis Lem is a defector,' Hauko said as he stepped into view. 'This is an *extraction* mission, brother.'

Lem indicated the alien corpse. 'My analysis of this xenos strain has uncovered implications that are… perplexing. It was my duty to the Omnissiah to inform the Ordo Xenos of the danger. Unfortunately, Secutor Strochan would not have complied and the skitarii were his.' The magos sighed – an entirely human sound. 'He was not a genuine seeker of knowledge.'

'You lie,' Branatar whispered.

The magos turned to Hauko, ignoring the fist poised above her head. 'Has my request been approved? It is imperative that I continue my work on the surviving specimens.'

'The Ordo has identified a suitable backwater world for your sanctuary,' Hauko replied. All traces of his cynical swagger were gone now. 'Construction of the facility has already begun. The inquisitor is sure it will exceed your specifications.'

'Acceptable,' Lem said. She indicated Branatar. 'And this variable?'

Hauko faced the Salamander. 'The mission is over, brother.'

'We are not brothers, Black Shield.'

'But we are both Deathwatch.'

'Were you working with the Techmarine?' Branatar pressed.

Hauko's black eyes were impenetrable. 'Stand down.'

Branatar hesitated, thinking of the comrades who had been sacrificed for this lie. Did Malvoisin still live? Was Thandios still falling into the infinite abyss of this cursed world?

'Do your duty,' Athondar whispered. This time there was no mockery in his voice. *'It is the path you must walk, brother. The path of true fire.'*

'Forgive me,' Branatar said, unsure if he spoke aloud. He dropped his hand and stepped away from the magos. 'Tell me of this new threat.'

'It's classified,' Hauko replied, 'but I'd wager you'll find out soon enough, Salamander.'

Branatar kept his oath to Icharos Malvoisin, but when he returned to the surface his friend's body was gone, along with his homer signal.

'Icharos?'

He expected no answer from the vox, yet he kept trying

as he searched, stalking back and forth across the barren plaza like a lost pilgrim. Perhaps his comrade had awoken dazed or half-mad and wandered into the greater necropolis beyond this dome. Or perhaps a pack of mutants had dragged him away...

'Athondar!' the Salamander yelled on impulse, but his shade was also gone.

The extraction operation was beginning, and soon afterwards his own departure must follow, but until then he would keep searching.

'I will forge a new weapon in your honour, my brothers,' he vowed to his lost comrades. 'A weapon of righteous rage and fire.'

Branatar's imagination was suddenly afire with possibilities. He had learned much from this mission, not least that carrying a *secondary* weapon wouldn't go amiss. Something else to bring purifying flame to the xenos.

Bitter and hateful, the hive shadowed the warrior who walked its avenues, tasting his thoughts and testing his soul for a way *inside*, but it found only fire.

Garran Branatar never found Icharos Malvoisin, nor did they meet again. But many years later he heard stories, and the stories were dark.

And by then the Angels Resplendent were no more.

THE KNOWN UNKNOWN

MARK CLAPHAM

'Retreat forty paces before firing,' said Jensus Natorian, his eyes closed. Here, on an empty deck of the Deathwatch strike cruiser *Lethal Intent*, he could taste the constantly recycled, stale air, smell the oil on his armour, hear his servant cranking the equipment into place.

'Forty paces, my lord?' asked Heffl, his primary mortal servant.

'That should suffice,' said Natorian. 'My aim will not go so far wide.'

'I am not concerned for myself, lord,' said Heffl. 'The payload here is quite large, lord, I worry that–'

'You overreach yourself, Heffl,' said Natorian sharply. 'It is only by pushing beyond our own capabilities that we can know ourselves. Now, be quiet until I give the order, or I really may come to harm here.'

'Yes, lord,' said Heffl, and Natorian heard him shuffle away indignantly. Heffl primarily assisted Natorian in the quieter aspects of his life, carrying books and maintaining equipment. It was unusual for the servant to be present when his lord was testing his combat skills.

But a Space Marine Librarian was far more than a preserver of sacred texts. Natorian dismissed these thoughts from his mind. He had left his gauntlets and helmet behind, but he still wore the rest of his power armour, wanting to test his own senses, his own fists. The plates of armour shifted as Natorian flexed his enhanced musculature, the armour an extension of his body. He had set his staff, the conventional extension of a Librarian's will, to one side. This was a test of his own biomancy, without weapons.

He looked inwards, into his own soul, forgot about Heffl, the cruiser, the smells and sounds of it. Instead he let his mind turn to the galaxy, the Imperium, its borders, and what lay beyond.

Threats: the terrible unknowns outside human space, lurking beyond the Emperor's Light. The creatures that humans knew of, but would always be unknowable to humanity and the Space Marines who walked amongst them: aliens – *xenos* – threatening the Imperium by their very vile existence. Natorian felt rage build up within him. He let his mind go to an ancient memory, a painful moment hidden within himself. He didn't let himself visualise that memory, but got close enough to the emotional wound of it, the ache within that fed his hatred. That hatred built inside him like a fire given fresh fuel.

'Now,' Natorian said, and opened his eyes. As he did so the crude launching device pointing right at him belched fire, propelling chunks of scrap taken from a recent battlefield in his direction. Half a dozen sizeable fragments of plasteel and ceramite hurtled towards him, solid and sharp enough to smash in his unhelmed skull.

He raised his left hand, letting his rage out in the form of bioelectricity that flowed down his fingers to be spat out in precise bursts of white-hot energy. Three, four, five bolts burst through the air, smashing into bits of debris, melting metal and shattering material, turning the projectiles into dust and smaller chunks that ricocheted harmlessly away.

One last boulder remained, a block of rockcrete larger than the Codicier's head, and Natorian brought around his right hand, forming a fist. He let the biomantic energy flood through the muscles of his arm, the punch moving with speed and strength incredible even for a Space Marine, every nerve and sinew inflamed with power. It was less than a second since the projectiles had been fired and Natorian was now moving at a speed where time seemed to slow for him.

As his foreknuckle touched the lump of rockcrete it sent a wave of cracks through it, each one infused with biomantic energy, the block shattering in mid-air.

Then time seemed to resume its normal course, Natorian's energy was spent, and the fragments of rockcrete, now sharp pebbles, maintained their forward motion, less dangerous but still slashing at the skin of his hand and bouncing off his armour.

'Very impressive,' boomed Captain Fakuno, approaching across the deck, boots clanging against the floor. Heffl bowed deeply as Fakuno passed him.

Fakuno, leader of Natorian's kill team, was a Salamander, one pauldron of his black armour still green-edged and bearing the crest of Vulkan's sons. Like every child of Nocturne, Fakuno's skin was onyx-black, and his pupils a simmering red. Those burning eyes did not lack humour, and Fakuno's face was cracked into a half-smile.

'You should train with us, Natorian,' said Fakuno. 'Not spend so much time alone in the bowels of the ship.'

'I spar with my brothers,' replied Natorian, binding the wounds on his hand. He tripped over the word 'brothers' as he spoke, the word sticking slightly in his throat, but Fakuno didn't seem to notice.

'This is not training,' he added. 'This is...'

He trailed off. He could speak of research, of the search for knowledge that was a part of every Blood Raven's life. Of the deep need to know himself and his capabilities. But he knew that Fakuno wouldn't understand, and would just nod formally in response, that half-smile remaining on his face. Besides, he knew Fakuno would not have sought him out just to chide him for his habits. Give him a breath and he would get to the point.

'Very well,' said Fakuno. 'Just never forget while out here on your own that you are one of us, a part of the team above all else.' Those red eyes caught Natorian's for a second, before Fakuno changed tack, as expected.

'We have a mission,' said Fakuno, taking a few paces away from Natorian as he spoke. 'Genestealers have been sighted on the space hulk *Endless Despair*. There are Space Marines present on the hulk already, but this xenos threat is of special interest to the Deathwatch, and we have already set a course for the hulk.' Natorian felt a tightening in his gut at the mention of genestealers. Fast and lethal, those exo-skeletoned, clawed monstrosities first encountered on the moons of Ymgarl were also one of the most mysterious species known to mankind, and had plagued the Imperium for a long time. They represented a dual horror to Natorian in their repulsive alien nature and their unknowable purpose.

His feelings must have been visible, as Fakuno slapped him on the shoulder.

'I see that has lit a fire in you, brother,' said Fakuno. 'Come join us when you are finished here, and we will discuss all the information we have on this infested hulk.'

Heffl was straining to lift the training launcher back on to a trolley as Fakuno walked past him, and without acknowledging the servant's existence Fakuno lifted the load up with one hand and placed it on the trolley. Heffl bowed again, muttering words of gratitude.

'If our company is not enough for you,' called Fakuno. 'Know that these Space Marines we join on the hulk are of your own Chapter, led by Librarian Captain Lanneus.'

Fakuno didn't wait for a response to this news, and Natorian didn't give one. He looked down at his bloodied knuckles, and flexed his hand.

Lanneus, he thought. What was Lanneus doing on a space hulk?

Weeks later, Natorian and Fakuno were on the bridge of the *Lethal Intent* as it approached the space hulk *Endless Despair*. The hulk filled the pict screen, and even through a fog of incense Natorian could make out where different ships and other space-borne structures had become fused together to make the hulk.

'Shipmaster, where are we to dock?' asked Captain Fakuno.

'Here, my lord,' said the mortal shipmaster in his control throne, and a crude white glyph appeared on the pict screen.

As the *Intent* moved closer to the hulk, it became clear that a cruiser was already docked with the section of the hulk they were approaching.

'This is why I wanted you here, Natorian,' said Fakuno. 'Do you recognise that vessel?'

'The *Burden of Proof*,' replied Natorian. 'A Blood Ravens strike cruiser, one of the Chapter's finest.'

'Then we are at least in the right place,' said Fakuno. There had been no further communication from the Blood Ravens since the initial call for aid. 'Shipmaster, hail the *Burden*.'

The order was relayed through the ranks, and the *Intent* attempted to contact the other cruiser. Then they attempted again. Tense minutes passed, but there was no response.

'Natorian?' asked Fakuno. 'What say you?'

'It could be a vox failure,' said Natorian. 'It would explain the lack of contact these last weeks. No Chapter is immune from such problems.'

'...or the signal might be disrupted,' added Fakuno, eyes narrowed in thought. 'These hulks are filthy with radiation and energies that interfere with communications.'

Neither stated the obvious possibility – that the genestealers had overrun the Blood Ravens, and everyone on the hulk and the *Burden* was dead already.

'Find us a place to dock, Shipmaster,' said Fakuno. 'Natorian, tell the others to prepare themselves. We will enter the hulk ready for battle.'

A short while later Fakuno, Natorian and the rest of their kill team were standing in an ancient airlock as it cycled the atmosphere before admitting them to the relic of a spacecraft that was their access point to space hulk *Endless*

Despair. Fully armoured, combat-ready, they stood in the huge airlock as machinery behind the walls hissed and ground.

'Inefficient,' said Stannos, flexing the fingers of his bionic hand impatiently. An Iron Hand, he judged all technology by his own harsh standards.

'No one comes to a space hulk to admire the facilities,' said Godrew. Beneath his armour he was the pallid counterpoint to Fakuno, his skin alabaster-white and his eyes jet-black. Natorian knew that beneath Godrew's helmet, those eyes were giving Stannos a withering stare. The Iron Hand and the Raven Guard clashed verbally all the time, but in battle they fought like a single entity, Stannos laying down heavy covering fire while Godrew finished off enemies with precise shots.

'Why would anyone come to a space hulk at all?' said Karlan, the last of their number and a Blood Angel. His exasperation seemed always on the verge of tipping into anger, but Natorian knew that the truly dangerous rage within Karlan was buried deep, and rarely came to the surface.

Karlan's question had been clearly intended as rhetorical, part of the constant letting out of steam that allowed the Blood Angel to keep lethally calm in battle, but Natorian considered it worth answering anyway.

'Knowledge,' he said. 'If Lanneus commands here, it is knowledge he seeks. Even by the inquisitive standards of my Chapter, his thirst for knowledge is unquenchable.'

'You know this Lanneus well, Natorian?' asked Godrew. Natorian saw that Godrew and the others were all waiting expectantly for an answer. Natorian realised that, unconsciously, he had neglected to mention that he knew

Lanneus through any of the discussions they had had about this mission.

It had not been secrecy or a conscious omission. Natorian had just presumed that these Space Marines from great lineages, all from Chapters of the First Founding, would not be interested in the internal concerns of the Blood Ravens, an obscure Chapter whose origins were long lost.

'He is... was... my mentor,' said Natorian. 'He trained me to become a Librarian, taught me the arts of combat, and how to direct my power and my anger. Everything I am, I owe to Lanneus.'

'Then to this Lanneus we owe gratitude and respect,' said Fakuno, looking up from adjusting his ornate combi-bolter, a customised hybrid weapon with an attached flamethrower. There was a ripple of assent through the others, a nodding of helmed heads. Natorian did not know how to respond to this, but was saved from awkwardness by the airlock's inner doors finally beginning to roll open. The kill team dropped into position, weapons raised, ready to open fire and withdraw to cover if genestealers swarmed into the airlock. Natorian felt the tension between his comrades, their intense focus. His biomantic powers rose within him in anticipation, causing the hairs on his arms to rise beneath his armour, his skin prickling.

The airlock door receded fully to reveal... nothing. An empty space, no signs of combat or damage. An empty loading bay, with heavy doors visible at the other side.

Fakuno nodded to the doors, and the kill team moved out, covering each other as they slowly moved across the loading bay.

The doors led to a wide corridor, and the kill team proceeded cautiously. The curve of the corridor seemed to Natorian's mind to be steering them towards some kind of hub.

It was in the next chamber that they found a figure slumped against a pile of crates, power armour scratched and scraped, a force sword in one hand. Natorian recognised him instantly, gesturing with one hand for the others to lower their weapons, or rather redirect them elsewhere.

For a moment, Natorian thought the Space Marine was dead, that they had reached the hulk too late. But as the kill team cautiously approached him, the helmed head slowly rose, and the slumped figure spoke.

'Jensus Natorian, my very old friend,' said Librarian Captain Lanneus, as if finding him like this were the most normal thing in the galaxy.

Fakuno had taken charge once Lanneus proved himself alive, asking short, sharp questions, his voice echoing upwards into the atrium above. Lanneus had answered lucidly and to the point – the area was secure, he was the only Blood Raven left alive here, the genestealers remained a threat. While Fakuno got his situation report from Lanneus, the others looked around them, checking for threats. They were in an open chamber overlooked by railings, a great atrium curving up into the ship over their heads, floor after floor. Natorian couldn't see anything move, though there was evidence of a struggle having taken place at some point.

'We hailed your cruiser yet received no response,' Fakuno said. 'Are there genestealers on board?'

'No,' said Lanneus, shaking his head. He was standing as if emerging from hibernation, stretching. How long had he been sitting there? 'A skeleton crew are still in place. I ordered them to lock down the cruiser until they received orders otherwise.'

'And you are the only Blood Raven who still lives?' asked Fakuno.

'Yes,' said Lanneus wearily, and as he removed his helmet he looked much older than Natorian remembered, his once silver hair now sheer white, hanging over the alabaster shoulder guards of his armour. That hair was receding on top, and the old Librarian's face showed many lines. 'My brothers fought well, but many died when we first encountered the genestealers, and none survived the sealing of this area. I am the last.'

'Then how are you still alive?' asked Karlan, and Natorian felt a spike of anger at the implied accusation.

'I do not know. It is an embarrassment to live so long in a life of war,' said Lanneus, without rancour. He turned to Natorian. 'You should not have saved my life so many times, young Jensus. I am sure you have done the same for your brothers in the Deathwatch in these years since, yes?' Natorian didn't know what to say under the gaze of both his Deathwatch brothers and his mentor.

'He has, Librarian Captain Lanneus,' said Fakuno. While Lanneus had removed his helmet and left his sword sheathed, Fakuno and the rest of the kill team remained on their guard.

'All of us have killed many xenos,' said Lanneus. 'But Jensus here brought slaughter down upon the alien filth the moment his talent emerged, a reckoning loud enough

TcoThe Known Unknown

to wake the black ships and Inquisitor Belicor. He rushed through the warp to see if this formidable power was enemy or friend, and finding the latter brought him to our Chapter, a child still soaked in xenos blood.' Natorian felt buried memories try to surface, but pushed them down. The truth of it was irrelevant to the story, and Lanneus meant only to compliment him.

'Chapter legend, nothing more,' said Natorian, trying to shrug it off.

'You do not wish to speak of it, you never did,' said Lanneus. 'Apologies, brother, long absence has made me forget my tact. Besides, we need not speak of ancient history when you have no doubt fought many great battles against the enemies of man with your new battle-brothers.'

Natorian did not know what to say to this, but Fakuno intervened.

'He has,' said Fakuno. 'Now if we might discuss the matter that brought us here…?'

'The xenos,' said Lanneus, all good humour fading instantly. 'We skirmished with them deeper into the hulk – that was when we lost most of our number. We lowered the bulkheads that connected this ancient ship to the rest of the hulk, and it was in sealing this ship that the remaining battle-brothers of my retinue died. I lowered the last bulkhead myself, and the genestealers have made no attempt to breach these barriers since.'

'You made no efforts to go back and eradicate the xenos yourself?' asked Natorian. 'Not even after they killed our brothers?'

He intended it only as a question, but fuelled by his own hate it came out more as an accusation. Natorian immediately regretted offending his master, even if he could not understand why all efforts were not made to purge the genestealers.

Lanneus did not react with anger at any offence; instead there was a disappointment in his eyes that stung Natorian worse than any rebuke.

'I am the only one left,' said Lanneus. 'The genestealer numbers are great, and my rapid death would have served no purpose. Furthermore, there was something in their behaviour that suggested that the Deathwatch might wish to investigate further, to increase their understanding of these creatures.'

'And what is that, Librarian Captain?' asked Fakuno. The Salamander's courtesy towards Lanneus was slipping, and there was impatience in his tone.

'Do you not see?' said Lanneus. 'The genestealers would normally pursue any human presence with murderous intent, yet here they only defend the edge of their territory, pushing no further. Why do you think that is?'

'It is unnatural for them,' said Karlan.

'They are guarding something,' said Lanneus. 'And if genestealers have something they need to guard, surely that is something the Deathwatch would want to identify and destroy?'

'It could be a weakness,' said Fakuno, his mind opening to the possibilities. 'Something we could directly target in future encounters. We will gather what intelligence we can, then end them.'

'At last,' said Lanneus, turning to Natorian. 'They begin to understand the necessity of knowledge.'

'We do not know anything yet, all we have is conjecture,' said Stannos bluntly.

'True,' said Natorian. 'But we know the shape of what we don't know, and that is a place to start.'

Lanneus agreed to be their guide to the genestealer territory, and a short time later he led the way. Natorian found himself walking besides his old mentor, slightly ahead of his kill team. The geography of the ship seemed familiar to Natorian, reminding him of Imperial ships he had been on before, but everything was slightly... off. The way the high ceiling of the corridor tapered off above them, the angle of the walls, all marginally different to the norm. There were no Imperial insignia to be seen, but neither were there symbols of traitors or other enemies of the Imperium.

'What is this wreck, Lanneus?' asked Natorian, quiet enough not to be overheard. 'Why are you here? I know that look, there's something here so valuable that these genestealers, even the deaths of our brothers, are a distraction to you. I can tell.'

There was a brief, difficult silence broken only by the sound of their boots clanging on the grated floor beneath their feet.

'Do you see the paintwork ahead on the wall?' asked Lanneus. 'What does it suggest to you?'

At first, Natorian couldn't see any paintwork at all, taking the reddish smear for rust. It was a rough, round shape, a thin central column twisting off at both sides, and curving at the top.

'It looks... like an avian creature,' said Natorian, 'a very indistinct rendering of a bird.' He tore his eyes away and kept walking, before the others caught up. 'Is this all you have? An image of a red bird? That could mean anything – the chances of it relating to our Chapter are infinitesimal, Lanneus.'

'There are other indicators,' said Lanneus. 'Signs that what is left of this ship, embedded here in the hulk, relates to the early years of the Blood Ravens. Scattered references to battles in our history match the path of *Endless Despair* through the galaxy. There are other–'

Natorian cut him off with a raised hand. 'If this comes to anything, then it will be a great day for our Chapter,' said Jensus. 'And on that day, I will share your joy. But my concern is with the matters of the Deathwatch. I cannot become too enraptured with dreams of knowledge yet unfound. I desire answers as much as you, old friend, but these matters cannot distract from my duties.'

Lanneus threw up an apologetic hand.

'You have become your own man, Jensus Natorian, and I am proud of that,' said Lanneus. 'It is good to see you stand your ground like this. But remember, it was you who asked me what my mission was, I did not provide answers unsolicited. There's plenty of Blood Raven curiosity in you yet.'

'I'm sure there is,' said Natorian. 'I'm sure there is.'

The kill team caught up with Natorian and Lanneus as they reached the bulkhead, and Fakuno had the others take position, bolters raised, as the two Blood Ravens opened the great shutters to the next part of the hulk. Natorian and Lanneus had to crank them open manually using levers at either side, and as the great rusty teeth of the bulkhead separated they could see ahead into a different space altogether, an unfamiliar architecture of twisted black metal and curved walls. Of the genestealers, at least, there was no sign, and all was quiet.

'This is no Imperial ship,' said Karlan, stepping through the gap, bolter muzzle twitching from side to side. The space they were walking into had tube-like corridors curving off in four directions, wide enough for two Space Marines to walk abreast.

'This is the work of xenos,' said Natorian, hissing with contempt. He could feel that familiar rage bubbling inside.

'What species?' asked Stannos.

'I do not know,' said Lanneus. The entire team was through into the alien ship, and he and Natorian began to close the bulkhead once more. 'We did not investigate far before the first attack.'

'It does not matter,' said Fakuno. 'The genestealers would not leave any other species alive.'

'This way,' said Lanneus, indicating a central tunnel after closing the bulkhead. He held the hilt of his force sword tight, and Natorian wondered how it felt to be here once more, close to where his brothers died. Natorian could feel the tension in the kill team as they moved further into the alien ship, but for Lanneus the expectation would be worse.

'Stannos, I want your eyes up front with Lanneus,' ordered Fakuno. 'Godrew and Karlan take the rear, if anything tries to block our escape route I want to know. Natorian, you're with me. Stay close – they will try to separate us so they can get their claws in, let us not gift them with the opportunity.'

There was an exchange of nods, and the kill team moved out, running from cover to cover, Lanneus and Stannos taking the lead.

The corridors were shaped more like pipes than access tunnels, curved and never entirely straightening out. Natorian had the impression that they were turning sideways and moving downwards, overall, but the layout had a way of baffling his sense of direction. Eventually they emerged into a wider open area with equally curved walls, arteries leading off in different directions. Natorian wasn't sure what to compare it to, he only knew its alien unfamiliarity stirred hatred in him.

'It is like walking into a fossilised heart,' said Karlan, as if responding to Natorian's unspoken question. The Blood Angel didn't sound impressed.

'Reading recent genestealer activity,' said Stannos. The bionic eye implant that protruded from his helmet saw traces and residues invisible even to the sharp eyes of his fellow Space Marines. 'Heat signatures everywhere, exhalation vapour in the air. Also older traces, burn marks from lasfire, evidence of bolter discharge some time ago.'

'This is where you were ambushed?' Fakuno asked Lanneus. The kill team had dropped into position as the Salamander and Blood Raven took stock, fanning out to cover all possible approaches. They were exposed here, and they knew it.

'I could not be sure at first, but I think so, yes,' said the Librarian Captain. 'This is where we first encountered genestealers. We fought them off easily enough. Apologies, captain, I didn't recognise the place. They must have cleared away their dead since then.'

Fakuno briefly twitched his head between Lanneus and Natorian, as if checking for a reaction. Natorian could imagine those red eyes burning behind the lenses of his helmet.

'A little advance warning next time we might be walking into a trap, Librarian Captain,' said Fakuno. 'Even if you are not certain, there is no harm in being over-prepared.'

Lanneus dipped his head in an apologetic bow.

'I will. Following our initial encounter we pursued a group of genestealers down this tunnel,' said Lanneus, indicating one of the exits. 'The xenos attacked in much greater force, and that was when we lost many of our number. The rest of us fought our way back out.'

'Then we should not go down there, if they're laying the same trap as they did for the Blood Ravens,' said Fakuno. 'Stannos, which is the coolest trail?'

'This one has virtually no readings,' said Stannos, indicating a tunnel to the right.

'Then that is where we will proceed,' said Fakuno. 'Let us show these genestealers that they are not the only ones who can pick off their prey.'

Natorian checked the readings on his helmet display as they moved out of the heart-shaped chamber, checking that his power armour's life support was functioning. He had a sensation of pressure, of the atmosphere thinning, darkness pressing in at the edge of his vision. Nothing life-threatening for a Space Marine, at least not immediately, but...

Nothing. Oxygen supply and air pressure normal. Then why did the walls seem to curve and tighten, like they were about to squeeze in and–

'Natorian?' asked Fakuno. 'Are you with us?'

'Yes,' said Natorian.

'You stopped,' said Fakuno. Natorian found himself looking down at his own legs. He had indeed stopped walking.

Fakuno nodded. 'We must keep moving.'

* * *

It was in another chamber, wider this time, that the genestealers attacked. Natorian barely had a sense of the chamber's details before they struck – of a larger space than the previous heart-shaped room, of a high ceiling with tunnels going off from high up on the walls, of barely visible tracks to those holes that could act as clawholds.

Then they came, almost in a swarm. Claws and hands reached out of those holes, and four-armed figures leapt directly at the Deathwatch.

The first one went straight for Karlan, a blur of limbs scuttling across the floor of the chamber. The genestealers had four upper limbs as well as two legs, bulbous heads and chitinous exo-skeletons. Hate-filled eyes stared out from beneath a ridged forehead; a stunted snout was barely noticeable over a wide mouth filled with sharp, curved teeth. Of the four arms, the top two ended in three viciously long talons, while the bottom two had more human hands, perfect for grabbing hold of an enemy and pulling them close to deliver a killing blow.

Lanneus and the kill team opened fire before the xenos could reach Karlan, and while the creature's armour was formidable, it was no match for the combined firepower of six Space Marines. Natorian was not naive enough to consider this any sign of the battle to come. The lone genestealer had surged forwards as a sacrifice, drawing the kill team's fire and allowing the rest of them time to swarm closer and attack en masse. Two dozen, three dozen genestealers moved in from all sides, and more emerged from the holes in the walls in a mass of scything claws and vicious teeth.

'Form a circle and pick your targets,' ordered Fakuno, readying the flamethrower attached to his combi-bolter.

'I will lay down alternating bursts of fire to keep them back. Concentrate your fire elsewhere when I am about to shoot. Godrew's position is forward.'

Natorian was on Godrew's right. He could feel the hate rising in him, and let out targeted bursts of bioelectricity at the closest genestealers. He restrained himself from unleashing the full extent of his power – a force this large needed to be worn down. If he burned himself out early he would be no use in the battle ahead. So he hit the first genestealer with enough power to cause serious damage but not destroy it. The creature flailed backwards, jerking and smoking, as bioelectricity wracked its body. He did the same to another, and another, whispering meditative words to try and keep his rage in check.

'Right flank,' shouted Fakuno, and on cue Natorian pulled back his staff and stepped back into the circle, allowing Fakuno to step forwards and release a wide arc of burning promethium. Nine or so genestealers were consumed with flame, stumbling blindly as they burned. As Fakuno shouted again and turned his flamer in the opposite direction, Natorian resumed unleashing biomantic attacks on the dying genestealers, cutting down the ones that got too close.

'That should have put the fear of the Emperor into them!' Karlan said with a snarl, and Natorian could see that while the genestealers were still entering the chamber from all sides they were moving more slowly now, trying to regroup under the onslaught of flame, bolter fire and psychic attack.

'We have the advantage,' said Fakuno. 'We must drive them back.'

Under Fakuno's command the kill team, supported by

Lanneus, began to drive the genestealers away, forcing a large group of the xenos towards one wall of the chamber. As Fakuno incinerated the cornered genestealers the rest of the kill team used bolter fire and searing biomantic lightning to drive back the other xenos. The creatures had begun to pull back, withdrawing to the holes in the wall from which they had emerged.

Over the roar of bolters, Natorian barely heard the distinct hiss of air escaping. Debris on the floor began to tumble towards Fakuno's position. Natorian glanced back to see that the wall behind the genestealers that Fakuno had incinerated was white hot, cracks running across it. Fragments were beginning to be pulled towards those cracks.

Natorian was about to shout a warning but it was too late. Fractures emerged in the wall at tremendous speed, hairlines turning into chasms within seconds, and the whole wall collapsed outwards, sucked away into the vacuum of space. The genestealers went too, limbs flailing as they were sucked outwards. Natorian found himself being pulled towards the abyss, but as he fell managed to find a handhold on the rough floor. He seized Karlan as the Blood Angel fell past, grabbing one of his arms and swinging him around so he could hold on to the floor too. As they began to pull themselves towards the nearest exit, Natorian looked around to see Fakuno and Stannos doing the same, but of Lanneus and Godrew there was no sign.

Ahead, the tunnel entrance began to close, the material of the walls contracting as if alive. Time seemed to stretch as Natorian and the others dragged themselves towards it, using precarious hand- and footholds to prevent themselves being sucked out into space.

Natorian and Karlan got through the gap first, and forced the entry to stay open as Stannos pulled Fakuno through. When the last of them had made it, they let it go and the opening closed entirely, the wall closing up as if the chamber had never been there.

'Godrew? Lanneus?' Fakuno was saying into the vox as he got to his feet. 'Can you hear us?'

Several seconds passed with only static on the vox, before finally there was a reply.

'We live, for the moment,' said Godrew. *'Lanneus and I are out on the hull, we are trying to find an entry back into the hulk. Where are you? How fare the others?'*

'We are still within, all together,' said Fakuno. 'Find a way back in, we will push on and regroup when we can. Stay alive, brothers.'

'By the Emperor's will,' said Godrew, and Fakuno cut the vox.

They quickly checked their equipment for damage sustained in the battle. Natorian looked at the readouts on his helmet display. Everything was in working order.

'No damage here,' he said.

'Battle-ready,' said Karlan.

'Lost some grenades to the vacuum,' said Stannos. 'Otherwise, fully combat-effective.'

'The luck of command, then,' said Fakuno inspecting his combi-bolter. 'The flamethrower is damaged. I will have to rely on bolter fire from here on out.'

Stannos tilted his head, looking at Fakuno's weapon, which had been passed down by many Salamanders before him.

'Crushed ignition, shattered tank... yes, that will need

some repairs,' said Stannos, reading whatever complex diagnostics his bionic eye showed him.

'Thank you for your second opinion, brother,' said Fakuno drily, checking his bolter's ammunition and looking down its sights. 'We need to minimise fire and explosives, if we are to avoid another breach. From here on out we aim tight for the head and body.'

'What manner of ship is this, with walls like eggshells?' asked Karlan.

'Perhaps it is not a ship,' said Natorian. 'It may be an artificial moon or station. Either way it is very old, very alien.'

He spat out the last words with disgust.

'Could the genestealers have built it?' asked Karlan.

'That would seem unlikely,' said Stannos. 'They are mindless creatures, not builders.'

'Whoever built this ship, they are long dead,' said Fakuno. 'While those genestealers are very alive. We need to rejoin our brothers, and finish this.'

There was only one way to go, and they ran in that direction, boots crunching through debris underfoot, constantly alert for a further genestealer attack. As they ran, the corridor opened out into a vast chamber, a high vaulted ceiling above divided by columns. Natorian had a gut sense that they were heading towards the threat, a familiar rising anticipation and tension.

'Some of this is bone,' said Stannos, looking down at the debris they were kicking and crunching through as they ran, his enhanced senses taking in information at a speed even other Space Marines could not comprehend. 'Also armour, spent ammunition.'

'I smell blood too,' said Karlan. 'Old blood, but blood.

Thick enough to get through these filters.' He tapped the muzzle of his helmet. 'No, wait... fresher blood, over here.'

They were approaching a pile of bodies, a huddle of humanoid forms entangled in a heap.

'Form a defensive position,' Fakuno ordered. 'These are not ancient bones.'

They halted near the bodies, Stannos and Karlan pointing their weapons outwards, searching for any movement, while Fakuno beckoned for Natorian to join him to inspect the corpses.

'What say you, Brother Natorian?' asked Fakuno, as he rolled over the top corpse. It was of a mortal man in red uniform, stained with a darker red.

'Servants of my Chapter,' Natorian said, though Fakuno would have guessed that just as Natorian had, the moment they saw fallen mortals. He helped Fakuno move more corpses. The servants' clothes were slashed, but also burned in places. Some seemed to have died in terror, others looked placid, as if death had come quietly. The corpses were in the early stages of decay, and very limp, as if their bones were shattered.

'Genestealers did not kill these people,' said Natorian quietly. 'Not all of them. They seem to have been dropped from a great height, perhaps after death...'

He looked up, but the darkness consumed any hole in the ceiling above from which the bodies could have been discarded into this sprawling crypt.

'If I wanted facts, Natorian, I would have used Stannos' eyes,' said Fakuno, a cold urgency to his voice. 'What do you *see*?' Natorian looked down at the bodies once more, and felt a series of fleeting impressions. Of fear, of confusion, of a sense of betrayal and that the universe was not as it should be. Of a powerful presence, strong enough to dominate weak and powerful souls alike. Natorian could feel that presence himself, above them now.

He shook off the impressions like a bad taste, filled with revulsion.

'Something terrible nests near,' he said, spitting the words. 'It can break the minds of men to its will and it cannot be allowed to leave here.'

The words seemed inadequate as he mouthed them. The impressions were so fleeting, vague, lost emotions of the dead. He realised he was offering no concrete threat, nothing tactically useful. But what need did they have for his advice, these scions of great Chapters, with their long history dating back to when the Emperor himself bestrode the galaxy?

'Whatever this evil is, we will find it and destroy it,' said Fakuno, and Stannos and Karlan gave an enthusiastic 'aye' of support. Natorian had offered them vagaries, yet they trusted his instincts implicitly. He realised that this was what it was to be part of the Deathwatch, part of the Adeptus Astartes even: that long history or pedigree meant much, but little compared to the bonds formed in battle, and the bonds between this kill team were stronger than any ancestral history.

They kept moving, and when Natorian passed a pillar bearing the faint signs of a red bird painted there long ago he only briefly paused. He thought to mention it to his brothers, but then decided against it and moved on, quickly and in silence. The dreams of the Blood Ravens were irrelevant to the Deathwatch.

* * *

At the far end of the crypt, they found stairs leading up, spiralling away into darkness, and they followed them. After the organic shapes of previous rooms, these steps were flat and angular, worn to a polish – countless foot-steps had passed this way over the millennia.

When they reached the top, they emerged into one cor-ner of a vast chamber of onyx, the floor chiselled perfectly flat, the walls reaching up in sharp, brutal columns, all intersecting high above where a sickly light fell from some unknown source. High on the walls were sprawling balco-nies and alcoves carved into the black, stone-like substance, and at the very centre of the room, protruding from the floor, stood a sculpture of twisting shapes and harsh angles, light gleaming off its many facets in impossible ways.

'It looks like an altar in a cathedral,' said Karlan.

'A black cathedral,' said Stannos. 'I have never seen a place like this built in worship of the Emperor.'

'There's no stench of heresy here though,' said Natorian. He knew the presence of Chaos, of daemonic influences and the heretical sects that bowed to them, but this wasn't that. It was alien, dead. As foul as this alien architecture was, it was not the source of Natorian's visions.

'This is not the work of genestealers,' said Fakuno.

'No,' said a new voice, and the brothers of the Death-watch snapped their weapons in its direction. It was Lanneus who spoke as he walked alone across the sheer black floor. His voice was cracked, his armour battered and scorched. He was alone.

'The genestealers moved in here from elsewhere in the hulk,' said Lanneus.

'How do you know all this?' asked Karlan. 'And where is Godrew?'

'Godrew did not reach the interior, I'm afraid,' said Lanneus. 'He struggled, but was lost to the wilds of space. And as for how I know, I simply observe, and apply my own knowledge. There is nothing that cannot be discovered if you apply your mind to it. Isn't that right, Natorian?'

'That is certainly our belief,' said Natorian, the words terse and hollow in his mouth. Lanneus' manner perturbed him.

'You bring us news of our brother's death, and lecture us on knowledge?' spat Karlan. 'How is he lost and yet you found your way back to us, Librarian?'

'Karlan, you... overreach yourself,' said Fakuno. 'Do you not see, this is no time for petty recriminations?'

'Karlan is right to feel angry,' said Lanneus, and Natorian felt a strange pressure building behind his eyes. 'This old Blood Raven does not blame him for his thirst for vengeance, for his outrage.'

'I do not need you to defend me,' snarled Karlan, his temper flaring. His words were beginning to slur.

'Karlan!' shouted Fakuno, standing between the Blood Angel and the Blood Raven. 'Enough!'

The rest of the chamber seemed distant now. Even Stannos, who had not spoken, seemed transfixed with the argument between Lanneus and Karlan. Something was sticking in Natorian's head: Blood Angels, Blood Ravens, blood, blood, blood.

Karlan let out a bestial roar and lunged at Fakuno. Stannos tried to pull him back.

Blood, thought Natorian. Blood will be spilt.

Blood had been spilt, long ago, when Natorian was a child. The blood of all he cared for, while Natorian hid. Red blood spilling across the floor, and over the bodies–

It had been aliens who spilt that blood, the blood of Natorian's family. Just as it had been aliens that he had fought across the galaxy ever since, fought with cold, hard, rage. Aliens all around them. A galaxy full of aliens to be fought.

Aliens to be fought now. Natorian's cold hatred of the alien cut through the thoughts of blood and burning, allowed him to see the truth.

They had all been beguiled, focussed on each other, their minds clouded.

The genestealers were all around them. Dozens of them, close enough to touch the Space Marines in their midst, closing in quietly. Natorian drew in a sharp, flat breath – how could they not have seen what was right in front of them?

There was only one way. That cold, hard rage flowed through Natorian, focussed into bioelectricity, into his weapon. Natorian slammed the base of his staff into the floor and unleashed a shock of bioelectricity that shot through the air to his target as he spoke the name.

'Lanneus!' boomed Natorian, and a bioelectric bolt hit Natorian's mentor in the chest, knocking him back. The genestealers scrambled out of the way as Lanneus reeled and stumbled between them, then closed their ranks.

Lanneus' influence broken, the kill team could see the genestealers all around them, and reacted fluidly. Fakuno and Stannos let go of Karlan, who shook his head and let out a low groan, but quickly regained his senses. Fakuno and Stannos raised their bolters, opening fire. Natorian focussed his anger, letting out a steady stream of bioelectric bursts into the genestealers, driving them back. They had held back while Lanneus had the Deathwatch under his influence, but now they responded to being attacked with slashing claws, jumping forwards to gouge and tear at the Space Marines.

'Fakuno to *Lethal Intent*,' Fakuno snapped, while firing bursts into the mass of xenos. 'We have located the genestealer threat and are being overwhelmed. I authorise an immediate neurotoxin strike to our position. Come about and target our beacon.' Stannos began to set up a homing device, his gauntleted fingers adjusting the sensitive equipment quickly and carefully.

'How did we not see them?' demanded Stannos as he worked, clearly unnerved that even his senses could be overcome. 'How?'

'Lanneus,' said Natorian. He felt no undue humility speaking to these First Founding Adeptus Astartes now. He was one of them, and he knew of what he spoke. This was the knowledge that mattered, the kind gained through hard experience. 'He influenced us all, drew us into conflict and blinded us to our own mission.'

'He filled my mind with anger,' said Karlan. His voice was weary and battered, but his bolter joined the fray, firing on the xenos surrounding them. 'Pushing thoughts of rage into my head.'

'How could a psyker blind us all?' asked Stannos.

'It was not Lanneus alone who did this,' said Natorian. 'Something else acted through him, something that got into his head and increased his abilities. It bent Lanneus' mind to its will, subjugated him.'

+Subjugated?+ said Lanneus. He was in Natorian's mind now, reaching out from somewhere among the genestealers. +I have been freed, my mind opened to new knowledge.+

From somewhere within the horde of genestealers a dozen chunks of debris were flung into the air, crackling with psychic energy as they rained down on the kill team at a velocity that would pierce even power armour.

'No!' shouted Natorian, wielding his staff upwards, a barely controlled bioelectric burst disintegrating the missiles before they could reach their targets. The burst pushed outwards as well as up, knocking half a dozen genestealers back, buying the kill team a precious few seconds before the next attack.

'The neurotoxin strike is incoming,' said Fakuno. 'The *Intent* will need to align with this section of the hulk first, so we must hold this position and protect the beacon until then.'

+You will be dead long before,+ said Lanneus in Natorian's mind. +I will crush you and your beacon.+

Genestealers themselves were swept forwards towards the kill team next, picked up in a wave of psychic energy that ripped slabs of stone from the sheer black floor and turned them into projectiles. Natorian felt spent from the effort of deflecting the previous wave but forced himself to block the wave of psychic energy, holding his staff with both hands, the shaft glowing white as he willed the projectiles to slow. The genestealers themselves kept moving forwards, and as his brothers fought the creatures hand-to-claw he found himself pushed unwillingly out of the defensive circle into the mass of xenos.

+Why bring me here to kill me, Lanneus?+ he asked with a thought.

+I summoned you before my eyes were opened,+ said Lanneus. +I wish I had not. To kill my own brothers was bleak necessity. Your death will weigh heavier still.+

Lanneus' thoughts had an edge of exhaustion, of frustration to them now. Natorian could feel the exertion of the psychic attacks wearing his mentor down, the contradictions of the lies the Librarian Captain had told himself to justify his betrayal pulling at his sanity.

A genestealer ran at Natorian, clawed limbs slashing. Natorian ducked under one blow and, bioelectric energy coursing through his muscles, punched the creature so hard its purple skull crumpled beneath the blow.

+Where are you, Lanneus?+ he asked without sound. +Stop hiding behind these creatures, let us resolve this like brothers.+

'I do not hide,' Lanneus said aloud, and Natorian spun around to face his mentor, raising his staff defensively.

Lanneus' force sword hit the centre of Natorian's staff, breaking it in two with a tremendous release of psychic energy that sent both Blood Ravens reeling.

Natorian stood facing Lanneus, the two halves of his staff in his hands. His mentor was panting, luminous mist rising from his mouth, his eyes white with psychic energy. He was truly lost now. This was a dangerous moment – the Blood Raven could open a rift into the warp itself if forced into a further psychic attack. Natorian could feel the presence of his kill team close by, fighting the genestealers. Lanneus' attention had slipped from them to his old apprentice, so Natorian needed to buy them time to protect the beacon.

Natorian let the broken halves of his staff fall to the floor.

'I surrender to your greater knowledge,' he said. 'Show me what you have seen, Lanneus.'

'I will show you, Jensus,' said Lanneus, walking towards

Natorian, one hand raised. His eyes were burning, tears streaking down his cheeks and searing the skin red. 'Open your mind to me, and I will let its will pass through me into you. It is a great, bestial intelligence, a power unseen since the primarchs walked the galaxy.' Natorian could not lie to his mentor to get close enough to do what had to be done. He chose his words carefully as he took off his helmet and dropped it to the floor. He could feel the primal intensity of the horror that possessed Lanneus reaching out to him. It was lusting after the direct physical contact that would make Natorian's possession so much easier.

'I will help you, Lanneus,' he said with his left hand outstretched.

Lanneus clasped Natorian's hand in his own with gratitude.

'Thank you for your faith, Jensus,' he said. 'Together we will–'

The sentence ended when Natorian brought his right hand around in a fist, every bit of biomantic power coursing through his arm, strengthening the bones and muscles beyond even the capacity of a Space Marine, streaks of bio-electricity crackling off the knuckles of Natorian's gauntlet.

The blow hit Lanneus' jaw with unnatural strength and speed, and an explosion of psychic energy was unleashed as Natorian's fist met Lanneus' face. The impact vaporised Lanneus' head on contact, a blinding light illuminating the chamber, but the blow also reverberated down Natorian's arm, the feedback shattering every bone in his arm and hand in multiple places.

The pain was incredible, beyond anything Natorian had ever experienced in his life of war, and as Lanneus' corpse fell to the floor Natorian stumbled backwards, his arm

limp and held together only by his power armour. He
fell to his knees, but as he did so the genestealers were in
agony too, blinded by the psychic explosion that killed
Lanneus, flailing and lashing. Natorian looked across
and saw the three survivors of his kill team, their armour
dented and slashed, but still alive. He was determined to
help them, but as he forced his body to move missiles
smashed through the outer wall of the chamber.

The barrage hit, neurotoxic agents rapidly spreading
inside as the chamber began to void through the ragged
punctures in the hull. Natorian could hear the distant
sound of explosions as missiles burst through into other
parts of the hulk, unleashing puffs of acidic poison into
the whole area.

As the genestealers began to reel, their flesh bubbling
and bursting as the toxic clouds consumed them, Natorian quickly scooped up his helmet with his good hand
and locked it back on to his head. The chamber was filling with roiling clouds of toxin in spite of the pressure
loss, and the flailing genestealers were kicking debris in
every direction as they ran.

'Natorian, withdraw,' Fakuno ordered over the vox, and
Natorian looked up to see the rest of the kill team clearing a path for him, releasing a burst of bolter fire on any
genestealers who got too close.

Lanneus' force sword caught Natorian's eye, and as a
genestealer lurched towards him, screeching in agony and
body boiling, Natorian swept up the blade in one hand
and decapitated the creature with one swipe.

As he ran to join the kill team, Natorian felt something
pull at his consciousness, and he looked across the chamber. There he could see a genestealer, to the eye barely

different to any other, but to a psyker like Jensus Natorian it was a burning presence, alight with psychic power. This was the presence he had felt before, much stronger than the psychic background noise of the genestealers, the terrible intelligence that had broken the mind of a once-noble Space Marine like Lanneus.

Then the creature collapsed to the floor, the rushing toxic mist consuming it, and Natorian's sense of its psychic presence was gone.

As detonations spread deadly clouds of toxins throughout the black cathedral, the kill team evacuated.

Natorian watched the bombardment of *Endless Despair* through a viewport on board the *Lethal Intent*. Explosive blooms lit up space as the cruiser's guns bombarded the hulk. Eventually, the Blood Ravens cruiser *Burden of Proof* was consumed by the spreading explosions. Natorian had argued that his Chapter should be contacted and allowed to retrieve the ship, but he had been overruled. The *Endless Despair* was to be marked on Imperial maps as dangerous, and to be destroyed by a larger strike force. The fate of all Blood Ravens on board would be listed as 'Unknown' in the Imperial archives, and no further expeditions into the hulk, or any ship connected to it, would be allowed.

Natorian's broken arm was bound as it healed, and he rested his shattered hand on the pommel of Lanneus' force sword, which now hung from a belt around his waist.

'Will you return the sword to the Chapter, my lord?' asked Heffl. 'The artificers hold a number of fine staffs of great heritage which might replace yours, I am sure they would be proud to–'

'No, Heffl,' said Natorian. 'I will keep the sword.'

'Yes, my lord,' said Heffl with a deep bow. He knew when his master wished to be alone, and he withdrew.

Looking on as the *Endless Despair* burned in silence, his hand on his dead mentor's sword, Natorian knew then that there would never be an end to it. From those blighted memories of his early life as the xenos had killed his family, to the life of war he had lived since then as a Blood Raven and a member of the Deathwatch, the different species of alien maintained a relentless onslaught on humanity, and they never stopped. They ravaged, they killed, they even had abominable psykers amongst their numbers that could corrupt noble souls like Lanneus to their repulsive purpose, forcing brother to slay brother. There was no end to the horror of the xenos threat.

They would keep coming, again and again, until the last light in the galaxy was extinguished.

CEPHEUS

BRADEN CAMPBELL

The chamber into which he walked was circular, high-ceilinged, and lit only by four immense candelabra – one that hung suspended over a small platform in the centre of the room, and three that cast down flickering orange on the watch captains. To his right, obscured within the shadows, was a scribe-servitor. It had quills for fingers and containers of ink mounted on its forearms. A seemingly infinite scroll of parchment protruded from its mouth and spilled across the floor, while its glowing red optics watched him unblinkingly.

Barefoot and dressed only in a heavy robe, he silently made his way to the platform.

The captains surveyed him coolly. It was a tradition that the petitioner neither wore his power armour nor carried a weapon. He was a Space Marine, just as they were, and as such, no longer experienced fear. Still, was it not written in the Codex, '*Look to your wargear, brothers, and let it never leave your sight. Your armour is your lifeward, and your boltgun is the Emperor's wrath incarnate.'* To be unarmed and unarmoured conflicted with his psycho-indoctrination.

He suspected that was exactly the point – for the applicant to rendered humble, to be made pliable and open to manipulation. Perhaps he might reveal some hidden truth or detail upon which they might pounce. Well, such tactics might provide fruitful results against a less experienced battle-brother, but there were very few who had lived a life as long and filled with war as he had. He had long since mastered every nuance of the nineteen implants that separated him from mortal men. He could not be manipulated or coerced.

He willed his body to quiet itself. His pulse slowed. His shoulder muscles relaxed. The memorised lines of the Codex Astartes that were calling for him to arm himself against the foe lowered their protestations to a whisper.

The watch captains were each seated in an elaborate throne ringed with a carved wooden desk. As he took his place in the centre of the chamber, thick servo-arms in the backs of their seats lifted them high above the floor where they could suitably lord over those called before them. The centremost of the three, a man with a short, grey beard, tapped a sheaf of parchment. The black surface of his armour was broken only by the bright green field on his right shoulder plate.

'This council is now come to order,' he said in the distinctive brogue of his home Chapter. Nearby, the servitor's quills began scratching against the parchment. 'State your name, rank, and Chapter of origin for the record.'

'Ortan Cassius, Chaplain of the Ultramarines.'

'Presiding are Watch Captain Bresnik, Watch Captain Seumas, and myself, Watch Captain Drusus.'

Cassius was familiar with Drusus and Bresnik, both of whom were stern but well-respected leaders. In their home Chapters, they each commanded a company of one hundred Space Marines, and both were adherents of the Codex. He fully trusted that they would find no fault in what he had done, for had they been in his place they would have done exactly the same.

He did not recall ever hearing Seumas' name before, however. Nor did he recognise the heraldry of his home Chapter; a yellow field emblazoned with a black, winged lightning bolt.

Bresnik rubbed his cheek. 'Chaplain Cassius, you have been called here today before a congress of your superiors in the Deathwatch because you have made a specific request. You are petitioning to assemble a kill team and travel to the Ghosarian System in order to locate certain members of your previous kill team, sent there on a mission of lethal investigation.'

'Yes,' Cassius said. 'There has been no communication with them for some time.'

'There are many possible explanations for why they have so far failed to report in,' Captain Bresnik said. 'The parameters of their mission might even forbid it.'

'I am responsible,' Cassius answered, 'and so it falls to me to discover what that explanation is. Not only was I their original team leader, but I was also their Chaplain.'

'Am I my battle-brother's keeper?' Seumas said quietly.

Cassius had never heard the Chaplain's duty put so poetically before, but he found that he liked the turn of phrase. All loyal Space Marines, regardless of their doctrines, beliefs, or traditions, were ultimately brothers – sharing a genetic lineage that stretched back through ten millennia of unceasing duty to the Emperor. It was easy in these turbulent times for the various Chapters to remain at odds, to be insular and isolated from one another. Yet, the Deathwatch was composed of recruits from many different backgrounds. Friend and foe alike had to learn to work together against the common xenos threat, to eradicate the alien from the face of the galaxy. The duty of a Deathwatch chaplain was therefore compounded beyond such parochial boundaries; he had to guard the spiritual well-being of the whole of the Emperor's family.

'Yes, watch captain. I am my battle-brothers' keeper.'

Watch Captain Drusus continued. 'We have considered your request, Chaplain Cassius, and are prepared to deliver a verdict.'

'But firstly,' Seumas interrupted him, 'I should like to review the events that took place in the Vadol Majoris System, Ultima Segmentum, at 859680.M41, referred to in your reports as "the Incident at Port Cepheus".'

Cassius frowned inwardly. To him, Seumas seemed callous and arrogant. 'I have already submitted my report in full,' he said, 'and given it my seal to verify the contents.'

'Yes, I have it here,' Seumas replied.

'Then what more can I tell you that you have not already read?'

'I beg your indulgence, Chaplain,' Seumas said. 'I have not had the same amount of time to pore over your report as my esteemed brothers have.' He laced his fingers together and leaned forwards intently. 'I would very much like to hear what happened in your own words. And perhaps you would consent to clarify a few things for me?'

'I am here to serve, my lords,' Cassius said.

'Excellent. It is my understanding that in your time with

the Deathwatch, you have undertaken… well, more field missions that I can readily count.'

'Indeed. It is *my* understanding that I currently hold the record for both the number of kill team operations, and tours of re-enlistment.'

'Quite true,' Captain Bresnik confirmed, 'and quite commendable.'

'Many decades of service,' Seumas said. 'Indeed, Chaplain, mankind is in your debt. You have done great things to keep the xenos threat at bay. You've been the death of orks, eldar, borlac, chuffians, hrud – and now, it seems, an Imperial space station.'

Cassius did not bristle at the implied attack on his character. He had calmed himself to the point where his hearts were beating a mere twenty-five times per minute. Watch Captain Drusus, however, was not so restrained.

'I will remind you, Captain Seumas, that your own teams have been far from innocent when it comes to the issue of grievous collateral damage.'

Seumas ignored him. 'Brother-Chaplain, do you feel your actions in this instance were absolutely necessary?'

'*Walls, trenches and towers are no obstacle,*' Cassius said, quoting directly from the writings of Guilliman. '*Lack of imagination and lack of will are obstacles.*'

'The Codex Astartes,' Captain Bresnik said in benediction. For a moment the chamber fell silent. Even the scribe-servitor ceased its transcription.

'As it is written, so it must be. I withdraw my previous comment.' Captain Seumas cleared his throat. 'Be that as it may, Chaplain Cassius, even you must admit that some of the elements in your report strain credulity.'

'Such as?'

'The creatures, primarily.'

'Their xeno-identity has been positively confirmed since the incident.'

Seumas paused, considering his next words. 'Does the name Chaegryn mean anything to you?'

'That is enough!' Bresnik shouted, slamming an armoured fist down on the desk before him. The wood cracked with a sound like gunfire. 'The Chaplain's report stands. Nothing further can be gained from inference and speculation.'

'Indeed,' Drusus said. 'Chaplain Cassius, after reviewing the details of your petition, the council has decided that–'

'Drogg Mordakka,' Seumas exclaimed.

Cassius' heart rate increased. 'He has been found? Dealt with?'

Seumas reclined into his seat, confident now that the inquiry would continue. 'Let the record show that the name Drogg Mordakka refers to an ork leader with an apparent predilection for salvaged Imperial technology. No, Chaplain Cassius, he has not been located or killed, in so far as I am aware. That task was given to you, is that not correct?'

'It was.'

'By whom?'

'Watch Captain Drusus.'

Seumas turned to face the elder captain. 'Perhaps Watch Captain Drusus could elaborate, then.'

Drusus, clearly annoyed, ran a hand over his beard once more. 'Drogg Mordakka began raiding Imperial settlements on the Eastern Fringe three years ago. Captain Bresnik and I were aware of him, but did not take any action against him until recently.'

'Why is that?' Seumas asked.

Bresnik answered. 'There were more important threats to deal with. That is, until he attacked the colony on Vinicus.'

'In the same sector as Port Cepheus,' Seumas said.

Drusus nodded. 'Bolstered by that victory, other green-skins rallied to his side. The surge in numbers prompted a re-evaluation, and termination was prescribed. His crusade of violence, the so-called "Waaagh! Mek", was defeated by a combined Imperial force which included units of the Deathwatch. Mordakka managed to escape destruction however, and Chaplain Cassius was tasked with hunting him down.'

'And so, Chaplain,' Seumas glanced down to his notes, 'your ten-member kill team arrived in the Vadol Majoris System onboard the *Veritas*, a Gladius-class frigate. And as soon as you exited the warp, you received the distress call from Port Cepheus.'

'That is correct.'

'They were under attack by xenos life forms.'

'Again, correct.'

'You ordered the *Veritas* to respond immediately, because you assumed that the port was being attacked by Drogg Mordakka.'

'At the time, it was the likeliest conclusion,' Cassius said.

Seumas leaned forwards again, marking carefully every word that was about to proceed from the Chaplain's mouth. 'But it wasn't the greenskins who were attacking the port, was it?'

'No, watch captain. It was not.'

Port Cepheus was typical of many Imperial refuelling stations. It had a tower at its centre that contained cogitator banks, command decks, and cramped living quarters for any crew or workers beyond mere servitors. From the base of the tower, four fat piers reached out into space. There was an open area on each where a mid-sized vessel could dock. Immense conduits and tanks ran along their upper and lower sides. At their ends were thruster assemblies of titanic proportions that fired occasionally to keep the platform upright and stable. Beneath all of this dangled dozens of pipes, each one several miles long, which vanished into the upper cloud layer of the gas giant that the port orbited. An outside observer might have been left with the impression of a jellyfish trailing its tentacles through the water.

Most of the time, it was a quiet place. Today, however, it was crying out into the void.

Cassius peered into the augur array. There were no enemy vessels on the scope, but sensors could be fooled. He raised his head and surveyed his kill team. There were nine of them standing around him; nine battle-brothers drawn from nine different Chapters. It was not the smallest flock he had ever been tasked with shepherding, but it was certainly the most diverse.

'The distress call is automated,' Cassius said, referring to the string of numbers, time and date stamps, and the two words that were issuing from the port's alert systems.

'*Hostica ignotus*?' Koden asked. The Space Wolf's oversized canine teeth made every consonant he spoke particularly hard.

'Imperial Navy shorthand,' replied Vael Donatus, Cassius' brother of the Ultramarines Chapter. 'And archaic at that. It means the station is under attack by unidentified hostiles.'

'It must be the orks,' Omid snapped. He made a fist with his left hand, the one painted a bright red.

'An isolated promethium refinery on the edge of the system is just the kind of target Drogg Mordakka would choose,' Captain Ectros added.

Jonat Teven wasn't as convinced. 'Why would they bother to attack this place? Greenskins like a fight – the bigger, the better. There seems little challenge here.'

'Perhaps they need the fuel,' Donatus offered.

'Who else might it be, all the way out here?' Omid asked.

'Brother Donatus,' Cassius said, 'inform the port that their message has been received and that we are inbound.'

'We would be wise to use an encrypted channel,' Omid offered, 'in case Mordakka is inclined to eavesdrop.'

Ectros gave a snort of derision. 'You give the orks too much credit.'

'No, he does not,' Cassius said sternly. He folded his arms and glared. The captain was as honourable and steadfast a Space Marine as any Cassius had ever met. He was a valuable member of the kill team, but he was too used to being in command. Here in the Deathwatch, his rank did not automatically afford him the same level of command and respect as he enjoyed in the White Consuls. Experience outweighed titles, and Cassius had lived twice as long as he. He gestured for Omid to give an explanation.

'Despite what many believe, greenskins are capable of trickery and subterfuge. I wouldn't discount the possibility that Drogg is hiding within the gas giant, ready to ambush us at a moment's notice. We've seen it before.'

Cassius nodded, and gestured to Ectros. 'You have served in the Deathwatch long enough now, Thaniel. Have you not learned that assumptions, especially where alien beings are concerned, can prove fatal? You must divest yourself of your preconceptions, and utilise the varied expertise of your team members. You will never become an effective watch captain until you do.'

Ectros' jaw worked, but he remained silent.

'I didn't hear you,' Cassius said.

'I understand, Chaplain,' he said tersely.

'Don't simply understand. Put it into practice – or else our time has been wasted.' Cassius lowered his arm again. 'Vael, contact the port. The rest of you, look to your wargear and prepare your hearts for battle. Insertion for this mission will be via drop pod.'

Ectros frowned. 'Respectfully, Port Cepheus can accommodate a ship of this size. Should we not simply dock the *Veritas* on one of the fuelling piers?'

Cassius' answer was a loaded one. 'Is that what you would do, brother, if this were your kill team instead of mine?'

Ectros took a moment to consider, looking for what he had missed. 'Granted, if there is an ork vessel lying in ambush, the *Veritas* becomes a stationary target if she docks. Conversely, if we use drop craft, not only is our deployment safe from possible interception, but the ship will remain free to act against any potential enemies. I see the wisdom of it.'

'Then hope remains,' Cassius said.

The others each saluted in their own ways and left the chamber while Donatus accessed the main vox-array. His brow furrowed. 'There is no response on any of the long or mid-range channels. Even their distress call is being routed through a secondary system. It could be a mechanical failure.'

'More likely, their communications have been purpose-fully sabotaged so that no one outside of their immediate vicinity will be able to hear them.'

'I had reached the same conclusion, brother.'

Cassius opened a channel and called down to the lower decks. 'Increase to best speed, and prepare for drop-deployment. Forward lance batteries at full ready.'

The *Veritas* had been designed to transport a single Space Marine unit, along with all the attendant serfs and vehicular support, rapidly across interstellar distances. Her engines were among the best in her class, and before long, the station loomed large beneath them. The vox-channels still registered nothing but empty static and background noise, and the endlessly repeating distress call that no one save the crew of the *Veritas* would ever be able to hear.

By the time Cassius and Donatus entered the cramped space within the drop pod, the other team members had stowed all of their weapons and locked themselves into restraining harnesses. Donatus took a moment to ensure that his prized Artifex pattern boltgun was safely racked before locking himself into place.

The deployment doors slowly closed. Cassius took his place in the sole remaining alcove and signalled to the bridge crew that all was ready. Deep reverberations came through the pod walls as cumbersome machinery was roused from sleep.

There was an anticipatory moment of stillness, and then they were away.

The pod rocketed from the ship with a velocity that would have pulverised most mortal men. The Space Marines were lifted upwards until their restraints creaked.

Cassius muttered the Liturgy of Freefall, asking the Emperor's blessing to be upon the machine-spirit of their transport. Otherwise, there was no sound but the dim roaring of thrusters beneath their feet, until Donatus spoke over the vox-channel they all shared.

'Brother-Chaplain, I've been monitoring Port Cepheus' short-range comms. Something is coming in.'

'Let's hear it.'

The kill team's helmets were immediately filled with a woman's strained voice. As she shouted, the background was filled with overlapping cries, the whine of turbine engines and staccato lasgun fire.

'...don't care, just secure the main door! Incoming Imperial vessel, I pray you can hear us. We are evacuating the station via Aquila lander. Repeat, we are evacuating the station.'

'Port Cepheus,' Cassius shouted back, 'this is Chaplain Ortan Cassius of the Deathwatch, commanding the starship Veritas. A relief force is currently inbound to your location. Remain where you are.'

Someone was screaming. The woman's voice called over the din to her would-be saviours. 'Not a chance. We're lifting off.'

Cassius cursed. Fear always drove mortals to act irrationally.

He called up the pod's exterior feeds. His helmet's visor display was suddenly filled with a scene from the landing scanners mounted at the base of the exterior doors. Port Cepheus seemed to be rushing up towards him through a halo of retro-rocket flame. As they had seen on the long-range augurs, three of the station's docking spars were vacant. On the fourth sat a bulk freighter – its hull was ancient, pitted and dull, and thoroughly unremarkable.

Then he saw the lander, near the base of the central tower. Its wings were spread like those of an eagle, but the rest of it displayed none of its namesake's gracefulness as it heaved up from the deck and began a wobbling climb.

'Aquila lander,' Cassius called, 'you will not be permitted to dock with our ship until we have ascertained the nature of your distress call.'

'There's no ti–'

The link went dead.

Cassius watched the Aquila as it began a drunken roll to one side, before striking the deck with its wing tip. The fuselage came down hard on the docking pier, and the fuel tanks inside the hull ruptured. Still within Port Cepheus' limited atmospheric envelope, the lander exploded, the short-lived fireball scattering smouldering hunks of armour plating noiselessly across the surface of the station.

The others did not respond, though many of them had also witnessed the crash. The pod signalled that it would impact in ten seconds.

'Weapons ready!' Cassius barked. He flicked off the external feed and drew his bolt pistol. 'Consider our landing zone hostile!'

And then, with a mighty, thundering impact, they were down. The restraining harness retracted from Cassius' shoulders, and the doors surrounding them all fell away with a flurry of locking bolt reports.

As he and the others exited the pod, it became immediately apparent that the port's gravitic generators had been sent offline by the force of the lander's destruction. The mag-lock plates in the soles of their armoured boots vibrated softly as they worked to keep each warrior securely bound to the space station's deck.

Cassius found himself flanked by Omid and his heavy bolter on one side, and by Donatus on the other.

'Auspex,' the chaplain barked. 'Scan for survivors.'

Koden moved up beside Omid, a portable scanner in his outstretched hand. He aimed the device towards the wreckage of the Aquila, pieces of which were already beginning to drift away into the void. 'No survivors. Nothing within fifty yards in any direction.'

'No life forms at all? What about from within the station?'

Koden shook his head.

Cassius surveyed the area. Port Cepheus' central tower lay a short distance to his left, but its viewports were dark. Beyond the crashed lander loomed the corroded hull of the bulk cargo freighter. What few windows the ship had were as black and lifeless as the station's. Huge, twisting pipes connected its cylindrical midsection to the pier's deck plating. White lettering, faded to obscurity, stretched across its bow.

'Brother Pranus,' Cassius called.

One of the Space Marines near the back of the formation raised his head. His right shoulder guard was a field of blue emblazoned with a skull and a twelve-pointed star. 'Brother-Chaplain?'

'Go with Omid and two others. I want a sweep of that freighter.'

'Understood, my lord.' Pranus gestured to the Space Marines on either side of him. 'I'll take Brothers Siegfric and Thalassi.'

Cassius nodded in agreement. 'Captain Ectros and I will lead the remainder of the team through the station on the chance that there are additional survivors. We will also retrieve the station logs and personnel files from the cogitator banks. Keep the vox-channel open at all times.'

'We are no longer concerning ourselves with potential eavesdroppers?' Ectros asked. The captain's voice carried a trace of cynicism that Cassius did not fail to notice.

'Mordakka is not here,' he said quietly.

'Can we be so certain?'

Cassius watched as Pranus, Omid, Thalassi and Siegfric made their way past the wreckage of the Aquila and towards the freighter.

'If he were, he would have attacked us by now.'

'*Hostica ignotus*. If not greenskins,' Ectros asked, 'then what?'

To that, Cassius had no answer.

The central spire's nearest voidlock stood open. Within, a blinking blue light futilely warned of complete depressurisation. Cassius and Donatus entered first, followed by Ectros and the others.

Beyond the open airlock was a large, darkened chamber filled with storage lockers, and a wide, circular stairwell. A ceramic cup surrounded by frozen droplets of some dark brown liquid twirled end over end in the absence of gravity.

Cassius pointed to Koden, who once again held up his auspex.

'Still registering no life forms,' he said. 'The station's atmospheric envelope has failed. This is hard vacuum.'

'Vael,' the Chaplain said, 'lead the way. The xenos must be purged!'

Donatus moved to the base of the stairwell, his bolt-gun at the ready. They began their climb in single file.

On the second level, they passed a space that had once served as a communal dining area. Chairs and long metal tables drifted aimlessly, banging into one another. Above that, they encountered floor after floor of empty hab-compartments.

It was on the seventh level that they encountered the remains of two makeshift barricades. Supply crates and empty fuel drums now floated freely, but Cassius could see how they had been used to block the stairs. An empty lasgun lay on the floor, secured in place by a frozen pool of blood. Tattered shreds of beige cloth drifted lazily, their edges stained red.

A nearby wall caught Cassius' eye. It looked as if something had exploded against it, leaving a dark stain. Tiny, jagged shards were embedded all around it. He pulled one of them out and held it between his fingers. It was deep indigo, shot through with veins of black.

'Up here!' Donatus called.

Cassius flicked the fragment away.

The command deck was located on the next and topmost floor. A set of thick blast doors, their external surfaces covered with deep scratches and grooves, greeted the Space Marines. Something – perhaps several somethings – had been trying desperately to get in here.

Cassius pushed past Ectros and the others to Donatus' side, and together they hauled the doors open.

The chamber was circular in shape, with archways to both left and right. In the centre of the room squatted a bank of bulky cogitator machines. Two of their front panels had been removed so that a nest of wires and connectors spilled from the open space. The wall opposite the blast doors was dominated by a long crystalflex window.

Wordlessly, Cassius signalled for Ectros and Koden to each search one of the adjoining rooms while he crossed to the window. Through it, he could look out on all four of Port Cepheus' docking piers. There was a second Aquila lander, he saw, sitting quietly on an elevated platform near the pitted freighter. The topmost viewports of the large ship were now brightly lit, and so he opened a vox-channel to the second team.

'Pranus, report.'

'Brother-Chaplain, we have completed a search of the lower decks and are currently on the vessel's bridge. We've seen no indication of hostile xenos or the vessel's crew.'

'What is the status of the ship itself?'

'Completely intact.'

'Are you able to rouse its machine-spirit?' Donatus asked. He had squatted down to examine the patchwork wiring more closely.

'Yes,' came the reply. *'Easily.'*

'What is the vessel's name?' Cassius demanded. 'Where did it come from?'

'The Pride of Ghosar. *An ore freighter from the Ghosarian System. It arrived forty-seven hours before we did.'*

'Has it been resupplied?'

'Yes, Chaplain. The ship is fully refuelled, and carries a full cargo load. A return course to the planet of Ghosar Quintus has already been plotted.'

Donatus pulled something free from within the tangled innards of the cogitator and stood up. In his hand he held a battered dataslate.

'Station logs?' Cassius asked.

Donatus nodded. 'Useless. Scrambled and corrupted.'

Koden emerged from the nearest doorway and said,

'Equipment storage. Thoroughly ransacked. There are compartments for fifteen environment suits. Half a dozen of them are missing.'

'Ectros?' Cassius called out.

The captain stepped back into the room. He held a rectangular device in his left hand. 'I found nothing of note, save for this.'

'A vox-corder?'

Ectros nodded and handed the box to Donatus. After a moment, he depressed a button on the side of the device, and the voice of the woman they had spoken with earlier filled their helmets.

'I'll... I'll try to make this as brief as possible. If for some reason we are unsuccessful in our escape attempt, then at least there'll be some kind of record. It's been nearly two days since the creatures appeared, and in that time more than half of the station's crew have either been killed or gone missing. I have no idea what happened to all the servitors. Maybe they just tore them apart so that they couldn't repair any of our communications systems.

'These things – we don't know what to call them – are smart. We thought they were just animals at first, but they disabled the primary power grid somehow, and slaughtered our astropaths. They intentionally cut us off from any kind of outside help, isolating us so that they could finish us off at leisure. Chameron was able to reroute a distress call through the secondary systems, though. He wasn't even sure that it would reach far enough for anyone to hear.

'I want it noted that the crew of Port Cepheus defended this installation to the end. I mean, they're mostly dock workers and menial mechanics, but they did the work of any Militarum guardsmen. They set up barricades on the floor below

us, and when the... things... rushed *them*... well, they kept...
they kept on...

'Well, there's only six of us now. Myself, Chameron, Chief
Medicae Gryr, Alexus and the Inge brothers. The blast doors
seem to have held the damned things off for now, but it's only
a matter of time before they find some other way to get in
here. So, we've decided to just run for it while we can... try
and get off the station and rendezvous with the approaching
Adeptus Astartes frigate. We'll take the lander – no way I'm
going anywhere near that freighter. It's no coincidence that the
infestation started right after it arrived. I know it.

'Anyway, I guess that's all there is to say. May the Emperor
have mercy on us. This is Overseer Lusi Arevik, Port Cepheus,
Vadol Majoris System.'

The recording ended with a click. The Space Marines
digested the information in silence for a moment.

'Pranus,' Cassius said, 'were you privy to that?'

'Yes, Chaplain. We heard it all.'

Cassius rifled through his memory. There were many
species in the galaxy that propagated themselves by
becoming stowaways. They would attach themselves to
the outer hulls of starships or hide away within their cluttered holds. Almost all of them were animalistic vermin of
one kind or another, and certainly couldn't have precipi-
tated a slaughter such as this. The only possible candidates
he could call to mind were–

'There's something else you should see, my lord – patching
through to your display now.'

Brother Pranus' rune-icon blinked up in Cassius' helm,
and his visual feed overlaid the visor. The Chaplain saw
the dismal interior of the *Pride of Ghosar*, all bare metal
bulkheads and worn decking. Nothing out of the ordinary.

Then Pranus turned to the rearmost wall of the bridge, and Cassius was filled with fresh hatred for all the unspeakable forms of xenos he had ever encountered.

Elegantly depicted in ageing fresco was a devotional mural of the Emperor of Mankind, defiled as though by some madman's whim. His teeth were fangs, and his too-many hands tipped with elongated claws. Beneath this abomination, rendered in crudely sprayed lacquer, were the words 'BLESSED BE THE TRYSST! ALL HAIL THE FOUR-ARMED EMPEROR!'

Blinking away the feed in disgust, Cassius returned his attention to the chamber in which he stood.

In that fractional instant, he caught the barest glimpse of *something* as it flew up the main stairwell and through the open blast doors – a blur of limbs and chitinous shell and teeth that hurled itself against Brother Koden's shoulders. The Space Wolf gave a grunt and stumbled forwards with the unexpected impact.

Cassius raised his crozius arcanum, the gilded power maul that was the symbol of his office, above his head. He meant to remove the creature from Koden's back with one fell blow, but he never got the chance. The crystal-flex window beside him shattered soundlessly as three more creatures forced their way into the control room. Like the one attacking Koden, they were multi-limbed and covered with an indigo-coloured shell. Their heads were dominated by mouths filled with teeth the size of knives.

Possessed of a hellish speed, they were upon the team before they could react.

The xenos slashed at Cassius' chest with their claws. One of them attempted to bite its way through the top of his helmet. With a cry of defiance, he swung the crozius. One of the monsters was struck across the face. Globules of dark blood sprayed out from between its teeth and spattered against the wall.

A pair of jaws clamped around his left leg. The reinforced plating of his greave buckled slightly but did not give way. Again he brought his maul down, and again he made his attackers bleed.

Still, the damnable things refused to die. Distantly, he realised that they were trying to render him defenceless by pinning him to the floor, and that it was only the magnetic plating in his boots that was holding him upright. He saw his brethren fighting back with the righteous zeal that befitted loyal servants of the Deathwatch.

He shouted an oath to the Emperor. Then a long talon raked across his faceplate.

Half blinded, Cassius swung his crozius on instinct. He felt reverberations up the length of his arm as an alien skull exploded across the weapon's weighted end.

A dark maw filled his vision as one of the creatures made to bite at his faceplate. He drew his pistol from the holster on his hip, and fired.

In the airless vacuum, he was denied the rewarding sound of a bolt leaving the chamber. Instead, he had to content himself merely with the sight of the monster's head exploding into ribbons and shards of bone.

Cassius wiped his eye-lenses clear. The last of his attackers had somehow sprung backwards and was now scuttling up the wall. Cassius fired at it three times, but it dashed out of the way towards the ceiling. In its wake, it left deep claw marks in the metal plating. When it was directly overhead, it sprang at him.

Its mouth was gaping in a silent roar. Its tongue moved like a snake.

Cassius drove the crozius past its lethal teeth and out the back of its skull in a blaze of concussive force. Its body, headless but still twitching, bounced away towards the storage chamber.

Cassius whirled around. Five more of the aliens drifted lifelessly around his men. Donatus and Teven were still on their feet, flanking the blast doors and firing down the stairwell with the boltguns. Koden was on his knees – he had apparently managed not only to dislodge his attacker, but cleave it in two with his power axe. But tiny jets of gas were venting from the back of his armour, evidence of a breach all the way to his sealed undersuit. Captain Ectros was standing over the body of Brother Radovan, whose right arm, Cassius noted, was now missing below the elbow.

His instincts had proved correct. Port Cepheus was infested with genestealers.

'Kill team,' he growled over the vox. 'Report!'

'We have two men wounded,' Ectros replied. 'One of them critically.'

'I'm fine,' Koden growled.

'Pranus here, my lord. We are on our way to you.'

Cassius shook his head. 'No, Brother Pranus – remain where you are. The xenos have the tactical advantage in this place.'

Ectros slipped an arm under Brother Radovan and lifted him up, while Cassius moved behind Koden. The Space Wolf's armour had indeed been breached in half a dozen places. His enhanced lungs would protect him for a while, but Cassius knew that not even the toughest of Space

Marines could operate at full combat readiness for very long in a total vacuum and expect to survive.

'Donatus, lead us out of here,' Cassius barked. 'And send word to the *Veritas*. We will clarify the extent of our operational jurisdiction. Mark my words, I shall not suffer this infestation to remain.'

At the top of the stairwell were five dead genestealers, each shot through half a dozen times. Donatus shoved their drifting corpses aside, clearing a path for the others. Retracing their magnetised path through Port Cepheus' dark, airless corridors, they passed the smashed barricades and habitation levels without incident.

They reached the second level, where the space was thick with drifting detritus. Cassius motioned for everyone to go ahead of him. Donatus, Teven and Koden started down towards the entrance level. Ectros, still carrying Brother Radovan, moved to follow them.

Suddenly, tables and chairs were being knocked aside.

Cassius had remained halfway up the step to the third level, where he could survey the cluttered room from on high. The control room, a confined space with limited firing avenues, had been an excellent place for an ambush. So too was this.

His diligence was rewarded.

There were five of them. They came at Ectros from all sides, but this time Cassius was ready for them. He shot two dead as they sprang from their hiding places. Then, bounding down the steps, caved in the skull of a third one with his maul.

Ectros kept hold of Brother Radovan as he spun around. Levelling his chainsword across his body, he caught the first of the remaining genestealers in its thorax as it leapt at him. The second one, however, ploughed into him at the hip, and wrapped its monstrous clawed hands around his abdomen. The ceramite gave like waxed parchment, and cooled gases vented from his ruptured plate.

Over the vox, Cassius heard a sound completely unfamiliar to him. It took a full second for him to realise that it was Ectros crying out in pain.

The captain brought his sword down, and severed two limbs off the creature attached to him. It twisted away, trying to save itself, but Ectros lunged and caught it in the chest, the chain-blade chewing its way between two bony, rib-like plates.

Cassius struck the final genestealer, collapsing its exoskeleton and covering the crozius' golden wings with foul ichor.

The wounded captain's breathing came over the vox in sharp gasps. 'Right through my armour,' he muttered. He inhaled deeply, altering the pressure in his lungs and commanding his enhanced body to start conserving oxygen. He gave a comradely nod to Cassius, and continued down the stairwell.

As they exited the central tower back through the void-lock, Cassius called to Pranus and the rest aboard the *Pride of Ghosar*.

'Brothers, activate the freighter's engines. Prepare it to leave the port.'

'*Yes, Brother-Chaplain,*' Pranus replied. '*I will have the others meet you at the starboard lock.*'

'No,' Cassius said. 'Once the ship is ready, you are to follow its return course back to its home system.'

A moment passed where none of the kill team members

said a word. Finally, Pranus cleared his throat. *'Chaplain, a kill team cannot be divided without higher authorisation.'*

'Inquisito lethale omni tempore,' Ectros said quietly. 'At all times, lethal investigation.'

'We *have* been commanded by a higher authority,' Cassius said. 'Our original mission stands – the *Veritas* and the kill team under my command are to pursue Drogg Mordakka and the remains of Waaagh! Mek unto their righteous destruction. However, Brother Donatus reports that the *Veritas* has received additional orders from a Watch Commander Vaerion. Do you know him?'

'I do not recognise the name,' replied Pranus. Ectros shook his head, glancing back as Donatus sealed the voidlock behind them.

Cassius continued. 'It matters not. I am to divide the kill team, and dispatch you to Ghosar Quintus on a new mission that will be relayed separately. The new team is codenamed Excis.'

No one else spoke.

'We are the Deathwatch, brothers. For us, this is more than a mandate, more than a mere mission. It is a holy charge! It falls to us to purge the stars of inhumanity so that mankind may inherit them once more. This was what our great master, the Emperor, began ten millennia ago, and we are the heirs of his undertaking. Drogg Mordakka still lives, and that cannot stand! The planet Vinicus must have retribution. The blood of millions cries out from the ground for us to avenge them, and we will oblige. I will find the greenskin leader, and I will end him. Yet, I cannot also ignore this new threat. Here too, Imperial lives have been taken and must be answered for, blood for blood.'

'Therefore, Pranus – you, Omid, Thalassi, and Siegfric will go to Ghosar Quintus. Whatever else Watch Commander Vaerion tasks you with, you will find the source of the genestealer infestation and you will eliminate it.'

'*Yes, Brother-Chaplain,*' said Pranus. His enthusiasm, stoked by Cassius' homily, was evident even over the vox-channel. '*We will go at once!*'

'And I will go with you,' Ectros said. 'We should divide the kill team equally.'

Cassius glared at him. 'If you are going simply to uphold protocol, then you need not bother. You are wounded, and we do not yet even know the extent of the mission to Ghosar Quintus.'

'I am going because my battle-brothers on that freighter need someone to lead them. I am going because it is what *you* would do.'

Behind his faceplate, Cassius smiled grimly. He raised the crozius arcanum above his head. 'Then go, Captain Thaniel Ectros, with all the blessings of the Emperor. Go with praise for His great name and damnation for His enemies, and He will be with you, yea, even unto the end of all things.'

Ectros passed Radovan to Donatus, saluted the group with the sign of the aquila, and headed towards the *Pride of Ghosar*.

'Shall I call the *Veritas* for retrieval?' Donatus enquired.

'If the ship were to dock, then the genestealers could find their way aboard. We cannot risk it. The port has one more lander. We will take that, and invoke full quarantine protocols upon arrival.'

'Then we will return and cleanse the station,' said Teven, 'once the wounded have been healed.'

'No, we will continue the hunt for Drogg Mordakka,' Cassius replied. 'That continues to be our primary duty.'

Donatus inclined his head. 'But what then of Port Cepheus?'

From the command deck of the *Veritas*, Cassius watched as the *Pride of Ghosar* slowly moved away from the station. He recited a prayer for those in departure, and then ordered the forward gunnery crews to obliterate the port's nearest stabiliser.

'The watch captains will question this decision,' Donatus muttered.

'But not my motives,' Cassius replied. 'Not my resolve. By this act, we purge any remaining xenos infestation. Had I more Space Marines and more time, I would do it with more discretion. As it stands, I have neither.'

The deck plates beneath their feet shook as the *Veritas*' weapons were readied. Then, searing beams of light shot out from her bow, cleaving into the station's flank in a cascade of explosions.

Port Cepheus, mortally wounded, began to tilt.

Three stabilisers were not enough to keep it aloft, and the gravity of the gas giant below began to drag it downwards. Farther and farther it fell towards the swirling cloud tops, picking up speed as it went. Mounting external pressures caused the superstructure to crumple in upon itself. The docking piers bent towards the central tower. Further detonations ripped along them as the promethium in their storage vaults ignited, ripping along the length of the intake pipes. Into the infernal, crushing, stygian depths, went Port Cepheus, compacting and burning with every mile, until it finally vanished from sight.

Only when he was certain that the entire station had been utterly destroyed did Cassius order the *Veritas* to break orbit and renew the search for Drogg Mordakka.

Only then did he send word to his superiors in the Deathwatch of what he had done.

'I trust that the Chaplain's account answers all of your questions, brother?' Drusus asked pointedly.

Seumas, deep in thought, looked up and nodded silently. Drusus wearily rubbed at his temples before continuing.

'Then, if there is nothing further, we will return to the issue at hand. Chaplain Cassius, there has been no distress call received from Captain Ectros, nor any other member of Kill Team Excis. It is to be assumed that they never reached Ghosar Quintus, most likely falling prey to gene-stealers while on board the freighter *Pride of Ghosar*, which also cannot be found. Your petition to assemble a new kill team and undertake a second mission in force to the Ghosarian System is hereby denied.'

Cassius' eyes grew wide with surprise. 'Then I will go alone.'

'Your dedication is an example to us all, Chaplain,' Captain Bresnik sighed, shaking his head, 'but there are other wars to fight, and other engagements that demand our attention. This is simply not a priority for the Deathwatch. Your petition is denied. May the Emperor guide you all the rest of your days. This council is adjourned.'

The scribe-servitor completed its hectic quill strokes. The three thrones of the watch captains lowered themselves to the floor, and the desk portions swung open. Bresnik rose and walked quickly out of the chamber. He did not so much as glance at Cassius as he passed. Seumas remained seated, his focus turned entirely inwards. Drusus got up from his throne, and walked to the servitor. He tore the length of parchment from its mouth, and rolled it into a tight scroll.

Cassius finally broke his stunned silence. 'Captain Drusus, I must protest.'

'The decision stands, Chaplain. Need I remind you that your original mission remains incomplete? Drogg Mordakka remains at large.'

'I am not one to question the judgement of my superiors, but–'

'Then, as your superior, trust me when I tell you that there is no need for you to travel to Ghosar Quintus. Return to your quarters, Cassius, and meditate upon the wisdom of this council. We cannot chase ghosts and phantoms through all the dark corners of the galaxy.' Drusus took the record of the inquiry and placed it into a pouch on his belt. As he left the chamber, he called back over his shoulder. 'It is almost certain that the *Pride of Ghosar* was infested with genestealers *after* leaving its home system.'

Home.

For a moment, Cassius thought of the magnificent mountain ranges and windswept lowlands of the Ultramarines capital world. It had been entirely too long since he had last set foot upon it, or been within the walls of the Fortress of Hera. He could return there now, if he so chose, and watch the golden domes of the Chapter monastery blaze in the light of the rising sun. He could once again walk through its vaunted halls, and praise the Emperor and primarch in the Temple of Corr–

'You'll never see it again,' Seumas said.

Cassius' head snapped around. He and Seumas were alone. 'Do you mean Macragge?'

The watch captain rose up slowly from his seat. 'The record of this meeting. Our Brother-Captain Drusus will either destroy that scroll, or bury it in a scriptorium so deep that it will never be seen again. Not by you or I, or any other living being.'

'Why would he do that?'

'Why indeed...' Seumas moved slowly towards Cassius. 'Do you uphold the sanctity of confession?'

Cassius blinked.

'It has been a long time since I have heard the confessions of any Space Marine,' he replied. 'Have you been derelict in your duty somehow?'

'No. Quite the contrary. But, in the course of serving the Emperor, I have had to... dissemble. I have had to keep information from my brothers-in-arms while I discerned which of them I could truly trust.'

'And you trust me?'

'After hearing about the incident at Port Cepheus first-hand, I do. I asked you earlier if you had ever heard the name of Chaegryn.'

'I have not.'

'Chaegryn is the name of an Ordo Xenos Inquisitor.'

'Very well. What does that have to do with me?'

Seumas began walking slowly towards the door. 'As I said, I have been keeping information. Collecting it. Sorting it. Finding connections, parallels, and... *unpleasant* coincidences. When your report came to my attention, I tried to corroborate some of its details. And, within the records of the Deathwatch, I came across a handful of mentions of the very star system that Captain Ectros went to investigate.'

'Ghosar.'

'It was a report from one Inquisitor Chaegryn. Heavily redacted. Entire sections of it had been covered up or erased. Still, there was enough left to provide a partial picture. It seems that the Inquisitor went to Ghosar Quintus to investigate an alien threat, one that drew a lot of unwholesome attention from his peers. Shortly after arriving, Chaegryn sent back a message saying that all was well, that there was no problem whatsoever, and that under no circumstances should anyone attempt to investigate the matter further.'

The watch captain halted. His gaze was cold.

'Brother-Chaplain Cassius, almost all other information regarding that star system has been purged. Were it not for your report and a handful of bureaucratic remnants, its very existence would be in doubt. And Ghosar Quintus is not the only such example. Over the past two thousand years or so, more than one hundred and twenty worlds on the Eastern Fringe have likewise reported the presence of genestealer infestations, and then all but vanished from Imperial records.'

Cassius did not know what to say. Seumas glanced around them before continuing in a more hushed tone.

'There is a conspiracy at work here, and the creatures you encountered at Port Cepheus appear to be integral to it. Sweeping portions of the Deathwatch are ignorant of these facts – either wilfully, or because they haven't taken the time to put together all the pieces of the puzzle. But I have. I can give you the requisition codes for the documents in question. It's all there, in the archives.'

Cassius stared. 'You're insane,' he muttered finally, and turned to leave.

'Then go to Ghosar Quintus. I'm sure you'll find all the proof you could ever want.'

'The other watch captains refuse to sanction my petition.'

'I know someone who could approve it anyway.'

Cassius froze, his hand hovering just above the door plate. He glanced over his shoulder as Seumas closed the distance between them once more. 'Who?'

'Watch Commander Vaerion.'

'And what of the kill team selection?'

'I would suggest that you begin your own preparations now. I would go myself, but that would raise too many questions. I have no idea how far this rot has already spread.'

'Are you so certain of what we will find when we get there?' Cassius asked.

'I am certain of the danger. You and I both know that there is far more to these beings than mere vermin clinging to hulls and hulks.'

Still, Cassius did not move.

'We both neglect our duty by doing nothing,' Seumas said. 'I can offer no further argument.'

'It is enough,' Cassius said as he left the chamber.

Vael Donatus was standing by a grand viewport on the embarkation level when Cassius found him. Through the armourglass, they could see the *Veritas* being prepared for departure. 'What did they say?' he asked. 'Did they approve the petition?'

'No,' Cassius replied. 'Yet, strangely, we will likely be going nonetheless.'

Donatus did not understand. Nor did he feel the need to. The Chaplain was including him in this endeavour, and that was enough for him. 'Then what must we do now, brother?'

'We must prepare a new kill team, you and I. But it must be done with caution and secrecy. We take only those skilled and experienced individuals in whom we have the utmost trust, and none of the watch captains must be aware of it. Not until we can contact Watch Commander Quovis Vaerion.'

Cassius saw Donatus' eyes narrow with unease.

'I know, brother. I too hate to undermine our betters. It is not for a Space Marine to be duplicitous, doubly so for two sons of Guilliman.' The Chaplain placed a reassuring hand upon Donatus' shoulder. 'But this is how it must be. Ectros, Pranus, Omid, Siegfric, and Thalassi – I sent them into a place from which, it seems, no one returns. They have become lost. And I must do all I can to find them… or avenge them.'

Donatus nodded. 'As always, I will stand by you. Whatever may come.'

'Then let us prepare,' Cassius said. 'The dark secrets of Ghosar Quintus await.'

ABOUT THE AUTHORS

Braden Campbell is the author of *Shadowsun: The Last of Kiru's Line* for Black Library, as well as the novella *Tempestus*, and several short stories. He is a classical actor and playwright, and a freelance writer, particularly in the field of role playing games. Braden has enjoyed Warhammer 40,000 for nearly a decade, and remains fiercely dedicated to his dark eldar.

Mark Clapham is the author of the Space Marine Battles novel *Tyrant of the Hollow Worlds* and the Warhammer 40,000 novel *Iron Guard* as well as the short stories 'The Siege of Fellguard', 'The Hour of Hell', 'In Hrondir's Tomb' and 'Sanctified', which appeared in the anthology *Fear the Alien*. He lives and works in Exeter, Devon.

Ben Counter is one of Black Library's most popular Warhammer 40,000 authors, with two Horus Heresy novels to his name – *Galaxy in Flames* and *Battle for the Abyss*. He is the author of the Soul Drinkers series and *The Grey Knights Omnibus*. For Space Marine Battles he has written *Malodrax*, and has turned his attention to the Space Wolves with the novella *Arjac Rockfist: Anvil of Fenris* and a number of short stories. He is a fanatical painter of miniatures, a pursuit which has won him his most prized possession: a prestigious Golden Demon award. He lives in Portsmouth, England.

Chris Dows is a writer and educational advisor with over twenty years' experience in comic books, prose and non-fiction. His previous works for Black Library include 'In the Shadow of the Emperor', and the first Zachariah story 'The Mouth of Chaos'. He lives in Grimsby with his wife and two children.

Peter Fehervari is the author of the novel *Fire Caste*, featuring the Astra Militarum and Tau Empire, and the Tau-themed Quick Reads 'Out Caste' and 'A Sanctuary of Wyrms', the latter of which appeared in the anthology *Deathwatch: Xenos Hunters*. He also wrote the Space Marines Quick Reads 'Nightfall', which was in the *Heroes of the Space Marines* anthology, and 'The Crown of Thorns'. He lives and works in London.

Justin D Hill is the author of the Space Marine Battles novel *Storm of Damocles* and the short stories 'Last Step Backwards', 'Lost Hope' and 'The Battle of Tyrok Fields', following the adventures of Lord Castellan Ursarkar E. Creed, as well as 'Truth Is My Weapon', and the Warhammer tales 'Golgfag's Revenge' and 'The Battle of Whitestone' for Black Library.

Steve Lyons' work in the Warhammer 40,000 universe includes the novellas *Engines of War* and *Angron's Monolith*, the Imperial Guard novels *Ice World* and *Dead Men Walking* – now collected in the omnibus *Honour Imperialis* – and the audio dramas *Waiting Death* and *The Madness Within*. He has also written numerous short stories and is currently working on more tales from the grim darkness of the far future.

Robbie MacNiven is a highland-born History graduate from the University of Edinburgh. He has written the Warhammer 40,000 novels *Carcharodons: Red Tithe* and *Legacy of Russ* as well as the short stories 'Redblade', 'A Song for the Lost' and 'Blood and Iron' for Black Library. His hobbies include re-enacting, football and obsessing over Warhammer 40,000.

Ian St. Martin has written the Warhammer 40,000 novel *Deathwatch* and the short stories 'City of Ruin' and 'In Wolves' Clothing' for Black Library. He lives and works in Washington DC, the US, caring for his cat and reading anything within reach.

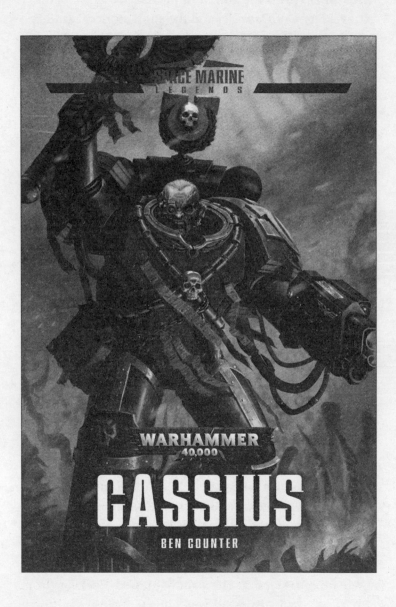

SPACE MARINE
LEGENDS

WARHAMMER
40,000

CASSIUS

BEN COUNTER

An extract from

CASSIUS

by Ben Counter

The engines screamed and the world called Kolovan screamed back, the howl of a toxic storm that roared and scraped at the lower hull of the drop pod. Cassius knew the violent sensations of a drop pod assault intimately: the chill wail of the thin upper atmosphere, the hammering of the retro jets firing up, the hiss and buffet as the pod punched down through cloud cover and the rising bellow of the jets fighting against the thickening air.

As the pod screeched into its final descent attitude, these sensations were as familiar as taking a breath. Leaning into the pod's lurches was like taking a step or speaking a word.

'Clear your minds, brethren,' said Cassius, trusting in the amplified vox-channel to carry his voice above the storm of the descent. 'Seize upon only that symbol that shall lead you to victory. The sacrifice of Lord Guilliman. A passage from the Codex. The sight of blessed Macragge from space. An emblem of all we fight for. Take it and focus on it, and your soul shall be ready for the fight. Be pure and steel-hearted! Be all that is fury and righteousness!'

He was making his descent to the surface alongside a Tactical squad from the Third Company. Sergeant Verigar led them, a grey-haired veteran whose temple and left cheek glinted with the dull sheen of bionics. For now his stern visage was hidden beneath the pitiless iron mask of his red Mark VII helmet, and he sat with the easy calm of a warrior who had been through dozens, hundreds, of landings like this. Cassius had not fought beside Verigar before, but Captain Fabian spoke highly of him. He knew the names and faces of the others, but had not yet ascribed particular value to any of them. He would see them fight, and then he would know them.

The grav-restraints tightened and forced Cassius back into the plasteel frame holding his armoured body in place. A moment later the drop pod slammed into the ground. The retro engines and shock absorbers did not completely cancel out the teeth-rattling impact, and Cassius' head snapped back and forth with the force.

The restraint around Cassius' right arm snapped free. The Chaplain drew his crozius arcanum from its compartment at his side.

He was armed. He was ready to kill.

The explosive bolts in the drop pod's upper hull fired like a series of gunshots. Light blared in as the hull split into four sections and fell away, exposing the Space Marines inside to the sun of Kolovan for the first time.

The star that hovered overhead and shone between clouds of filthy brown toxins was a painful, acid yellow. It fell on a broken plain, as if the surface had been baked hard by that sun and then shattered by a vast hammer.

Deep fissures broke the land up into patches of scorched ground, and fingers of pale rock broke through, the bones of the planet, where the ground had been particularly tortured. A distant line of smouldering mountains spoke of the geological activity that had torn this place up over and over again.

More drop pods bearing the colours of the Third and Fifth Companies were thudding home, raising splintering showers of broken earth. As the crafts' bolts fired, squads of Ultramarines leapt out, weapons raised and ready to kill, the blue of their armour discoloured by the sickly filter of Kolovan's sun.

Cassius' grav-restraints snapped open, and he jumped from the drop pod as his men disembarked alongside him. A thousand battles' worth of experience flooded through him and he took a tally of the landscape around him in the space of a few seconds.

Broken ground, difficult to move over swiftly. Rises and breaks in the earth could serve as cover. The rest of the strike force was making landfall closely-grouped, for the crew of the ship *Defence of Talassar* had performed their task well in launching the drop pods from upper orbit.

The air was toxic. It would have dropped a normal man in a couple of minutes. A Space Marine's constitution could survive it initially but it would build up over time, and so Cassius wore a rebreather unit over his mouth and nose. The toxins stung the skin that still remained on his blasted face, the wind that carried them sharp with the dirt whipped up by the drop pod's impact.

'We're east of the drop zone!' came a vox on the command channel from Captain Galenus of the Fifth Company. 'The xenos are massing from the south.'

'*Sigillite's teeth,*' swore Captain Fabian of the Third over the vox. '*We expected no resistance here.*'

'Do I detect dismay, brother-captain?' said Cassius. 'This is but a drop in the ocean compared to what will come. Let the men test their fury. It will do them good.'

Cassius turned to the battle-brothers emerging from the drop pod. 'The tyranids were not so distant as we feared,' he said. 'They mass and respond from the south. We take the southern ridge, and we hold it until our main force makes landfall.'

His squad nodded gravely. Gauntleted fingers rested on weapon studs. Blades were checked and stowed. They were ready.